EXILES

EXILES

DANIEL BLYTHE

First Published in 2019 by Fantastic Books Publishing
Cover design by Gabi

ISBN (ebook): 978-1-912053-05-6
ISBN (paperback): 978-1-912053-04-9

ACKNOWLEDGEMENTS

I would like to thank my family for putting up with my endless periods of silence and absence while writing this book – the longest one I have written so far. Rachel, Ellie and Sam are endlessly supportive and an inspiration to me every day. Many friends and other writers have proved very helpful in discussions during the writing of *Exiles*. I would especially like to thank Chenab Mangat and Susan Elliot Wright for reading and commenting on earlier versions of the text. As ever, I am also indebted to my hard-working literary agent, Caroline Montgomery at Rupert Crew Ltd., whose dedication to duty and care for her authors is exemplary. Finally, my thanks to all at Fantastic Books for taking *Exiles* on and giving it a home.

May you all consider yourselves and your descendants to be honorary members of the Chapter of Continual Progress.

PRELUDE

A sharp sound breaks into her thoughts.

She makes a grab for her pistol on the bedside table – then, she realises it's the buzzer on her pod's outer door. Someone trying to get her attention. She pushes open the bedroom door, kicks through the clutter on the floor of the living-area, rubbing her tired, aching eyes. She presses the intercom button.

'Who is it?'

There is no reply from the small black grille beside the door. She stabs at the button again. 'Hello? Someone there?'

Again, no reply. She feels her fingertips tingling, telling her something's wrong.

The indicator light is not on – for some reason, the intercom isn't working, at least from her side. 'Something else to get fixed.'

She slides back the bolt which opens the door, allowing a chink of light in from the curved corridor outside, and puts her eye to the space to see who her caller is.

She smiles in relief.

'Oh. Right … It's, um, not a good time, all right?' She is about to seal the door shut, and then she relents. 'Oh, what the hell. Come in.' She slides the bolt to release the door all the way. 'Don't mind the mess.'

She is aware of how silly that sounds. She bends down to throw a handful of clothes away in her cupboard, and the outer door slides to behind her as her visitor enters the room.

She hears the soft click as the door seals itself, and she straightens up.

'Right,' she says to the newcomer, her voice flat and emotionless. 'What can I do for you?'

There is another click.

Something flashes in the dimness.

Her expression freezes. Her jaw drops and her face drains of blood, unable to believe what she sees facing her.

She does not even have time to scream.

1
PLANETFALL

I

Engines screamed as the ship died.

The echo of clattering feet, of alarms, shouts and yells. The din rattled the capsule, shook her body, even though she was firmly strapped in. Beth could smell hot metal. Pungent, angry.

Someone had dragged her, pushed her into this capsule. She could not remember who. The inside of the capsule was drenched in red light and the klaxon sounded to warn her that she was about to be ejected.

A force like a punch from a giant fist slammed her back into her seat, sending pain through her already-broken body.

She could smell burning flesh. She didn't know if it was her own.

She was screaming inside. Beth knew the scene from a thousand safety visuals. In her mind she saw the ship, a vast slab covered in twinkling lights, a flying mega-city, now in flames.

Burning itself to death.

Slowly breaking up, chunks spiralling off into the blackness on plumes of smoke and tails of flame. The round hatchway opening in the belly of the giant, her round life-capsule popping out like a cork from a bottle, spinning away from the destruction, into ... into what?

The Universe.

The unknown, endless Universe, screaming past her.

She gasped out loud. Hot blood was pouring down her

face but she could do nothing about it, both her arms pinned to the chair as the capsule hurtled through space. The instrument panels were meaningless to her.

Dimly, she wondered who else had managed to get to the bays. Who had dragged her from the wreckage of Circle Twelve and got her inside a capsule? She wanted to throw up, but somehow swallowed the bitter, acid taste back down.

Something was flashing on the panel. Desperately, she tried to ignore the pain in her body and attempted to focus her mind on what was in front of her.

Information was pouring on to the circular panel, showing the alignment of the nearest star system.

>>> REGION: Galactic Edge
>>> HABITABLE LOCATION DETECTED.
>>> Planet 4: atmosphere Earth-similar: 78% nitrogen 20% oxygen.

Habitable location. That was her last and best hope. Beth remembered the expression the Teachers had used on board *Arcadia* – 'Goldilocks zone'. You had to search, hope for it.

>>> Some lightly acidic precipitation.
>>> Limited but adequate UV light cover.
>>> Gravity 98% Earth normal. Land masses: 17. Oceanic composition: largely saline water, other non-harmful matter.

>>> Polar ice caps: permafrost. -40 degrees Celsius. Equatorial zone: dense jungle and swampland. 80+ degrees Celsius. Large desert/plain regions. 2 small satellites.

>>> Equatorial radius 4412 Km.

>>> FLORA AND FAUNA: largely non-hostile.

She didn't like that word *largely*. But she could not see what other choice was available to her.

>>> STATUS: Explored/abandoned

>>> REASON FOR STATUS: Unknown

>>> NOTIFICATION: Electrical activity detected. Residual tachyon energy detected.

>>> NOTIFICATION: Some low-level seismic activity.

>>> NOTIFICATION: One small low-level technological settlement Level 3, located on 6th largest island land mass.

>>> ATTEMPTING TO LOCK ON.

>>> PROCEED?

Yes. Yes, proceed.

She didn't know where it was, or what was waiting for her when she got there. But there was a Level 3 settlement. And that meant humans, or something at least compatible with humans.

It had to be better than burning up or suffocating in the

endlessness of space, out where the galaxy spread into nothingness, emptiness.

Yes! Proceed, yes!

She realised she had opened her mouth to give the command, but nothing had come out.

The capsule was shaking, screaming in pain. *What if it broke up before landfall?* Her mouth had never been so dry. Her whole body shook in fear.

And then, she could do it no more.

Great Power, she said inside her head. *Great Power, ChapterSister Bethany Kane needs you. Please save me. Help me.*

Redness crept in at the edge of her vision as the capsule accelerated, and she felt a strong, terrifying dizziness take over. Everything turned black, her head fell back and she lost consciousness.

>>> PROCEEDING
>>> LOCKING ON
>>> STAND BY FOR ATMOSPHERE ENTRY
>>>

>>> CLOSING DOWN ALL SYSTEMS
>>> CORRECTION
>>> ALL SYSTEMS BAR LIFE-SUPPORT

>>> ENDS

>>> ATMOSPHERE ENTRY IN 5

>>> 4
>>> 3
>>> 2
>>> 1

>>> ATMOSPHERE ENTRY ACHIEVED

>>>

>>>

>>> PREPARE FOR IMPACT

>>> IMPACT IN 5
>>> 4
>>> 3
>>> 2
>>> 1

II

Mia reached the top of the ridge. Her boots kicking up the blue dust, she scrambled the remaining distance at an impressive pace, panting in the heat and the muggy air.

From her vantage point on top of the cobalt-blue rocks, she could see the smoke-trail cutting through the jade sky, getting wider as it approached the planet. She held the viewer up, toggled the zoom and the filters, following the object down on its entry path.

She pulled out a chunky two-way radio. 'I've got a visual on the trail.'

There was a crackle at the other end, and then a weary-sounding male voice. *'What's all this "I've got a visual" crap? Can't you just say you can see it?'*

'Sorry, Zach. Approximately thirty degrees in the Northern sky. I'm guessing landfall in about five.'

'Then go and see what it is!'

Mia tutted in irritation. 'Send me two Drones, at least. And get me some of the others over here. I don't know what the hell it might be.'

'It's probably rock again … Remember Shan got us all excited fifty cycles ago about a chunk of space-dirt.'

Mia Janowska straightened up, the glutinous sunlight framing her on the ridge. On Earth, she would have counted her age as fifteen. But that was meaningless now they went by the rhythms and cycles of the Edge, with its twenty hours of light and ten of darkness. She was a tall, skinny girl, with toned arms beneath her plain white vest and combat trousers, and her body gave the impression of taut strength. Her hair was sun-bleached, dry and split-ended, her skin tanned. There was a hardness about Mia, as if she had seen things beyond her years – a touch of cruelty in the downturn of her mouth and the set of her jaw. Like her fellow Hunters, she had a personal adornment, a symbol of herself – Mia's was a dark-blue pair of stripes across each cheekbone, semi-permanent warpaint made from a paste dug out of the deep mud near the lake. She also wore a necklace made of ragged, broken animal teeth threaded on a leather braid.

'I dunno,' Mia said thoughtfully into the radio. 'I'm not sure it's rock.'

She watched as the smoke-trail cut the sky about four kiloms distant from her, near the mountain foothills. She was sure she could hear the whine and hum of motors, echoing across the ravaged dunes and cracked stones in front of her.

'Zach, I think it's coming in on gravity buffers.'

There was a crackle on the other end of the radio, Zach presumably relaying this information and consulting with the others. Mia grinned, despite her apprehension. She liked giving him something to think about.

'*Welcoming committee coming over. Three of us and— bzzzt bzzt.*'

Mia thumped the radio in irritation. 'Why does nothing *work* properly around here ...? Say again, Zach, you broke up.'

'*Three of us and two Drones. Whatever it is, keep your distance till we get there.*'

'Oh, don't worry,' she said. 'I intend to.'

She cut the radio and lifted the viewer again.

It was almost visible in the haze of heat and smoke, as it descended. Yeah, she thought, definitely buffers. It wasn't dropping like a stone, and yet the Edge's gravity was comparable with Earth's, even if it made you feel slightly heavier when running.

She watched it slice through the sky. She tracked the glowing silver object as it disappeared behind the foothills. There was no impact or explosion. So, if it was buffered, that meant an escape-pod. And that could mean life.

Visitors.

They never got visitors, here on the Edge.

So it would not be a willing arrival. A refugee, perhaps, from a disintegrating ship – maybe one caught up in the galactic skirmishes. They sometimes made out flashes in the night sky like shooting stars, and did not know what they might be. Perhaps whole empires were falling out there. And so a pod, here on this wasteland on the fringes of the known Galaxy, could mean danger. Mia was prepared.

She set off at a brisk trot. Her face grim, she drew the silver Magna pistol, checking the green bar of light on the tube which displayed its charge. Almost full.

They'd been amazed when they found the guns, broken out of the base's hold shortly after the crash. Somebody, Zach had joked, was obviously hoping they'd all kill each other. Mia hadn't found that funny.

She checked her watch. She estimated she'd reach the landing site in about five minutes, and that the others would be another five minutes behind.

Whatever the visitor was, they were going to be ready for it.

The impact pod sat in a pit of scorched earth.

Standard Class X escape, she thought – a rugged, gun-metal-coloured sphere with few comforts. The person inside would probably have survived, but wouldn't have had a smooth ride. The pod had carved a scar out of the rocky basin, stone and mud ripped up as easily as soft chocolate, a ploughed furrow marking the last few moments of descent.

Mia winced. What had happened to its buffers? Not a comfortable landing at all. She ran down the slope, avoiding the spiky, dry plants which protruded like red knives from the blue soil.

Smoke rolled like mist in front of her as she eyed up the battered sphere. She coughed, blinked. Even at this distance, heat radiated out, and she could smell the scorched sand. The heat was not intense enough to prevent her from approaching, but it brought her out in a sweat, prickled on her forehead and under her arms. Mia wiped her forehead, hawked and spat into the sandy blue ground. She levelled the Magna pistol as she approached.

At last, she heard the whining engines of the jeep above and behind her, and she half-turned, lifting one arm so they could see her, but keeping an eye on the pod.

The battered black jeep, its six massive sturdy wheels churning the sand, hit the top of the basin and surged across it with confidence, powering downwards with Zach at the wheel. It juddered, jolted but held hard. It scrunched to a halt behind Mia, spraying up a broadside of earth and shale.

She took in the arrivals in a couple of seconds. Zach, their leader, tall and blond, a spiral tattoo on each forearm. Dark, lean Shan, his expression keen and alert as ever. Skinny Maddi with her nose-ring and short, bright red hair. All armed.

Behind them, floating on their glowing engines, came the two gleaming silver Drones. They were glossy metal spheroids, a single red sensor-eye glowing on each. They made a 360-degree scan of the terrain, emitting their usual whirring and buzzing.

'Anything moved?' said Zach, striding towards her.

'No. Came down pretty hard. Poor bastard inside could be dead.' She paused. 'With any luck,' she added.

Zach was having none of it. 'We have to act as if it isn't.'

'Yeah, all right. I'm not stupid.'

'Wouldn't dare imply it.'

Zach swung round to the others, indicating that they should spread out in a wide semicircle around the pod. As they did so, there was a hard clanging sound from within. Mia looked at Zach in alarm, but kept the gun level.

'Steady,' said Zach, holding a hand up. 'Steady, now.'

There was another, louder clang, and this time the circular access hatch on the side of the pod vibrated. Scarred, blackened and pitted by the descent, it almost shook free of its housing. Then there was a third clang, and the hatch flew open, thudding on to the sand.

For a couple of seconds there was a terrible, tense silence.

A battered figure emerged from the pod, straightening up. Slim, bipedal, clad in a scorched, tight-fitting black atmosphere-suit. It had a metallic belt with a wood-handled knife.

Human.

They had a second or two to register that the new arrival was female, slightly-built, her jet-black hair tangled with sweat. Crusted blood smeared on a pale, frightened face. She swung from one side to another, blinking, trying to focus. She put an arm up to her face.

'Light adjustment,' said Mia, remembering something they all took for granted. 'She needs–'

Zach was already there. 'Visor,' he said. 'Quickly.'

Maddi was already on to it – she'd grabbed a green-tinted visor from the Jeep and threw it to Zach, who held it out to the new arrival.

The girl eyed it suspiciously.

'You need to wear it,' said Maddi. She put two hands up to her face, simulating the action. 'Wear it.'

The newcomer hesitated.

'Put it on!' Mia snapped. 'Or you could damage your sight!' She wondered if the girl had understood. Did she even speak English, or Panglish, or any of the other old Earth languages? She was about to try her very rusty Common Collective, but then the girl took the smoked-glass visor and pulled it on.

The new arrival swung her head to look at each of them in turn, as if she had never seen people before.

'You ... you do not have them,' she said, her voice cracked.

Mia, Zach and the others exchanged a look. *English*. Part of the Galactic Collective, then, part of Earth's great outreach into the stars. The Collective – that great body of which Earth, ironically, was now no longer a part.

It was Maddi who answered, giving the girl a warm smile which Mia would not have bothered with. 'You don' need it after you've been here a while. You adjust. Long as you don't spend more than a few hours in the sunlight, you're fine.'

'Who *are* you?' snapped Mia. Her pistol was still pointed unwaveringly at a point above the new girl's heart.

No way was she going to drop her guard or start being friendly to this person, not until they had more of an idea about her. Resources were scarce here. Mistrust was Mia's default position.

The girl had dropped to her knees, obviously exhausted. Through her cracked lips she was able to whisper, 'Bethany … Aurelia … Kane.'

Earth name, Mia thought immediately.

Shan had been holding up his scan-pad – a small, black, hand-held device – monitoring the new arrival's life-signs and biological make-up. 'Where are you from, Bethany Aurelia Kane?' Shan asked, speaking for the first time, not looking up from the readout.

The girl turned her head, presumably trying to associate a face with this new voice. '*Arcadia*,' she said. 'Colony ship.'

'Where were you headed?' Zach asked.

'Celestia. On the Outer Rim.'

Celestia? thought Mia. Never heard of it. But then that was true of a lot of places. The human race had become pretty scattered, even in her short lifetime.

Shan was looking at the readout, data flowing on to the scan-pad screen in the form of 3-D patterns, numerical readings and heat sourcing. 'Pretty obvious she's human,' he said. 'Oh, and female. Did I mention female?'

Mia looked witheringly at him. 'No. *Really*?'

'Sustained some tissue damage. We ought to get her taken care of.'

'This journey you were on,' Zach asked. 'How long was it?'

'Twenty years. We've … we had … two years left to go.'

'What happened?'

'I do not know.' She fell forward, her palms flat on the blue soil, her breath ragged. 'Some kind of impact. It was … It was chaos … Please … Do you have any water?'

Maddi came forward with a flask, holding it gently to the girl's lips. She tried to gulp down more than she could manage and coughed it up, the water splattering in an arc on the dry, dusty land.

The girl wiped her mouth with the back of her hand, staggering to her feet. 'That tastes disgusting,' she said.

'Somethin' else you get used to, 'fraid. Filtered rainwater.'

'And it doesn't rain an awful lot here,' Mia added, keeping her voice level, 'so you soon learn not to *waste* it.' She wrinkled her nose at the stain on the ground, hoping the girl would have got the message.

The girl stood with her arms clutched to her chest, as if hugging herself for protection. She looked around the rocky basin, then at the others one by one. Her stance was guarded, Mia thought. Cautious, but still ready to spring into action. 'And where is … *here*?' she asked.

'Welcome to the Edge,' Zach said.

'The Edge …? The Edge of what?'

'Civilisation,' said Mia. 'Life, the Galaxy, call it whatever you like.' She scowled at Beth. 'Passing through, were you? Hell of a place to bail out.' Everybody else, Mia thought, was being far too polite to the new arrival. Why were they not more suspicious of her intentions?

'Come on,' said Zach. 'Let's get her to Town. She needs food and water and rest.'

The Drones buzzed around like giant, agitated insects, recording everything, as Maddi and Shan helped the injured girl to the jeep.

Zach hung back, peering curiously at the battered door of Bethany's impact pod. Mia hovered at his shoulder, hands still nervous and sweaty on her pistol. She wasn't happy about any of this, and if she didn't say something it would be too late.

'So, what, we're inviting her home?' Mia muttered. 'What are we, now, waifs-and-strays central?'

Zach thumped the sturdy inner casing of the pod, as if searching for something. He deliberately avoided Mia's gaze. 'What do you expect me to do? Leave her out here?'

'Give her food and water, something for a shelter, and send her on her way.' Even as Mia said it, she felt a shudder of guilt, knowing it wasn't the right thing to say. Here, in this hostile wilderness – really? To send someone out to fend for themselves? But she had said it, and she bit her lip, trying not to seem too regretful, wondering how she could save face here.

'One night out in the wilderness could finish her off, Mia. Left to be pecked clean by the Klaa.' He pointed to the sky, where a cluster of whirling, pterodactyl-like creatures could be seen. 'Do you really want to abandon her to that?'

Mia grabbed his arm, holding it. 'Forty-six, Zach,' she said. 'Forty-six, and you know what we said about last winter? Remember?'

She knew Zach wouldn't say. But they both remembered it, thinking it out loud together, in private.

If five of us hadn't died … we'd have been in trouble by now.

'I know,' he said softly. 'But she's *one* person. And she's new. We've not had anyone new … Remember how we thought there might be? At first …? People with news, with information, maybe even some way off this dump?'

Mia felt Zach's muscles straining beneath her fingers, but she did not slacken her grip. 'That doesn't mean–'

'She won't get an easy ride. We question her, find out what happened. And we give her the choice. If she wants to be part of Town, it's on the same terms as everyone else. Or she leaves and makes her own way.'

Mia still did not release her hold on Zach's arm. 'Or we could sort this right now,' she said. 'We don't know who she is, or where she came from. Only the four of us have seen her alive.'

She could barely believe what she was saying. It was as if she had allowed herself one unthinkable thought, and could only justify it by going further still.

'What are you saying?'

'As far as everyone else knows, it could have been a very nasty, fatal crash.' Mia paused. 'No survivors,' she said.

'Mia – *no.*'

'Why the hell not?' Mia actually felt a shiver of anticipation at the thought, like the first time she'd crushed a beetle under her boot. 'We deal with the problem. It ends.'

'*No.*' He pushed her hand away, holding a finger up, admonishing. Mia felt anger rising in her, a prickling inward heat.

'She may not be a problem,' Zach said quietly. 'She may be a solution. Have you thought about that?' He thumped the inside of the Pod again. 'We need to strip this for parts. Get a team on to it.'

He strode back towards the jeep and the others.

Mia glowered after him. She didn't push it. For the moment.

III

Beth felt bruised, scorched. She tried to ignore the terrible, angry throb in her head, the cramp in her limbs and the salty tang of nausea in her mouth.

The wheels scoured the ground, sending great, billowing blue clouds of dust into the air as the jeep headed for – where? Nobody had told her.

Hot, evil-smelling particles were coating her skin, hair and tongue. In brief moments when the fog settled or cleared, she glimpsed endless stretches of rocky sand and shale, its hues of ice-blue and aquamarine darkening to royal-blue in the hollows. There were great, dark gashes in the earth, from which walls of pungent yellow steam gushed upwards – the jeep dodged to avoid these.

Spiky vegetation loomed like monsters in the dimness. Some kind of winged creatures wheeled in the sky, sharp-beaked like pterodactyls. She caught flashes of snowy peaks in the distance, forests hugging the mountainside. There were jagged, upthrust ruins, too, clusters of old buildings which could have been a once-great city. There was an acrid, battery-like smell in the air, mixed with the metallic stink of the jeep.

She had picked up the names of her travelling companions. Zach, the taller of the boys, at the wheel – close-cropped hair, high cheekbones, whirling spiral tattoos on each upper arm – seemed to be in charge. Next to him was the other boy, Shan, with darker skin and blue-tinted glasses, his hair cropped so short he was almost bald. He had barely uttered a word. Maddi with the ragged crimson hair and nose-ring, the girl who'd given her the visor – the only one of them to have smiled at her so far – sat beside Beth on the hard seat in the back of the jeep, facing forward. And opposite them, her finger never far from the trigger of the bulky, battered pistol she carried, was the hard-faced blonde girl, Mia, with the stripes on her face, the one Beth knew had taken a dislike to her.

New people. New names.

She was aware of how small the jeep felt against the vastness of the land and sky. It seemed to stretch forever.

On *Arcadia*, you were never far from the steel sky. You had to climb – up the Thousand Wishing Steps, maybe, or one of the Tall Trees – but you could do it. You could touch the inside skin of the *Arcadia*, feel it as one with you. You'd know it was your home, your place of safety. The world was hollow, and you could touch the sky.

For another two years. Until you reached Celestia.

The destination she had been waiting for, planning for all her life.

She had always known that she would be a young

woman of sixteen summers when they reached Celestia. 'Maybe ready to pair-bond, Bethany,' her Uncle Victor had said. 'Ready to be a mother to a child of your own, bring it up in this new world?'

That had all been wrenched away from her. Instead, she was here. In a place terrifying in its vastness, its openness. The Edge, they had called it.

Here she was in a cramped, juddering metal jeep with four complete strangers, and not knowing if her life had another six months, or six minutes, or six seconds.

She had no idea of how long they'd been travelling. Twenty minutes, maybe. But the light had begun to thicken, shadows stretching.

She could no longer make out their two accompanying Drones – they'd been skimming along behind them, not quite as fast as the jeep. She marvelled at the accomplished ease with which the small robots floated. The Drones on the Arcadia had been simpler, moving on spindly legs or caterpillar-tracks.

'How do they do it?' she mouthed at Maddi. She pointed behind to the Drones, and made her hand flat in imitation of their gravity-defying gliding.

Maddi leaned in, her breath hot. 'Micro-neutron engines!' she shouted over the noise of the jeep. 'Gives 'em a buoyancy column. And they're useful for carrying machinery and stuff.'

'Shame they can't carry us!' Beth's remark sounded flippant as soon as she uttered it, but she was just saying whatever came into her head. Maddi, though, took the comment seriously.

'Yeah, people are a bit trickier. Their equipment's not adapted for that.'

'How many Drones do you have?' Beth asked.

'Twenty.'

'And how many of you?'

'Fif– forty-six.'

Beth noticed the correction.

The jeep whined and rattled, thumped and bumped over shale and broken rocks, careered down gullies. Grinding and groaning, it climbed steep slopes with enormous power. Zach, at the wheel, made no concessions to those in the uncomfortable back seats – his firm, muscled arms controlled the machine with ease.

The dust-clouds receded, but the ragged gashes still ripped through the land ahead, gushing their yellow steam, like monsters buried deep in the earth.

'How does this thing work?' Beth shouted to Maddi. 'You have fuel?'

'Nah. Solar cells. Neutron-boosted. They're pretty much inexhaustible.'

They passed giant clumps of shiny, toffee-coloured fungus. Hunched, twisted trees with crusty red bark. Endless slopes and hollows of blue sand, blue rock. There was the odd muddy pool, even a narrow track under a waterfall. They splashed straight though the curtain of cold, silvery water, and Beth could only allow it to swish over, soaking her.

Despite the water she'd had earlier, her throat was ragged and parched. And she was trying to ignore another, more familiar sensation. A tingling in her head, a combination of senses which simultaneously made her head ring as if with the sound of distant bells, brought a smell of burning metal, and made her teeth hyper-sensitive as if she had bitten on ice.

The jeep rattled on.

The sun, an eggy yellow blob, was sinking rapidly in the sky. The sunset quickly infused the land with a bloodied tinge, casting misshapen shadows. Even in the tight, lined atmosphere-suit, Beth didn't fail to register the sudden drop in temperature.

The roar of water, the crashing of breakers. The jeep, she realised, had reached a shoreline, and before them was a wild, dark-blue, tempestuous sea.

Accelerating down the slope, wet blue sand gushing up on all sides, it hit the beach at a fast pace.

Before them was a great, raised causeway made of the dark blue stone, linking the land to what looked like a forbidding rock just visible out in the sea. The jeep hit the causeway at full speed, and she watched with interest and fear.

Maddi glanced at her. 'We're almost home,' she said.

'What's home?' Beth asked fearfully.

'You'll see. Hold on tight.'

With a roar and a thrust, the jeep powered along the causeway. Beth realised that the rock they were heading for was an island several kiloms across – a natural one, she assumed, although the causeway was probably artificial. The island seemed to consist of jagged, blue-black outcrops and wild, stark trees, sloping down to cyan-and-white shores dashed by the aquamarine waves. They drew closer and closer as the jeep thundered along, the great dark cliffs casting a chilly shadow.

As they came off the causeway, the jeep climbed the blue sand-dunes, groaning and grinding, sand spraying up as they headed to the top of the island. They emerged on to a plateau fringed with vegetation – spindly trees, spiky red bushes, green cactus-growths bigger than a human. Giant sheets of rock stuck up from the plateau at odd angles, stark against the violet sky, like broken teeth in a wide-open mouth.

The jeep came to a halt outside a chain-link fence, the whine of the engine subsiding to a gentle hum, the dust-cloud settling.

Beth's gaze settled on the rusting structure on the far side of the fence. It dominated the centre of the island, where a tree-lined slope coasted gently down towards a tangle of crimson vegetation. It was like a steel mountain, she thought, a battered bluff of metal. She recognised a Planetfall Class ship immediately, its stubby engines and spiky clusters of external instruments giving it away. The six towering landing-extrusions seemed to have smashed into the rock like giant fists. In places, the metal was peeling away like the skin of old fruit, even crumbling into fragments, revealing gashes in the structure, darkness beyond.

About fifty emms from the ship was a compound of a dozen or more geodesic domes, varying in size, squashed together like soap-bubbles. The two biggest, like giant greenhouses, loomed over the others. The vermilion light hit their triangular plexiglass segments and bounced outwards, scattering with a glancing beauty.

Set apart from the compound on the other side from the ship, a tower jutted upwards, a spike of rock and metal topped with a windowed hexagonal platform and a battered, primitive radar dish. Some kind of observation point, she thought.

Beth sniffed the air. New smells, not planet-smells but those which indicated the presence of Humanity – fire-smoke, hot metal, even roasting meat.

At first, Beth did not notice that Zach had turned round in the driver's seat, one arm over the back of the head-rest.

'Welcome to Paradise,' he said. 'Also known as Town.'

'You can prob'ly take the visor off,' said Maddi kindly. 'Light's not so bad, evenings.'

Beth lifted the visor, pushed back her wet hair. Then she gazed at the vast, crashed ship and the gleaming domes.

'It's … impressive,' she said after a few seconds.

'You reckon so, Spacegirl?' Mia joined her, the expression on her painted face giving nothing away. 'Give it a few weeks and you'll think it's a shit-hole like the rest of us do.'

'Ignore our resident philosopher.' It was Shan, speaking for the first time since the jeep had left the crash-site. 'To us, Town's just home.'

'Did you build it?' she asked in awe.

'No. It used to be a scientific base, decades ago,' Shan

said. 'Dunno why it was abandoned, but the Drones, well, they kind of renovated it. While we slept in semi-animation. Then the computer woke us up.'

The enormity of Beth's situation was growing in her mind, hope of rescue slipping away in the dying light.

'How ... long have you been here?' she asked.

Behind them, the round, pale Drones floated into view, having finally caught up with the jeep. They hovered, the small red discs in their front panels pulsing gently like the eyes of watchful animals. The dull whine of the Drones – almost inaudible – seemed to Beth to mingle with the sound in her head which was making her teeth hurt.

No, she said inside her head. *Not now.*

'Two hundred and forty-two cycles.'

'What does that mean? What's a cycle?'

'A day and night. Like an Earth day and night, only longer.'

'So ...' Beth did a quick calculation. 'About eight months?'

'In Earthtime? Nearer ten months,' Zach replied casually, punching a code into the keypad on the gate. 'But you lose count.'

'The days and nights – the cycles – they're longer than Earth's,' explained Shan. 'Equivalent to about twenty hours and ten hours. You get used to it. It's better suited to the human body ...'

'You had Earth-sim on your Ship?' This was Maddi, asking as if she already knew the answer.

'Yes.'

Earth-simulation, intended to mimic the light and climate rhythms of a central European day, was a key feature of *Arcadia* and her generation of colony ships. Beth had spent her entire life on *Arcadia* and knew nothing of Earth beyond what she had seen on the endless, detailed Lumi-casts, but she still felt it was her home. She had been one of the first of *Arcadia*'s children, born a few years into the voyage.

Her head was spinning.

She had no context for this. It was like a nightmare she was due to wake up from any second.

Except she wasn't. She never would.

Everything was gone.

The Tall Trees, the Teachers … Uncle Victor and Auntie Gwen … all the ChapterSisters and ChapterCousins … she didn't remember seeing any of them after that first explosion and the confused, screaming rush.

Great Power, why did she not remember what had happened to them all?

The grief punched through her body, physically taking strength from her.

Her legs became useless. The ground was spinning as it came up to meet her. The nausea, combined with the weakness in her limbs, was altogether too much, and she vomited copiously on the ground – mostly water at first, but then a pungent, steaming flux of bile, splattering the dust and the rocks. Gasping, sobbing, she felt the retching twist her body, her vision blurring, not knowing or caring what any of the others were doing.

Some sensation returned to her. She wiped her dry, hot mouth, and tried to stagger to her feet.

The Drones had swivelled as one, as if assessing the situation. They hovered closer, motors whining softly, a hot metallic smell in the air as electronic eyes darted back and forth. It was almost as if the robots were *concerned*.

'I'm fine,' Beth said, almost jokily. 'Thank you for asking.'

And then something rushed at her. She felt herself lifted, slammed against the rock. The impact knocked the breath from her. Someone was shouting. Regaining focus, she found herself staring up into the cold muzzle of Mia's gun.

'I don't care what you say, Zach.' The girl's voice was cold, hard, unyielding. 'She's a liability. We don't know anything about her. She could be anything, anyone.'

'Mia!' Maddi's voice had acquired an edge for the first time. 'What the hell–?'

Mia spat into the dust. 'All she's done since she got here is whine, snivel and puke. Do we need this?'

Beth trembled in fear. She pictured her uncle's face, and the rough bark of the Great Home Tree. Time stood still. In the silence, a chilly, distant howling – neither wind nor wolf, but something colder and more haunting than either.

In a second, it was gone.

'Put the gun away, Mia.' Zach's voice was soft but powerful as he strode to stand behind her. 'We don't do this.'

'Come on, Mia.' That was Maddi, backing him up. Shan, though, leaned against the jeep, smoking some kind of rolled-up black leaf, not saying a word and not getting involved. The Drones, at the edge of her vision, were bouncing up and down – in what could have passed for agitation.

'Give me a better reason,' said Mia coldly.

'Because I say so.'

'Oh, you're my daddy now, are you? Yeah, well, you can't tell me what to do any more than he could.' Mia's gaze did not move from Beth's face. 'It's easier this way.'

'Put it *down*, Mia.'

Mia grinned. Beth noticed how gleaming white her teeth were, like exposed bone. 'Put it down?' she mimicked, and moved the gun closer to Beth's head. 'Yeah. Like an animal.'

Beth tried not to panic. She had instinctively known they were all somewhere around her age, biologically – Zach slightly older maybe, the others a bit younger. But there was that hardness about them, a desperation. She could see it in Zach's expression, in Mia's toughened skin and sun-split hair, in Maddi's lean intensity. Only Shan seemed lithe, almost relaxed, at home in his dark and lean body. They all had good teeth, she noticed, white and firm. They didn't exactly look malnourished. So she guessed she wasn't going to starve here, if she lived. But there was one more thing she had noticed, one small thing which gave her a chance.

They were frightened.

'Please,' she said, holding her hands out, palms flat. 'I have no idea where I am, or what I'm doing here … But please. I am as scared as you. I'll do whatever I need. I need to survive. *We* need to survive.'

Mia did not slacken her grip on the gun.

But she did not tighten her finger on the trigger.

Beth forced herself to look past the cold metal of the gun, to ignore her churning guts and aching limbs. She heard her voice speaking, and it was like someone else's voice, like something outside her body.

'Mia,' she said. 'I don't think you want to kill me. You are a good person.'

Mia's nostrils flared.

'Please, Mia. You have survived, here, in this place, all of you. I do not know who you are or where you came from … I do not know what I am doing here. But I think I must be here for a reason. That is what I believe in, everything having a reason.'

Mia's eyes opened a fraction wider. Beth went on, gabbling desperately.

'Until yesterday, I thought I was heading for a new world called Celestia. And, well, I am here. The Universe, the Great Power I believe in, has given me to you, and you to me. We should not waste that. Let's show the Universe what human beings can do.'

There was an unbearable, tense silence. Everyone held their breath, and even the Drones stopped moving for a second.

Mia slowly, almost imperceptibly, raised her chin, as if Beth's words had hit her with a physical impact.

And then she lowered the gun.

Beth allowed herself to breathe out.

Mia made as if to turn away. And then she launched

herself forward, an elbow thudding into Beth, slamming her with powerful force against the metal fence. She gripped her by the collar, staring intently at her.

Shan took a step towards her. But Zach stopped him with the lightest of touches on his arm.

'You better be right,' Mia said softly, her eyes open wide, full of darkness and sadness. Her face was so close to Beth's that Beth could feel her breath, hot and rough. 'You better be right, or we're not done.'

And then she tapped Beth gently on the cheek, gave her a cold smile, and let her go.

Beth slowly unpeeled herself from the fence. 'I am fine,' she said, sarcasm finally burning through her polite Chapter veneer. 'I have only been fired through space, almost burned alive and smacked into this rock in the middle of nowhere. Do not bother asking.'

Shan gave her a sudden, unexpected grin. 'It's a bit like that round here,' he said. 'You get used to it.'

She rubbed her neck, glowering at the back of Mia's head. *I do not think I am going to get used to her in a hurry*, she thought.

The gates slid smoothly open, and they all piled back into the jeep.

Zach, glowering at Mia, gripped the wheel. 'We don't exactly get visitors in Town,' he said, trying to sound casual. 'Don't expect the red carpet.'

Nervously, Beth lowered herself into the seat again, clinging on. Mia deliberately didn't look at her.

The jeep entered the compound, followed by the watchful Drones, and the gates clanged shut automatically behind them.

There were more young people on the other side of the fence.

Beth caught a fleeting glimpse of battered clothes, of pale faces staring at her as the jeep made its way across the dusty enclosure. Some were tinkering with bits of machinery, others kicking a ball between them. A small knot of boys and girls was stoking a metal crucible with wood so that blood-orange flames leapt high. But she only caught fleeting glimpses of each group.

They juddered towards a pair of doors in the nearest dome, some kind of loading-bay. Tally-marks, in groups of five, were scratched into the metal – the cycles they'd been here, she presumed. She didn't have time to count.

On the left, in a dip in the earth where the land was so dark-blue it was almost black – a cluster of stark, white plastic crosses in the ground.

Her heart beat faster as she counted them.

Five, she told herself. *Five dead.*

And then the crosses dipped out of sight, and she was inside the big doors, swallowed up by darkness.

∞

2
HOME

I

Every day, Zachary Tal found it hard to believe how normal this place seemed – especially given how it had started out.

A bunch of no-hope kids. Fifty-one of them at first, living and breathing here on this island, in this strange place they called The Edge. Now there were forty-six. And they were all alone in the night, alone at the edge of civilisation. The edge, even, of existence itself.

He scanned the tables – taking in the various Towners trying to relax. Chess-players, card-players, those sitting, talking, drinking. The Drones buzzed around, bobbing on air, going about their usual tasks.

Zach had grown up in Olympus City on Mars, a town of two million souls. It was a settlement only three generations old, and their technology hadn't been great. Their Drones were wheezing, clapped-out old things which either walked on stilts or trundled on wheels or tracks. Those here were like something from the future, the most advanced Drones which Zach had seen.

He knew Maddi and one or two others had run into Synthets, the almost human-like Drones, in their earlier lives. He was silently grateful that they didn't have those here. From what he'd seen of them – only in holos and Lumi-casts – they were creepy, unsettling. Human but not human. A technology which humanity's Collective had decided to abandon, because it was getting dangerous, and because the question of rights and morals had raised its head too often for the Collective's liking.

The most advanced Synthets – only a hundred or so of them in existence – even behaved like humans: ate, drank, sweated, spat, excreted. They fought, loved, hated, remembered and wept. All of it. And some, it was rumoured, a handful, so closely resembled humans – complete with memories of a false life they had never had – that they were not even aware that they were Synthets at all. Zach found that idea very disturbing.

When he left Mars, under arrest, the last newscasts he heard had been full of the Synthet issue. The decision had been taken to ease back on the development of Synthets and retire those still in operation, before any of them did anything to 'bring humanity's future into question'. That was the euphemistic phrase they had used. He had the idea that the Collective was scared of them.

It was reassuring, then, to have these old-school Drones here – primitive yet advanced enough. Without their labour and expertise, the Collective would certainly have been sending the young exiles to their death on an empty world. There was no way the authorities could pretend otherwise. Giving them the Drones, this semi-abandoned base, the tools to build a new world – that had been the concession to the Chapters and other rights campaigners.

The nod to a kind of humanity. One glimmer of hope. They needed to build on that.

Blue Team was on catering duty today. Zach lifted a hand to the green-haired boy at the bar, Robbie. Zach leaned on the bar, arms flexed, trying to allow some of the tensions of the day to ease away.

'I hear it's a girl,' said a velvety, slightly mocking voice.

Ella Dax. Sitting along from him, hands round a steaming mug of something, she raised her eyebrows inquisitively.

She was a tall, athletic, strikingly beautiful girl, full-lipped and high-cheekboned, her dark skin burnished by the soft light. Blue dreadlocks twisted into a fantastic shape above her high forehead, the sides of her head shaved. Ella's beauty was marred only by a jagged, raw scar across her left cheek – a remnant of the past, one which she did not discuss. Only when you drew close to the girl could you see that her dark skin was inlaid with a fine, silvery mesh, the most delicate of filigree patterns. It covered her, neck to toe, and made her glitter uncannily in the light. She dressed in unadorned black, and had a blood-red Magna pistol jammed into her belt.

'Her name's Bethany,' he said. 'Bethany Kane.'

He liked and trusted Ella. She was the next oldest in the community, by just a handful of cycles, and she'd had his back a good few times this year when things were bad.

'What's she like?' Ella asked, loudly enough for him to hear above the noise. Her voice was soft, but commanding.

He indicated his thanks to Robbie as he was served his drink. 'Fifteener, at a guess. Nervous. She's got that, you know, ChapterSister way about her ... kind of proper, Old Earth. Seems pretty smart, but you can tell she was shaken up by the crash.'

For a second, the lights in the Rec Hall area dimmed, flickered, threatening to go out. Zach and Ella looked up, holding their breath – and then the lights flared brightly once, and settled back to their normal level.

Ella narrowed her eyes. 'I don't like that. This place is keeping us on our toes … So where's she from?'

'Colony starship, headed somewhere called Celestia. No idea what happened. She said it broke up, but we haven't had any junk come down.'

Ella took a thoughtful drink. 'Strange times,' she said softly. 'There could be territory battles. Anything could be happening up there.'

'Before …' He stopped. This was a word they rarely used, but he trusted Ella enough to feel safe using it. 'Before,' he said again, and she gestured, showing he could go on without any need to be more specific. 'There was talk. On the rail-rings. Traders out beyond the Outer Planets with rumours of something big, of something …'

'Like a war?'

'They said … the sort that makes stars burn and planets vaporise. And they said it wouldn't start with war, or even rumours of battle, but instead the kind of thing that might seem … almost normal. Cargo raids, squabbles, skirmishes. And then it would be … something else coming out of the night.'

He paused, had a drink. Time seemed to stand still. Ella was watching him carefully.

'You think something happened up there that's part of something bigger?' she asked. 'That this girl … wasn't meant to get away?'

'Ask yourself this,' Zach said. 'Why have we not had any others?'

Ella leaned back. 'I was asking myself that.' She gave a

sudden, unexpected smile, gleaming like a switched-on light. 'Anyway – she pretty?'

Zach made a non-committal noise, and tried to hide behind his drink.

'Aaaaaaah.' Ella's big grin did not diminish. 'That'll be a yes, then.'

'Stop it, Ella. She's part of our community, whether we like it or not. However she got here.'

'New blood, though,' said Ella mockingly. 'New … flesh. When did you last get any, Zach?'

'You're disgusting,' he said, but with a grin. 'Anyway, she's Chapter. I'm not going there. She'll have … prohibitions. We should respect that.'

Ella laughed. 'Chapter girls aren't nuns, you know. I was almost one myself.'

'Really?'

From high above them came a crackling noise, and a buzzing like angry wasps. The lights flickered again, this time with half a second of darkness between each flicker, and then finally stuttered back into dim life.

Zach looked upwards, worriedly. 'Get someone to sort out that circuit, will you?'

'Me? Do I have to?'

'That's what I like about you, Ell. You never complain.' Zach finished his drink in one go and slammed the mug down. 'Got stuff to do,' he said with a grin, and slipped into the shadows.

II

Ella had no intention of doing the job herself, even though she was more than capable. She knew the person to take it on. She pulled out her radio and keyed the channel.

'Mia, *darling*. Can you do somethin' for me?'

There was a hiss and crackle, and then Mia's tired, jaded voice came through. '*What is it? I was asleep.*'

'Oh, good. I got a job to wake you up. Go take a look at the junction boxes in the ducting for D section, will you … ? We got a … reluctant illumination problem.'

There was a resentful silence, and then, '*Fuck off. Seriously?*'

'Yes, Mia, seriously. Unless you want everyone to be eating in the dark tonight, honey.'

A long, drawn-out groan. '*All right.*' There was a scrabbling noise at the other end, presumably Mia either starting to get dressed or pulling some equipment together. '*Give me ten minutes.*'

'If you make it five, dearest,' said Ella, 'I'll be so grateful.'

She snapped the radio off.

As she reached for her drink again, Ella felt the air shift next to her, and heard the scrape of a wooden stool.

'Colm,' she said without turning round, 'you move like a Hunter.'

'How'd you know it was me?' said a male voice in mock outrage.

Ella turned gracefully, leaning on one elbow. 'I got eyes in the back of my head.'

The young man who had moved to sit beside her was bony-lean, pointy-faced. His teeth were white and firm, his black hair tousled as if it hadn't seen a brush in weeks. Colm Dale was handsome, but in an untrustworthy way. His gaze flickered back and forth all the time, always checking out the rest of the room, never resting on the person he was supposedly talking to.

'Right, then,' he said. 'Didn't have a tiff with lover-boy, did we?'

Ella scowled.

She and Zach had never been lovers, not in any real sense. 'The chances of our making it to a second generation here,' Zach had said to her on Cycle Two, as they worked together, tightening bolts on the stanchions of the main stairway, 'are almost nil.' And she had said with a grin, pushing her hair back, 'Definitely nil, if none of us ever find the time to sleep together.' She and Zach had laughed, and that had been the start of their understanding, as they called it.

There were some romantics here, she knew, some who still believed in a thing called *love*. Not Colm – he was an opportunist, an old-school seducer. But Maddi, she was one, and Ella knew her genuine sadness now that Leila was gone. Mia, well, Mia was as conscience-free as Colm, but more honest in her seduction, giving the physical act freely to anyone she desired enough, but never deceiving, and never allowing any to possess her heart. There were some who seemed to have bonded, to have genuine feelings for each other: Dionne and Hal, Aisling and Brad, a few others who darted in and out of what might be called love. Maddi and Leila – until Leila went. But in a place like this, with the available population so low, what were the chances of it truly being real?

They knew one thing. If this place was to be the start of something, the beginning of a new mark on the Universe, a new fingerprint of life and not the guttering of a dying flame, then they would need something for the future.

Something to ensure humanity continued on this planet.

The chances of our making it to a second generation.

Nobody had been brave enough to try. Nobody wanted to be the first. As far as Ella knew, anyway.

'Ohhhhh. Sensitive subject?' Colm sneered. 'Don't worry. I won't pry. Lot on his mind, young Zach. Lot of responsibility. It'd drive a lesser man mad.'

'You mean you?' Ella suggested, sipping her drink. But there was nobody else at the bar, and talking to an irritant like Colm amused her more than her own company. Anything, in this place, was usually better than solitude – although Ella, for her own reasons, often chose it more than most.

'Me? *Pfffft.*' Colm made a dismissive sound. 'I'm not lesser, or greater, or anything, Ella. I'm me. Holding out for a way off this dump.'

'Ohhhh, you'll like the new girl, then. Poor kid thinks she's getting rescued.'

Colm laughed. 'Avenging angels gonna hoist her up into the sky, are they? Carry her off to live in luxury on Galaxy City?'

Ella shot a derisive look at him. 'You ever go there?'

'May have done.'

'Oh, right.' Ella left a suitable pause. 'They got quite a trade in low-lifes, I've heard.'

'Ella-bella. Every time you open your mouth, you betray your total and utter devotion to me, d'you know that? Why not give into it and be mine for a bit?'

'I'm not anybody's.' She didn't like the way this conversation was going.

'Not what I've heard. The opposite, in fact.'

Ella moved at him like a lioness, sweeping his metal tankard aside with a clatter and splashing the cheap, greenish *plaan* beer across the counter, making young Robbie jump back in alarm.

She grabbed Colm's wrist in a firm, tight grip, enjoying the change in the boy's expression as he became more and more uncomfortable. 'Ow!' he yelped. 'What are you doing?'

There was a gentle hissing sound as her fingers tightened. The silvery mesh on her body seemed to flicker with an inner light. Even her irises appeared brighter, sharper.

Ella spoke calmly, 'I want to make sure I have your attention.'

'Yeah … You've got it. Seriously.'

'In all the time we've been here, Colm, you have made thirty-eight provocative, suggestive and, you know what, downright *dirty* comments to me. I only have so much patience for that kind of thing.'

'Oh, good, Great. I'll try and respect that. Seriously, could you not hold my wrist so tight?'

'All I want to do,' said Ella, still calm, 'is make absolutely sure you understand there is no way *anything* is going to happen between us. The only way you're ever getting inside me is if I kill and eat you. And if you carry on like this, that might happen.'

'Okay, okay … Can you … let go now …?'

'Watch yourself, Colm. One day,' she said, 'that tongue of yours is going to get you into trouble.'

'We've got something in common then. *Aaaaagh!*' With inhuman strength, she had bent his wrist back at an angle it shouldn't go, and the rest of his body was twisting in sympathy, almost sliding off the bar-stool.

'We got one more to feed here, Colm. Who knows? Zach might decide it's one in, one out. And we have to decide on who goes, I don't fancy your chances much. Do you?'

She let him go with a sudden, theatrical wave of her hand, deciding he'd probably had enough.

He rubbed his wrist, still trying to make light of it, but less successfully now.

'All right, all right. Jeeeez. No need to assault a boy for a bit of banter. I'm happy to say you're an angel and always have been, if you promise never to do that again.' He glanced down at his fallen tankard and the spray of green beer on the bar top. 'That's a waste of – hell, I'd like to say *good* beer, but you and I both know it tastes like Lantrill piss. But it's booze, and that's the only way a lot of us stay alive in this place. I mean, who cares about a liver?

Concentrate on living. Can I get another there, Robbie Roberto?'

'Don't give him one,' said Ella firmly. 'He's leaving.' She fixed Robbie with her firmest stare, and he withdrew, grinning.

Colm glowered at her, still rubbing his aching wrist. 'You know, I think you might have broken it. What do I do if you've broken it? I should sue you. Only – oh I forgot. There aren't any lawyers here, are there? And no money. So what use is that, eh?' He grinned. 'I'll have to drown my sorrows.' He winked at Robbie. 'C'mon, Roberto. One more.'

Ella raised her mug in mock salute. 'You should try camomile tea. Much better for you. It's how I stay so calm.'

'Really? Ella, darling, I thought it was the natural, perfect balance of serotonin and dopamine in your brain. I'm disappointed.' A Drone bobbed in at Colm's shoulder, arriving soundlessly as usual. 'Now, what do you want, buddy? Don't tell me you've turned into a portable drinks dispenser? That would be useful. Tell Zach.' Colm wagged a finger. 'That would actually be really useful.'

The underside of the Drone flipped open and a small, spongy pad on a metal rod pressed against the bar, wiping up the spilt beer and simultaneously spraying a fine mist of cleaning fluid, so that in seconds no trace of the spillage was left. With an almost-inaudible whirr and clunk, the cleaning-rod retracted and the panel in the Drone flipped closed. It flashed a light once to show its task was complete, and bobbed off across the bar, weaving in between the metal pillars which supported the roof.

'There you go.' Colm eased himself off the stool. 'You need a skill like that,' he said to Ella. 'Might make you useful. You could be somebody's lovely wife. What a prize.' He reached out as if to stroke her face, but she smacked his hand down with force, her expression cold and hard.

'You won't take a friendly warning, will you?'

She gave her voice more of an edge. Insidious bastard, she thought. I can take care of myself, but there are other girls here, girls old enough for his type to notice. Two hundred cycles can make a lot of difference. And Colm's noticed, all right.

He held his hands up in mock surrender. 'I'll go and … find something useful to do,' he said.

'You do that,' Ella told him.

She watched him stride off, not allowing herself to look down until he had disappeared up the steps and through the top door.

Then Ella allowed herself to breathe out, and took a long drink from her mug.

III

'I hope you don' mind, but … they burned your clothes.'

Beth spun around at the soft voice.

It was the red-haired girl, Maddi, smiling hesitantly. She was standing there with some clothes over her arm – a pair of sleek black trousers, a plain, round-necked white shirt and a battered, military-style, leather-look jacket. She was holding a pair of sturdy lace-up boots. 'Hope these are your size.'

Beth didn't quite know how to react. Then she realised Maddi was being kind and she nodded – briefly, awkwardly.

For the last hour she'd been kept in isolation in this bare room somewhere deep in one of the domes of Town. She'd been pointed towards a shower unit – inside it, brownish but warm water had pounded and massaged her body with surprisingly soothing force, and then hidden air-ducts had dried her with blasts of air. A mouthwash nozzle had bombarded her mouth with sweet, minty granules, making her teeth feel smooth and fresh. Confused thoughts bombarded her mind, and she tried to focus them by working out the distance between here and the site of her crashed pod, based on the speed of the jeep and the time they had taken – it had to be about twenty, maybe thirty kiloms.

Two fair, wispy-thin girls even younger than her, who had shyly introduced themselves as Cait and Livvy, had helped to dress her cuts and bruises. Her body, under a thin towel, was speckled with patches of white gauze, as if her skin were the board for some bizarre game. An older girl, Luciana, who they called Lulu, had examined her like a doctor – shining various instruments into her throat, ears and eyes and scanning the strength of her bones and muscles.

Then they had left her here.

'I am not *diseased*,' she said, somewhat resentfully, pulling the towel more tightly round her body.

'Yeah, well. Y'know what people are like,' said Maddi, putting the clothes down. 'The Twelvies patch you up?'

'Twelvies …? Oh, the two girls? Yes, they were very kind.'

Maddi tossed her a sealed plastic packet containing some very basic white underwear. 'Sorry, don' run to anything fashionable. You'll … find they don' really care much about that stuff here.'

Beth was grateful for the girl's flippant comments, knowing she was trying to put her at her ease. 'You have spare clothes lying around?' she said, picking up the jacket and admiring it. The jacket was well-made – rough, but solid, with dull metallic buckles and metal studs which seemed built for action.

'Kinda. They was Leila's. She's … well, she was about your size.'

The crosses. Beth remembered.

She looked up at Maddi steadily. 'Leila was one of …'

'Yeah. One we lost. Special, Leila was.'

'I'm … sorry.' Beth paused, uncertain if she had picked up on the nuance. 'Special … to you?'

Maddi rubbed her thumb and forefinger together, awkwardly. 'Yeah, well.'

'I'm sorry. You were pair-bonded?'

'Pair-bonded?' Maddi laughed. 'Oh, that's Chapter talk, right?'

'I suppose so.'

On board, many would find a lifelong mate with whom they expected to settle and start a family when the ship reached its destination, or even before. The Chapter Elders and the Teachers played a part in the matchmaking, and sometimes, these pair-bonds were chosen in childhood by the Chapter. In honour of the Great Power, the couples would dedicate their lives to each other and any future children they might raise.

'Nah,' Maddi said. 'We … really liked each other. But that's life, innit? Or death.'

'You're sure this is …' Beth paused, chose an Old Earth word, one she thought Maddi might use herself. 'Cool?'

'Hell, yeah, it's cool. Leila was … well, she was kind. She thought about others. She'd've wanted you to have it. Oh … ' Maddi handed her a black plastic packet. 'The other stuff you had. Got a bit scorched, but … still yours.'

Beth opened the plastic envelope. There were several items inside: a ring, her belt made of closely-welded titanium cylinders, and the oak-and-vanadium knife which had been a present from Uncle Victor. She had a brief flash of memory – carving wooden figures with him in the Sky-Park.

'Thank you. Some of these things, they … they mean a lot to me.'

She wanted to ask how Leila and the others had died. One for later, she thought. Her head was spinning. *So many questions.* How did this place start, how had they survived, how did they all get together?

Maddi folded her arms, put her head on one side. 'You was pretty upset back there,' she said, peering out from behind her crimson fringe.

Beth sat down heavily. She was still half-convinced that this was all some dreadful, very intense and detailed nightmare – and that in a second, she'd be back in her Homeglobe, with the Lumiscreen showing its shifting patterns of

EarthHome and the soft multisensory aura-music shimmering in the background, tingling her body into wakefulness.

These memories of life on the ship came back to her like this, as broken vignettes. Patchy, fragmentary. She supposed it might be the effects of shock.

'I'm guessin', yeah,' Maddi went on, turning away to give Beth privacy as she dressed, 'there's a hell of a lot goin' on in your mind. I can't … really remember what it's like. Comin' here for the first time.'

Beth slipped awkwardly into the clothes, pulling on the surprisingly comfortable shirt and trousers. 'Well … It's different for you, isn't it? I mean, this is your colony. It may not be perfect, but you chose it.' There was a silence. 'It's all right. You can turn back.'

Maddi's expression was troubled, shifty. 'Not exac'ly,' she said.

'You crash-landed too?' Beth asked, remembering the battered ship she had seen outside, looming above Town. She pulled the jacket on. It felt comforting. She guessed it was polymer, but it had the warm, feral odour of real leather.

'I'll … let Zach explain. Oh, here …'

Maddi picked up the other package she'd brought with her, a small, open metallic box divided into two. In one half there was a green mush, sprinkled with various herbs and spices, and in the other a passable stew with what appeared to be meat and pulses in a thick, red-brown stock.

Beth took it nervously. Emptying her stomach earlier had left her feeling drained – and now that she'd recovered from that, she realised how hungry she was.

'There's water too,' said Maddi. She put a silver flask down beside Beth on the table. ''Fraid it's the same stuff you had before. Tastes bad at first, I know.'

'You are being … kind,' said Beth. It sounded ridiculous – a small, empty word against the magnitude of all she had lost. The steam coming off the stew had a hot, meaty, aromatic smell – not unpleasant – but the mash was a lurid green and seemed to be full of stringy, tough coils of stewed vegetation. 'Um … what am I eating?'

'Lantrill stew with dried pulses … Not a good time to tell me you're a vegetarian. You don' really get that luxury here.'

Beth prodded the meat. 'No, no, it … it's fine,' she said, uncertainly.

'Goes right through you the first time you have it. Don't worry, we've got decent sanitation.'

Beth shuddered. 'And what's … Lantrill?' she asked.

'Sorta boar creatures. Live out in the forests. Well, almost jungle really. We've found a few good hunting-grounds.'

'You *hunt*?' Beth was astonished. She'd viewed Lumi of the clamour and clatter of old hunts, from long after the time when people chased animals for food – from a barbaric time when it was a sport and pleasure. To her it seemed a totally alien idea. She flipped the pieces of meat over with her fork, uncertain. The reddish meat fell apart easily, soft flesh crumbling into smaller, layered chunks in the sauce.

Maddi grinned. 'Some things you gotta do. Processed

protein was never gonna last for ever … Hey, the Hunters may ask you to join them. That's a good knife you've got there.'

'I am afraid I am not much of a huntress. It's more of a … well, a memento.'

'Do you fish? We spear them from the causeway, and we've got nets too. Some freshwater lakes, too, good ride away. Some edible fish in them.'

'Well, I know the principle … How do you know what is edible and what is poisonous?' she asked in wonderment.

'You bio-scan a sample,' said Maddi. 'We got the equipment. You can simulate the effect on the stomach. Even program in any known allergies.'

'That's amazing.'

'Yeah, doesn't often go wrong. We've only ever had a couple o'people throw up after a bad one.'

'Right,' said Beth faintly.

Maddi pointed at the green mush. 'And that's *plaan*, the cactus stuff.' Beth remembered the giant, twisted cacti rearing out of the dust. 'It's good, actually,' Maddi went on. 'Like marrow. Bit chewy, but … Few extra bits in there, too – proper veg from Hydroponics. Beans, tomatoes, carrots.'

That, at least, gave Beth hope. There had been huge, splendid hydroponic areas on the *Arcadia*, providing fresh vegetables for its entire population, lovingly tended by the gardening Drones. She could see it all clearly playing out in front of her, as if she was there. And yes, she remembered, as they came into Town on the roaring jeep, seeing two massive domes, at least five times the size of the habitation areas, squatting behind all the others.

Carefully, she tried a forkful of the *plaan* mash. It was stringy, like old leeks, but it wasn't bad – there was a dash of something sharp, a bit like fennel, in there too. She gave a cautious thumbs-up.

'I'll leave you to it. Zach's gonna come and get you. He's callin' a Gathering about you.'

'Maddi?'

'Mmm?' The girl paused at the door.

'Did anyone … I mean … have you seen any others?'

'Others?'

'From the *Arcadia*? Did any other pods make it?'

Maddi frowned. 'Nope. You, you're the only thing what's broke through the atmosphere since our last load of space-junk. An' that were like, hundreds of cycles ago.'

Beth felt her stomach flip, disappointment coursing through her like a poison, weakening her body. 'Really? Not … not even any debris?'

'Look … don't be too hopeful. The computer in the Ship does a regular orbit-scan. And we've got basic radar. That's how we spotted you, babe.'

Beth frowned. 'But I crashed, what, twenty or thirty kiloms from you?' She recalled how she had worked this out while showering. 'Someone else could have landed on the other side of the planet.'

'Nah. A Class X Pod like yours, sensors will have homed in on our tech-emissions, right? Brought you in, close as possible. So anyone else woulda landed nearby too. Unless the pod sensors failed, in which case … They're dead anyway.'

Beth didn't allow herself to think about that. 'I want to get back. If I can,' she said firmly. 'I know you're being … well, kind … but … I need to know what happened to the *Arcadia*. I have to get back.'

Maddi gave a tight, humourless grin. 'Yeah, well. Nobody leaves here.'

The meaty stew stung her mouth and slid down her throat, where it tingled, fizzing angrily. 'What do you mean?'

'It's … this place, it's … You don' leave, yeah? However bad it gets …' Maddi didn't meet her gaze. 'This place is your new home. It's not paradise, but it's not hell. Stuff keeps breaking all the time, but we get by. You'll get used to it.' Her voice was not unkind, but there was an impatient edge to it. 'Seeya later.'

The door closed, and there was silence.

Beth tried to forget what Maddi had said.

She forced down several mouthfuls of the tingly stew and the chewy, spicy *plaan*. Survival instinct had kicked in. She knew that, whatever was to come – and something told her it might be unpleasant – she needed to eat and drink. She took several gulps of the water, swilling it round in her mouth. It didn't taste so bad this time. She swallowed it, hoping it stayed down.

There was silence in the windowless room, humming in her ears like static.

Beth lay down on the bed and stared at the grey ceiling. She stretched her arms out, admired the smooth, almost alive texture of the jacket, the sharp clicks of the magnetic snaps on the cuffs. It was a strong, warm, solid garment, like both a comfort blanket and battle armour at the same time.

Thank you, Leila, she said to herself. *I'll never know you, but I'll try to make myself worthy of your jacket.*

But the thought kept coming back.

These people are keeping something from me. They'd helped her from the pod, dressed her wounds, given her food and water and clothes, but they hadn't given her the full truth.

It wasn't lost on Beth that she hadn't, as yet, seen any adults. Maddi and Shan were about her age, give or take; Lulu and Mia were older, maybe sixteen or seventeen. The quiet girls, Cait and Livvy, were twelve. The oldest person she'd seen here so far was Zach, who surely could be no more than eighteen.

Mia intrigued and scared her. Jumpy, frightened Mia, who had wanted to kill Beth where she stood. Put her down like an animal. Even Zach, with his natural air of authority, had only just managed to stop her.

Was it Mia? Or was there more to it?

Beth knew enough, she thought, about the colony worlds – had read about them in the *Arcadia*'s library, had attended the Teachers' modules and watched many Lumi displays about their history. Earth's first tentative, jittery excursions into space … all the accidents and disasters and setbacks … All in just a few hundred years of spacefaring history. She'd heard about colonies which failed in a year, in two years, in ten. Through famine, plague, conflict with the indigenous life-forms – or by being beaten down by a war of attrition against the environment in which they found themselves. It was hard enough to find worlds in other systems' 'Goldilocks Zone', worlds suitable for sustaining life. To ask also that they should be Eden-like and tranquil was pushing it too much.

She sensed tension here, crackling in the air like static. They were edgy, uncertain, as if they were constantly on the brink of ... something ...

And then there were the graves.

Nobody leaves here. What could Maddi mean by that ... ? Beth had a creeping feeling in her body. An unnameable irrational idea that she had crashed somewhere that would put her in even more danger.

Her head was still aching, tingling from within. She tapped it. 'No,' she said. 'No!'

The tingling continued, like an insistent alarm-clock at the edge of her hearing. She tried to sleep. Tried to block out this new, difficult world and these strange people, trying to let her mind relax and her heartbeat slow.

IV

'You can see the smoke, still,' Zach said. 'Where the pod came down.'

'Yeah.' Lulu could see. Out there, beyond the great curve of toughened glass, past the rocks and the undulating trees. Across the causeway and the dark, churning sea, a wiggly exclamation mark of grey-black rose up into the violet sky. They could see it even through the gouts of steam from the fissures. 'Pretty big impact.'

Lulu had found Zach on the Sky-Gallery, a semi-circular platform high up in the main dome, offering a view as far as the horizon. He was staring out across the darkening sea to the forests and mountains beyond. She slid a hand on to his shoulder, and he planted a soft kiss on her close-cropped head.

'Don't pretend you like me,' she said, turning away with a mock scowl.

'Hey, who said I liked you? You stop me going mad sometimes. That's all I need.'

'I'm honoured.'

The evening lights had kicked in, a dull, liquid-orange gleam from the discs inlaid into the high ceiling above them.

Two Drones, their plaques reading 158 and 006, buzzed busily past her, going about their business, one carrying a toolbox with its arm-attachment. Lulu stepped out of their shadows with an exaggerated flourish. Always something to do, she thought wearily. It's never finished.

Lulu leaned against the rail beside Zach, briefly slipping a hand across his.

She glanced over her shoulder at the chasm of the Atrium below. Yellow team was on duty, bustling back and forth between kitchen and Rec Hall – she picked out Linzi, Carsten, Joel, Mahala, Dionne. A team of five Drones, the size of buttons from up here, buzzed between them, holding trays piled high with crockery, cutlery and flasks. There was always a noise in Town, always a bustle, no matter what time of the day or night – a background hum, punctuated with cries and clattering, which Lulu had slowly become used to. She heard sobbing, too, on more than a few occasions. Usually, she managed to ignore it.

Luciana Fox was one of the most vital members of Town – a Late Offworld seventeener with AMT, or Accelerated Medical Training. A prodigy at the Deimos MedStar Station, she'd been trained in her skills by her father. Her downfall was spectacular and well-known. She was, she insisted, framed for causing the death in mysterious circumstances of a Senator, who had been found dead in the family apartment. She knew that Zach, who had grown up in Olympus City on Mars, had known of her – the case had been that notorious in the Martian Federation.

The matter had never been settled to anyone's satisfaction, and – despite her influential father – Lulu was tried and found guilty. Within a few days, she had gone from a dazzling MedStar to the lowest of humanity, taking the final place on a long-haul voyage from Deimos Station into the unknown – alongside killers, robbers, thieves, political prisoners, dreamers and the plain unlucky.

Her hair had been long when they first arrived here, a sweeping curtain of dazzling gold – but as a statement, a way of telling the Universe what she thought of it these days, she had trimmed it down and down. It became first a bob, then a spiky crop. It was now dyed blue, setting off her elegant, high-cheekboned face.

'Maddi gave her the stuff?' Zach asked quietly.

'Yeah.'

'How does she seem? In good shape?'

'Don't think it's quite sunk in yet. I think she still believes someone's coming to rescue her.'

Zach snorted. 'Yeah, well. She can dream on.'

There was an awkward silence, during which they saw Maddi coming up the spiral stairs from the level below.

'So?' Zach asked her. 'What do you make of her?'

'Ahhh … well, she's cute,' said Maddi.

Lulu laughed. 'There you go. One-track mind.'

Zach was impatient. 'Yeah, I could have told you that myself, thanks. I mean, do you buy her story?'

Lulu was shocked. It had never occurred to her, at any time in the last few hours, to disbelieve Bethany Kane. She had assumed the girl was simply too frightened and too overwhelmed by everything to have lied. Now that the cynical, analytical Zach mentioned the possibility, it opened up a whole realm of new possibilities in her mind.

'Not really thought about it,' Maddi confessed. 'Lu?'

'We have to trust her.'

'Maybe,' said Zach. His voice was level, not betraying any emotion. 'Just wondered if you'd like to think about how credible she is, that's all.'

'No need to be smug.'

He gave them a quick, taut smile. 'Not being smug. Practical. We've got to bear in mind the possibility that she may not be who she says she is.'

'Right,' said Lulu. 'So what do we do?'

'Keep a close eye at first. Make her welcome, but don't let her in too much.'

Maddi wasn't sure. 'I don' really like that. It's like … we're not trustin' her. I mean … surely you gotta trust people sometime, Zach?'

At first, he didn't reply.

'Have you ever stood up here at night,' he asked after a while, 'and watched the moons rise? That's when you really start to feel it. That sense of being out here on the edge of *nothing*. That's when it really starts to mess with your mind. That this place is all there is for us. For ever. It's not at night. Night's fine. Night's the same anywhere, except the stars are different from home …'

'What you sayin'?' Maddi was puzzled. Normally he was so straightforward, assertive, decisive. She had not seen him like this for a while.

'He gets like this, sometimes,' Lulu murmured. 'All philosophical.'

'I'll take your word for it,' Maddi said.

Zach's green eyes were sharp and clear. Lulu smiled up at him.

'We've built something here,' she said. 'Something fragile, but it works, yeah?'

He nodded. 'And now *she* arrives. So I'm not just thinking, what good's she going to be, let's burn the dead wood, like Mia was. And I'm not just thinking, how are we going to help her integrate here? I'm thinking – *what does this mean?* Something brought her here. She speaks like a sister of the Collective, says she's from a Chapter, but … who knows?'

'Who knows what?' said Maddi.

'Where Bethany Kane's really from. Space-junk's one thing. Space-junk with a living being inside, that's something else. Call it fate, call it … destiny, whatever. Something brought her here. The girl who fell out of the sky.' He grinned. 'Almost magical, isn't it? Some people might say.'

'We always knew it could happen,' Lulu pointed out.

'Yeah. But it has … We play it safe.'

'You're sayin' we keep Beth at arm's length?' Maddi asked.

'While we check her out.'

'So how exactly do we do that, then?' Lulu asked. 'We can't look up her records. Not out here.'

Zach was quick to answer. 'Sooner or later, she'll do or say something. People who are lying slip up. They can't keep it up. They say something that doesn't tally with something else. They do something odd you can't quite put your finger on. So be alert.' He paused. 'And, Mads … don't …'

'Don't what?' Maddi answered sharply.

'Don't … get too close. I know what you're like.'

She snorted. 'Yeah, as if.'

'You *did* say she was cute.'

'Yeah, well, so did you,' she reminded him.

'Point taken. Anyway, I've scheduled a Gathering. Twenty minutes. It's time for everyone to make up their own mind about her. Me, I think this place can always use an extra pair of hands.'

'And an extra mouth to feed,' said Lulu, instantly guilty. She knew it was wrong to think like that. There was something likeable about Beth, something instantly trustworthy. The prim, precise way she spoke was odd, but that was her upbringing. She seemed a good person.

Zach thumped the rail of the observation platform. 'You know what? Never mind twenty minutes. Let's do it now.' He snapped his fingers at the nearest Drone, number 044, who floated obediently over. 'Sound the Gathering klaxon for me.'

V

The bass note shuddered through Beth's body as Zach led her through dimly-lit corridors to the Rec Hall. She scurried to keep up with his long, confident strides.

Through every Drone and speaker-grille, it sounded: a great booming noise overlaid with a shrill trilling, as if designed to reach every point on the range of human hearing.

The Hall filled up. Those working elsewhere in Town left their posts, those relaxing put down footballs and cards, and one by one they drifted in from the various corners. The Towners teased and bent the law here on the Edge in many ways. But nobody ever ignored a summons to a Gathering.

The Rec Hall was a vast, glassed-in space, reaching up almost as far as the top of the Main Dome, its height broken here and there by platforms and mezzanines. Giant pillars, like crimson tusks, met at the high, circular Sky-Gallery surrounded by its metal barrier. A swirling spiral staircase in the centre of the room led up to the different levels, ending at the gallery.

At the top of the steps, with Zach beside her, Beth huddled in the jacket, trying not to show she was quaking in fear. She tried to count as they came in, and also to see what range of people made up this strange community on the edge of nowhere. Murmurs, clatters, whispers and bantering cries echoed through the Rec Hall as people tried to find places to sit – on benches, on tables, on the floor. There was the occasional electronic squawk from a Drone as they buzzed around, almost anxiously.

The Towners jostled, thumped each other, whistled, cat-called. The youngest were scraggy girls and boys of no more than twelve, their faces unnaturally tough and knowing for children so young. Then there were teenagers of all sizes, although pretty much everyone was lean and bony – barely a gram of fat on anyone, Beth thought. Either they ate and exercised well, or they were always hungry.

Nobody's skin and hair was unhealthy, exactly, but she recognised the look of people who spent a lot of time in the blast of the sun and the wind – a tanned, weathered appearance, hair sun-bleached or in some cases shaven to the skull. Pretty much everyone had done something to their body: a tattoo somewhere, a garish earring or nose-ring, a lurid dye on hair or hands. Some of them were grubby, she thought, hair bunched up or in need of a comb – but nobody was actually *dirty* as such, and there wasn't an offensive smell of unwashed bodies, more a kind of fusty warmth. Beth was grateful for that.

She picked out the faces she recognised. Maddi, her face warm and friendly under her shock of red hair. Shan, slender and dark and mysterious, lounging against the wall, his expression slightly knowing. Right at the back, lean and lithe and dangerous, was Mia, her face unreadable behind jet-black sunshades. Sitting at the front, the two young fair-haired girls who had helped her shower and dress her wounds – Cait and Livvy. Then there was Zach, of course, tall and commanding beside her. She kept glancing surreptitiously at him to take in his firm jawline and smoothly muscular arms. And then telling herself to stop it.

All names, faces registered and logged. She knew her memory never let her down.

Beside Zach, hanging back on the step above like a guardian or a right-hand woman, was the black girl with the glittering skin and scarred cheek, introduced to her briefly as Ella. She carried a natural air of authority and made Beth feel a kind of alien coldness. She didn't seem friendly at all.

One by one, they all noticed she was there.

The whispers and shouts and babbles and scrapes and clatters all stopped. There was stillness and open-mouthed silence. Expectant, the young Towners stared at the new arrival and waited for their leader to speak. To explain.

Zach waited for total silence. Like one of the Teachers, Beth thought, at a Schooling back on *Arcadia*. He seemed older than he was. When he spoke, he didn't need to project – the Rec Hall carried his soft voice easily, and everyone hung on his words.

'Brothers and sisters,' he said. 'Thank you all. This Gathering is in session.' He paused briefly. 'We've been here, making sacrifices, working hard, pulling together to show them that we *could*. Because, make no mistake, brothers and sisters. We were not sent here to *survive*. We were not sent here to live. We were not sent here to flourish. Yes, we had the salvaged tech, and yes, we had the Drones to help adapt this place, the place we call Town.'

Only three or four Drones, Beth noticed, bobbed in and out of the crowd, going about their maintenance or cleaning business. The others seemed to have withdrawn elsewhere, as if they knew a Gathering was for the humans and not for them.

What puzzled her was how this benighted outpost had an advanced class of Drone. Twenty of them, she remembered Maddi telling her, although the way they jetted about in a perpetual state of agitation made it seem as if there were more. They were smooth, spherical, with one single-lens eye and, from what she had seen, a variety of extendable tools tucked away beneath concealed openings and hatches. They were individualised as well – by the three-digit number-plaques, but also in the way each one was put together. The riveting, the finish on each was subtly different, and no two Drones were exactly the same shade of metal: there were silver ones, red ones, blue ones, some a gleaming gold and some a dull coppery hue.

'In all that time,' Zach said, his voice still strong and clear, 'we've never had any connection with the outside world. No patrols, the occasional bit of debris – sometimes rocks, sometimes burnt-up pieces of spacecraft from whatever the hell is going on up there. But …' He gestured towards Beth. 'Fate, or destiny, or luck – call it what you will – has brought us Bethany Kane. She's fallen from the sky, and she survived. For the next couple of cycles, she will need our help, and our understanding, and our patience, as she tries to come to terms with her new surroundings.'

He paused. Beth's face burned with embarrassment. She hardly dared to make eye contact with anyone in the crowd. She listened to Zach as he introduced her, passing on to the group the little she had told her rescuers about herself since arriving.

'Beth is a survivor from one of the Great Ships. She's from the *Arcadia*, which was on a twenty-year journey to a habitable world on the Outer Rim. Beth was born on the Ship, and she's spent her entire life there so far.' He glanced at Beth for a second, reassuringly. 'Our systems … haven't been able to detect any other remains of the *Arcadia*, or any indication of where it might have gone. We can only assume that Beth's pod brought her a long, long way from what has been her home so far. Think about that, brothers and sisters. She hasn't come here the same way the rest of us did, but she's ended up in pretty much the same situation – she's alone, she's determined to survive, and she realises she may never again see the people she grew up with. Her family. Her friends.' Zach raised his voice. 'Just like us, yeah …?'

There were murmurings in the crowd. Some, though, were exchanging uneasy looks, not saying anything at all. Beth's fear grew.

'And so,' Zach said, 'now Beth's here, I don't want anyone

resenting her presence, or making things difficult for her. She's one of us. She's our sister. And I know … I know that she will pull her weight, and want to be one of us, and want to be part of this community. Because we're all she's got.'

There was silence for a second, and then several different conversations broke out at once in the crowd. A tall, lissom girl of about fifteen, with brown skin, her hair in a jet-black plait, stood forward, raising her hand.

'I think lots of us want to know a lot more about her,' the girl said. Then she appeared to change her approach, and addressed Beth directly. 'Sorry. About *you*. We don't really know who you are, or where you're from. You could be anyone. You could be a spy, or a SecureTech agent, sent here to observe us. Report back on us.'

'That's pretty unlikely, Baljeet.' It was Shan who spoke. 'You think anyone gives that much of a damn about us?'

Shan was right, thought Beth. Why would spies or SecureTech be interested in this ragtag colony on the edge of nowhere? Or was there something that made them important – something, again, that she didn't know?

Baljeet looked Beth up and down – curiously, but not unkindly. 'Why don't you speak, Beth?' she said. 'Don't let Zach or Shan or *anyone* put words in your mouth.'

There were murmurs of agreement from some of the older Towners.

Beth stepped forward, her mouth dry, all the faces in front of her a blur.

For some reason, she fixed her gaze on the bobbing Drone at the back of the room, staring intently at the winking red light on its curved surface. She found its presence oddly comforting.

'I did not come here wanting anything,' she said, softly at first – and then, remembering the words of the Teachers when it had been her turn at a Presentation, she lifted her chin to seem bold and determined, deliberately gave her voice a new, confident fullness. 'There is nothing I am hiding from any of you.' She opened her arms to the audience, another trick the Teachers had helped her to remember. 'I crashed here. I cannot remember very much about the past few hours. Days, even. I am ... I'm ... touched by your kindness. Grateful for the clothes, the food, everything. I really am. I know ... I need to work, to be part of this place. I know ... that's how you ... how you do things. I want to fit in with that. As Zach said ... I do not have anything else.'

She paused, swallowed hard. There was an intense silence in the Rec Hall as she spoke, buzzing in her ears like static electricity.

'I have nothing else at all,' she repeated.

She took the time to gaze around the room, firmly, making eye contact with some of them. It was important that they trusted her.

'My name is Bethany Aurelia Kane. I am fifteen, almost sixteen. My mother, Jamilla Kane, died in the early days of the *Arcadia* voyage. I barely remember her. She was not with my father – he left her when she was still on Earth. I never knew him. I was brought up by the Blessed Chapter of Continual Progress, an order dedicated to peace, human understanding and scientific research. We believe in the Great Power – a harmonising influence throughout the Universe, expressed through human love and understanding. My guardians are … were … my uncle, Victor Kane, and his wife Gwen. They have … they had … no bio-children of their own.'

She paused, feeling her eyes growing hot with tears. Should she be talking about them in the past tense? Did she even dare talk about them at all?

'I am a quick learner. I can cook, clean … I have computer Resonance skills, learned over many years. And I want nothing else from you. I have no secrets, no agenda. I came here by accident. There's nothing I can do to change that. So you can hate me … Or you can accept me. If you do not accept me … I will make my own way. Out there.'

She gazed out at the darkening forests and mountains. It was a brave boast, she knew. Roaming among the Tall Trees on the *Arcadia* was one thing, but surviving in the hostile wilderness of an unknown planet? Finding food, water, shelter? It would be completely beyond her, and they knew it. One or two sneers and derisive laughs from the audience confirmed as much to her.

She was cold inside, and wanted to get off the steps, to go and hide somewhere she couldn't be seen. But she felt Zach's hand on her arm – for a second.

'That won't be necessary,' he said, gently. 'All right, everyone, that's it for now. Get on with your designated tasks.'

The small crowd began to break up, some of the children

still staring curiously over their shoulders at the new arrival. Cait and Livvy waved, which reassured Beth. She smiled back.

The crowd thinned out, but one person stood fast, arms folded, and didn't show any sign of moving.

'Can you use a gun, Spacegirl?'

It was her. Tall, angular Mia Janowska with her sun-bleached hair, stripes and cruel mouth. She'd got off her perch and was swaggering through the dispersing crowd. People moved aside to let her through.

Beth was so surprised at the question that it took her a second to get her voice back. It came out as a croak, and she had to clear her throat. 'Um …'

'Can you use a gun?' Mia asked again, coldly. She came right up to the steps, climbed them, stood face-to-face with Beth. She lifted her shades so Beth could see her eyes – cold, set, heavily ringed, the skin around them crinkled as if she was forty-five or fifty.

'I think so,' said Beth cautiously. She tilted her head slightly, as if recalling something. 'There was … an impact range on board the *Arcadia*. But it was mostly for recreation. I have never hit a moving target.'

Mia seemed to consider this. She unholstered her weapon, still not breaking her gaze, and handed it to Beth.

'Oh … no. Really, no.'

'Take it.'

Such was the force in Mia's voice that Beth found herself obeying.

'Mia,' said Zach sternly. 'What are you doing?'

'I'm seeing if Spacegirl can be trusted,' said Mia. 'It's what you want, isn't it?'

'Yes,' Zach murmured. 'But not like this.'

The conversation passed over Beth's head as she hefted the gun in her hands. It was much heavier than she had expected, like a bulky piece of machinery, oily and metallic. The butt was a gleaming silver, the barrel and power-pack a dull iron-grey, and it smelt of engines, of death and burning.

There was something angry about it, something decisive.

'It's a Magna 242,' said Mia. 'You won't have seen anything much like it on your ship. It's an old colony weapon. They go back well before Earth even joined the Collective. They fire flares of superheated plasma with a range of two hundred emms. Can you estimate that in your head?'

Beth tried to give her face a cold, hard determination that she didn't feel. 'Maybe,' she said.

Mia sneered. 'If I'm taking someone out on a Lantrill hunt, I don't want to know that they can *maybe* hit it, or they've *maybe* got my back. I need certainty.'

Beth hefted the gun. She closed her fingers over it. Tried to make it feel familiar, less alien. 'All right,' she said. 'Yes, then.'

'Better.' She snapped her fingers, and Beth instinctively handed the gun back. 'Right,' Mia said. 'Get some sleep. I'll train you when you feel up to it.'

And to Beth's relief, Mia gave her a taut, brief twitch of a smile.

∞

The new girl has fire in her. Watch her.

She acts the passive, simpering one, and yet there is something in her which shows a fighting spirit. Hidden depths which she cannot control. The others do not yet realise what she has to offer.

And there is something else. A hint of something she dares not speak about. A fragment of the past, contained in a piece of the future.

Her mind is not totally her own. This may be useful.

In such a closed world, the stranger is feared. The one who is different, new, unusual. It is always the way.

They will seek out someone to blame, to hurt. When the time comes for recriminations, for violence, they will lash out at the outsider.

She may yet prove to be the key.

3
SECRETS

I

The Table was a remnant of the Ship.

It was a huge disc of dark, burnished metal, standing on a spindle as thick as a barrel. On Zach's instructions, the Drones had assembled it in their first few hours there. He had been remembering an old Earth legend, about a king who sat at a round table with his knights so that they were all equal, nobody at the head.

His mothers, both influential citizens on Mars, had once taken him to the Council Chamber in Olympus City, where they'd done something very similar – the Council table made from a disc hewn from the reddish-brown crust of the planet, in the dead centre of a high room surrounded by tinted glass, above the city and the plains. It was a good reminder, Primary Mother Anj had said, of their responsibilities and the scale of the decisions they had to make.

So, when he was elected leader that first cycle, it had been one of Zach's first thoughts – something big, obvious, memorable, something which would show everyone what kind of leader he was. He had stood and watched the Drones slice the perfect disc from a sheet of metal. Two of them cut it free with laser-torches, and four others fixed themselves to the hull with magnetic clamps and pulled the disc free. A team of ten Drones buffed, assembled and secured the Table in less than an hour. It was Zach's first exposure to the efficient, clean power the small robots contained.

Lulu was already waiting in the Council Room, bare feet

up on the round Table, when Zach and Ella came in. Zach stood, while the others were seated. He leaned on the Table, toned arms firm and strong, asserting his natural authority.

'Lu, tell us what the scans showed up.'

Lulu flipped her scan-pad over on the Table, showing them all a 3-D projection – a human form picked out in shifting patterns of blue light, a depiction of Beth Kane's inner workings. 'Physically, she's in great condition. Amazingly, in fact, considering all she's been through. A few abrasions, bruises. Nothing broken. No evidence of any surgical procedures.' Lulu caressed the Table and the image zoomed in on the figure's head. 'Apart from … this.'

She toggled the focus again, and on the Table the scan of Beth's head flipped, whirled into an overhead view. They were looking at something which seemed to be a city, a labyrinthine network of tall steel passageways and buildings connected by walkways.

Zach's face was impassive. 'Tell me what we're seeing here.'

It was Ella who answered. 'Chapter implant. Am I right?'

'Standard procedure?' asked Lulu.

'Well, not quite,' said Ella. 'Not always.'

Zach was not happy. 'You've got to have more than that. I'm not getting this.'

Lulu smiled – seemingly enjoying the feeling of confusing Zach with her advanced knowledge.

'The Chapters,' said Lulu, 'aren't quite the sweet and harmless brigade they like to paint themselves as.' She toggled the focus again. The image broke up, and Lulu cursed, thumping the side of the scan-pad until the picture re-formed. It pulled back, showing a 3-D rendition of the square of circuitry, a full overview of the implant. 'This is no more than the size of … I dunno. A grain of rice? Masterpiece of engineering. But it's there for a reason.'

'That reason being?' Zach asked.

Lulu waved a hand. 'You're the tech expert, Ell. You tell him.'

Ella leaned forward. 'If the Chapters can't guarantee obedience … if they're dealing with someone who's been a bit … difficult … Doesn't go along with what the Great Power supposedly stands for … then their engineers can see to that. It doesn't affect the personality. Well, not much. But it can suppress stuff. Dissent, rebellion. You know, all that kind of thing.'

'How do you know all this?'

Ella was uncomfortable for a moment. 'My dad was involved with some of the research. He was part of the tech team that sold it to them. I studied it. Thought it might come in useful.' She grinned.

Zach sat down now. He leaned back, steepling his fingers and frowning. It didn't help, but he had seen important people do that back in Olympus, and he'd found that it was one of the things which people respected. *Keep quiet, Zach is thinking*. It made him feel like a leader.

'This doesn't change anything,' he said. 'Not really.'

'Why not?' Ella's voice had an edge to it.

'So the Chapter had a problem with her,' said Zach. 'Built

in a restraint to her rebelliousness. It's not our concern, is it? She's still one of us. Still part of this community.'

Ella leaned back in her chair, avoiding Zach's eye. 'If you say so,' she said, a steely tone in her voice.

'I do say so. We need to make her feel welcome. Give her stuff to do. Right? Maintenance. Tech. What she said she was good at.'

Zach got a nod from Lulu, and then, reluctantly, from Ella.

'I'll get on to sorting that out, then,' Ella said, looking from one to the other.

'Thanks,' said Zach. 'I appreciate that.'

After she left, Lulu slid elegantly into his lap, arms around his neck. 'You know,' she whispered, nuzzling his ear, 'your word used to be enough round here. People getting edgy? Don't let it get to you.'

'I don't,' he said.

She drew back, pouted, scanning his face for the sign of any hidden emotion. 'You can't always keep it all in,' she said. 'Talk to Maddi. It's what everyone else does.'

'Maddi doesn't solve everyone's problems.'

'No,' said Lulu, and she touched the tip of his nose. 'But she can talk. Empathy, remember? Empathy, not strategy.'

'I want strategies,' Zach said. 'Every time.'

She drew close to his face. 'Even with me?'

'Yes,' he said. 'Even with you.'

'And what's your strategy with me?'

'Give me time. I'm working on it.'

She kissed him gently, teasingly. And then, less gently, and more eagerly, delighting in feeling him respond, his arms sliding around her waist. A second later, she slid out of his grasp and stood up, reading off her scan-pad.

'Got stuff to do,' she said. 'Ricky's arm needs looking at. And Mahala's cramps are worse.'

'Your work is never done.'

'Seems that way.' She made her way to the door, deliberately taking her time, knowing he was watching. She glanced over her shoulder. 'See you later.'

II

The plasma-bolt slammed into the boulder.

A fountain of earth whooshed into the air. The bolt carved a gash into the ground – well beneath the intended target, which was the small plastic container perched precariously on top of a rock on the cliff-top, twenty emms from Bethany Kane.

Beth squinted through her visor. 'Did I hit it?' she asked tentatively.

Mia uncurled her tanned legs from the cable-drum on which she was sitting. 'No, Spacegirl,' she said, striding languidly into Beth's line of vision and pointing at the rock. 'Third time in a row. You went wide.'

Beth had adapted to a new routine. She slept in the Ship, despite having checked out the comfortable sleeping-pods – each with their own bed-cubicle and living area – in the Main Dome. She wondered idly why they had any going spare, and then she remembered the crosses.

She did not want to sleep in a dead person's Pod. But her main reason for being in the Ship was a deliberate distance, borne not out of coldness but perhaps caution. These people had welcomed her on one level, but there was an undercurrent of tension, of threat. She felt that by staying in the Ship, she would avoid treading on anybody's toes for now.

It was cold. She shivered, reaching for the jacket. It scraped across the floor, and she instinctively shook it before putting it on. Huddling herself into it, she went to the main airlock, stared outside. The domes sat in front of her, lit from within by a crimson glow which spread across the sand like blood.

When she told Zach she had decided to carry on sleeping inside the clattery, rusting hulk of the Ship, he was concerned.

'Come on,' he said, 'it's not even watertight any more. The storms can be pretty vicious sometimes. And it gets quite cold. Close to zero, some nights.'

'I will be fine,' she'd said. 'I barely feel the cold. Really. I have hardly any possessions to speak of, I have no home. It feels … right, somehow. Nomadic.'

And nobody else had the slightest desire to return to the cold, rusting, ghostly Ship.

Breakfast, she had worked out, was at dawn – you got up, or you missed it. Water flavoured with pulverised fruit, whichever was currently being extracted from the hydroponic domes. An actually quite tolerable coffee-substitute made from the bark of a tree called *zort*, and some hunks of bread, maybe dried meat if there was any. There were variations on types of fish and seaweed too. She'd expected it to be a mad scramble, but it was all very civilised. They'd obviously decided a while ago that they were all going to get further and live longer if they agreed to co-operate rather than fight. Mostly.

Meals were rowdy, sociable occasions where she learnt a lot of names, picked up on gossip, backstories, rumours. Tales of pacts around the fire, secrets swapped on the hills or out on Lantrill hunts.

She tried to study people, to learn their body language, to read them. Nobody was straightforward. Leader Zach seemed in control, assertive, but was oddly indecisive and didn't like people getting to know him all that well. Colm was sly, sardonic, selfish, treated girls appallingly, but was intelligent and a useful ally. Under Mia's callousness lay fear, and beneath that lay warmth and an uneasy kindness. And so on. Beth wondered if these people knew how easy they were to read – or was it her position as an outsider that made it easy?

With the work required – cooking, cleaning, maintenance, security – people took it in turns in groups assigned by colour – so one cycle it would be Blue Team on, the next Red, and so on. Everyone seemed to know what colour they were. And everyone had to muck in. 'Nobody's a passenger here,' Zach had said to her. Ella was nominally in charge of security, but this seemed to be something she had assumed, rather than any kind of official title.

Beth had also spotted the cobbled-together mixture of technologies. Some of it was new, but some of it seemed literally centuries old. Advanced Drones and an ergonomic living-space, alongside hydroponics, wind turbines and solar electricity, straight out of the fabled Last Days on Earth. Jeeps powered by solar cells. Then the familiar stuff: hand-held scan-pads, circuit-trackers in the corridors showing the locations of energy surges and drops. But basic two-way radios from even further back, a rusting radar dish, rifles straight out of Earth's first colonial expeditions … It was as if the Edge was unsure where it sat, straddling several times at once.

The Drones, they were always around. Making their quiet sounds – buzzing, whirring, clicking. They tidied, fixed and mended. And there was a lot of mending, because things here, as Beth had quickly learned, broke an awful lot. The other night, she had even seen a couple of them slicing pieces of metal up for some purpose or other, buzzing around it like big silver insects, bright red cutting-beams making sparks dance in the darkness. She wondered if they were happy, and then told herself not to be so stupid. Robots didn't have feelings.

The oldest Towners took it in turns with her, showing her how things worked here. They were her rescuers – Zach, Mia, Maddi and Shan – plus Ella, and occasionally Lulu, Baljeet or Colm. They were all around her age or older. There were others, thirteen or under in Earth years.

She had seen the vast, gleaming domes of the hydroponic centre. Baljeet, who seemed to have warmed to her, took her for a stroll along the walkways, pointing out the various vines, trees, beds and cultivation pods. Beth understood some of this had been grown from extracts brought from the Stations – again, evidence that the Collective wanted the colony to survive – while some was taken from the forests and lakes around, only cultivated after being extensively tested for its nutritional content and lack of poisons. *Plaan* was one such plant, the cactus-like stuff, and *zort* was another, the reddish bark from one of the trees in the jungle. 'Tastes like crap at first,' Baljeet had said, 'but you get used to it.'

And then, the various domes for storage, accommodation, recreation and so on. One of the most popular areas was a makeshift football pitch on the edge of the compound, with goals made of girders from the ship and vine netting, and lines sprayed in paint on the reddish-blue, dusty ground. A lot of the younger boys and girls could be found there during the day when they weren't on duty. There was a tournament too, and endless group-game between the four colours of Work Teams – at one end of the pitch was a giant board made of battered metal, each quadrant daubed a different colour, with tally-marks scratched into it for games won. Red Team seemed to be the solid champions at the moment.

She had learned not only the geography of Town, but its history too. The names of those who had died, for example. In order: Kai, Leila, Janie, Faiz, Thom. All had succumbed to various infections – or in Janie's case, a rare lymphoma which they didn't have the treatment for. 'In her last few cycles,' Maddi said, 'she used to sit out on Lunar Beach, by the beacons, and watch the sun go down, and we'd all take it in turns to go out and talk to her, take her water. It was all we could do.'

Mia and Shan's job, along with Lulu, was to make sure Beth was physically recovering, and indeed fighting fit. It was Mia's task to teach Beth to shoot accurately, and it wasn't going well.

'Try again,' Mia snarled.

Her expression was masked by her reflective sunglasses, but the reproach in her voice was clear.

'Oh. Must I?' Beth pulled the visor off, wiping the sweat from her brow. The heat and humidity were getting to her. The gun was heavy and making her hands smell of metal, and there was an odd fizzing noise inside the barrel and a burning smell coming off it. She sniffed at the gun. 'Are you sure this is all right?' she asked Mia.

'No,' said Mia. 'It's gonna blow up in your face.' She snatched the gun irritably from Beth, hefted it in one hand, barely seeming to aim, and fired. Beth yelped, physically jumping. Mia had blasted the plastic cup off the rock in a shower of dust and liquid plastic. 'You have to focus,' she said. '*Become* the gun. I thought you said you could use one of these things?'

'I am truly sorry!' Beth sank down on the blue soil in despair. 'Don't shout at me!'

'Something distracting you? Again?' asked Mia, her voice sharp with suspicion.

'It is different from the ones I used on the *Arcadia*. Heavier. And the ... beam ... or whatever it is, seems to go off at the wrong angle.'

Beth had handled guns on the *Arcadia* – narrow-beam lasers in the Impact Range. They were light as air, with no recoil. Almost like toys. Somehow, she didn't think the oily, dirty, battered Magna pistol would be quite the same, and she was right. It was more like an engine than a weapon. She found it almost impossible to hold steady and fire straight at the same time.

'Bethany,' said Mia wearily, 'my half-brother used to say this thing, yeah? "A bad workman blames his tools." He said it was an old Earth expression.' Mia fired again, three times in rapid succession, blasting chunks out of the rock with loud retorts. 'Nope. Working fine. It must be you.'

'I want to go home,' said Beth miserably, uncovering her ears. She sneezed at the acrid smell of burnt rock, blinking as smoke drifted from it.

'Don't we all, precious,' said Mia, with unexpected softness. She unhooked a tin flask from her belt, took a swig and made an appreciative sound, then handed the flask to Beth. 'Go on. It can't make your aim any worse.'

Beth took the flask and sniffed at it, wrinkling her nose. 'What is it?'

'*Plaan* and almond whisky. From my personal stash.'

'I'm … not sure I should drink alcohol.'

'Oh, for …' Mia hawked and spat on the ground. The saliva sizzled in the sun like hot oil in a pan. 'You and your purity. Mummy Chapter's not here, you know. You're not on a stayout licence. You're gonna be here till you die, so you may as well get used to the things that make life bearable.'

Beth sniffed at the bottle again. She thought the whisky smelt not unlike petrol, with a slight dash of urine. 'Is this poison?' she asked. 'You tried to kill me not so long ago.'

Mia laughed. 'Yeah. Sorry about that. I was … having a bit of an episode.'

'Episode?'

'Look … I go weird from time to time, all right? My shrink said I was psychotic. I used to have medication, but … there's none of the right stuff here.'

'Oh. Right,' said Beth politely, unsure how to respond. 'Sorry, your … *shrink*?'

'Sorry. One of my half-bro's Old Earth words again. My family had a thing about them … My psycho-med. Or whatever the hell she was. A woman who sat in a room and talked to me.'

Beth took another sniff of the flask. It didn't smell so bad this time, but she still didn't want to risk it. She handed it back to Mia. 'Why did you have a psycho-med?'

Mia hopped off the drum and took a few steps away from Beth. Framed in the morning light, taut and jittery, she was exciting and dangerous, Beth thought – like some caged animal ready to be loosed on the world.

'I killed someone,' Mia said eventually.

'Oh,' said Beth. Her stomach lurched and she hoped that she wasn't going to be sick again. It would be embarrassing to keep doing it.

There was a long silence.

So, there was the answer to one of her questions, at least. Some of them were murderers. And for one of them to be

Mia – that didn't surprise her. She wondered how many others were.

A smirk creased the warpaint stripes on Mia's face. 'Don't worry. It's not something I do randomly. If you don't piss me off, you'll be fine.'

'Right,' said Beth. She handed the flask back to Mia. 'How ... how old were you? When you did it?'

'I can't really remember. Maybe a Thirteener?' She grinned, her teeth bright and sharp. 'Anyway, she betrayed me. I had to do it.' She snapped her fingers. 'Get up. Aim the gun.'

Beth scurried to obey, hurriedly brushing the earth off her trousers. She fumbled with the gun, but managed to swing it up so that she was levelling it fairly steadily at the distant rock. She squinted at the churning, dark sea beyond.

'Is there anyone else here ... like you?' Beth asked cautiously. 'You know ... someone who's ... killed?'

'I expect so,' said Mia. 'I haven't asked.' She sounded genuinely as if she didn't care.

Her heart thudding, Beth squinted down the barrel of the gun. The weapon still seemed so heavy – it wouldn't even stay still in her hands – and the distant rock so far away in the haze. She was never going to be able to hit it. Her mind wandered again.

'So I was thinking,' said Beth. 'About the people who died. You said about not having medication.'

'We've got some. Only what came with us. It won't last long. Another couple of years, maybe.'

'And what happens,' Beth asked, 'if someone gets ill?'

'They get better,' said Mia, lighting another of her black roll-ups. She blew a jet of green smoke into the air. 'Or … they get worse. And die. 'We've got Dr Lulu. She does her best. She's got AMT.'

'AMT?' Beth had not heard of it.

'Accelerated Medical Training. But she's not really a doctor. I mean, she's only, like, sixteen, seventeen, right?'

Beth didn't have any suitable reply to that.

'Actually,' Mia went on, 'it's thanks to your lot that we've got anything at all. The Collective would have been happy to launch us into space with nothing, but there were still a few of your Chapter advocates on the Judiciary. Bit keener on human rights than the others.'

'I am pleased we are good for *something*,' said Beth, and she dared allow her tone to be reproachful for once. It seemed lost on Mia, though.

Beth raised the heavy weapon again, tried to forget she was holding a strange, alien-feeling piece of deadly tech. Tried to think of it as an ordinary, everyday object.

She squeezed the trigger – lightly, she thought.

Before she even realised she had fired, the gun kicked in her hands, so hard it almost fell. The plasma bolt scoured a gash from the rock, chips of blue stone spurting up in an orange-and-white cloud. As the smoke settled, Beth could see she had hit the target.

She lowered the gun, trying not to show her sense of triumph.

For a second, Mia seemed taken aback. Then, recovering her composure, she grinned in approval.

'Getting better, Spacegirl. Getting better.'

Beth exhaled deeply and pushed her damp hair back from her forehead. 'I'll ... try not to let you down,' she said, handing the gun back to Mia.

Mia didn't answer. Beth sat on the ground again, hands around her knees.

'So who did you kill?'

It was a daring question, and as soon as it left her mouth she wondered if it had been the wrong thing to say. She was not sure she really wanted to know the answer.

Mia took a long swig from the bottle, hooking it back on the belt of her denim shorts. She holstered the gun.

'My mother,' she said.

'Your–' Beth grew cold. 'Your *mother*?'

Behind the sunglasses, Mia's expression was unreadable, but Beth thought she heard her voice crack. 'Yeah,' she said. 'It's like I said ... she betrayed me.'

Beth, cold with fear, didn't say anything.

'Come and get something to eat,' said Mia. 'You must be starving ...'

She began to stride away across the compound towards the main dome. Beth hurried to keep up.

III

Maddi prodded the massive cauldron of the fire-pit, throwing in more gnarled, dry branches for the flames to consume. Above her, the vast bulk of the spaceship blotted out much of the sky.

It was still beautiful, Maddi thought, the hunk of space-faring metal which had sailed across the stars with its sleeping crew. Silent and beautiful. Rusting, with twisted plants choking the hull, but still with a towering dignity. In the flickering firelight, the Ship was a mountain of metal, picked out in gold and reds and burnished orange.

This girl, she thought. Coming along and stirring up feelings, memories …

There was something of Leila in Beth Kane, she thought – a deep, knowing kindness. Leila had been a Faith-reader too, not a ChapterSister like Beth, but one of the old-school. Hindu mythology, she was into. Ancient stuff from Old Earth. Vishnu the preserver and Siva the destroyer. They'd laughed about it together, Maddi never sure how seriously Leila took it all, and Leila saying that you could believe in it metaphorically if you wanted to – that the old texts gave particular names for universal forces.

You could try and explain everything with science, Leila used to say, but where's the fun in that? And Maddi had smiled, not wanting to argue. For science, in its way, had both destroyed and created the Earth she knew. It was both Vishnu and Siva.

On her last days on Earth, as a child of twelve, Madeleine Vanderbilt would sometimes escape to the abandoned Inland. She would ride the old rails and sit high up on the crumbling, rusting top of the great four-pillared arch of girders – a sculpture she and her friends used to play in, something from the Wartimes which her father had said used to be called High Fall. She could see why it was called that. The thing had a sheer drop from the platform which topped it, unfenced, rusting away. She wondered if it had been beautiful in the old days, if something had been built around the structure of girders.

Her friend Xander's older brother told her there used to be other platforms on top of it, rising to a pinnacle, but they were lost in the war – the High Fall had been shattered, destroyed like most of the world's art and monuments. Nobody went near the place these days. Everything in the city centre was supposed to be contaminated. But Maddi carried her own radiation detector, and she could tell from the readings that it was pretty safe. The scariest things about it were the huge scorpions and mutated rats which scuttled around, scavenging. If you kept out of their way, you were all right.

These old, abandoned cities were worthless. The billion who had remained on Earth after the Exodus – the great abandonment of Earth following its departure from the Galactic Collective – had more space than their ancestors could have dreamed of. The Arcs, the sky-parks, the Ocean Platforms: great pinnacles of civilisation, shining testaments to human endeavour. Nobody needed to go back Inland much any more, certainly not into the remains of the cities. Some people said the places should be restored, preserved, but most of Maddi's generation didn't see the point. Relics from the time when Earthers almost destroyed themselves, monuments to power and passion and terror – they were best left as ruins. All the knowledge from those times was preserved, so the physical structures were irrelevant. In another hundred years they would be dust, engulfed in plants, with some of the Inland's strange animals roaming around, still scavenging for food.

Maddi, in her explorations of the ruined city, knew how to avoid these creatures. The deer with five ears, the six-legged dog-things. Sometimes she'd sneak out one of her dad's old flare-guns – the sizzling shot would send the odd, deformed animals scuttling back into the shadows.

High Fall was her favourite place. She would often stand in the vast space beneath its rusting girders, or sit atop it and gaze out at the shattered, misty city, trying to imagine it full of life, of people and shops and petrol-driven vehicles. Paree, the place had been called in the oldentimes.

It was on one such expedition, on an autumn evening as the sun was sinking below the shattered city, that they found her. Police Drones, blue-and-white globes two emms across, floated down to cut off her access on all four sides, and a hard, grating voice barked from one of them:

—THIS IS A RESTRICTED ZONE. PUT YOUR HANDS BEHIND YOUR HEAD AND GET DOWN ON THE GROUND—

'Mads? You all right?'

Her reverie was interrupted. There was a movement beside her. The shape took form as it emerged from the shadows – tall, dark, tinted glasses.

'Shan! Don' creep up on me like that. Arsehole.' She punched him playfully.

'Sorry,' the boy said, with a flash of white teeth. 'Good fire. Always decent when you do it.'

'Thanks. I have my uses.'

They stood together for a while in the warmth, watching smoke and sparks lifting against the alien sky.

Out beyond the sea, the Howling Mountains were singing. None of them had worked out, yet, why the mountains sang, but a few of them had reasoned it was something to do with magnetic fields, or some other kind of energy. Whatever it was, it could often be heard, usually after dusk and before dawn, like the sound of the planet singing a soft, ambient electronic song. It was unearthly, but at the same time strangely comforting.

'You know,' Maddi said, 'it's really scary if you stop thinkin' about lookin' *up* at the stars. When you think that the only thing that keeps us anchored on this rock is, like, gravity ...'

'Yeah. Good old gravity.' Shan jumped up and down. 'Never breaks.'

'But what if we're lookin' *down*? Into the abyss.' She spread her arms as if embracing the sky, and whirled around the fire. 'Into the deep, dark, endless Universe.' She stopped spinning, and laughed. 'Imagine if this place, like, let us go. And we'd fly. Fall and float for ever into nothingness.'

'Or freeze to death first,' Shan pointed out. 'Or burn up. Or have all your capillaries explode because of the pressure differential.'

'Oh, Shan. Where's the poetry in your soul, mate?'

'Never had none. Don't think I've even got a soul.'

'Oh, *Shan.*'

Shan laughed out loud. 'Hey, you know what? The new girl likes you.'

'I *know*.' It made her feel comforted, but also responsible, carrying a duty she didn't really want to have. 'Why me?' she wondered aloud, prodding the fire-pit thoughtfully.

Shan didn't answer her. 'Must be hard for her,' he said. 'I bet she's still disorientated.'

'Weird that we ain't seen no wreckage. None o'them detectors picked up anythin' in the atmosphere.'

'Which means?' Shan asked idly, taking a drink from a metal bottle and offering it to Maddi.

She held up a hand to refuse. 'Either the *Arcadia* dissolved into atoms, or … it broke up a long way from here … or …'

'Or she's lying,' he said.

'Yeah … Why would she be lyin', Shan?'

'I dunno.' Shan, whose gaze was fixed on the Ship, slowly screwed the cap back on his bottle and slipped it into his pocket. 'Who else is out here tonight?' he asked softly.

'Nobody, far as I know.' Maddi felt a sudden chill, despite the roaring fire. 'What? What is it?'

'Nothing, I …' Shan narrowed his eyes behind the blue glasses. 'Thought I saw something, that's all.'

'Gettin' old and tired,' said Maddi with a grin, and she poked the fire again, making the sparks dance. 'Ain't we all? This place ages us.' She thought her quip had lightened the moment, but Shan still seemed perturbed. He had moved round to the other side of the fire-pit and was staring into the vast hulk of the Ship, peering into the shadows. 'Seriously, what is it?'

'The Lantrill never come up this far,' Shan said thoughtfully.

'Nope. And they'd never get through the fence. Well, maybe a really determined one with sharp teeth could.'

Shan scrambled right to the edge of the Ship's hull. He thumped the access portal to open it, peered inside.

'Here,' Maddi said, scurrying after him, and pulled her powerful flashlight from her back pocket. The bright white beam cut through the darkness, into the metal cavern.

'Take a recce?' Shan suggested.

Together, Maddi and Shan advanced into the cathedral-like space. The fire-pit receded behind them, the flames becoming a flicker, a lick of orange, a dot in the darkness as they left it behind.

Maddi was swinging the torch around so that it shone like a lighthouse, picking out an arc of their surroundings at a time. The place still stank of metal and burning, of rust and decay. She shivered.

'Must have been imagining things,' he said, and his voice echoed in the vaulted space.

'Coulda been a Lantrill?' she asked, still swinging the torch like a weapon.

He would not meet her gaze. 'Nah.'

'Klaa?'

'No way. Not this late at night.'

'What, then?' Maddi was worried. 'Shan, you ain't one of the dumb ones. You don't imagine things, yeah?'

'We're all jittery since she arrived,' he said. 'Chasing shadows. Hearing noises in the night, seeing things at every turn … You can't live like that. You've gotta get on. Pull together. Show the universe you're someone who can fight, and work, and live.'

Maddi grinned. 'You're right.' She started marching back towards the glowing lights of the domes. 'C'mon.'

'Yeah. No problem.' Shan followed her, after one last look around.

Maddi stopped, stared. 'Is that a jeep on the causeway?' She lifted the viewer. Lights on the causeway, approaching fast. 'It is. Who'd be out at this time?'

As they emerged into the dim light of the compound, they were dazzled by the arrival of the jeep at the perimeter gates. Shan and Maddi watched as it entered, its lights sweeping in an arc across the bonfire. Only when the motor and the lights cut did they recognise the tall figure jumping from the driving seat as Baljeet. Her Magna pistol was slung across her chest and she wore her visor hanging loosely at her neck. This suggested to Maddi that she'd been out for a while, out on the brighter, exposed mountain slopes where they rarely ventured. Baljeet raised a hand in greeting.

'All well, guys?'

'Yeah,' Maddi said. 'We … thought we saw movement. Out by the Ship. We … well, there was nothin' there.'

Shan, more direct than Maddi, stared in a not-quite-friendly way at Baljeet. 'Where you been?'

'Reconnaissance,' she said, hauling her backpack from the jeep.

'For what? And why you back so late?'

Baljeet hoisted her backpack on to her shoulder, and strode up to Shan. Both tall and slim, they stood eye-to-eye. The smaller, slighter Maddi looked up at the taller two in slight trepidation. Like two Lantrill about to butt horns, she thought.

'You ask a lot of questions, Shan,' said Baljeet.

'I tend to,' he said. 'When I don't get answers.'

Maddi stepped between them, feeling almost comically out of place. 'Cool it, guys,' she said. 'Zach said ages ago, no unauthorised trips, right?'

Baljeet's face hardened. 'Whatever.'

'So what was you lookin' for?' Maddi surprised herself, but she knew she got answers out of people through her soft, quiet determination. Back in the early days, when some of the younger boys had been stealing bread and fruit, Zach had made her interrogate the potential culprits, and her approach had been effective. 'Well? C'mon, Balj, we don't wanna do secrets, right?'

Baljeet dropped her rucksack with a thud, leaned against the jeep. 'Wreckage,' she said.

'Of Beth's ship.' Shan understood immediately.

'Nothin' was picked up.' Maddi was growing irritable.

'Yeah, but do we know that?' Baljeet snapped back at her. 'It could easily have been missed.'

'Did you find anythin'?' Maddi asked.

'Nope.'

'So there you go. Pointless exercise. You comin' in?'

'Suppose so,' Baljeet said, hoisting her pack again, not looking either of them directly in the eye.

She and Shan walked on ahead.

Maddi hung back. Baljeet had been lying about something, Maddi, thought – that much was clear. But what was it?

After giving the fire-pit one last prod, she slowly followed the others inside, with the song of the Howling Mountains echoing in her ears.

IV

Beth and Zach stood on the steps down to the Rec Hall.

After dark, the Hall came to life. Busy, crowded. Full of shouts, cheers, the slamming of cards on tables. The clink of metal cups, and occasional bursts of old songs, although there seemed to be no instruments. Thumps and slaps, shouts and whistles. Casual kisses, promises of more. Pungent smoke drifted up the steps. Soft lighting cast long shadows, made the place full of dark recesses like some low spaceport tavern.

'A city of criminals,' she said out loud, rather tactlessly.

'We're all here,' he said, barely glancing at her. 'It doesn't matter *why* we're here, does it?' He faced her, challenging, legs braced.

Beth took a step back, swallowed hard. 'Um … no,' she said.

Of all the planets she could have ended up on, she thought bitterly. Not only was it a desolate backwater, it was also one which nobody was expected to leave – ever. Once again the sheer desperation of the place hit her like a physical impact, the realisation that there was no safety net, nobody to run to, no emergency services or authorities. It was a wonder Town was as ordered as it was.

She learned that there had been an expedition, of sorts, after the first few dozen cycles when things seemed desperate. Ten of them, led by Ella, had loaded up the jeeps and headed North, in search of anything that could improve their lot – resources, shelter, even a potential new location for the colony. She gathered it had not been successful, and they had returned with hardly anything of use.

'Bit different from your comfy *Arcadia*, isn't it?'

'Very,' she said. She decided not to allow herself to be riled by these comparisons. She knew they would keep coming thick and fast. 'So where did you grow up?' she asked defensively.

Zach grinned, leaning back against the wall. 'Aaaaaah, well, long story. More dragged up. In the red dust.'

'Mars,' she said, and immediately felt stupid for stating the obvious.

'Jewel of the solar system, ChapterSister.'

She scowled. 'You're used to life on the edge of civilisation, then.'

'It wasn't that bad!' Zach laughed derisively. 'Olympus is a big city. The biggest off Earth. There were sky-parks, lakes, towers, a stadium. Not like this place.'

'Sorry. I … I always thought of it as the edge of nowhere.'

'Tactful, aren't you?' He gestured down the steps, into the hubbub and fug. 'Go and socialise, then. Meet a few people.' He moved off.

'Zach, I–'

'What?' There was tension in his face, barely held back.

'Will you come with me?'

'Things to do. Go and find Maddi and Mia. They'll look after you.'

Beth steeled herself. 'Right,' she said. 'Thanks.' Would she ever adjust?

Zach and Ella had asked her questions. Endless questions in the Council room, around that big wheel of pitted metal. Like an inquiry. A Drone bobbed up and down, recording her, while they tried to get as much information from her as they could. Everything about the journey, about the *Arcadia*, about her life so far. It was exhausting. Beth talked herself hoarse.

They hardly offered any word of encouragement. The only one to do so was Maddi, who sat in, and who would dart a frown at the others if their questioning grew too aggressive. Maddi, it seemed, had been charged with Beth's welfare and moral well-being. Maddi, Beth realised, was Good Cop – listening to her, understanding. Bringing her drinks unasked, making sure she had her back, that nobody gave her any trouble. Small, graceful Maddi did not have Mia's gritty toughness, but she had the respect of many. That, Beth noted, went a long way in a place like this. People came to Maddi with their problems, and she either solved them or gave them a way of coping.

In the Rec Hall, Beth allowed herself to breathe for a moment, taking in the soft discs of the lighting, the din of the place.

And the smell of it – what was that all-pervading odour? It was like the freshness of crisp, newish technology, like on the *Arcadia*, but overlaid with something earthy and human, something rich, rough and raw. Like old vegetables allowed to rot. The odour of decay, or maybe of uncensored living.

Slowly, she walked down the steps, acknowledging all the new faces. Some raised metal beakers to her, others gave her mock salutes, cries of 'Spacegirl!' Mia's nickname for her seemed to have taken hold quickly. She gave cautious, awkward waves to faces she recognised.

Even though the population here was a fraction of what she had been used to on the *Arcadia*, it seemed like a huge, boisterous crowd because they were all so noisy, so ebullient. And probably drunk, – or worse – she realised, seeing Mia laughing uproariously at a nearby table as she took a drag on an evil, greenish-black roll-up. Beth coughed at the pungent smoke.

'Beth!' Mia bellowed, shoving a red-haired boy off the end of the nearest bench to make room for her. The boy swore at her, but laughed as he got to his feet, gesturing in a mannered, mocking way for Beth to sit on the bench. She did so, nervously. Mia shoved a metal beaker her way, topping it up from a nearby jug.

She put a drunken arm around Beth's shoulders, planted a kiss on her forehead. 'So you don't drink in your Blessed Chapter? That really not allowed?'

'Um … well …' Beth held the beaker at arm's length at first, then drew it closer and sniffed it. The green drink was pungent and minty, but also had an underlying earthiness, a wet smell like soil after rain.

'Great Power,' she murmured. 'What … is this?'

Mia clinked her cup against Beth's. 'Tell us if you like it first,' she said, to laughter around the table.

'She don' have to drink it if she don' like it.' From along the table, among the group of card-players, came the softer, lilting voice of a new arrival – Maddi. She slid into place, raising her eyebrows at Beth in friendly welcome.

Beth, grateful for the intervention, put the beaker down. 'I … no, I really don't think–' she began.

'Go on,' laughed Mia. 'You may as well get used to it, if you're gonna stay.'

'*If* she's gonna stay?' said a new voice from behind her.

The mocking face of Colm Dale. Colm was handsome, Beth had thought with a brief surge of interest – but there was something sly about him. Untrustworthy.

Colm brushed her cheek with his fingers. 'You are so *soft*. Not had a soft one here before.'

'Colm!' Mia snapped. She glared at him.

'Like the jacket. Suits you. Cute.'

'Thank you.'

Beth blushed, irritated. Of course, he was a flatterer. Why did boys like him have to comment on her appearance, un-invited? She would have found it – what was that old word? – *creepy*, if he was not so … so … Oh, no. She admonished herself. That was the *wrong* way to think. She knew the Teachers would have had words about that … The Teachers, who were scattered across the galaxy as burning ash and dust.

Colm was on a roll. 'I can say a girl's pretty if I want to, can't I, Mia? Just 'cause you're a rough old bitch these days, no need to get in a huff about it. You don't mind, do you, Beth?'

'I ... well ... I ...' She smiled, trying to stay polite.

'See? Beth doesn't mind. Have a drink, Beth. You're all right, you are.'

Mia scowled. 'Colm, d'you ever think about putting yourself in the pulveriser? We could feed a shit-load of tomatoes with you.'

There was appreciative laughter around the table.

Beth was embarrassed, although she thought she ought not to be. 'It's all right,' she said, smiling nervously. 'It must be ... strange for all of you as well.'

She kind of knew what Colm meant, though. Her skin, now that she'd had a chance to clean up, was baby-soft pink as if she had emerged from some kind of container keeping her fresh. She wasn't sun-hardened, work-toughened like them. Her whole body spoke of the sanitised environment of the vast Ships. Places where you could if you wished, sail along the moving pavements admiring the Tall Trees and the vastness of the World Below.

The air, she remembered – the air had always smelled so clean and sweet, even though it had been recycled tens of thousands of times over. The light was as close as you would get to Earth's sun, beamed through by a hundred thousand glowsources and refractive filters, designed to mimic the passing of the hours and the days and the seasons in Earth's Northern hemisphere. Their sister ship, the

Venetia, was tuned to the southern hemisphere in the same way. She wondered if the *Venetia* was still up there somewhere – and all the others which had set off before them. She had no way of knowing.

Colm sat next to her, slipped an arm around her shoulders. 'Well?' he said, gesturing at the metal beaker in front of Beth. 'Tried it yet?'

She moved his hand from her shoulder. Then she reached out and took a sip of the green liquid.

Beth had never tasted anything like it. At first, it seemed innocuous. Sweet, smooth, almost heavy on her tongue. Then, as it slipped down, it fizzed up her nose, burned her mouth. She slammed the mug down on the table, her body wracked with coughs. She put a hand over her mouth, wanting to spit but not daring to. Somehow, she swallowed the rest of the scalding liquid. It slipped down inside her, warming her body. Her eyes watered, making everything blurred.

Mia and Colm laughed uproariously, but Maddi didn't find it as funny. She slid across to Beth, put a gentle hand on her arm. 'All right?' she asked.

Beth, wheezing and coughing, waved a hand. 'I've … had worse,' she croaked eventually. A lie, but she had to save face.

Everyone at the table laughed. 'Welcome to *plaan* whisky,' said Mia.

Beth eyed the cup warily. 'An acquired taste, I am sure.'

It left a metallic after-taste. But the way it numbed her throat and zinged down through her body, fizzing in her stomach, was curiously refreshing.

'So do you actually, like, *pray* to this Great Power of

yours?' Mia asked curiously. 'I've never really met a ChapterSister before.'

'No, no.' Beth was keen to have the chance to be on home territory, to banish some common myths. 'It's not like … *God*. Not an old religion. It's more of a … bonding force. A feeling that, if everyone does right and justice is seen to be done, the Universe will align and good things will come to all. A sort of … link between people, if you like. A universal harmony.'

'I quite like that,' said Colm, and lifted his cup in salutation. 'Comes down to *don't be a dick*, right?'

'Well, you fail on that,' Mia shot back at him.

'Love you too, babe.'

Mia tutted. 'C'mon, then, Spacegirl,' she said. 'What you wanna know? You've got the three best brains in the colony at your disposal. Ask away.'

'Three best brains?' Colm was milking the moment for all it was worth. 'Sure enough, I can see me, but–'

'Does Mia keep you around as a sort of pet these days?' Maddi asked, and Colm grinned, holding up his cup again.

Beth's gaze wandered. Beside her, the red-haired boy Mia had pushed off the table was jostling and scuffling with another, a skinny, lithe, dark-haired boy.

What did she want to know? She had found out most of the important stuff, as far as she knew. That they didn't know the real name of this planet – and it wasn't where any of them had ever expected to end up. There were forty-six of them, aged between twelve and eighteen in Earth years – although a lot of them were not entirely sure how old they were – and they all, in one way or another, had incurred the wrath of the authorities.

This place had been their destination after a journey in the auto-piloted ship, during which they had all been passengers in semi-animation pods. The Drones had renovated this old scientific base, transformed it into Town while the young humans still slept. By the time their awakening was triggered – several cycles after arrival, they seemed to agree – they had somewhere to head for in their blurred, dehydrated confusion. Nobody seemed to want to talk about those first few cycles, and that didn't surprise Beth. And now they had been here, as Zach had told her, for two hundred and forty-two cycles. Two hundred and forty-two sunrises, each heralding a new chance to survive.

Nobody used the words *penal colony*. She wondered what crimes everyone had committed. Some of the youngest here were barely twelve.

'Has anyone ever tried to escape?' she asked, glancing nervously over at the altercation between the two boys. They were shoving each other quite hard, bitter words flying back and forth.

They laughed. 'With what?' Colm asked. 'Levitation?'

Beth blushed again, feeling silly for having asked the question. 'And you're not guarded in any way?'

Colm pointed upwards. 'By the best walls ever. Millions of K of sky.'

'Better than locks or warders,' said Mia bitterly.

'I see … I'm sorry. You must think me very stupid. Some of the things I say.'

Colm was studying her expression carefully – rather enjoying her discomfort, she thought. 'Apart from anything else,' he went on, 'we're too many light years out from the centre of stuff for anyone to cause any trouble – even if we did find a way off this rock.'

'Yeah,' said Mia. 'All the Collective had to do was find a rickety ship designed for one pre-programmed, sub-light journey, and one alone. Easy, eh?'

Colm agreed. 'Those engines are Starform Class impulse units. Old exchangers. Five years old at least. To say it's a bucket is putting it mildly.' He leaned back and grinned. 'You can't turn an old wreck into a goer, boys and girls. And believe me,' he added, winking at Mia, 'I've tried.'

There was laughter around the table. Mia narrowed her eyes at him. 'Are you attached to your bollocks? Really? I can do something about that, you know.'

'All I get here is abuse,' Colm said to Beth. 'Abuse! You see it, don'cha?'

She was finding their lewd banter hard to keep up with, so she held her hands up in defeat. 'I am new here. How could I comment?'

Around them, clapping and chanting grew to a crescendo, as the tussle between the two boys became scrappy. The two of them were snarling at each other like dogs. People had moved themselves and the benches aside, creating a mini-arena for the fight. Beth started to feel tense.

'Yeah, so, basically … Easy to forget us!' said Colm, raising his voice over the tumult. 'Easy and cheap.' He spread his arms wide. 'The planet's the prison.'

The planet's the prison. Beth let the words resonate in her head, trying to ignore the fight. 'Did you ever think to rig up a distress beacon?' she asked. 'I mean, it would not be that difficult ...' She tailed off, aware that Mia was rolling her eyes. 'What? What have I said?'

Maddi answered, softly and almost apologetically. 'We had a sub-light pulse-beacon runnin' since Cycle Three. Transmits to four beacons on Lunar Beach. Powered from the old neutron converter. Problem is, it uses up a hell of a lot of energy, so it can't be on all the time.'

'I'm sorry,' said Beth, abashed. 'I did not mean to imply that you had not thought of these things.'

Maddi waved a hand. 'It's fine. It was about the first thing we thought of. There's hyperwave, too, but we can't sustain that. It needs more power for a minute than we'd use in a month. We can't risk it.'

'There's always the exchange booster,' said Mia. 'Like I keep saying.'

'Yeah,' said Maddi. 'Buried in a swamp somewhere.'

'Sorry?' Beth said. 'What is the exchange booster? And why is it buried in a swamp?'

Colm lifted his hand, moved it in over the table, simulating the flight path of a ship. '*Whooosh.* Baby comes in to land on autos. Last few minutes, enters the atmosphere, ditches all non-essential items.' He turned his palms upwards. 'The deflectors, tracking, exchange booster. All it has to do is get down. It doesn't need any of that stuff.'

'We think we know where it is,' said Maddi. 'The exchange booster, at least. It's still active. Shan picked up some emissions on his scan-pad. Not worth the trouble of divin' to fish it out, though, right?'

Beth tensed, embarrassed. There was a singing sound in her brain, and a metallic taste on her teeth. She clenched her fists. She needed a distraction. Her gaze alighted upon Ella, who was deep in conversation with Robbie at the bar. As she watched, the black girl did a fist-bump to Robbie and left the Rec Hall on some mission of her own, nodding briefly to their table as she passed.

'All right,' Beth said. 'Tell me about Ella. What's the deal there?'

Mia, Maddi and Colm exchanged glances. 'What exactly d'you wanna know?' Mia asked cautiously.

'She had an accident. That much is clear. It's some kind of semi-organic support mesh, isn't it? I've seen things like that for broken arms, and so on, but never so extensive.'

'It was years ago,' Mia said, 'as far as any of us knows. Ella keeps her past to herself, but … there was some accident.'

'It were pretty horrific,' said Maddi. 'That's all we know. The mesh, it keeps her body intact, yeah? Like, held together. It's the latest in micro-surgery. Thousands of tiny fibres, strong as steel, in her body. Stoppin' it from falling apart.'

'She's stronger than any of us,' muttered Mia, and the others murmured their agreement. She stubbed out her cigarette on the table, stretched her taut body and sprang up, sliding across the table to Beth. 'Ever killed anything, Spacegirl?' she asked, amused.

Beth opened her mouth to reply. Then she closed it again, looking away.

Mia laughed. 'You will. We're Lantrill-hunting tomorrow, me and Shan and some others. You can come if you like.'

'I'd rather not,' she said, in a small voice.

Mia leaned forward, kissed Beth's forehead and tapped her on the chin. The gesture was a curious mixture of affection and threat. 'You will,' she said. 'Maybe not tomorrow, but soon. When you're better at shooting.'

'Maybe,' she said, taking another cautious sip of the burning whisky. Her cheeks flushed. She had to get used to these people and their ways, she realised. Nobody was coming to rescue her any time soon.

There was a sudden cheer from the Towners watching the fight. The red-haired boy, thrown back hard, smacked into their table, spilling several drinks. Beth started in alarm, realising the scrap had become a proper, full-on fight.

'Whoa!' Mia leapt up, and her pistol was drawn.

All around, the audience calmed down, the mood changing rapidly. The clapping and cheering subsided. Some of them made a rapid retreat to the far corners of the Rec Hall, or headed for the exits. Beth watched, her heart thumping. The boy who had landed the punch was small, wiry, dark, with curly hair and a determined expression.

'Gabe, get up,' Mia said wearily. The red-haired boy, wiping a bloody nose, was slow to move. Mia grabbed him by the collar, hauling him to his feet. 'Get *up*!'

Beth's heart was racing at the brutality of the scene. Tension fizzed in the air. She did not like it at all.

Mia swung the gun between the two of them. 'Reza,' she said to the wiry boy, 'you calm it. What the hell's all this about?'

Neither of the boys moved. They hovered nervously at either edge of the cleared space, both still fizzing with tension and energy.

'Ask him,' Reza spat, pointing at Gabe. 'What he said.'

Panic rose inside her. The metallic taste, the singing in her ears … Would Mia actually *shoot* one of them to keep order? Colm was languidly amused, Maddi worried and biting her lip.

'You two are trouble,' Mia said. 'Keep away from each other. Right? Unless you want a spell down in the Coolers.'

'I am sure they did not mean to cause trouble.' Before Beth knew it, she had spoken, her voice sounding squeaky and awkward. She had got to her feet. Everyone was staring at her. 'Did you?' she said to the boys.

'What's it gotta do with *you*?' snapped Reza, glaring at her with shameless hostility.

'Stay out of this, Bethany,' said Mia softly. She kept her gun steady, held at a point between the two boys. The Rec Hall was clearing rapidly.

Behind Beth, someone murmured, 'Go and get Zach.'

Mia's voice was like a whiplash. 'No! *Don't* go and get Zach!'

Xara Belazs, the ragged blonde girl who had said this, took a step backward, abashed. Beth glanced at her, trying to smile, but Xara wouldn't look her in the eye.

'We don't need our Glorious Leader every time someone's a dick. Right, boys?' Mia swung the gun on Reza, who stepped back alarmed, then towards Gabe, who didn't appear quite so worried. 'We can sort this out.'

There was a tense, electric moment. The silence

hummed in Beth's ears. And then Reza relaxed his aggressive stance, spread his hands.

'Whatever,' he said.

'Whatever,' Gabe agreed, his freckled face rueful.

Everyone relaxed. Beth sensed Colm leaning back, heard Maddi exhale, saw her take a deep, long drink.

The two boys acknowledged each other, awkward but no longer hostile.

'Right,' said Mia. 'All done here.'

The boys walked away in separate directions, but as they did so, Gabe glanced over his shoulder and spat, 'Wanker!' at Reza's retreating back.

Reza snarled, moved like a hunter, launching himself forward. His fist connected with Gabe's nose, sending the boy sprawling in a shower of blood. Mia reacted instantly, grabbing Reza in a firm armlock, twisting him, forcing him to his knees with a scream.

'Get Lulu,' Mia snapped at Maddi, and she immediately began rapping instructions into her radio.

Colm, Beth noticed, leaned back and watched with amusement.

Gabe, his face streaming with blood, tried to launch himself forward for a free kick on Reza.

And now Beth moved. Without really knowing what she was doing, she grabbed the boy's hair and pulled him back, twisting him.

There was a cheer from the onlookers, whooping, clapping. Gabe snarled, trying to twist free, but Beth had copied Mia, holding the boy in an armlock from which he could not escape. She felt quite a sense of satisfaction, although her brain was screaming at her to stop.

Mia grinned at Beth, impressed. 'Nice one, Spacegirl. Very handy.'

The pain in Beth's head had intensified, as if all her teeth were being drilled at once. She ignored it. 'What do we do with them?'

Mia addressed the Rec Hall. 'All right, show's over. All of you. Go on! Go and do something else.' There was hesitation, a hint of mutiny. However, it didn't take much to bring them back into line. 'Go!' Mia barked.

The Towners jostled, dispersed, some of them still whooping and catcalling over their shoulders. Only Mia, Beth, Maddi, Colm and the two struggling, snarling boys were left.

Lulu arrived, hurrying down the steps, medikit satchel on her shoulder as ever. 'What's up?'

'Low tranqs on these two,' said Mia. 'They need settling down.'

Beth watched in fascination, holding Gabe firmly as he wriggled. The whining in her ears was subsiding, the electric pain in her teeth ebbing away as if anaesthetised.

Lulu pulled out a small packet of thin black discs, and slapped one on to Gabe's neck. The boy instantly slackened in her grip, his legs buckling. Within seconds, he had slumped, and Beth realised she could let him go. He keeled over slowly to the floor, as if falling asleep.

Reza's eyes bulged as Lulu approached him, smiling.

'Don't worry,' she said. 'It doesn't hurt.' She slapped a similar disc on to Reza's neck. He struggled and tried to claw it off, but within seconds he had gone the same way as Gabe, falling first to his knees and then over on to the floor. 'Well, not much,' Lulu added apologetically.

'Testosterone,' said Mia, holstering her gun. 'You'd think the little dicks would know how to cope with it.' She curved her hand, made a shaking gesture in the air which made Colm and Lulu laugh and Beth turn away, blushing.

'I dunno. Boys, eh?' said Colm, swinging off the bench. He saluted in mock admiration. 'Well, you ladies seem to have it all in hand, so, ah, I'll say goodnight.'

'What … what *are* those things?' Beth asked in wonder. The throbbing in her head was easing off, as if she had taken a shot of concentrated painkiller.

Lulu grinned. 'Good, aren't they?' She showed her the transparent packet of discs. 'Left by the last owners. High-density tranq-pads. They're an augmented form of flunitrazepam. Very useful when we get troublemakers.'

Mia strolled over to Beth and clapped a hand hard on her shoulder. Beth winced. 'You moved pretty fast there, Spacegirl,' she said, staring at her, whisky-befuddled. 'Bit handier than you let on, are you?'

'What happens to the boys?' Beth asked.

'I think we'll get them benighted,' Mia said. 'I'll check with Zach. Should teach them a lesson.'

'Benighted?' Beth didn't understand.

'You'll see,' Mia said, and didn't elaborate.

∞

4
THE HUNTING PARTY

I

Ella dimmed the lights in her room and flopped on to her bed.

Her living-pod, like all the others, was set into the outer ring of the Habitation Dome. Each had the bedroom against the outer skin of the dome, so they could see out across the surface of the planet, through a tinted porthole. Each person's quarters was divided into two, with the tiny bedroom, no more than a cubicle, leading off a living area. Everyone had an electronically lockable door, which led on to the communal corridors and social areas.

Not for the first time, Ella thought it was pretty good for a cell.

The pain was not too strong today, her inter-organic fibre network doing its business. The tiny electrical stimuli worked in a drug-like way, interacting with her body, building strength.

The new girl worried her. She folded her hands together and stared at the ceiling. And Colm was becoming a problem. And those power fluctuations. She wondered how much thought Zach gave to any of it. Did he delegate and forget? He never seemed to follow anything up. Zach, she knew, was a leader by the force of his charisma – not through any natural organisational abilities.

She knew there were rumblings. That a good few people thought someone else ought to be leading them. When the time was right. When Zach slipped up. Maybe there would even be a breakaway group.

Would they ever dare? And where would they go?

She remembered that expedition she had led in those early cycles.

They left the island at dawn. She had taken Shan, Amber, Aisling, Malachi, Joel, Caleb, Nasreen, Brad and Freya. Five boys, five girls, with a mix of skills and ages. That convoy of three jeeps and five Drones, sleeping under the stars, always with fires burning. Taking it in turns to be on lookout, edgily watching the darkness with its strange smells. Listening to the murmur of the sea, the distant song of the Howling Mountains.

They had covered several hundred kiloms, had sent Drones out to cover a lot more. They had gathered endless recordings and readings of forests, lush valleys, dark lakes, jagged gorges. They found the crumbling ruins of an ancient civilisation, proving that this place had not always been uninhabited. Twisted, jagged stubs of spires and towers protruding from acid-blue lakes. The shell of what might once have been a citadel, built from stone and metal, overrun with vines, crumbling to the touch.

Here and there, the bleached, semi-fossilised bones of giant creatures were half-buried in the rock and sand. They walked around inside them, the skeletons like giant, echoing cathedrals of bone.

Two vast, weather-beaten statues flanked a gorge; sharp-toothed, many-eyed creatures carved into the rock, a hundred emms high. What tragedy had befallen this world? What had caused this empire to rise, then to crumble and fall, hundreds if not thousands of years ago? They would never know. All they knew was that it was theirs now. Theirs to make the best of, or die trying.

Mostly, the place was a wilderness. They had gone right to the edge of this land-mass, mapping landmarks and distances as they went. They reached another dark, shining ocean, where frothing, creamy-yellow breakers curled and smashed on the rocks. There, they found beaches of indigo sand and glassy silver pebbles. Endless coastlines of hard blue rock. A hazy horizon where a glutinous sun broke the golden clouds, spreading like a mark of death, staining the water crimson.

Strange screeching sounds and darting green lights, which they assumed to be some kind of magnetic effect, had transfixed them for a while. They had quickly become unsettling, though, as if the planet were bombarding them with a barrage of light and sound, forcing them back inland.

That, then, had marked the limit of their world.

The party had one final fire and meal on the beach, then headed home to the island.

They brought back the news that Town was, all things considered, in the best possible place. Which was, of course, both good news and bad. *This is as good as your life's ever going to get.* People didn't always want to hear that.

And there was, as far as any of them could tell, no other sign of intelligent life on the planet. The Towners were alone.

Ella touched a wall-pad, dimmed the lights further still.

In the red glow, her metal-laced skin glittered. She lay there, twists of blue hair splayed out on the pillow. Deep in thought, allowing tiredness to flood her body. The web inside her tingled, firing off the tiniest impulses, fizzing and crackling in her, renewing her. She was used to this, and found it soothing.

There was a soft, low beep, indicating someone was pressing at the comm panel on her door. Irritated, Ella turned over. 'Oh, go away.'

The beep sounded again.

Ella tutted in irritation, sat up, pulling the sheet around her as best she could. Modesty wasn't that much of a big thing here on the Edge, but she didn't know who it was going to be. She strode the few paces to the door and flipped the switch. 'Hello?'

There was silence.

Annoyed, Ella flicked the switch again. 'Zach, is that you? I'm sorry, I need to be alone tonight.'

There was silence.

She didn't know why, but an instinct kicked in, some piece of primal self-preservation. She pulled open the grey-steel drawer in which she kept the few things that were precious to her, and took out the red Magna pistol, the one she always kept for her own use. As head of security. Not that she'd ever been appointed that – it had fallen to her.

Ella approached the door, slowly.

She held her breath.

Slowly, carefully, she moved her flat palm closer and closer.

She swooped, slamming her hand on the bolt, sliding it back in one swift movement. She was braced, gun ready.

There was nobody there.

Ella's heart was thumping, adrenaline coursing through her. For a second, her arms tingled, almost with pain, and she winced. She stepped out into the softly-lit, curving corridor, turning in a full circle. No sign of anyone.

Annoyed with herself, she went back into her room, secured the gun again. She sat down hard on her bed, drawing a deep, shuddering breath.

A shadow fell across her door.

Ella jumped to her feet, gun levelled. And then, as the familiar, bobbing shape of a Drone came into sight, the relief flooded through her like a drug.

'What do *you* want, sunshine?' she asked, patting the small robot like a dog.

Drone 016 swivelled towards her, its single red eye glowing, its motor whirring. The eye seemed to survey Ella inquisitively, as if wanting to know something.

'Go on. Tell me.'

The Drone's lower cavity flipped open, and its telescopic arm extended, grasping a cylindrical item, about the length of a human forearm, made of battered, scorched metal. It offered the item to Ella, who frowned, taking it slowly in her own hand.

Her expert fingers caressed the indentations and scratches in the burnt metal. It was like a small, tubular rocket, stubby, surprisingly heavy in her hand. From the marks and burns, it was evident to Ella that the thing had fallen through the atmosphere at high velocity. So small, she imagined, that it had passed undetected by the Comms tower. So much for vigilance.

'So,' said Ella uncertainly. 'Are you gonna tell me where you found this?'

The Drone withdrew its arm, flipped its panel shut and blinked its eye at her once.

'Course not,' Ella said. 'You can't speak. Can you *show* me where you found it?' She put the cylinder down on her table, and unrolled the rough map of the island, the sea and the surrounding country which she, Maddi and Zach had put together from scans and expeditions. 'Show me? Here?' She unrolled the map on the floor.

It hovered over the map, swivelled. Its red light intensified, stabbing down on a cluster of contour lines on the edge of the Howling Mountains.

'Right near Sharp Ridge ...?' Ella murmured.

But the Drone's light was circling all around the map, not indicating anywhere in particular.

'What ... You don't know where you found it?'

The light stabbed down again. Into the circles on the map which represented Town.

'Here? You found it *here*?'

The Drone bobbed up and down. It seemed to be casting about the room for something.

'Of course. Wait.' Ella rolled up the map and grabbed another from her desk, unrolling it quickly. This was a large-scale plan of Town itself, which she and others had drawn up in their first cycles. 'Where?' she said. 'Show me.'

The light stabbed down on to the map, moving across the yellowed paper, until it reached the small circle indicating a particular Habitation pod.

'Habitation 2/13 ...' Ella racked her brains, and then it came to her. 'Baljeet's pod.'

The Drone buzzed, as if in agreement.

'You're saying yes ...? You know who Baljeet is, right? Do you even know who any of us are?' Ella realised she was voicing an idea which was only really coming into her mind now. 'Can you ... even tell the difference between us?' she asked slowly, amazed that she was thinking this for the first time, let alone asking it. 'Do you *know* our names?'

The Drone's light pulsed. Was that agreement or not? She didn't know.

'Right ...' Ella rolled up her map. 'Very interesting. Thank you.'

The Drone bobbed, as if curtsying, and floated out of Ella's pod. She frowned, watching it go.

Then pain, like an electric shock, sliced up her right forearm.

She screamed, dropping the map on the floor, falling to her knees. She grasped her arm with her other hand, her breath coming in ragged staccato bursts.

No. No, please. Not this again.

The pain cut through her as if acid were flooding her veins. She gritted her teeth, groaning, dimly aware of her own voice echoing in her room. She gripped her arm tightly enough to cut off the flow of blood. She began to feel cramp in her spinal cord, her body curving and twisting.

She screamed it out loud, this time. '*No!*'

And then, astonishingly, mercifully, the pain abated. The artificial receptors inlaid in her body did their job.

Acclerated endorphins flooded her, racing through her, giving her a drug-like rush. She tilted her head back in relief. She did not know how long she knelt like that, but she finally allowed herself to release the grip on her arm, and to stagger to her bed and beg sleep to take her.

As she allowed exhaustion to engulf her body, Ella drifted through a half-reality, one in which she was hurled again and again into the wall of a Z-class shuttle, her body shattering, bones breaking.

Finally, sleep beckoned her, and she knew she had to succumb.

II

Beth sat up, gasping.

She blinked hard in the blackness, wondering if she was blind. It came back to her – a slow, wobbly reorientation. She remembered where she was, and another kind of darkness swept through her, this time from within.

She staggered to her feet, pushing off the light foil cover, and, rubbing her eyes, went to the reinforced window through which she could see the purple sky.

The two moons, one dark blue and the size of her fist, the other with an orange tinge and three or four times that big, dominated the horizon. There was a rich, velvety hue to the light, the palest of smudges hinting at the sunrise.

She could see a couple of swooping, diving Klaa – the pterodactyl-like birds which wheeled high in the sky, never coming close to town. The other creatures, the boar-like

Lantrill, occasionally ventured to the fence in the early days, but she had learned that a few well-aimed shots had seen them off, and they now rarely came close.

They had all been ensconced in the Ship for longer than any of them cared to remember, Beth had learned, in a semi-animated state to allow for long-distance travel. 'Semi-Anna', as it was scathingly called on the big colony ships, was thought of as dangerous and borderline illegal these days. It had started as a way of transporting livestock between trading planets – the idea of using it for humans seemed barbaric to Beth. She sensed that nobody really wanted to talk about the journey, and so she hadn't pushed it.

'You can sleep in the Main Dome, Beth,' Zach said to her after three cycles had passed, still puzzled about her choice of accommodation.

'I know, but I feel I would be taking up someone else's space.'

'We've got spare sleeping quarters,' Zach argued. 'We're not short of space here.'

'Thank you. Let me sleep in the Ship for a few more nights, will you? I will let you know how I get on.'

She didn't like to say, but she still wanted to keep her distance. Even now, if there was some way to get rid of her, some of them would – she knew that. There was a deep, cynical, un-Chapter-like part of her which had wondered if some of them hoped she'd get herself killed. Well, Beth told herself, she wasn't going to let that happen. Something – the Great Power, maybe – had helped her survive the *Arcadia* disaster. That had happened for a reason.

So she liked to be at a distance. The observer.

She could see the power of the bonds of friendship here, and of affection, sometimes very demonstrative, and the occasional burst of casual passion. With nobody to regulate this, why would any of them be in any way restrained? It was not as if the Chapter was there to disapprove. In a way it was much like the turmoil of relationships in Academies, but without any adults to sanction or forbid anything. So she tried not to react when she observed the various pairings and betrayals happening.

She had seen Aisling casually placing her mouth over Brad's as he worked, caressing him unashamedly so that he blushed. And then, two hours later, she had glimpsed the same girl pressed against the hangar with Caleb, half-undressed, engaged in one another so fiercely that they didn't even notice Beth pass by. She had seen Dionne and Hal similarly wrapped up in one another, while Colm and Zach always seemed to have various girls hanging around them. Zach was indifferent to them, but Colm relished their attention. One of the most popular Thirteeners was a slim, mixed-race girl called Amber Salem, very striking, with a tumultuous mass of purple hair and a gleaming jewel in her eyebrow. She was a thief, but also a fixer and mender of everything from jeeps to alarms, and flirted endlessly with everyone as she worked. Beth, observant and thoughtful, noted all of this, learning something new every cycle.

Maddi, she had come to realise, was different, a genuine, sensitive soul. She had been closely bonded to Leila, and had taken her death very hard – which made the gift of her jacket all the more special.

'I know where you're going.'

The Twelvies jumped. The two small, scruffy girls, their faces painted with tribal stripes in imitation of Mia, seemed startled and guilty. Cait tried to stuff the water-can into the belt of her skirt, making an unsuccessful attempt to hide it.

Beth grinned. 'It's fine. We can go together.'

'We didn't–' began Cait.

'It's not–' said Livvy.

Beth had seen the two slim, pale figures scurrying around outside in the half-light. She smiled as she recognised them. It took her only a few seconds to grab her knife, slip it into her belt and head through the airlock towards the exit ramp. Reason, she thought as she slid open the exit door, letting the dawn-light in. Reason and purpose. She had followed the two girls silently right to the edge of the compound, feet hardly impacting on the blue sand. She had waited before announcing her presence.

Beth pulled her battered jacket on, strode over to the girls and ruffled both their tangled nests of hair. 'It's good,' she said. 'I'd do it too. Come on.'

There were two boys on watch outside the Main Dome, she could see, armed with wooden stakes and not guns, but they were more interested in some makeshift gambling game with pebbles and cards. The girls moved swiftly, almost silently, until they came to a large, ragged gash in the chain-link fence.

'Did you make this?' Beth asked the girls, staring in puzzlement at the hole.

They shook their heads, as one.

'What, it was already here?'

The girls nodded, again in unison.

'Someone cut it,' said Cait.

'We couldn't do that,' added Livvy, apologetically.

Beth decided not to argue. 'Right,' she said. 'Well, whoever did it, it's very convenient for us. Come on, then.'

They slipped through the gap and were out on the open slopes, the rough untrodden sand and rock beneath their feet. She followed the two Twelvies across the moonlit dust, occasionally glancing back at the soft lights of Town. They headed upwards, up to the island's highest rocks, where the air was salty and pungent.

Cait had a scan-pad in her hand, its directional indicator showing in luminous green. Like the lamps, the scan-pads were solar-charged from a store in Town. 'This way!' she said confidently, and scurried on ahead.

'Did you steal that?' asked Beth, laughing.

Cait didn't answer, but instead led the way up the incline, through a gap in a misshapen, arch-like rock.

Livvy kept pace with Beth. 'You all right?' she asked. 'All them cuts and bruises …'

'Yes, I am healing. Thank you. Bless you two, really. It was very kind of you to take care of me.'

'Maddi and Zach said someone should.'

'Well, then, bless them too. The Great Power is at work, even in this place.'

Cait and Livvy didn't say any more in response. Partly, Beth suspected, because they did not want to get into a conversation about the Great Power – which she could understand – and partly because they had arrived at their destination.

At the top of the jagged rocks, six long poles had been fashioned into two tripods, lashed together at the top with thick twine. The poles were firmly embedded into the ground and wedged with rocks. A pole lay along the top. Reza and Gabe, pale and drawn, hair matted, were each lashed to the horizontal pole with twine around their wrists, their toes touching the ground. The sea, watchful and endlessly roaring, kept guard beyond.

So, this was a Benighting, thought Beth. It didn't seem very pleasant. Zach had to have a harsh side to sanction this.

'We've brought you some water,' said Cait, and she raised the canister to Reza's lips first.

'It's almost dawn,' Beth said apologetically. She gazed at the dark purple horizon, which was awash with green streaks. The two moons were already becoming paler, and below them the muscular, stealthy shape of the sea was beginning to emerge from the gloom. 'I expect they will let you go soon … Great Power, I am so sorry. This is barbaric. It is not the punishment I would have chosen.'

Cait handed the water to Livvy, who took it over to Gabe.

Reza, defeat in his face, tried to meet Beth's gaze. 'That's Zach for you,' he said, licking his cracked lips. 'Don't like people stepping out of line, yeah? And Mia's his guard dog.'

'Mia secured you?' Beth hardly needed to ask. She could almost imagine Mia enjoying it.

Reza could barely respond, face drawn with tiredness.

'Gabe doesn't look good,' said Livvy, coming back with the water. Beth could tell the girl was worried. 'He needs proper rest.'

Beth took in the boy's pale skin, the dark rings under his eyes. Her unease turned to anger. So, this was the way they did things here? The way they imposed discipline? It made them no better than those who had sent them here.

She unsheathed her knife, and the gleam of the blade made Cait and Livvy exchange an uncertain look.

'They've suffered enough,' said Beth. 'Time to cut them down.'

'Zach won't like that,' said Cait.

'Sometimes, girls,' Beth said, stepping forward and beginning to hack at Reza's bonds with her sharp vanadium blade, 'life is not about doing what the man in charge says. It's about doing what you think is right.'

She sliced through the twine, and Reza's freed arms jerked down as it unravelled. She moved over to Gabe and did the same. The two boys, rubbing their chafed wrists, eyed each other warily in the grey dawn-light.

'So,' said Beth. 'No fighting, no swearing. Pretty easy, no …? Shake hands.'

The boys looked curiously at her, then back towards each other. Cait and Livvy watched, grinning.

'Shake hands,' said Beth again, firmly. 'It is what people

do. After a conflict is resolved.' She was astonishing herself. 'Go on,' she said to the boys.

Reza shot a confused glance in Beth's direction, but he still stepped forward, offering his hand to Gabe. After a second's hesitation, Gabe took his hand and shook it awkwardly.

'A job done,' said Beth, and holstered her knife. 'See how easy it can be?'

She knew she would have some explaining to do.

III

Dawn over the forest.

Square columns of rock reached upwards from the mist and the trees, splaying outwards like the fingers of a stone giant. The rock was enmeshed in crimson and blue vines. There, deep in the tangle of alien vegetation, the two small figures scrambled and climbed. The tiniest of creatures, alien invaders in this jungle paradise. Humans. Mere specks on the dark, wet stone.

Mia knew she was faster than Shan – even though her head was still thick from the previous night's drinking.

Her lithe body honed by numerous hunts and chases, she moved like a sure-footed Lantrill herself, finding handholds and footholds fearlessly and without pause. The pressure-gloves helped, but only up to a point – you still had to know where you were putting your feet. With the knife gripped between her teeth, saliva building up behind it, Mia could feel her body slick with sweat, and her exposed skin scratched and barbed. The sweet-smelling vines were as thick and tough as cables, though – she had never known one to break.

Shan was at least fifty emms below her, his scrambling shape framed against the white of the jungle mist. Mia barely wasted a second checking on her companion. She kept going. Above the strange, unearthly singing of the winds, she could hear the bleating of the Lantrill cub, out of its comfort zone on the high rock.

In the jeep, in the growing light, the four of them – Mia, Shan, Ricky and Amber – had tracked the family to its lair. Mia and Shan were armed with a Karson rifle and a Magna pistol, the younger Towners with sharpened wooden stakes. With two shots from the rifle, without even leaving the jeep, Shan had easily slaughtered the slow tough parent Lantrill. The bodies fell, great slabs of meat. They hoisted the steaming, purple flesh into the trough on the back of the jeep, trying to ignore the oily, hot death-smell of the bodies.

It was then that Mia had spotted the scuttling young, making a break into the wet swamplands around them. Shan had been all for leaving them, coming home with the good haul they already had, but Mia knew the value of a kill. Lantrill meat, tough as it was, could be preserved in the molecular chamber for up to twenty cycles, by which time it fell off the bone like the finest young lamb. And the young females, although small, were fleshy, their stubby thighs and round breasts providing glistening smooth almost bone-free meat. She wasn't about to turn down the chance. So the younger kids, Ricky and Amber, stayed with the jeep, while Shan and Mia set off in swift pursuit.

Mia had fired a warning shot, sending the young animals scuttling and splashing through the muddy swamps. They snorted in terror, heading for what they thought was the safety of the rocks. It seemed the Lantrill, even after all this time, still didn't remember the versatility and persistence of the human invaders.

Shan squatted in the stinking mud, firing shot after shot at two of the scuttling creatures, managing only to blast three twisted, black trees to a pulp. The wood collapsed inwards, falling with a slurping, belching noise into the swamp.

Mia wiped spatters of putrid mud from her face. She had seen the other young Lantrill make for the Great Rocks.

'We go after it,' she'd said.

'Don't be insane,' said Shan. 'We've got enough.'

'You drive back if you want to.' Mia slung her rifle on her shoulder and drew her knife. 'I'm getting it.'

There was a brief moment's pause, with the mist billowing around them, the only sound the echoing, singing screech of as-yet unseen jungle creatures. Even after all this time, there were things they didn't know about deep in its recesses, things which cowered from noise and light but which might emerge if feeling bold. Some especially nasty things, Mia knew, lurked in the ruined cities, the remnants of this planet's old civilisation. She didn't like to speculate as to why.

'Well?' she said.

'All right,' he said reluctantly.

She knew, of course, that he wouldn't want to return to the jeep alone.

They hurtled through the putrid swamp, their boots thudding and sloshing, spraying up stinking water and mud and algae on all sides. Bespattered, they reached the slick grey rock, activated the pressure-gloves and began to climb.

Without the technology of the gloves – thick gauntlets which moulded themselves to every small crevice, fixing with a temporary molecular bond each time the wearer moved their fingers – two humans, even fit and young ones, would have had no hope on the slippery rock. The vines would have afforded some handholds, it was true, but there were flat stretches and overhangs as hard as worked metal, smooth and unpitted. Here, only the gloves and a strong, physical effort helped a climber to progress.

Mia was first on to the ledge. She could hear the snuffling and grunting of the Lantrill cub. She could smell its fear.

And there, as the mist briefly swirled and parted, she saw it, nestling into a dark fissure, trapped, unable to go further, six of its ten chubby blue legs flailing helplessly. She could see its glowing red eyes, flaming like coals – with fear, she presumed. Its tusks were chipped and worn, one of them almost broken in two.

Mia squatted on the ledge. One glove, with a hiss and a squelch, attached her to the slick rock. Steadying herself, she took the knife from her mouth and prepared to throw it. Up here, she was not going to risk the Karson – they were powerful weapons, but not contained. A single blast could take out the Lantrill's heart, but could as easily splatter its organs all over the rock, making it useless for food – or even shatter the rock, turn the ledge into dust and send her spinning down.

Behind her, Shan was puffing and panting as he hauled himself on to the ledge, his tread firm but stealthy. She kept the knife level.

'It's hurt,' Shan said.

'What?' Mia turned her head slightly.

'The rock.'

Mia made out the fresh, glistening, steaming trail of glutinous blue blood, thick as paint, leading along the rock to the crevice where the Lantrill cub squealed and thrashed. The wound, below its neck, spurted gouts of blood.

'Then this'll be easy,' she said. 'This thing will make thirty meals.'

Mia had a suspicion that the Collective had always intended the small group simply to live as long as they could on the small stash of food-sub pills, and then die. She didn't think the authorities had ever imagined that, tough as they were, they'd learn to hunt, and kill, and cook. The thought of the transgression made her blood surge with primal passion. Every hunt, every kill, was a win. A strike back against the authorities.

Shan pulled back, flattening himself into the rock wall. 'Go on, then,' he said. 'Get it over with.'

IV

'Bethany.'

Striding back across the compound towards the Ship, Beth stopped at the sound of Zach's voice. She put one hand on her hip as he approached her, took a slow and deliberate swig of the brackish, too-warm water from the canister.

She could not read his face behind the mirror-shades, but his body-language left her in no doubt that he was not happy.

'Good morning, Zach. I trust you had a good sleep?'

She offered him the water-can, having learned already that this was a gesture of trust and friendship in conversations here. But he did not accept it.

'I've had better.' His tone was curt, abrasive. 'I gather I wasn't up as early as some people.'

'Ah. News travels fast, I see.' She tucked the water-can into her belt.

'In a place like this, yes. I'm surprised you didn't realise that.'

'Oh, I did.'

She deliberately kept her responses laconic. Beth knew what to do when you were in trouble, when you were cornered. Say as little as possible. Let the other person speak, and let them tell you exactly how much they know and what they are angry with you about. Never put your foot in it.

'Did you think I wouldn't find out?' said Zach, moving close to her but not looking directly at her, in a way that made his body-language more hostile.

'Find out what?' said Beth breezily. 'That I like an early morning stroll by the sea?'

'Don't play games with me.' His hand moved fast, gripping her forearm, half-shoving, half-twisting her. Her stomach flipped in alarm, and her hand went instinctively to the hilt of her knife.

'Games?' she said, hating the tremor in her voice. 'I'm not playing games.'

Zach slowly, deliberately looked down, making it very clear that he'd seen Beth reach for her knife. 'Quite handy with that, aren't we? ChapterSister's not so unworldly, is she ...? Useful in a bar fight, too, I hear.'

She blushed, and removed her hand from the knife. 'It's ... instinct. I know how to take care of myself.'

'I'll have to tell Mia. She could do with that *instinct* in her hunting parties. I wonder if you could hit a Lantrill at fifty emms with that knife?'

She laughed. 'No, I'm useless. I'm rubbish, really. Didn't Mia tell you? I couldn't even hit a tin can with a Magna at twenty–'

Zach's grip on her forearm tightened. 'I'm not a fool, Beth,' he said softly.

'I'm sure you're not.' She swallowed hard, realising how uncomfortably close he was to her. The heat of his body. His broad chest and flat toned stomach almost pressing against her.

'I'm the leader here,' he said softly. 'I was *elected*. If someone wants to stand against me, rules say they need a supporter and a seconder, and it goes to a vote. Right?'

'Very democratic. The Chapter would approve.'

'Oh, the *Chapter* would approve. How very *nice*.' He let go of her arm, roughly pushing her. Her mouth turned paper-dry, her heart thudding. 'This is the Edge. This is Town. You're not on the *Arcadia* any more, Bethany Kane. You want to fit in here, you do things our way.'

She rubbed her bruised arm. 'Zach, come on. They are *young* boys. They were out there–'

'It was their punishment as agreed by–'

'–all *night* with no water, Zach! Cait and Livvy–'

'This is not about Cait and Livvy. They've been told.'

'Told?' she repeated. He sounded more like an angry parent than like one of the group, she thought.

'They transgressed, Beth. It's an agreed punishment. I don't need bleeding-heart Chapter refugees coming in–'

'Bleeding-heart …' She spread her hands in astonishment. 'Great Power. I can't believe this.'

'–coming in and reading the Galactic Rights Act at me! … *Understood*?'

'I wanted to give them hope, rather than fear. Hope can be good, you know.'

'Hope? I can't say that's ever brought very much.'

'You'd be surprised. Cities have been founded on less.'

He made a disgusted face. 'You and your Chapter words.'

She held her ground, trying not to recoil from his anger. 'You hurt me,' she said, rubbing her arm.

Zach's face was hard, unsmiling. 'Then I apologise. But if you undermine me again, you can expect worse.'

Blood drained from her face. 'Zach, to hear you speak …'

'What? To hear me speak, *what*?'

'Nothing.' She waved a hand. 'Really, nothing.'

Tension hung in the air for a second, and then he broke it with a dazzling smile. 'All right,' he said. 'Well done.'

'Well … done?' she repeated, puzzled.

'You stood up for yourself. Defended your actions. In a way, I admire that.'

Beth scowled, sensing she was being played. 'Admire all you like.'

'But next time,' he said, jabbing a finger at her, 'you *ask*. I might have said yes. I probably would have, in fact, if you'd made a good case.'

'You were asleep.'

'I rarely sleep,' he said, sounding as if he meant it. 'Occupational hazard.' Zach's radio crackled and he scooped it up, walking away from Beth as he answered it. 'Go ahead.'

She hurried into the shade of the Ship. She had the feeling an understanding had been reached there, but she wasn't quite sure what it was.

As she made her way back, there was a low whistle behind her. She turned, angrily, squinting into the sun. In the tar-black shadow between the dome and the hangar, she could see the outline of a shape sitting on a rock.

'So what's the deal, Sister? Making a name for yourself already, are we, babe?'

Colm. He was sharpening some kind of wooden stake, expertly slicing tiny shavings off with a hunting-knife.

She strolled over to him, joining him in the shadows so she could stop squinting into the intense sunlight. 'I am not your *babe*. What are you doing?'

'Just a diversion.' He grinned, held up the wooden stake for her to admire. 'You never know. The guns won't last for ever. Who knows? In five years we might be back to sticks and stones. And you know what they say about those, eh?'

'They break your bones,' she said, remembering the old rhyme. 'Are you planning on breaking anyone's bones, Colm?'

'Ah, maybe not. Depends if anyone gets on my nerves.' He nodded to her belt. 'Good knife you've got there. Vanadium?'

Her hand went to the handle, instinctively. 'Yes,' she said.

'Bet you're better with that than with the gun, aren't you?' He smiled, but only with his eyes. 'Saw your altercation with Zachy-boy there. Ahh, don't be too scared of him. He likes to act the Mr Big-bollocks, but he's all talk.' He winked at her.

'I shall bear that in mind, Colm. Thank you.'

'Have a good day,' he said, and carried on sharpening the stake. 'Oh, and watch out. I hear there are some bloody criminals round here, you know.'

'Thanks for the warning,' she said drily.

V

Inside the Ship, Beth relaxed.

She had explored the place to her satisfaction. As she had expected, she had found an inert, dusty flight deck. There was a full pilot's and co-pilot's instrument panel, stark and silver. Several chairs, still covered in plastic and unused, sat beneath the control banks. The Ship was designed, she had already worked out, to be fully-automated on the voyage, but with an emergency provision – like all space-faring vehicles of this type, barely more than a glorified Semi-Anna cattle-truck, it could still be switched over to human control if the need was there.

The computer interface was a tall, matte-black pyramid in the middle of the flight deck, seemingly inert – but when she touched it, there was a tingle in her fingers and her temples. The pyramid began to pulse with a soft, red glow.

Resonance. Something she could do.

Quickly, she withdrew her hand. Time for that later.

She strolled out to the gantry above the cargo silo, surveying the Semi-Anna capsules. There was a humming noise coming from down there.

She drew her knife, silently and stealthily. Colm was right, she knew. She was still far more comfortable with it than with a gun. In the dim light below, a disc-shaped shadow formed. Beth swallowed hard, gripped the knife. The whining sound increased in intensity.

She could make out a dull blue glow in the darkness, and she realised what had arrived. With relief, she shoved the knife back into her belt and leaned on the gantry.

'What are *you* doing in here, eh?' she said cheerfully.

A Drone had hovered into view, one with a coppery-red casing. Slowly, it lifted so that it was level with her. Its number-plaque read 356. It whirred and clicked at her in agitation, swivelling, bouncing.

'I wish you could tell me what you wanted!' Beth muttered.

The Drone stopped swivelling. It reacted like an animal, she thought – like a dog, responding to the call of its mistress. The thought alarmed her. That was insane. They had millions of neural receptors, but they were all essentially variations on logic gates, on the binary coding which had powered machines since the very earliest computers. The Drone couldn't think for itself any more than a protein analyser could, or a jeep. Or a gun.

Could it?

Beth lifted her hand as if in greeting, then she moved it slightly to the right.

The Drone's electronic eye flickered to her right, following the movement of her hand. She brought it back again, moving left, and the eye followed.

'So,' she said softly. 'You're trying to tell me something, 356. And it can't be as simple as data, or you'd have plugged into a scan-pad and displayed it.'

The tingle in her head again. That tickling sensation which made her mouth and teeth feel metallic. She hated it. She knew what it was and tried to ignore it.

The Drone moved forward. Closer still, not bobbing but gliding as if on a flat surface. It came right up close to Bethany Kane, its electronic iris opening. Eyeballing her.

'What do you want, 356?' she murmured. 'What do you need?'

The tingling sensation increased. Beth gritted her teeth in anger.

'No,' she said. 'Go away!'

The Drone did a small bob of acknowledgement, then

fired its thruster and zoomed back down into the Semi-Anna silo, all in the space of two seconds.

'No!' she cried, leaning on the rail. 'Not you! Come back!'

But the Ship was silent, and she was alone again.

VI

In the vast, cold, warehouse-like space of the Storage Dome, Zach was up on a metal stepladder, fixing a light-source. Lulu watched, helping. They could have asked a Drone to do it, Zach knew, but they had endless maintenance tasks, and the Towners had learned it was often quicker to do the small things themselves.

'Sonic probe,' he said to Lulu, holding out his hand.

She passed him the slim silver tool from the box. 'Thought it was a dud bulb?'

'No,' said Zach, peering curiously into the cavity in the wall where the light-tube sat. 'Something wrong with the connectors. Think they've burnt out.' He lowered the probe. 'That's really odd.' This place, he thought. Always something going wrong, always something to do.

'I don't like this,' Lulu said. 'The power-losses, all this stuff breaking … This doesn't feel like … normal, Zach. It feels like …'

Neither of them wanted to say the word. 'Sabotage?' Zach offered. There was an uncomfortable silence.

Lulu scowled. 'This is not good, Zach. It feels almost like someone's trying–'

She got no further. An alarm screeched into life, echoing through the whole dome, loud enough to make their ears tingle.

Zach had leapt down from the ladder and was already tapping at the screen of the nearest tracking-point.

'The generator room. Come on!'

He grabbed her hand, almost forcibly indicating that she should follow. Lulu dropped her tools and ran to keep pace with Zach, following him through doorways to two sections as the blare of the alarm cut through the air. They both hit the downwards stairs at a run.

In thirty seconds, they hit a solid metal door. They could hear the alarm screeching from inside. Zach jabbed again and again at the control, but the door would not open.

'What's up?' Lulu asked.

He kicked the door in frustration. 'It's bloody jammed!'

Lulu thought quickly, grabbing her radio. 'Amber, come in. Amber, we need you urgently in Lower Storage 4!' She looked up at Zach. 'Some days it's good to have a thief around,' she said.

'*Yeah, what is it?*' Amber's sleepy voice responded.

'Get here now. Storage 4. And bring your box of tricks. *Now*, Amber!'

Zach thumped repeatedly on the door in the next two minutes, as the alarm became ever more shrill and insistent.

'What the hell do you think's happening?' he asked Lulu.

'I don't like to think. If it's the generator …'

Neither of them said it, but they both knew how serious this could be. Seconds later, Amber clattered down the stairs, rubbing her eyes, her toolbox swinging from her fingertips.

'All right, what's the fuss?'

'Get this open, *now*,' said Zach.

She squatted down, lifting her purple curls out of the way and putting her ear to the door. 'Jammed solenoid override? Seems like it. Wow. Someone knows what they're doing.'

'But can you get it open?'

'Patience, yeah?' She held up a hand, while in her other she had already produced a small, silver pen-like device with a digital scale inlaid into it. She skewered the lock-panel with it. 'Case of finding the right echo tremble, innit?'

Zach balled his fists and thumped the wall, making Lulu jump. 'Can you get on with it? Please?'

Amber had her ear to the door, listening carefully while monitoring the readout on her device. She held up a finger and grinned. 'You can't rush an expert, boss. You want this doing properly, or quickly?'

'Both,' said Zach. 'Both, *please*.'

'Do you know what you're doing?' Lulu asked.

Amber scowled. 'Bitch, please. I been breaking into shit since I was, like, eight. This is nursery stuff ... Aha! Gotcha.' The girl gave her lock-device a twist, and gestured like a magician as the door rumbled very slowly open. Zach and Lulu rushed inside. 'It's fine,' Amber said, sauntering in behind them. 'Don't thank me. Oh – you didn't.'

Behind the door was the small, underground chamber housing the tall silver cylinder of the neutron generator, inlaid into the wall. In a second, Zach took in the two things in the room which were not right – the panel on the side of the generator which was pulsing cherry-red, and Ella lying on the floor, apparently unconscious. He skidded as he ran over to her, Lulu following closely behind.

'She's breathing.'

'Let me,' said Lulu, touching Ella's neck. 'Do something about that alarm!'

Zach went over to the generator, reaching out for the glowing panel. An intense, searing heat was coming off it, preventing him from putting his hand anywhere near it. He winced, pulling back.

'We've got a problem. Is she all right?'

'I'm going to give her a shot of adrenozam,' Lulu said. She was focused, flipping open the medikit she always carried. She took out a syringe and started to draw off the relevant chemical.

Amber was watching from the door, concerned. 'She gonna be all right?'

Zach was on the radio. 'Anybody, I need a Drone with a heat-shield in the generator room!'

There was a clattering on the stairs – a small group, headed by Colm and a wiry, blond Thirteener, Finn.

'What in hell's happening?' Colm asked.

Lulu was brisk, pointing at the prone Ella. 'Finn, Amber, you'll need to support her head for me.'

'Why?' Finn asked in bemusement.

'Just *do* it!'

Zach was still shouting instructions into the radio. 'And

get that bloody alarm turned off! It's doing my head in!' He turned to Colm. 'Is there a Drone nearby?'

'I think so ...'

'Well, *find* one!' Zach's calm demeanour was shaken, and the others visibly quailed at his anger.

'Okay, gotcha.' Colm backed off, holding his hands up. 'No need to shout, boss.'

Lulu prepared the shot of adrenozam as Finn and Amber, cradling Ella's head, watched in alarm. 'What's going to happen?'

'With any luck, she'll wake up very suddenly. I need someone to support her so she doesn't do herself another injury.' Lulu looked sharply at the young Towners. 'Ready?'

As Lulu was about to plunge the needle into Ella's skin, Ella gave a deep, throaty gasp, her eyes opening wide as if she were seeing nightmarish visions, and she sat bolt upright. Lulu and Finn did their best to calm her.

'Ell, Ell ... It's all right. You're fine, Ell!' Lulu patted her on the cheek. 'Do you feel all right? Can you see me?'

Ella nodded.

The blare of the alarm cut off.

The requested Drone had finally appeared, bobbing in through the door, twirling and buzzing urgently. 'Got your little fella, here,' Colm said, from behind it on the stairs.

'At last!' Zach snapped. 'Where have you been, you metal moron? Get *that* pulled out,' he pointed to the glowing red panel, 'and find out what's wrong!'

The Drone obeyed. From its cavity popped something rather like a metallic grey umbrella, expanding to protect it from the intense heat. It then extended various probes, tools and pincers around the umbrella to remove the glowing red panel, in a shower of sparks and smoke. With remarkable efficiency, the Drone pulled out the charred circuitry and frazzled wiring, and began effecting a repair. Intense cutting and slicing were punctuated by brief bursts of cold yellow sealant.

Zach went over to Ella. 'Feel all right?' he asked quietly. She nodded, smiled weakly.

'Nasty bump on the head,' said Lulu. 'We'll get that seen to, don't worry. Try not to move too fast for a few minutes.'

'Do you remember anything?' Zach asked. 'Anything at all?'

She looked from side to side, as if panicking as she tried to recall.

'I … I heard the alarm … I came down and saw that.' She nodded to the inspection panel, which was now a twisted knot of molten metal on the floor. 'It was glowing bright orange … I got my radio out to call someone and then …' Ella closed her eyes and shuddered. 'I think … I think I saw someone out of the corner of my eye, but I can't be sure. A movement. A shadow.'

Colm squatted down beside Zach. 'Any idea who it was, Ella-bella?' he asked gently.

Ella kept her eyes tightly closed. 'I don't know,' she said, her voice soft and strained. 'I couldn't see clearly.'

Colm touched her cheek gently. He was alert, though, scanning the room – looking for what others, perhaps, had missed.

'Well, there we go, guys,' Amber said, lounging against the wall with her arms folded. 'You see? Who said a misspent childhood was useless?'

VII

Mia judged the throw.

The Lantrill squealed and thrashed, red eyes flashing like lamps. And then, without warning, it jerked itself free.

Startled, Mia almost fell backwards, but Shan steadied her. Mia's heart thumped as the small blue furry scaly creature clamped itself to the rock, its gashed wound steaming.

The wedge-shaped jaw opened in a silent scream to reveal stubby, yellowing teeth beside the sharp tusks. The creature's meaty stench hit them with enough force to bowl them over. It was screeching, yelping. It scuttled along the ledge towards the young humans, eight of its legs good, the others mashed and bloodied stumps.

Mia was paralysed – not with fear, but with astonishment that the creature dared to confront them. This was new. The usually timid Lantrill fighting back, barking and yelping, drooling. Her knife-arm slackened.

'Go on, then!' Shan hissed in her ear.

She hurled the knife – badly.

It missed.

The blade bounced off the rock and hurtled into the chasm below, before Mia had a chance to grab it. And then the Lantrill squealed, and was off along the ledge, scuttling to safety, dragging a steaming trail of blood behind it.

'Stay here,' Mia snarled, and began to climb. 'I'm going to blast it from above.'

She barely heard Shan's, 'Be careful,' because she had already gripped the rock with the pressure-gloves. She was climbing, her booted feet scrabbling for a hold on the wet rock, the mist thickening, obscuring her vision in the dim light.

Up and up she climbed, covering ten, twenty emms. She scrambled across, using vines to help her, trying to find somewhere to stop and angle the gun. Mia sneezed as the irritating, salty mist found its way up her nose, loosening thick mucus which she hawked up and spat out in stringy gobbets.

She could see the creature's red eyes on the rock, about ten emms below her.

She had to risk the shot, so it had to be good, clean – and she could not risk dropping the weapon into the jungle below, or her own hold slipping.

She knew the Karson rifle would be no good here. She drew the Magna and fired once, deliberately wide, so that the plasma burst hit below the Lantrill, searing off a curtain of vegetation with a whoosh of flame. As Mia had expected, the creature screamed and began to scramble upwards – towards her.

It covered the distance remarkably quickly for a wounded animal.

Mia slammed her booted feet into the nearest available holds – one in a tangle of vine, the other in the smallest hole in the rock – and stuck her gauntleted right hand on to the rock, where it squelched and held firm. She had to draw the gun with her left hand, which felt awkward.

Five emms below her, on the ledge, the Lantrill cowered, scrabbled with its good legs. She could see its fur shimmering, its teeth gnashing, the steaming gash of its wound gouting blood into the chasm.

For a second, its eyes met hers.

She pointed the pistol. At this range, even one-handed, she could not miss.

She fired.

Its head split open like a ripe fruit. Blood and offal fountained upwards, some spraying so far that it spattered Mia's legs. A scream echoed across the valley, bouncing off the rocks – a terrible screech of death. The creature, its gashed head glistening, reared up, thrashing in its dying throes. A second later it slumped, dead, on the ledge – thankfully not falling off the rock entirely.

Mia gave a grim smile of satisfaction.

And then, slowly, with a hideous squelching sound, the pressure-gauntlet unpeeled itself, one finger at a time, from the rock wall.

Mia's world became slow-motion. She grasped, desperately, for rock that was not there. Her palm unstuck itself and she toppled backwards.

She screamed out loud as the world gave way beneath her, and she fell, twisting into cold, empty space.

∞

The smallest of tests. The most fleeting of problems. Slowly, they build into a coherent whole. This place, these people, this community is under a greater threat than ever.

First, the world around them falls apart. The technology, the objects they take for granted. And then ...

They will soon come to realise that nothing is as it seems.

That the worlds they have constructed around themselves are about to come crashing down, and the darkest of emotions will be unleashed.

And so it begins.

5
FRIENDS AND ENEMIES

I

A metallic creaking and scraping. Like someone trying to move around in the darkness of the silos outside her make-shift sleeping-quarters. Beth drew her knife, pressed herself up against the cold metal wall.

The Drone returning? No, this was different.

Sturdy boots on metal. Trying, and failing, to move stealthily. A long shadow fell across the red light, and a shape stood in the alcove, its head moving, casting light in front of it. Dry-mouthed, heart hammering, Beth tensed, not daring to move.

The arc of light swept through the room, across her meagre possessions, growing closer and closer. She swallowed hard, gathered all her resolve, tried not even to breathe. But she knew that, in seconds, she'd have to let out a breath or her lungs would explode.

The shadow stepped into the room.

Beth pounced. In the gloom, she didn't really know where she was going, but she jabbed with the knife, hoping the blade would glint.

'Stand still,' she said.

There was a sharp intake of breath, and the new arrival stepped back.

'Turn that light off,' Beth ordered. 'Now.' Her heart thudded as she levelled her knife at the shadowy figure.

'All right, all right … jeeez … you're a jumpy one, missy.' It was a warm, lilting voice, one she recognised. The figure reached up and toggled the head-torch, just dimming it rather than switching it off altogether.

'Throw it to me.'

The figure obeyed, and Beth caught the torch one-handed. She flicked it on full and shone it into the newcomer's face. He recoiled, blinking, holding his hands up.

'Yeah, yeah, all right – dazzle me to death, why don'cha?'

Beth lowered the torch. 'Colm. Don't sneak about like that.'

Colm grinned. 'Charmed, I'm sure … Thought I'd come and see how you were. If you wanted anything.'

'I am … fine,' she said guardedly.

Her limbs still ached, but the broken, nerve-shattering tiredness had eased. It was normal, she knew, for a body to go into shutdown after a traumatic experience, to heal itself with a kind of deep, cleansing mega-sleep.

'People are worried about you.'

'I am well.'

'You did a good job before. Helping Mia sort those lads,' he said.

'It was nothing. I can see there is the need for order here, for rules. One cannot live in anarchy.'

'Nice one. So, not a rebel, then?' He grinned.

'I did not say that. We are all rebels, Colm, in our own way. But some revolutions do not involve fighting, or damage. Some rebellion is just in the mind. Some rebellions are rebellions of kindness.'

'Very deep. Oh, of course … you've been playing the saint, too.'

'What?' She missed his meaning at first.

'Water for our naughty prisoners …? Your friendly mission of mercy out there with the pixies?'

'Oh, that.' She was embarrassed. 'Yes, I believe authority should always be tempered with mercy … You seem to know a lot.'

He grinned. 'I bribe the Twelvies with booze and weed. They tell me stuff. I'm happy, they're happy.'

'That's … enterprising.' Beth tried to put contempt into her tone, but wasn't quite sure she succeeded. 'Are the boys in good health?'

'Oh, yeah. They'll have sore wrists and blurred vision for a bit, but hey. Show me a Thirteener who doesn't.'

Beth wrinkled her nose. 'I *think* that is disgusting. Possibly.'

'If you want it to be, Princess … So. Good set-up here.' He swaggered in, more confident now she wasn't shining the head-torch directly into his face. 'Got the big old space-ship all to yourself?' He thumped the black metal wall, and it rang like a broken bell, echoing up into the high steel roof. 'The big, old useless bloody spacey-ship.'

'Did nobody ever think to try and get it going?' Beth asked curiously. Their voices were no more than whispers, but they carried up, echoing spectrally in the high criss-crossed lattice of girders above them.

'Nobody's got the skills. This old hulk? To use a technical term, gorgeous, this ship is buggered.'

'Highly technical.' She threw his torch back to him and holstered her knife. 'But you strike me as inventive, Colm. Sure you couldn't … jump-start it?'

'It's not a bloody jeep, you Old Earther. Takes more than hot-wiring and a prayer, so it does.' He flicked the torch back on, dimly, so that they could still see in the gloom.

'Sorry. Only asked … The computer's on standby, you know.'

'Yeah, but if the ship won't fly … So Zach and the others, they talked about it, you know? But even with the Drones … it's not about patching the thing up to make it space-worthy again.'

'It is not?'

'Hell, no. It's a case of fuel, supplies … And hull integrity. Remember? Starform Class impulse units, five years old. This bucket would clear the atmosphere, and then …' Colm spread his hands. 'Big boom.' He gave her a wide, winsome grin. 'Who wants to die floating in a tin can? When I go – hopefully not for a looong time yet – I'd kinda like to go a bit more prettily than that. Drunk, maybe, in the arms of three beautiful girls.'

Despite herself, Beth couldn't help smiling. 'Three seems a bit greedy.'

'Oh, well. Two, then. But only if one of them was you.'

She laughed. 'How very smooth. I have a knife, re-member?'

'Whoa. So you do. Yeah, you'll fit in fine round here.' Colm jerked his head towards the shadowy, girder-crossed interior of the Ship. 'Can we move out there? Bit more space to breathe.'

Gantries criss-crossed in the darkness above the gigan-tic, cold silo. Beth and Colm leaned on the rail as Colm gestured down into the gloom, where iridescent, teardrop-shaped columns stood in ranks like upright coffins.

'Not a lot of fun, Semi-Anna travel,' Colm muttered moodily.

'So I gathered. How does it work?'

Colm pointed to one of the capsule doors, where the ripped-open, dangling remains of tubing and wires could be seen, clustered around a human-shaped indentation. 'Kept alive by intravenous nutrients. Pipes and wires shoved in places you *really* don't wanna have them. Then when we landed, an automatic dose of coolant gas to wake everyone up.'

'Uncomfortable,' said Beth, shuddering.

'Yeah, that's an understatement ... Fancy a stroll?'

'A stroll?' Despite herself, she was intrigued.

'Putting one foot in front of the other? It was quite popular with the human race back on Earth for a long time, before they invented petrol.'

'All right, then. As long as you do not make any more ... *suggestions*.'

'Cross my heart. And hope to – no, we'll leave it at cross my heart, if that's all the same to you ... Coming?'

'Yes, of course.' She followed him down the steps to the main airlock. 'Where are we going?'

'Gonna show you one of my favourite places,' he said.

II

With a thud, a hard object hit the workbench in front of Ella Dax.

She glanced up from the Drone she was fixing. Her right eye was covered with a small, high-intensity scan-pad, like an advanced eye-glass. It made the newcomer pixellated and blurred at first. She adjusted the settings.

Mia was standing with her arms folded and a grim, set expression on her face. She seemed even more angry than usual. And the object on the table was a pressure-gauntlet.

The throbbing in Ella's head was starting to recede, but the memory of the attack was not becoming any clearer in her mind – and now there was another incident right on the heels of it. One which could be connected.

She had also been ignoring the pain which occasionally crackled through her arms and legs. It kept coming back, with enough intensity to remind her that it was still there. It had happened once before, that feeling, when they were out on the exploratory mission – she had said nothing then, either.

'What's this about?' Ella asked, putting down the piece of circuitry she was prodding.

However, Ella knew exactly why Mia had come to see her. News travelled fast in Town. She had just wondered how long it would take.

'You may well ask,' said Mia, sliding on to the bench. 'For once in my life, I find myself in need of your expertise, Ella, *dearest*.' Mia gnawed at the hunk of rough-grain processed bread she'd got herself for lunch, pushing the pressure-gauntlet across the bench.

Ella frowned, staring at the glove as if it was something dead. 'Problem?' she asked, trying to sound casual.

'Only that someone tried to kill me,' said Mia indistinctly, chewing her bread like a hungry animal.

Ella frowned. 'Explain.' She pushed the silver globe of the Drone aside, and picked up the glove, turning it over.

'On a close hunt with Shan, right? We had the 'trill cornered on the Sky Rocks, yeah, high up.'

Ella raised one eyebrow and she sprawled back languidly. 'Sky Rocks …? Interesting. Out of your comfort zone.'

'We'd chased the thing up there. The cub of the pair we brought back.'

The adult Lantrill, Ella knew, had already been stowed in the molecular chamber. This would, over the course of several cycles, eviscerate and bone the bodies and cook and dry the edible flesh. Nobody had thought any less of the hunting party for only bringing back two fairly tough specimens. At least twenty of the Towners had been on a Hunt at some time, and nobody had done as many as Mia. If two was her haul, then two was all it had been possible to track down on this occasion.

'I see,' said Ella, holding the gauntlet up to the light. 'So you put yourself and the rest of the party in unnecessary danger.'

Mia leaned forward and slammed the table. 'Listen, Ella. I knew what I was doing.'

'*Ground level* hunts, Mia. It's what we agreed. No point

getting yourself killed for meat. Just to be Alpha Female hunter-gatherer.'

Ella knew her calm languid sarcasm infuriated Mia, but she couldn't help it. Mia leaned back, scowling, the stripes on her face creasing as her face darkened in fury. 'You don't wanna know, then? How I almost died?'

'I'm fascinated,' Ella murmured, putting her eye-glass back in and beginning to prod around the wrist of the gauntlet with her micro-probe. 'What exactly happened?'

'One minute I was fixed to the rock, yeah? I could feel the grip. No worries. I aimed the gun, hit the 'trill square on. Then about a second later … The glove stops working. I'm falling off the cliff.'

Ella peered right inside the glove. 'No evidence of any malfunction that I can see. I'll test it properly in the workshop.' She took the eyeglass off and leaned back. 'That's all I can do.'

'It stopped working, Ella.'

'Well, it's working now.' Ella slipped the glove on, and slammed her hand against the Drone next to her. With a creaking, metallic squelch, the glove moulded itself to the robot's curved surface, giving Ella a perfect grip on the slippery metal. She picked the Drone up, holding it like a bowling ball, and it gave an electronic whine which sounded almost like a squawk. She flipped her hand over. Gravity meant the Drone should have dropped to the workbench, but it remained attached. 'Satisfied?' said Ella.

'I don't like it. Things haven't gone wrong like this before.'

'Things fall apart, Mia. You heard of entropy?'

Mia laughed hollowly. 'Yeah, yeah. The depressing collapse of the Universe? Everything working towards becoming piles of dust?'

Sometimes, Ella found Mia's directness refreshing, but at this time of the morning it grated. 'You could put it like that. Change and decay. Sometimes things … like I say … stop working.'

She placed the Drone back on the bench, allowed her fingertips to caress the glove to release it, and peeled the glove off again.

Mia snorted, folded her arms. 'Yeah, well, maybe I'll go all *entropy*. I'll stop working. How would people like that, Ell? They'd soon notice if I didn't go out hunting.'

'I understand. You don't get enough gratitude.' She tried to stay flippant. 'Would you like Zach to call a Gathering about it?'

Mia jabbed a finger at Ella. 'Don't tempt me … Let me know what you turn up.' She got up to leave.

'So …' Ella ventured, spreading her hands, 'are you going to tell me?'

Mia frowned, paused in the act of turning away. 'What?'

'Well … isn't it obvious? Given that this,' Ella prodded the gauntlet, 'was presumably all that was holding you stuck firm to a sheer cliff face, I wondered – out of idle curiosity, you understand, not out of any concern for your welfare – why you aren't an ugly wet smear on the jungle floor?'

Mia gave a sideways smile. 'Oh. That.'

'Yes,' said Ella patiently. 'That.'

'No great mystery,' she said. 'I slipped, I fell.' She swung her leg up, plonked her foot on a stool to show Ella the silvery bandage around her calf. 'I lost my footing, but I stayed close to the cliff. Grabbed some vines. The rock took off a good slice of my skin, but I hung on in there, shouted to Shan. He was already right behind me. Hauled me back up.'

'I see,' said Ella, steepling her fingers.

'You can go and ask Shan. And Lulu. She patched me up when I got in.'

'I know,' said Ella. 'I've already spoken to Shan and Lulu. I wanted to hear it from you.'

'Oh.' Mia was confused.

'Don't always assume people don't believe you, Mia. Paranoia's not a very attractive trait.'

Mia tutted, but managed not to give a retort as she swung her leg back down.

'You fine otherwise?' Ella asked. 'Not too shaken up?'

'Hey, it's me you're talking to.'

'I know, but … From a purely selfish point of view, we can't afford to lose you.'

'It's nice to feel wanted.'

'Indeed.' Ella put the glove into the multi-pocketed bag she carried with her. 'I will get this analysed. I'll let you know what turns up. And try not to go climbing any rocks in the near future.'

'Yeah, yeah. I'll try.'

Ella sealed the bag, pressed her fingers together and rested her chin on them, looking intently at Mia. 'This isn't an isolated incident.'

'It isn't?'

'The power drains … And a couple of hours ago,

someone gave me a whack on the head and tried to over-load the generator.'

'Seriously?'

Ella watched Mia's reaction carefully. Of course, the Huntress had been out of Town when it happened, she knew that. But it was still interesting to observe. She was trying not to over-react, Ella thought. But maybe that was Mia. It was how she was. Ella leaned back, put the eyeglass in and picked up her micro-probe again to get on with her work, effectively dismissing Mia. 'Oh, and Balj wanted you,' Ella added casually. 'Out at perimeter point four.'

'Me? Why me?'

'Well, you're nominally on security detail this morning. I told Zach to let it slide in view of your … incident. But now I can see you're all right … Go and be useful.'

Mia gave a mock salute. 'Yes, Miss. Anything else?'

'Try not to get yourself killed.'

III

'What do you s'pose they're up to?' Amber asked Robbie.

The two Thirteeners were taking a break, slouched in the shade of the jeep Amber was supposed to be servicing. The vehicle was up on hydraulic jacks, wires from its underbelly exposed. She even had a creeper-board cobbled together with parts from the Ship – a flat panel of Perspex, a foam head-rest, metal wheels. Amber was chomping on a tomato she'd stolen from Hydro when she was last on duty.

Robbie pulled his collar up, wiped stinging sweat from

his brows. 'Who?' he said, looking where Amber was pointing.

'Them by the fence.'

Robbie squinted across the compound. A couple of Drones, some boys play-fighting, Cait and Livvy building a sculpture out of broken components. He tried to focus. He could make out two figures gesticulating by the fence. He thought it was Baljeet and Finn. 'Dunno,' he said. 'You bothered?'

Amber stuffed the rest of the tomato in her mouth. 'Nah, not really,' she said indistinctly. 'Avoiding getting back inside this bastard.' She slapped the metal underside of the jeep, and it clanged like an empty drum.

'New girl sleeps in the Ship,' said Robbie.

'Yeah. Weird, ain't she?'

'I quite like her,' Robbie said with a sly grin.

'Oooooh! Get in.'

Robbie wrinkled his nose. 'Not like *that*. No, I think she's all right. She sorted Gabe and Reza out the other night.'

'I heard she cut them down from the Benighting,' said Amber thoughtfully. 'Zach was seriously pissed off.'

'Still,' Robbie said, 'it's weird. Having someone new here. Maybe her *Arcadia* will come back for her.'

Amber snorted. 'Yeah. And *maybe* I'll go back to Phobos Platform and become fucking President.' She took a small green canister out of her pocket and inhaled from it, leaning back with a blissful expression on her face. 'Ahh. *Breakfast.*'

'What the hell is that?'

'Filter propellant. From that jeep we cannibalised. It's

170

not bad.' She giggled. 'Yeah, it's working. Can't have too much or you start seeing flying purple dragons.'

'Bloody hell, Ambs. You do this a lot?'

'Only when I'm feeling sad and lonely,' she said. She tossed him the capsule, and he caught it turning it over and lifting it up to the light. 'So, yeah. A lot.'

'Did you just ... steal this?'

'Course I did. It's what I'm here for, after all. Girl needs to use her skills.' She got up, stretching her long limbs. 'Best get on. Who knows? This time tomorrow, like, we could be rescued. Imagine that. Being out of here.'

'Or out of your head,' Robbie said, concerned. He pocketed the capsule.

Amber grinned. 'Spaced-out. The final frontier.' She yawned, reaching up to the morning sky, letting the propellant-induced euphoria bubble through her, flowing out as uncontrollable giggles for a minute or two. Then she relaxed and opened the tool-box once more, ready to slide back under the jeep on her makeshift creeper.

'You know you and I are going to die here, Amber,' said Robbie matter-of-factly.

'Course we are.' She pulled her visor on, blanking her expression, as they both watched Mia stride purposefully from the Main Dome. 'We're all gonna die here.'

She waved a photon probe at him, and then she slid back under the jeep until all that could be seen of her was a corkscrew of purple hair. From under the jeep, her muffled voice said:

'But not today.'

IV

Mia trudged across the compound, trying to ignore the jabbing pain in her leg. She took a deep, warm swig of the gritty *zort* coffee from her steel mug, hoping it would kick her into wakefulness.

'Right, then,' she said, striding towards Baljeet and Finn at the chain-link fence. 'What's up?'

'Seems like it was cut,' said Baljeet, straightening up to reveal the long, jagged gash in the wire of the fence. Two Drones were buzzing up and down, one recording the damage from every angle, its twinkling red sensor lights playing over the fence, while the other extruded various cutting and soldering tools, getting ready to patch the fence up.

Mia wiped her mouth with the back of her hand. 'You what? *Cut*?' she repeated.

Baljeet gestured again at the jagged gash in the chain-link fence. 'See for yourself.'

Mia bent down. The break in the fence was as tall as her, and wide enough to accommodate a human form. Pushing the maintenance Drones aside for a second, she swept her hand up and down where the gap had been, gauging its height and width.

This new development would have made her uneasy – especially coming so soon after her narrow escape. However, she knew exactly who had cut the fence and why. She wasn't going to tell Baljeet, though.

Baljeet stood next to her, arms folded. Beside her, Finn,

a scruffy and sullen blond boy with bright intelligent blue eyes, was more interested in sharpening a wooden pole into a stake. He was making a very loud, irritating scraping noise with it.

'You didn't see anything at all?' Mia said.

Scrrape, scrrrape, scrrrape.

'Did the usual patrol. Nothing out of the ordinary.'

'Yeah. Nothing.' Mia stepped aggressively close to Baljeet. 'Except maybe your eyesight. Maybe you should get the Drones to make you some glasses.'

Scrrape! Scrrrape! Scrrrape!

'Not funny, Mia. What were we supposed to do?'

'Well, how about guards actually being on *guard*, for example?' Mia practically spat her response. 'That would be good, Balj. That would be a *start.*'

The remains of her anger and frustration from her near-death still burned inside her. And then there was the way Beth unsettled her, too. It wasn't so much that she resented the newcomer – she seemed harmless enough. But the change, the sudden intrusion into their routine, made Mia resentful. They had survived so far by sticking to a rigid way of doing things.

She realised she had been closed even to the possibility of anyone, or anything, coming from outside. Then, the sky had ripped open and deposited Bethany Kane, orphan of some distant conflict. A reminder of other worlds, other lives, other places.

And things had started going wrong.

She knew she was taking out her frustration on Balj and

Finn, and they didn't deserve it. Her only bit of fun was to wind them up about the fence.

'It wasn't there yesterday,' said Mia, aware she was stating the obvious.

'No. It wasn't.' Baljeet's reply was sharp, sullen.

The scraping sound stopped. Both girls turned around as one to Finn.

The boy had glanced up from his sharpening. 'I wanna know,' he said, 'what are we actually guarding *for*, anyway?'

'What?' Mia snapped.

'What we guarding *for*?' the boy repeated, as if it were the most obvious question in the world. As if he was amazed nobody else had thought to ask it. He straightened up, holstering his knife, brandishing his newly-sharpened stake. 'I mean, there's nobody else on this damn planet.'

'Well, it's true,' Baljeet said with a grin. 'Can't argue with that. The Drones did a sweep, didn't they? Us, the 'trill, a few Klaa and useless river-creatures and insects. If we weren't alone here … we'd know about it.' She folded her arms and glared at Mia. 'Unless there's something the precious Council isn't telling us all.'

The sun, bright and blinding, was appearing properly from behind the hills, spreading bright tendrils of light across the land. It was already getting warm. Mia brushed the sweat from her forehead.

'Like he says, there's nobody else on this damn planet,' she said. 'Trust me. Who'd be that stupid?'

'Apart from the new girl,' Finn said sullenly.

'New girl's been holed up in the Ship,' Baljeet answered

curtly. 'Like we frightened her off. I reckon she might not hang around.'

'Maybe,' said Mia. 'Maybe not. Anyway, where would she go? I hope she doesn't, actually. I find her kind of … amusing.'

'You don't trust her,' Baljeet said accusingly. 'Shan told me–'

'Never mind what Shan told you.' Mia moved forward fast, shoving Baljeet hard in the chest. The two girls were of equal height and weight, but Baljeet, caught off guard, staggered and almost fell. 'People say a lot of things round here,' Mia snapped, jabbing a finger into the air. 'Did you notice we've got two eyes and one mouth? There's a reason for that. Start looking a lot more and prattling a bit less.'

'Oh, yeah. Because it was all our fault, obviously. Anything else, while you're here?'

'Yeah,' Mia snapped. 'Try to get through this cycle without cocking anything else up.

'You seriously need some anger therapy, bitch.'

'No,' said Mia coldly, 'I don't need *anger therapy*. I just need people to stop pissing me off.' She flicked the button on her radio. 'Zach, come in.'

As she stalked off across the sandy earth of the compound, back towards Town, she was aware of Baljeet's hard gaze drilling into her back.

V

The waterfall was three kiloms or so from Town, on the far side of the island.

Beth was fascinated as Colm led her across a high plateau of grassy blue meadows. The grasses were dotted with odd, nodding, twirling red and white flowers with bell-shaped clusters of petals. The scent up here was overwhelmingly sweet and fresh, so different from the stifling fug of Town.

They found a hidden, twisting stone stairway in a crevice in the rocks. Colm knew where he was going, so Beth followed. She thought the steps seemed worn and ancient, almost as if hewn from the rock centuries ago. She could hear the distant rush of water, glimpsed a foaming torrent through the trees and undergrowth.

At the top, the stairs led to a rickety wooden walkway with a metal rail. Above and below them, the glacial waterfall thundered, hitting the water a hundred emms below with clouds of foaming white. On the far side, a steep, twisting path led down through the spiky undergrowth to the beach below.

Beth presumed the scientists who had once been here had put the walkway in for some purpose other than a decorative one, but it was refreshing to stand there and feel the cold spray in the air, smell the slightly salty tang of freshness. She sensed the feeling of life, of vibrancy in the planet here. A sense of a place which had been here long before them, and would be here long after they – or their descendants – had gone.

'Did you have any say in how this place was set up?' Beth asked curiously. 'In where you were to live?'

'You must be kidding. We wouldn't be consulted, because we're basically scum.'

'*Scum*?' She wrinkled her nose, unfamiliar with the term.

'Low-life. Cast out of the Collective.' Colm smirked. 'In my case, for "inappropriate consorting", whatever that means. I got involved with the wrong guys. I ended up taking a hell of a lot of blame for something that wasn't my fault … Well, only partly my fault.'

'Everyone here might say the same, do you not think? That they are all wrongly convicted? Victims of injustice?'

'Yeah … Well, I prefer to think of us all as misunderstood. As people who, for one reason or another, it was helpful for those in power to get rid of.'

'The authorities can be ruthless,' agreed Beth. 'On *Arcadia* we often talked of this. There needs to be law and order, surely?'

'Yeah, but come on. Earth's crazy, but … well, they don't shoot *kids* in cold blood there. At least, not openly.'

'I see.' She gazed into the foaming heart of the waterfall, beginning to realise she had been cushioned from the Galaxy's harshest realities over her fifteen years.

'So,' Colm went on, 'every so often, they use this "humane" idea, yeah? Shipping reprobates off in Semi-Anna to a pre-programmed destination.' He exhaled deeply. 'Preferably one on the edge of the Galaxy.'

'Washing their hands of you,' Beth said quietly.

'Yup. Give us Drones, living space, the means to grow food, and make sure the world's one that's been catalogued and registered Z-class. Basically, one left abandoned as having no value to Earth or the Collective whatsoever.' He stared at her. 'I thought everyone knew all this.'

Beth avoided that question, and instead asked the one she had wanted to ask for a while. 'Is anyone … you know … *dangerous*?'

Colm swaggered across the walkway towards her, a hand on the slippery rock above him. 'Oh yeah,' he said quietly. 'That's the fun thing. Only … we dunno who, do we? Nobody asks, nobody tells. It's one of the *rules*.'

'I barely believe it. You cannot all be criminals.' She thought about the Twelvies with their cheeky smiles. 'Those *kids*?'

'Sometimes, with the younger ones, yeah, it's that the parents were wasters, y'know? Or troublemakers. Those guys ended up on the streets and … got into a mess. Frankly, they're better off here. We watch out for each other.'

'I can understand that.'

'Plus … there are a few inherited sentences.'

Beth frowned. 'A few *what*?'

'If someone dies before they've completed their sentence, it passes to their descendants. So some of these kids – Cait, Livvy, Finn, Gabe – they aren't criminals. They're the *children* of criminals.'

A cold blackness spread through her as she allowed that to sink in. 'Are you serious? That's *insane*?'

'Yeah, well. One of many shitty things to come in after Earth left the Collective … Despite all the sensible people saying, don't, because it'll all go to shit. And we left, and what do you know? It all went to shit.'

'Why did Earth leave? I still don't really understand it.'

'Dunno. Politics, stupidity. Usual reasons stuff happens.'

Beth shook her head in dismay. 'And you?' she said, lifting her chin. 'What exactly did you do, then, Colm? What is "consorting", exactly?'

'Ah, well … That's a matter for me.'

He moved closer to her. He was caught in a stray glint of sunlight, and she could see the ragged stubble on his face, a hardness in the set of his jovial mouth. He seemed older than sixteen. She watched him against the endless, cascading curtain of water.

'Don't worry about me. But there's a few you've got to keep an eye on. That Ella? Watch out for that one. She's … one of the unpredictable ones.'

'And Mia,' Beth said without thinking. 'I think I … got on the wrong side of her.'

Colm laughed. 'Mia's a polecat. And a pussycat. She can be growling and squealing and pissing out her territory one minute, and then the next she's nuzzling up to you for a stroke.' He paused, head on one side. 'Or … oh, was that only with me?'

'If you are trying to be disgusting again,' Beth said primly, 'it will not work.'

'That's a shame.'

'I had full Personal Health Education on *Arcadia*, you know. I might be a ChapterSister, but I am a full Initiate, not some shockable novice from the Outer Closed Orders.'

'I don't doubt it,' said Colm. For a second, Beth felt a skipping, almost sick, but excited sensation. One she didn't fully understand. 'Where does your Great Power stand on that, these days?'

'The Great Power's not a–' But no. She decided to ignore the goading. 'Anyway, um …' She gazed back up the stone steps. 'Mia was going to give me some more shooting training. And I should see Zach, find out what I can do around here. I don't want anyone thinking I am some kind of … *freeloader.*' She said the word awkwardly.

'Cool. I like your attitude. *Can-do*, eh …?' He moved closer to her, slid a hand on to her arm. 'Let me give you a tip, Bethany Kane. Round here, you need to know who your friends are.'

She lifted her chin and hoped she wasn't betraying herself in her expression. 'Well, that does help. Yes.'

'And if what you need is … y'know … someone to talk to, someone to trust … For various reasons, I'm not always Mr Popular. So I understand about being an outsider.'

He was close to her, so close she could feel the warmth of his body, and she was struck with an overwhelming urge to reach up and stroke that annoying, stubbly face.

A strange, jittery weakness rippled through her, one which was really not at all unpleasant. The thundering water made her feel as if they were in their own world, here, isolated from the others. They could do what they liked.

'Well …' she started, and was aware it came out as a croak. She cleared her throat. 'Possibly. I am not sure.'

Colm tilted his head slightly. 'Trust me,' he said, and winked.

Something happened then. The Universe seemed to spin on its axis, and she tried to forget where she was. To forget that she was light years away from everyone and everything she'd ever known, beside a mountain waterfall on this rock on the edge of the Galaxy, battered and bruised and confused and lonely.

Because she couldn't heal her body any more quickly, she thought, as her mouth moved closer to his, but she could *pretend*. And she couldn't heal her loneliness and desolation, but she could act like a person who was not alone, desperate.

She could pretend she wanted this. Something new.

From the Lumi-casts she'd watched, she knew a Thing to do right now. She glanced down as they drew close, making her eyelids heavy, feeling her lashes flicker. And almost, but not quite, smiled.

It seemed to work.

It seemed to work very well.

His mouth was warm against hers, opening and closing in a way that sent shudders all the way down from her lips to the rest of her body. She quivered as he stole an arm around her waist, didn't even flinch when it sneaked up to her breast. His tongue explored hers, and, knowing that this was what people did, she allowed her own to respond in a probing, teasing fashion, breaking the seal of their lips very slightly every second or two to allow their hot breath to mix. Her body prickled with heat and sweat. Her own heart thudded against his, the roar of the thunderous water echoing in her ears.

Stealthily, he touched her above the waist, where her top was not quite tucked in, where a sliver of bare flesh poked out.

And then he slid his hand lower.

She jumped back as if stung, gasping, stepping backwards and putting an arm's length of space between them.

'I … I think … you had better go,' she heard herself muttering. Again, a line she knew she had learned from somewhere. Something those impossibly shiny women in the Lumi-casts said at moments like this.

Colm grinned. 'C'mon, Space Princess. Go with it. You'll enjoy it.'

'No!' She folded her arms angrily, lowered her head in what she hoped was a threatening pose. 'I am sorry, Colm, I … That all went too fast. I do *not* want this right now.'

He narrowed his eyes at her, as if not quite able to believe what she had said. 'You don't *want* this right now?' he repeated. The usual carefree, cheerful sing-song of his voice had gained a steely edge.

She sensed the shift in tone, and it filled her with defiant strength. 'No,' she said, lifting her chin. 'I do not.'

'Awww, c'mon.' He took a step or two closer to her, hands sliding around her waist. She tensed. 'It gets very cold in the Ship at night,' he said softly, and raised his eyebrows meaningfully.

'Colm!' This time, she not only pulled away but gave him a shove, sending him staggering back against the walkway rail. It squeaked and creaked alarmingly, and her heart leapt in sudden fear, wondering if she had sent him plummeting into the chasm. But he recovered, righting himself.

'All right.' His voice was harsher, his face angrier. 'Gods, you're a scrappy one, aren't you?'

'I should like you to go.'

'Okay,' he said. He lifted his hand, his finger jabbing the air, emphasising every word. 'But remember. This is a small place. People can't avoid each other.'

'I'll bear that in mind.'

But his face, half in darkness, was more threatening. 'You think you're someone? Here? Remember you're nobody, yet.' He laughed to himself. 'I dunno. Thought you'd be different. Not one of *those*. Oh well. Can't have it all.'

'What do you mean?' she asked with a frown, folding her arms defensively. 'One of *what*?'

Colm swaggered forwards, invading her space, forcing her to back up against the cold, wet rock. Her mouth was dry. She tried to appear steely and confident, tried not to betray the turmoil she felt.

'You know,' he said with a whisper. '*Teases.*'

Her mouth gaped. 'That is *not* appropriate.'

'Maybe.' His voice was colder. 'Well … you had your chance.'

'And you had yours,' she responded, equally coldly. 'Well, I'm sure you've got things to do.'

'Plenty,' he said softly. 'Oh yeah. I've got *plenty* to do.'

He turned and headed back along the walkway, up the slippery stone steps to that intoxicating plateau of grass and flowers, heading back towards Town.

She exhaled, and gripped the wet rail in front of her, frantic heartbeat slowing.

This place, thought Beth angrily, was becoming so *complicated.*

She knew she had to get back to the Ship, though. There was something there that she needed.

VI

'Where have *you* been?'

Colm, walking back across to the Main Dome, turned at the sound of Zach's voice. He was standing by the ramp, arms folded, a dark and threatening figure against the light.

'Well, hello there, Zach. Are you having a good day?'

'I asked you a question.'

Colm strolled forward, feeling the heat of the morning sun on the back of his neck. He spread his hands. 'So you did. I kind of … think that's between me and my conscience, don't you? And last I looked, Zachy-boy, you weren't my conscience. It's a bit better-looking than you, and, well, I gotta admit – more fun.'

He moved to go up the ramp, but Zach blocked his way, giving him a shove. 'I asked you a question, and you answer it.'

Colm laughed, prodded him. '*Bzzzzt.* Wrong! C'mon, Zach. We don't all have to account for ourselves round here, you know. It's one of the few perks of the place. Loosen up.'

Zach nodded towards the Ship. 'And paying visits to our

new friend Bethany? Are they one of the perks of the place, too?'

'Ahh, I seeeee.' Colm walked as close to Zach as he dared, and gave him a knowing wink. 'I get where you're coming from. You want Miss ChapterSister kept under control. And so, like you always do, you're playing a little game. Well, fine.' He patted Zach's shoulder. 'Not a problem. I'm happy to tell her you've got the biggest dick in this place.' He turned to move past Zach. 'Sorry, did I say *got*? I meant to say *are*. My mistake.'

Colm pushed past Zach, bumping against his shoulder. Despite his bantering, his mouth was dry, and he was wondering if he'd pushed things further than he should. He heard the rush of air behind him, and so he was ready when Zach grabbed his shoulder and spun him around.

'Get over to Hydroponics, *now*. See if Shan needs any help with the coolant regulators.'

'Oh, that'll keep me out of trouble.' Colm grinned.

'Yeah. It will.'

'Zach,' he said, 'remind me again. Who made you the boss of me?'

'Everyone,' Zach said coldly. 'I was elected leader. The stones people put in the tin, remember?'

'Oh, yeah … that … I abstained. But if it makes you happy …' He lifted his hands in mock-surrender. 'I'm glad to help. Don't have a fit about it. Lead by example, Zach!'

He was up the ramp and heading into the Main Dome before Zach could field a riposte. Only when he got inside did he allow himself to unclench his fist and breathe out.

He made a habit of sailing close to the wind – enjoyed it, even. But sometimes he felt he pushed things too far – even for his own comfort …

VII

'Strong one, Robbie,' Baljeet said, slamming her gun-belt and satchel down on the bar.

She noticed the Rec Hall was quiet at this time. The pale sun was casting tendrils of shadow out in the compound. Ella was tinkering with some pieces of circuitry over in the far corner, while some of the younger ones – Hal, Dionne, Gabe – were playing cards. Colm was heading through the hall, not stopping, seemingly deep in thought.

Robbie grinned, pouring Baljeet's drink into a tin mug and lifting the jug high, allowing it to build a frothing, whitish-green head. 'Tough day?'

Baljeet glared at him. She rarely smiled at anyone, and today was no exception. 'Tough year, Roberto.' The boy slid the drink over to her. 'I've had a tough *life*,' she added.

Not everyone would have agreed with Baljeet on that. Her father, Rohit Midda, had been a rich businessman, whose fortune had been made on trading Deep Minerals with the outer colonies. He had invested in the Synthet market, too, although that could be risky.

They had it good, they were comfortable. And then, when Baljeet was thirteen, it all fell apart. She still didn't really understand what had happened – he had made a deal with the wrong kind of people, she understood, and had

186

lost everything. Earth left the Collective, and new rules had come in. Their houses in Londinium Sky-Park and the New Delhi Arc were impounded by the government, along with most of her father's other assets, while his bank accounts and investments simply dissolved overnight. All of her father's influential friends seemed to have something better to do, or disappeared quietly from his life and could no longer be contacted.

They had found themselves in a succession of sky-hotels, until the money ran out, and then, finally, on an offworld shuttle to one of the City Stations – her father's emergency accounts emptied for a last, desperate throw of the dice. A chance for a new life.

Everybody seemed to have forgotten who Rohit Midda and his family were – and nobody seemed to believe him when he told them.

Baljeet remembered the life ebbing out of her father, the joy disappearing from his face. He seemed to age twenty years in their first year on the City Station. People still needed his skills – in diplomacy, negotiation, business management – but at a much lower level than before. His income was, she imagined, a tenth, maybe a twentieth of what it had been. They could pay for somewhere to live and didn't go hungry, but it was frightening to think more than six months ahead and wonder where they might be.

Baljeet found ways of making a living in the City Station – not all of which she told her father about. There were people from all over, from Earth and the Mars colonies and even further afield. Strange new modes of dress, languages she had not heard before. Sounds and sights and smells like nothing on Earth, all contained in a ring of reinforced steel revolving slowly around a ragged asteroid.

She made new friends in the dark streets of the Station, the streets where putrid steam rose from vents, and where the high buildings obscured most of the light. She remembered Kala, and Logan, and Trix. Her new friends or, more accurately, associates. Accomplices. Members of the small gang of blackmailers, extortionists – and, where needed, petty thieves – which she had fallen in with.

It had not lasted. One false set-up, one betrayal. Baljeet remembered staring into Trix's dead face for a second – and not even having time to react, to cry out, before she was grabbed by the Lawguards, hauled away.

She remembered, too, the shame in her father's face as she stood in the tingling electrical field of the restraining dock. And the words of the Judiciant, echoing in her ears: 'To be transported to an Assigned Destination, for the duration of her life.'

Assigned Destination, she knew, was part of that special, euphemistic language they liked to use. A prison planet. A place where any normal young woman of refined breeding would struggle to survive. But Baljeet knew she was more than that. She was still strong. So there was still defiance, steel in her as she was led away. She saw her father's aged face showing despair, his eyes crinkled and deep-set with care behind the red-tinted lenses. She read the accusation in his face and, despite her bravado, it chilled her to the heart.

He watched her as the Lawguards took her away. She tried to maintain eye contact with him, tried somehow to convey to him that it was going to be all right. That she would survive this. Maybe even escape. Then one of the Lawguards, out of nothing more than pure malice, twisted her head away so she could no longer see the public gallery, forcing her to her knees as they entered the elevator. She tried to look up, but a truncheon smacked her down with enough force to blur her vision. She cried out.

The elevator doors swished shut, blocking off the courtroom. She never saw her father again.

And now she was here. A criminal, like all the rest. One more lost soul trying to make the best of a place none of them would ever have chosen. Exiles from Earth. Exiles from the Collective. Exiles from life.

'Think we'll ever get off this rock?' Robbie asked, as he busied himself replenishing the jugs of beer and whisky from the barrels stacked at the back of the bar area.

Baljeet was surprised that he even raised the subject. 'You don't really think that's an option?'

'I dunno,' Robbie said thoughtfully. 'I never really did … but since *she* arrived …'

Baljeet tutted, took a long gulp of her drink. It was pungent and refreshing, with a strong kick to it. 'What's she got to do with it?'

'Well, she gives us a kind of hope, doesn't she?'

'I wouldn't cling on to that, Robbo. She's stuck here as much as the rest of us.'

'Maybe. We'll see.' He looked over towards the steps of

the Rec Hall, and Baljeet followed his gaze. 'Someone's not happy.'

A familiar small slight figure, her red hair scruffy and spiked-up today, as if she had just got out of bed, was marching down the steps and making her way over to Baljeet with a determined expression.

'Hiya,' Maddi said, sliding on to a seat at right angles to Baljeet. 'Got a minute?'

'All the time in the world,' said Baljeet languidly. 'Not going anywhere until I rot, am I?'

'I wondered,' she said, 'about the other night.'

Baljeet tried not to look at her directly. 'What's that?' she asked.

'You and your haul of wreckage …? You went out across the causeway in the jeep, remember?'

'Oh, that,' said Baljeet dismissively. 'Yeah, I told you, I didn't find anything.'

Maddi gave her a long hard stare. 'Balj,' she said. 'Come *on.*'

Baljeet realised Maddi was not going to stop asking until she got an answer that satisfied her.

'Right,' she said, leaning forward. 'I found something. Out by Sharp Ridge. I go scavenging a lot, yeah? Most of the time there's nothing. Odd bits of space-rock make it through the atmosphere. Never anything remotely tech … Until …' She held a hand up. 'Wait.'

She lifted her bag, put it on the bar. Robbie and Maddi peered forward interestedly as Baljeet rummaged in her bag.

'Well?' Maddi asked impatiently.

Baljeet drew back, confused. 'I had it,' she said. 'It was there. I don't understand.'

'This what you're looking for?'

Ella had come over almost silently from her side of the Rec Hall, and she was holding something in her hand that Baljeet recognised. Ella tossed it on to the bar, where it landed with a thud. A small, tubular, rocket-like object, battered and scorched as if from intense heat.

'Where did you get that?' Baljeet asked in astonishment.

Ella, arms folded, raised her eyebrows. 'Might ask you the same question.'

'Yeah, but … It was in my bag. In my room.' Baljeet stood up, squaring up to Ella, and shoved her lightly. 'You been going through my stuff, bitch?'

'Steady,' said Ella threateningly. 'Don't you push me.'

'Guys, guys! Seriously!' Maddi held her hands up placatingly. 'Can we not …? Ella, what happened with this? Did you steal it from Balj?'

'If you must know,' Ella said haughtily, 'one of the Drones brought it to me.'

'One of the … Why?' Baljeet was perplexed. 'What do they want with it? And why the hell bring it to you?'

'More importantly,' said Maddi, leaning forward and prodding the small rocket interestedly, 'what even *is* it?'

They all crowded round, peering at the dull metallic object on the bar.

'Some kind of space-probe?' Robbie suggested.

'If it is, then …' Maddi looked up in excitement.

191

'Someone could be … This could be in response to the beacons! Our first sign of life in this system!'

'I dunno,' Baljeet said. 'It could just be junk. All kinds of stuff floats around up there. It could have been drifting for years.'

'If it was drifting,' Maddi said quietly.

They all drew back in silence.

'We need to tell Zach about it,' Ella said.

'You take care of it,' Baljeet said to Maddi. 'Everyone trusts you.'

'Really?' Maddi sounded surprised.

Baljeet looked at Ella. 'What do you think?'

'Yes,' Ella said. 'Sounds a good move.' She clapped a hand on Maddi's shoulder. 'Sorry, Mads. You're too honest. That's your burden.'

VIII

Maddi flopped on to her bunk, tiredness coursing through her.

She felt something hard in her pocket, and remembered the piece of space debris. She picked it up, sniffed it, held it up to the light. It didn't seem to be doing anything much. She threw it on to the table.

Leaning back, she folded her arms across her chest. From across the sea, deep in the valley, she had heard the rumbles of thunder as the storm gathered. It seemed to be getting closer. Rain spattered her window. Maddi yawned, stretching out on her bed, watching the clouds in the darkening skies.

She was haunted again in her dreams by the memory of the police Drones which had picked her up at High Fall in the ruined city of Paree.

The silver globes with their grating voices. —THIS IS A RESTRICTED ZONE. PUT YOUR HANDS BEHIND YOUR HEAD AND GET DOWN ON THE GROUND—

And there, marching out of the misty shadows behind the Drones, four sinister figures in stylised uniforms. Armed and walking in unison.

Synthets.

Maddi had heard of them, but until then she had never seen the sleek stark bipedal Drones. But for their glossy faces and low blink-rate, they could have passed for human. The most advanced Synthets, she knew, could even deceive a scan-pad. They were routinely used for factory work and driving, as well as the faux-celebs of Lumi entertainment. They could mimic all the functions of Humanity, needing only an occasional recharge period akin to a long sleep. But to have them involved in the routines of law-enforcement was a recent innovation.

Maddi had heard rumours that some of them genuinely believed themselves to be human, with false identities and constructed histories. The idea filled her with a gaping, hungry emptiness.

She shuddered as they marched her back to the car, her heart thumping and her flesh prickling. Not until she was sitting in front of a real, human Interrogator – a superficially friendly woman with blue glasses and white hair – did she finally allow the tension in her body to slacken. The

Interrogator was kind, brought her drinks and coaxed answers out of her.

'Why did you enter the city, Madeleine …? Have you broken any other rules, Madeleine …? Have you had issues with your parents …? Tell me, what political meetings have you been to? Who were their leaders?'

Her questions assumed Maddi's guilt from the start, making it clear that it was unlikely she would remain on Earth. Maddi had already resigned herself to this thought.

In the weeks that followed, Maddi's life spiralled into a nightmare. She could not see her family. She was kept in a holding cell somewhere in the depths of New Londinium, possibly under the Pyramid. Whatever her father was trying to do behind the scenes to rescue and protect her, it wasn't working.

And she knew, deep down, what this was about. It was not about trespass in a restricted zone – nobody *really* cared if anyone went into the old cities. There were no guards, no physical barriers. It was about other *transgressions*. Thoughts she had put into words at the Academy, on the Networks. Questions which had challenged authority. Student politics. The hidden meaning of certain braidings and tattoos.

She had, in twelve years, become someone it was useful to get rid of. It didn't take them long, these days. In the post-Collective years, everyone on Earth had become spikier, less tolerant of difference. The politics of hate was now the politics of normality.

*

On her bunk in Town, she was toying with an idea.

Maddi was honest by nature, and deception – even by omission – did not come naturally to her. She swung herself off the bed, grabbed the radio. From the curved triangle of her window, she could see the stark, metallic edge of the Ship, squatting there above Town, like a giant metal guard-dog against the skies.

Odd that Beth chose to spend her days there, but then why shouldn't she be different? It didn't necessarily mean anything bad about her.

Maddi called the Ship on her radio. She knew she would come through on the general comlink in the control room and with any luck, if the relays were still working, the call might be patched through to wherever Beth happened to be inside the giant structure at the moment.

'Beth? It's Maddi. Can you hear me?' Her voice was still croaky with tiredness.

There was silence, overlaid with a gentle wash of static. She tried again.

'Beth, I know you're in there. I need to talk to you. It's really important. It's …' Maddi hesitated, not quite sure how she should phrase this. 'It's about something I said before,' she ventured. 'Something about space debris.' She paused, frustrated with her inability to find the right words. 'I'm tired. I can't do it over this … But come and see me. I'm in Habitation 2/7.'

Still silence. Maddi flicked the radio off. Perhaps, she thought, she'd make the short walk across the compound, go and see Beth herself. Or maybe she was still asleep. Maddi hesitated.

A sharp sound broke into her thoughts.

She made a grab for her pistol on the bedside table – then, she realised it was the buzzer on the outer door. Somebody trying to get her attention. She pushed open the bedroom door and kicked her way through the clutter on the floor of the living-area, rubbing her tired, aching eyes.

She pressed the intercom button. 'Who is it?' There was no reply from the small black grille beside the door. Irritably, Maddi stabbed at the button again. 'Hello? Someone there?'

Again, there was no reply. Maddi's fingertips tingled, telling her something was wrong. She realised the indicator light was not on – for some reason, the intercom was not working, at least from her side. She tutted in irritation. 'Something else to get fixed.'

She undid the bolt which opened the door, allowing a chink of light in from the curved corridor outside, and put her eye to the space to see who her caller was.

'Oh. Right … It's, um, not a good time, all right?' She was about to seal the door shut, and then she relented. 'Oh, what the hell. Come in.' She slid the bolt to release the door all the way. 'Don't mind the mess.'

She was aware of how silly that sounded. She bent down to throw a handful of clothes away in her cupboard, and the outer door slid to behind her as her visitor entered the room.

There was a soft click as the door sealed itself, and she straightened up.

'Right,' she said to the newcomer, her voice flat and emotionless. 'What can I do for you?'

There was another click. Something flashed in the dimness.

Maddi's smile froze. Her jaw dropped and her face drained of blood, unable to believe what she could see facing her.

She did not even have time to scream.

∞

These are children, unformed, groping their way in the darkness.

They have had to learn to grow, to trust, to build. Slowly and surely, they will learn to wither, to mistrust, to destroy.

Once this is set running there is no going back. These people protect their own. It will be like the dropping of a stone into a pool, the ripples growing and growing ...

These are children, lost in the terrors of an adult world.

This will be the beginning of their nightmares.

And it will be beautiful.

6
LUNAR BEACH

I

At dusk, Colm hurried through the compound, hoping nobody would see him and ask him to do anything.

He smirked to himself as he thought about Zach's arrogance, his casual assumption that everyone respected him. They didn't, and he sometimes needed to be told. Standing up to him was one of the few pleasures this place afforded.

Colm's existence on the Edge was characterised by looking after Number One. He had some affection for a few of the worldly, feisty girls, and he kept up his banter to irritate Ella. But he was generally careful not to like anyone too much.

One person, though, he thought of as an equal. And with this one person, he was almost honest. And he knew where he'd find her tonight.

Colm ducked behind the parked jeep and the piles of crates, checking around him for signs of activity in the compound. The fire-pit was flickering, and he could see Zach strutting about as ever, giving orders to younger Towners. Over by the Main Dome, Ella and Baljeet were deep in conversation about something. Colm grinned when he saw Amber, violet hair bouncing in the pale evening light, fighting with Finn, the two of them getting quite a battle going with sharp wooden stakes used like swords. A couple of Drones buzzed past Colm, but they barely spared him a glance.

He removed the thermal lance from his jacket pocket – liberating it from Lulu had been easy, and Colm had found their resident medic almost enjoyed being distracted. He put it on the lowest setting and cut through the fence again, in a place a short distance further on from where he'd done so before. The chain-link glowed, blistered, melted like butter. When there was a hole big enough, he slipped through.

He could have got authorisation, easily – the cycle's gate-passcode was held by Zach and he shared it with anyone, as long as he knew where they were going. But Colm didn't like Zach or his authority, or his rules. Slicing his way out through the fence every so often was his small rebellion. He knew the person he was going to see would approve.

He kept up an even pace across the rocks, dodging the fissures and their gouts of yellow steam.

Mia was surprisingly easy to track. Her footprints were distinctive, but there was also, once he got near to the dunes, the curl of green smoke. The pungent aroma of it grew stronger as he descended towards the shore.

Lunar Beach was a stark, beautiful crescent of azure sand and white shale, a good twenty minutes' walk from the compound. It was approached through banks of undulating blue-green dunes whose grasses were blood-red, sword-sharp, bristling as they reached into the sky, tall as a human. As Colm skittered down the dunes, he could clearly see the beacons relaying the sub-light pulse signal into space. White globes, each half an emm or so across, they sat in the dry sand, evenly spaced across the bay, each a hundred emms or so apart. Like two giant pairs of eyes on the beach, gazing up into the stars.

Mia was sitting on a flat rock, and didn't turn round, but he could tell she knew he was there. Gentle breakers washed the sand with a low, rhythmic hiss. Like the planet breathing in and out.

He plonked himself down beside her, without a word.

'Hiya, polecat,' he said.

'Hiya, dickhead.'

Colm grinned. He knew Mia well enough to know that this passed for affection in her world, and a willingness to talk. If she wanted to be alone, she would have stormed off – maybe after shoving him flat on his back in the sand first.

'You getting on well with that?' he asked, looking at the burning cigarette in her hand.

Her mirror-shades meant he couldn't see her eyes, but he sensed from her relaxed demeanour that her pupils would be pretty dilated by now. 'Trying some different leaves,' she said. '*Plaan* on its own was getting boring.' She passed it towards him, but he declined with a polite wave. 'Gets you more drunk than stoned. It's good.' She took another puff herself, the home-made cigarette glowing pur-plish-red in the twilight. 'Good to escape this place the only way we can.'

'Yeah.' They exchanged a complicit grin. As was often the way, they were in harmony, understanding each other. 'I know the feeling, polecat.'

'Will you stop calling me that? I do have a *name*.'

There was no aggression in her reprimand, though – it was listless, curling, like a dried-up leaf in the harsh sun.

Colm and Mia's uneasy alliance went back about sixty

cycles. After a long period of being two people who barely spoke, eyeing each other across the compound or from opposite sides of the Rec Hall, they had got mildly drunk together one night by the fire-pit, and Mia had taken his hand and led him nonchalantly, wordlessly, to her room. It had happened several times since. They understood one another, knew no emotional attachment was required. Neither of them felt their casual bond was especially wrong, or right. It existed. Since then, they had talked a lot, verbally circling around each other, neither giving much away to the other.

'Sorry. Mia.' He shifted position awkwardly. 'So … you worked all these stars out?'

In the purple-blue sky, the swirling, scattered Universe was already beginning to imprint itself on the night, pale stars peeking out. The two moons were rising, milky discs watching them from the vastness of Space.

'Yeah, piss-easy.' She lay back, her finger randomly pointing to star-scattered swirls in the night sky. 'That's the … Giant Space Hog, that one's the Random Huntress, those two are, phhwww, Castor and Bollocks. I really have no idea. Do you care?'

'This could be our home till we die. I thought we should know.'

'Maybe.' Mia pointed upwards again. 'This is true, though. I saw lights earlier.'

'That's nothing new.' They were always seeing strange things in this alien sky. Shooting stars, suns burning themselves out …

'It was off to the edge of Big Moon, up there. I wondered if it might be a battle.'

'Starships?' Colm's interest was briefly stirred. 'Something's going on up there. Zach talks about stuff like this all the time.'

'We'll never know,' said Mia. 'Still. For centuries, people used to live on one planet all their lives, didn't they? And it didn't kill them. And they had to share it with billions of others. And pollution. And wars and terrorists.'

'Mia Janowska. Are you going a bit New Terran there? Being all starry-eyed idealist? Is that what that stuff does to you? Makes you almost tolerable.'

'Shut up. I mean, yeah, this place is a shit-hole. But it's *our* shit-hole. We've got it all to ourselves.' She turned to him, her pupils big and deep and intoxicated. 'That's scary and wonderful at the same time.'

'Sure … You know, it's quite a beautiful shit-hole, really.'

'If you say so.'

Colm stretched out his legs and lay down beside her. 'I always used to lie on the roof at home and gaze at the stars.' He rubbed his nose awkwardly. 'It was the best way of getting away from my dad.'

Mia glanced towards him for a second. 'Oh, yeah. I remember you saying. What did yours do again?'

'Ahhh … y'know … Minor random acts of violence. Some not so minor … He'd have loved the thought of me being sent to this place.'

'My half-dad used to hit me for fun,' she said, almost casually. 'Sometimes … There would be worse.'

'I know … Shit. That sounds … I'm sorry.'

'You said that last time.'

'I know. Hell.'

'And my mum skulked in the corner. On cushions. Blue silk cushions. Usually high on something. And she'd watch. And watch … And watch.' Mia took a long, hard drag on her cigarette, and exhaled the greasy green fumes in a spouting plume, which almost coalesced into a ring high above her before dispersing. 'And when he left, because he found better entertainment elsewhere, it was her I killed. Weird, that.'

Colm was nervous in Mia's presence, but oddly energised. There was something reassuring about her bluntness, her casual acceptance of violence. 'I must make sure never to piss you off,' he said.

'Yeah. Too right.'

'Do you actually like me, Mia?'

'No, you're a dick,' she said, laughing. 'A selfish, sexist arsehole.'

'Flattery gets you everywhere.'

'But that's why I trust you,' she said, rolling on to one elbow.

'Really? Trust *me*? That's bullshit.'

'No, really. I basically know you, right? You're a trickster. I'd never trust you with my life, or with an important secret. Oh, and you treat some of the girls here like dirt. But, hell, that's not my problem …'

'Go on.'

'You're like me, Colm. You look after yourself, because at the end of the day, that's all we can do here.' She tossed her cigarette-butt into the sand and ground it under her boot, the sparks scattering and dying. 'You insult me all the time. You're a total shit, and yet … I know where I am with you. And …' She levered herself upright, hands clasped around her knees.

'Yes?' he said.

'That first time … You … well, you were … you were good to me. I didn't know it … even could be like that.'

It was a backhanded compliment, but Colm was prepared to take it. He knew, deep down, that everything Mia said was true.

She straightened up. 'I've got an appointment with the boss. Somebody knocked Ella out. Did you hear?'

'Yeah. I was there, actually.'

'So, make yourself scarce.'

'Sure, and I think I'll stay out here,' he said. 'Nobody'll miss me.'

'You're right,' said Mia, but she threw a smile over her shoulder as she stretched, got to her feet. 'Fence cut in the usual place?'

'Usual place, babe.'

She grinned. 'Baljeet's having kittens about it.'

'Let her. She needs something to keep her mind off being an officious bitch.'

Mia laughed. 'So what do we–' She broke off. She jumped up, tensing. 'Did you hear that?'

'No.' Colm scrambled to his feet, alert. He knew Mia didn't get easily spooked, and he automatically trusted her instincts.

Mia's gun was already drawn, and she was crouching, one hand on the rock, scanning the blue-purple dunes and ridges around in the gathering gloom. She held a finger to her lips, gestured to Colm to move away down the beach. He did so, feet skittering, sand spraying up.

She slinked up the dunes, almost silently.

And then she leapt, snarling.

With a flash of one long arm, she pulled the listener out by his hair. He was squealing, thrashing, fists punching the empty air. Mia hurled him on to the sand, and Colm winced in sympathy with the boy as his hands went to cover his face. Mia, spitting, kicked the boy in the ribs, and Colm hurried up, restraining her.

'All right, Mia. That's enough, isn't it?' Colm grabbed the boy's hands, revealing his face, and was astonished to find himself looking at young Reza.

'Well, well,' said Mia, coldly, hands on hips. 'One of your Twelvies? Come to spy on you for a change. What you doing skulking out here, Reza?'

'Nothing! Let me *go*.' The boy sat up, trying to get away, but Mia shoved him down again.

'Wait, hang on,' said Colm. Mia's savage violence was all very well sometimes, he thought, but there was a time and a place for it. 'Reza? Something wrong?' The boy was skittish and hunted, his body language conveying tension and uncertainty. 'Reza?' Colm stepped forward, squatting down slightly so he was on a level with the boy. 'What's up?'

Reza scrambled quickly to his feet. Before they could

stop him, he fled up the dunes, a cloud of sand glimmering behind him in the pale evening light.

Mia started forward, but Colm put an arm out, quite firmly, like a barrier in front of her. He kept the disappearing boy in sight, and didn't need to look at Mia to sense her anger – he could feel it. A second later, his arm was wrenched round and he was slammed up against the shale at forty-five degrees, with an impact that knocked the breath from him. Mia pinned him down, her face up against his, her breath hot, her gun jammed at his throat, her face full of anger.

'I could have *caught* him!' she spat.

'Like old times, this,' Colm quipped, raising his eyebrows.

She bared her teeth, and prodded him hard with the gun. '*Why* did you do that?'

'It's not the right time. You'd have scared him.'

Mia glowered at Colm for five seconds, both of them breathing heavily, hearts hammering. Their mouths were close, hot breath mixing in the night air.

Colm was uncomfortably aware that Mia was equally capable of kissing him or killing him. He could feel his heart thudding against her warm chest. Distant cries from Town drifted up towards them, as the evening fires were lit.

Finally, Mia released him, unsticking her body from his, taking longer about it than she needed to.

'Lucky, this time,' she said, and gently kissed his forehead. 'Better head back.'

Coolly, casually, teasingly, knowing exactly what she was

doing, she allowed her hand to trail down his chest and linger for a second on his crotch as she rolled off him.

'Bitch,' he said quietly, sitting up, and laughed.

Mia straightened to her feet, gave him a casual middle-finger gesture as she headed off into the dunes. Colm offered a wave in return.

Rather than watching Mia's retreating form, Colm sat and gazed out across the moonlit sea. He was still thinking about Reza. Wondering why the boy had been skulking about like that, watching them.

No answer that Colm could come up with was at all a reassuring one.

II

Zach thumped the battered, charred hull of Beth's escape-pod, then patted it thoughtfully. He walked all the way around the pitted sphere, sizing it up. It was covered in gouges and dark patches – like a giant, bruised, silvery fruit.

Two Drones buzzed around the hangar, zooming inside and outside the pod, recording all aspects of it, occasionally extending probes to take samples of the metal. Amber was monitoring them, her tangle of purple hair tied back for once.

Pensively, Zach traced a finger down one of the jagged scars on the object's metal skin.

Bethany Kane was holding back. Of that much, he was certain. She had gone against his authority once already, and now she was being less than honest with him. About what, he didn't know, but he intended to find out. The power-drains, the malfunctions and the attack on Ella – it hadn't escaped Zach's attention that these had all happened after the arrival of a newcomer. And he didn't like the fact that Colm was spending time with her, either, maybe finding out things that he couldn't himself.

'These things,' he said to Amber, 'are built to withstand everything deep space can throw at them. Bounce through atmospheric re-entry with minimum damage to the organics inside.'

'Organics?' Amber wrinkled her nose as she took readings on her scan-pad. 'You got a funny way of saying *people*.' She grinned, and gave Zach a wink which he totally ignored.

'Whatever.' He thumped the side of the pod again. 'Solid design. Chapter tech … Got to admire it really.'

'What *is* a Chapter, anyway?' Amber asked.

Their resident thief, Zach knew, had grown up in the slums of the Phobos Platform, a structure built above the rugged satellite of Mars. She had not experienced much beyond her day-to-day, hand-to-mouth existence, and had learned her skills in order to survive. Ideal preparation, really, for life on the Edge.

'Sort of mystical order. Hers is the Blessed Chapter of Continual Progress, which is more, kind of, science-based than a lot of them. They believe in the Great Power. This idea that we're all bonded together by a bunch of people all being nice to each other.' Zach grinned at Amber. 'Dunno about you, but that's never got me very far.'

'I can think of worse ways to be.'

'Maybe.' Zach had not had much time for Chapter people before, thinking them a bunch of hard-edged zealots. He had to admit, though, that he was starting to have a sneaking admiration for their engineers.

Drone 121 bobbed at his shoulder, buzzed.

'Oh, sorry, pal.' Zach gave an over-exaggerated gesture. 'Be my guest.'

The Drone's lower section flipped open and a small drill-attachment, sharp and silver, plunged into the side of the pod, creating a hole. It then withdrew that, and a second later a thin, tubular arm swung down, reaching into the hole and sucking up metallic dust from within. Amber took the readings from the Drone's probe, and moved inside the pod to carry on scanning.

Mia strolled in, dishevelled and languid as usual. Her legs, he noticed, were sparkling with azure sand. He knew where she had been, then.

'Getting anywhere?' she asked, leaning against the wall of the hangar.

She sounded almost insolent. She had a dangerous edge, the keen huntress. That was how he needed to carry on thinking of her. Another born survivor.

'Stripping this thing back. About time we did.'

Zach watched the Drone in fascination. They were re-markably efficient little things – he'd never quite got over marvelling at them.

'Watch out,' said Mia. 'Here comes the Spacegirl.'

Zach followed her gaze. Beth was approaching across

the floor of the hangar, her gait self-conscious and awkward. 'Be nice,' he muttered.

Mia spread her hands, opened her mouth in mock-offended fashion. 'Hey, I'm *always* nice.'

'I was talking to myself ... Had a good sleep, Beth?' He enjoyed mimicking her opening gambit from their earlier conversation.

She folded her arms defensively, and he immediately felt guilty. 'I am still recovering,' she said.

'Sorry. Yes. How are the war-wounds?'

'Not bad.' She took off her jacket, revealing the gauze med-patches stuck on her bare, pale arms. She held her gaze steady, almost smiling as she removed the jacket. Zach knew she was watching him carefully, so he tried to show as muted a reaction as possible. 'I think these are doing the job nicely.' She peeled off one of the med-patches, revealing clear, unblemished skin beneath. She did the same to another, then another.

Beneath all the med-patches, Beth's formerly lacerated and discoloured skin had returned almost to normal, smooth pinkish-white.

'That's ... bloody good tissue regen,' said Mia. 'You Chapter kids are pretty healthy, right?'

Mia widened her eyes as if she wanted him to say something. Almost imperceptibly, he shook his head. Outside, thunder boomed again, and they all instinctively looked through the window. Thick, scarlet clouds were boiling against a darkening sky.

'Nice going, Beth,' Zach said, still watching the skies.

'You took a battering in this pod. You owe it your life, though. It doesn't sound as if anyone could have survived that explosion.'

Beth shuddered. 'No,' she said. 'It was horrible. It's all … very hazy. I keep … getting flashes of it. In dreams, and when I am wakeful too. As if it is never going to leave me.'

'Probably never will,' said Mia – not unkindly, Zach thought. She was being blunt and matter-of-fact as ever.

Amber emerged from the pod, waved the scan-pad. 'Got all the readings,' she said. She smiled up at Beth.

'Great,' said Zach. 'We stripped out as much instrumentation as we could,' he explained to Beth. 'Some of it will be useful …'

'I do hope so.'

Beth's face was full of innocence. A girl, he thought, who could flit from flirtatious teasing to childlike candour in a breath. He knew the type well, and was practised in the art of not letting his guard down with them. Again, that instinct nagged at him – that feeling of wanting to keep Beth Kane at arm's length.

'Amber, you show her.'

'Come and see,' Amber said.

Inside the pod, the glossy surface was cracked and burned in places. Panels had been ripped out, wires dangling. Ella and her salvage team had done their job with enthusiasm, if not decorously.

'What will happen to the pod?' Beth asked.

'If it's all right with you …' Zach paused. 'We'll melt it down, break it up. We can always use metal.'

'You can?'

'Sure. I mean, it's not like up there.' He pointed to the ceiling, and they both understood his meaning – the sky, the stars, the worlds beyond. 'It might have scrap value. But that's useless here. We're not exactly going to trade with the Lantrill or the Klaa. And there's nobody else on this damn planet … So, we've got to think how it would be useful.'

'And how will it be useful?' Beth asked.

It was Amber who answered. 'Repairs, renovations, testing … We can always find use for good materials and components.'

Zach approved. Young Amber was pretty handy, he thought, at least when she wasn't getting high on drugs. A lifetime of stealth, of breaking things open and taking them apart was being put to good use.

'That's fine by me,' Beth said. 'I have no … emotional attachment to it.'

'Great!' Zach shot her a quick glance. 'Well, we'll keep scanning. We *might* be able to find out what happened. If it was destroyed, or if not, how badly damaged it was. And if anyone else survived … You want that, don't you, Beth?'

'Of course,' she said softly. 'Of course I do.'

Zach clenched his fists, lifting his chin. 'Yeah,' he said. 'Course you do.'

He wondered what was going on behind that pert, innocent face of hers. What she was hiding. She'd already openly undermined him once. He wasn't going to let that go, no matter how much he might have tried to make light of it.

'You going out again later, Mia?' he said, not breaking his gaze from Beth.

'Got to. Last haul was pretty shit, all things considered.'

'Who you taking?'

'Shan … Maybe Caleb, Finn.'

Zach grinned. 'All your favourite boys.' He patted Beth on the cheek, and she flinched. 'Take Sister Bethany here with you. She could do with the exercise. Now that she's *all better*.'

Beth was alarmed. 'But I'm no good with the gun. I could barely hit–'

'I think you're better than you know,' said Zach, coldly interrupting. 'Good with a knife, aren't you?'

Beth turned away, embarrassed.

He gave her a cold, tight smile, enjoying her discomfort. 'It's all right. We won't make you until you're ready.'

'Thank you … Can I go and get my stuff from the Ship?'

'Be my guest.'

Beth shrugged herself back into the jacket, and stalked out of the hangar without a backward glance.

As soon as she was out of earshot, Zach turned towards Mia, while Amber was busy consulting with the Drones some distance away. 'I don't trust her. The weird stuff's all started since she got here.'

Mia frowned. 'Oh, come on. Yeah, she's odd, but … she's all right, really.'

'Her best friend now, are you?' Zach leaned against a nearby workbench.

'You don't like what she did with the Twelvies and the Benighting. Got one over on you, there.'

'It's not only that.'

'Yeah. If you say so.'

'Think about what's happened since she arrived.' Zach started counting off on his fingers. 'Your pressure-gauntlet lets you down. Ella's assaulted. Someone tries to overload the generator. Three weird things … Plus all the power fluctuations.'

'Yeah, but …' Mia folded her arms. 'That's the way it is out here. Things fall apart.'

'I know. Entropy. None of it's built to last.' He spread his hands. 'I dunno, then. Could be paranoia … We keep watching her, okay?'

'Understood,' she replied.

'Be careful.'

She gave him a mock salute. 'Hey. I'm always careful,' she said with a grin and a wink.

In the distance, across the sea, thunder rumbled.

A light drizzle was hazing the air outside, and dark evil black clouds had gathered around the mountains. Zach gazed out at the forbidding landscape. 'I really don't like the look of that.'

III

Beth climbed the ladder to the flight deck, booted feet clanging in the cavernous darkness.

The sleek, black panels seemed inert. The tall, pyramidal central computer was matte-black and forbidding. She had the sense that it was still working, still sitting there thinking and processing information.

She placed a hand on the pyramid again – and instantly, as before, she could feel it, as if alive. It glowed softly from within, making her hand pale and transparent, the veins standing out. The surface was vibrating.

'*System. Online,*' said a soft, feminine voice.

Shocked, she withdrew her hand.

'*System. Offline,*' said the voice again. The glow faded.

Resonance. That was what it was called, back on the *Arcadia.* Human and machine in unity. To get a computer to do what they wanted, Beth had learned, a skilled crafter of the interface did not punch keys, program, construct architecture in two dimensions to be applied in three. You would cajole, almost persuade the machine. Have a conversation with it. A combination of logic and mental rhetoric.

She placed both hands on the panel.

'*System. Online.*'

She closed her eyes.

She remembered one time on the *Arcadia*, long ago, her mother's hand reaching out. It had rings on it, she remembered, many rings, silver and inlaid with green and blue jewels. Her mother had died before she was three, so it had to be one of her earliest memories.

Her mother's hand was reaching … to steady her? Pull her? She remembered a gap, a wobbly chair. She was jumping down from the chair to the floor, uncertain, scared, even … She remembered her own hand, and how small it was, and how firm and strong her mother's hand had been. She took her mother's hand in hers, and closed her eyes, and jumped.

She opened her eyes.

These memories … were they trying to tell her something? That she had to be strong, brave, take a leap in the dark?

She looked at the panel again.

A new computer, she knew, took a long time to resonate with. It was a case of building up a relationship over time. This one, unsurprisingly, was cold, unused in her mind. Like a flame left to burn low, or a creature left to scavenge. The layers of its programming were chunky, fragile, the subroutines ragged and dull. But still Beth moved her hands across the panel, and still she explored, and still she learned. Introducing the computer to her mind, her personality.

Including the tiny part of it she did not speak of. The part which was not … wholly her own.

'Interface. Engaged.'

Not everyone could do Resonance that well. It was like learning to play a musical instrument – a mixture of skill, time and practice. She presumed nobody else here was able to do it.

Ten thousand hours, Beth knew, was what you needed to become really proficient in anything. But you could only do it if you had the skill and the inclination to begin with.

She closed her eyes again, and opened her mind to the computer.

Darkness. A great, unending void, and in it she stood alone. She held her hands out in front of her, making sure she could see herself. Gleaming and ghostly.

She appeared to be standing on nothing. That could not be right. She focused, concentrated.

The darkness was not completely black. She could see the shimmering walls of intricate, closely-packed circuitry. Woven in a web, so close and tight that it appeared to be velvety blackness. She reached out, touched it. Her hand flared with light, and so did her surroundings, lighting up in a fan of electric-blue in front of her, exposing the billions of intricate circuits. She felt the tingle inside her head.

Determined, she walked through the darkness, concentrating. She stopped once or twice to close her eyes and make sure she could still tell the difference between having her eyes open and having them closed.

There was a small white dot ahead of her. It grew larger as she grew closer, and she started to see detail. It was not white at all, but radiant, a sharp cobalt-blue, like a hologram.

It was the spectral, shimmering outline of a pale girl with dark hair, in slim-fitting dark trousers and tightly-laced boots, wearing a battered leather jacket covered in zips and buckles. Leaving traces of herself behind, like flickering after-images in the void.

Beth stopped.

Her image stopped.

Beth tried to speak. 'Hello,' she said, unsure if she was speaking in her head or with her mouth.

'Hello,' said the image, in her voice.

'So ...' Beth gestured at the digital facsimile of herself. 'Why this?'

The other Beth folded her arms. 'Why not? The interface aims to create a restful, non-threatening environment, one in which it is represented by something which the Resonator finds acceptable. In this case, it has chosen the most appropriate image.'

'Right,' she said. 'Do I really sound like that?'

The other Beth laughed, not unkindly. 'Is that all you came in here to find out?'

'No, no ... I ... I wanted to ... explore, test something.'

'You want information.' The other Beth sauntered forward, perched on an invisible chair, crossed her legs. 'Go ahead.'

Beth's mind was buzzing, her head beginning to ache. She could not spend long in here.

'I want to know about the *Arcadia*. If anything has been found.'

'The colony only has limited scanning procedures available. You know that. If they find anything, they'll tell you.'

'I know,' she said miserably. 'It's just ... There should have been something by now.'

'All available information has been given,' said the other Beth.

'And this place ... it's really so far from anywhere that nobody picks up a signal? Is that possible?'

'That is possible,' said the other Beth.

Annoyed with herself, she realised she had phrased the question wrongly. 'All right, but is it true?'

'This planet is on the edge of known Space. It is of no value to the Collective. It has no necessary mineral deposits or other exploitable wealth. Other planets with similar habitable climate are far more accessible from Earth's solar system and the Outer Planets. This place is …' The image shrugged. 'You could say, unnecessary.'

'Great place to put a bunch of young criminals.'

'It is the safest place.'

'Is there anyone else on this planet? Any other humanoid life?'

'All reported scans have been verified.'

That, thought Beth, was something of a weasly answer. The pain thudded in her head, the image began to blur and flicker. She knew she would have to pull out at any minute.

'One more thing,' she said. 'Is there any other habitable world in this system? Anywhere that might have picked up a message, be able to relay it?'

'All reported scans have been verified,' it said again.

The other Beth was shimmering at the edges now, blurring like a bad transmission. Beth let out a growl of frustration.

The image gave her a small, comical wave, then seemed to turn in on herself, becoming a thin, fizzing line of white pixels, and then contracting to a dot, and popping out of existence entirely.

After a time – it could have been minutes, or hours – she eased her mind out of the computer's architecture and gently removed her hands from the panel.

They were still tingling.

She took a deep breath. She was drained, dehydrated, which was not unusual after Resonance.

So that was it.

She had not really been 'talking' to the computer, of course. It had collated her information in the most easily-accessible way, and presented it in an interface which, her subconscious had obviously thought, found it palatable.

It was not going to help.

A flash of red caught her eye.

Something was flickering high up in the bulkhead above her – a trapezium-shaped red light. She frowned, putting her fears to the back of her mind for a moment, curiosity taking over. One red light was flashing on and off, sending a cone of glowing red up into the latticework metal of the flight deck.

Beth sat herself down in one of the plastic-coated chairs and located the source of the light.

Her mouth dry with excitement, Beth flicked the switch beside the light.

A voice crackled from a speaker. A recorded message, crackling into life. She recognised it straight away.

'Beth? It's Maddi. Can you hear me ...? Beth, I know you're in there. I need to talk to you. It's really important. It's ... it's about something I said before. Something about space debris. I ... I'm tired. I can't do it over this ... But come and see me. I'm in Habitation 2/7.'

The message excited and puzzled her. Maddi was an ally here, so she could trust what she said. Perhaps she ought to go and find out straight away what she wanted.

She stood on the gantry overlooking the vast silo with the Semi-Anna capsules, all standing exactly as they had been left the day that the unwilling passengers emerged.

Beth had to feel sorry for these people.

She was aware of the irony in doing so, because she was in exactly the same position as them. But the Chapter side of her wanted to see the good in people, wanted people to be given another chance. She did not believe that these people, these kids, deserved to be treated this way. People who hadn't toed the line, had uttered the wrong thoughts. Packed on to a shabby, shoddy transport vessel and shipped into space, sent to a bleak outpost where they had to fight to live or die. It was barbaric, Beth thought. It was like what they used to do to convicts in the bad, old, pre-industrial days.

So this was what Earth had gone back to, since leaving the Collective. It wasn't exactly progress.

The acoustics of the silo were eerie, grabbing every footstep and breath of hers and firing them all around, bouncing them off the walls. She strode down the steps, practising being confident, keeping her chin up. It was easy to do when nobody was around.

She walked along the rows of abandoned capsules, inspecting more closely than she had with Colm. They were all dark, upright teardrop shapes, all fitted with human-sized foam recesses and endless tubing and wires. She could see that the insides were stained with a mixture of fluids, long ago drained away – the stuff of life, Beth presumed. The nutrients which had kept the fifty-one young people alive on the flight to this desolate world.

Fifty-one.

She thought again about that number.

An odd number, she thought. Both as in not even, and as in a strange number. Beth walked up and down the aisles between the tapered, lozenge-shaped capsules. Deep in thought, she reached out and caressed the external skin of one of them. It was incredibly smooth, cold to the touch like marble, almost liquid, frictionless. Her hand slid easily off it.

Beth walked the entire length of the silo, counting. Then she walked back, counting again, to be sure.

There were exactly ten rows of five Semi-Anna capsules. Ten times five.

Fifty. Not fifty-one.

Thinking she had to have miscounted, she paced the aisles again, counting carefully, touching each one. 'Forty-eight ... forty-nine ... fifty.'

She went back to her backpack, took out her notebook and pencil. She drew a rough plan of the silo, then counted a third time, marking off each of the capsules as a circle and numbering it as she counted it.

She tore the paper off, held it up. She stared out at the fifty capsules and frowned. Something was wrong there. She wasn't sure if they knew, but–

Out of the corner of her eye – a movement.

'Hello?' she called. 'Who's there?'

Beth dropped the paper, her sketch forgotten. She ran to the halfway point of the silo, where she had seen the flash of movement. She glanced up and down. There. In the reflective surface of the furthest capsule. Was that the edge of a slim young form, ducking into the darkness?

Beth's blood ran cold. 'Hello?' she called again. 'It's only me. You know. Beth Kane. The new girl. I don't want to hurt you. Come out and talk to me.'

She advanced slowly up the aisle, treading as softly as she dared. Shadows ducked and dived, tricking and bewitching her. She kept glancing over her shoulder, convinced that something was about to leap out from one of the capsules behind her.

On the gantry, Beth turned round as a loud, reverberating clang echoed through every corner of the silo. Light spilled in from outside, scattering through the metallic mesh of the gantry floor, and she drew the unfamiliar, horrible Magna pistol from her belt. Images of her wayward shooting-skills flashed across her mind. Of her ungainly unaccustomed hands holding the thing, and of Mia's despairing expression.

There was a low, whining sound, and a smell of hot metal. With an ironic laugh, Beth lowered the gun as the coppery-red Drone, 356, hovered into view again. The spherical robot bobbed and swivelled.

'Come in,' she laughed. 'Make yourself at home.'

The Drone's electronic iris widened, as before. It bobbed up and down once, as if in acknowledgement of her.

Then, the panel in its lower hemisphere flipped open. Beth watched curiously as the bowl-shaped section this formed lowered on a metal rod, until it almost reached the floor. There was a package on there, wrapped in cloth.

She stepped forward, crouching down.

'May I?' she asked.

The Drone's light pulsed once.

Beth reached out, took the small package and un-wrapped it. Three small, powdery biscuits and some vitamin pills.

'Someone wants to take care of me,' she said to herself. 'I wonder who sent you? Maddi, maybe. Or Zach. I can't imagine anyone else caring enough.'

The Drone swivelled this way and that. Beth had learnt not to read anything much into the robots' jittery, agitated movements. There did not seem to be any correlation between that and any message they might be wanting to send, or anything which was going through their electronic minds.

Biting on one of the biscuits and slipping the rest of the package into her pocket, Beth was struck by a sudden, un-likely thought.

'356?' Beth said, straightening up and chewing on the biscuit. She didn't like to call it 'Drone', after all, and she wanted to address it as *something*. 'Did … *you* decide to bring me this?'

The Drone remained entirely impassive. No buzzing, no jitters, no bobbing, no pulsing lights.

It was a ridiculous thought, decided Beth. A Drone was not capable of spontaneous kindness, any more than it was capable of malice. They didn't feel. It had to have been in-structed by someone to bring her the package. The Drone itself could no more think and react emotionally than a door, a gun, the *plaan* processors or the moisture regulators in the hydroponic centre. Could it?

She had a sudden flashback to her vomiting attack at the fence, when she had first arrived. How the Drones had buzzed around her, seemingly concerned.

She dismissed the ridiculous idea.

'Well ... thank you,' said Beth. 'That was very kind.'

The Drone gave a small, courteous bob, then whirled round and floated away on its invisible cloud.

Beth watched it go, curiously.

IV

Deep in the jungle, Mia stood on a grassy ledge, staring down into the foaming crucible beneath her.

The water was fine, she knew that – it had been one of the first things they tested. Saltier than Earth freshwater, with a high sulphur content, but still safe for an invigorating, if pungent, bathe, especially after a rainfall. Even so, it still filled her with trepidation each time.

The enclave was a good twenty kiloms from Town, in the heart of the jungle. It was a deep, narrow gash in the rock, drenched in yellow mist, canopied by huge, gnarled, twisting black trees. A thunderous waterfall, much bigger than the one on the island, descended from somewhere high above her. It foamed into the lagoon thirty emms below. Broad leaves almost blocked out the light, while hanging vines as tough as cables hugged the rocks. The gorge smelt of mud, a peppery pungency, an earthy wetness. The mist, like yellow steam, swirled everywhere.

The place was only accessible on foot – and hardly

anybody else had Mia's strength or stamina. Even if they tried to follow her, they'd give up. And, this close to an oncoming storm, nobody but Mia would have risked venturing out.

Mia stretched out, arms lifted high.

She allowed the foaming torrent of water below her to fill up all of her senses. She breathed in the life-giving fumes, having trained herself over a hundred cycles or more not to sneeze and cough at their sulphurous harshness.

Stretching, stretching high, Mia reached for the sunlight. For the skies where they would never again travel.

Then she swung her arms down hard, brought her fingers together, braced herself and leapt.

The jump, she knew, took anything between two and three seconds.

It was always a shock when she smacked into the embracing water, even after all this time.

Beneath the cold surface she dropped, dropped, kicked upwards, seeing the familiar plants and rocks. She kicked, powered for the light at the surface, confidently holding her breath. Mia broke the surface in delight, spitting water, the yellow steam gathering like ghosts around her. She was about to kick off for her usual swim when the mist parted for a second.

Two glowing, red circles there in the black rocks.

Mia jolted. Her heart hammered as she trod water, pushing her soaked hair back and squinting across the bubbling lagoon.

She saw, a second later, that it was a Lantrill. A young

one – not quite a cub, but not one of the grizzled elders. Its sleek fur was still glossy blue, its limbs firm and taut, its tusks still shiny and white, not yet yellowed with age. It was crouching on the rocks. Watching her. Eyes burning like coals.

Mia frowned. The Lantrill didn't approach humans if they could help it. But this one was neither timid nor bold. Rather … it seemed *interested* in her.

Mia unfurled herself gracefully in the water and swam with broad, deep strokes towards the shore. It took her less than half a minute to reach a handhold on the slippery black stone and haul herself upwards, her tanned body immediately starting to steam as it dried in the hot daytime sun. Rocks slick beneath her hands and feet, she almost slipped for a second, but grabbed a clump of plants and righted herself on to a flat surface of polished rock.

She rubbed the water from her eyes, fully expecting the Lantrill to have fled.

But it was still there. Watching her.

Unbelieving, Mia cocked her head, like an animal listening for predators in the forest.

And the creature did the same. It put its shaggy, blue head on one side, its eyes glowing a deeper red.

Her heart thumping, her body taut, primed and ready to run at any instant, Mia opened her mouth in an O shape.

The Lantrill parted its snout, showing sharp white teeth.

'No,' said Mia softly. 'You shouldn't be able to do that.'

The creature turned towards the lagoon for a second, then back at Mia, and then up the rocky path towards the point thirty emms above where she had launched herself off.

'What?' Mia said, confused. 'Up there? What?'

Once again, the creature swung its head back and forth. Then, with a grunting and wheezing, accompanied by the odd squeak, it turned, great clumpy clawed feet finding a hold on the muddy rock, and began to plod its way up the incline towards the top of the rocks.

It understood me, Mia was thinking. *That's not supposed to happen.*

She was not at all comfortable with the idea of these creatures being more intelligent than they had suspected. If they'd not had the Lantrill to hunt and kill, it would have been a diet of *plaan* soup and vitamin pills until the hydroponic centre got up and running.

There was something animal-like in Mia, something instinctive and feral, and it made her leap across the rocks like a young gazelle, scrambling barefoot after the creature. She could see its blue pelt through the mist and the vegetation, as it hauled itself upwards, claws easily finding a hold on the black rocks. She climbed after it, desperate not to lose sight of it. In the distant skies, thunder grumbled and growled – Mia knew she didn't have long.

At the top of the rocks, she hauled herself on to the grass. Her ragged white top and her shorts were where she had left them, and she pulled them on hurriedly over her damp body. Her gun-belt lay there untouched too, and she clipped it back on, feeling immediately reassured by the presence of the cold metal Magna pistol against her thigh.

'So,' she murmured, 'where did you go?'

There was a scuffling and a scratching in the rocks, and the vegetation shook. The creature's snout and tusks re-appeared, almost comically. Mia had drawn her gun immediately, hunting instincts kicking in. For a second or two, she and the Lantrill eyed each other cautiously.

Mia levelled the gun at the creature. She could easily have shot it. The easiest hunt, the easiest kill. The creature had pretty much walked into its own death, and Mia was confident she could carry it home over her shoulder, tied to a small, stripped tree-trunk.

Except she wasn't going to kill it.

She somehow knew. It was there in her head, the certainty, enclosing her brain like a gloved hand, dulling her killing instinct.

The creature turned very slowly and shuffled off into the forest, and Mia, not quite knowing why, followed it.

It was easy for her to follow the Lantrill. The rain-washed ground was softer here, and the animal didn't exactly try to hide, or cover its tracks. For ten minutes she hacked and slashed her way through thorny vegetation – keeping an eye out for some of the nastier things she knew lived in this part of the forest. Warm, squashy blue mud splashed up her calves. Her breath was ragged and harsh inside her head. Cursing, she asked herself why she was doing this.

As Mia was about to give up and head back for the rocky plains and the hour's jog back to Town, she emerged into a muddy hollow. The ground dipped so quickly and alarmingly that she almost lost her footing, but she was able to right herself in time to hunch her body into a scrambling position and half-skitter, half shuffle down the muddy slope to the bottom of the hollow.

The depression was bowl-shaped, about ten emms across. Here, it was cooler, and the mud was thicker, cold, dark. Twisted, thorny red trees swept up in corkscrew shapes above Mia's head, and broad, flat blue leaves formed a canopy high above. A secluded, hidden part of the forest.

Lurking in the shadows at the other side of the hollow was the Lantrill she had been tracking. It snuffled, squeaked, pawed the ground, carving great gouges in the mud. Its eyes flared red.

'All right,' said Mia softly. 'I think you brought me here for a reason. So what was it?'

Amazingly, again, the Lantrill seemed to respond to her voice. It trotted around the edge of the hollow, snuffling and snarling at a great, dark tree and a mass of tangled vegetation on the far side.

Mia hurried over, her gun cautiously levelled.

And this time, the Lantrill reacted as she would expect. It squawked, skittered on the muddy ground and then fled, scrambling up the muddy incline back into the shelter of the forest.

Mia watched it go, her mind feeling oddly lazy.

I could have killed it three times over. And yet it didn't seem scared. Almost as if it knew I wasn't going to.

Mia had never seen a dog or a cat, but she knew about them – animals kept in homes of the wealthy, almost part of the family. She remembered from Lumi-casts about how these creatures instinctively trusted humans, had almost a telepathic connection with them.

Mia shuddered for a second, thinking of the Lantrill cub she had been about to kill when the glove gave out on her.

Something gleamed under the thick, knotted vegetation which hung from the tree. The tree's roots hung over the edge of the hollow, forming a kind of irregular woody cage which the vegetation had taken a hold of.

Mia dropped to a crouch.

She wasn't going to waste a shot until she was certain. And whatever it was, it didn't seem to be moving. She reached out, clutched a handful of the rubbery, spiky vines and pulled. They were swept aside fairly easily, revealing a smaller hollow within the depression.

Mia advanced cautiously, taut and tensed, ready for fight or flight.

In the darkness under the gnarled tree-roots, the thing which was gleaming revealed its shape. At first it seemed to Mia like a smashed, silvery egg. Fragments of it lay on the ground, embedded in the mud.

She climbed further in. The egg-thing had a shell which curved above her. Something adjusted itself, fed the right signal to her brain.

It was not an egg.

It was a capsule.

Mia, hardly daring to breathe, climbed into the space under the tree and allowed her hand to trace a pattern on the worn surface of the ovoid pod. Its surface was covered with a dull grey metal, burned and pitted and scarred in places as if it had been seared by intense heat. Halfway down, there was a clear crack where the fragments had fallen, and there was darkness within.

She fumbled in her pocket, pulling on the LED head-torch she always carried. And, steeling herself, she crawled inside and panned the light around the interior of the pod.

She had to put a hand over her mouth, as the capsule smelt of damp and decay, an almost fecal reek. Simple navigation instruments lined the walls, dusty and cracked from years of abandonment. Nature had begun to encroach upon the abandoned pod, with vines and thorns eating their way through the glossy, technological surfaces, strangling the control panels. Glowing blue fungi nestled in the higher reaches of the interior. Mia vaguely wondered if they might be edible, and thought about taking a sample back to Town for the Drones to analyse. Then she told herself to concentrate on the matter in hand.

The beam of icy blue light swept across the whole of the inside of the capsule.

And a second later, she jumped as the light picked out the unmistakable bleached white of bone.

'Holy hell!' she whispered out loud, and the curse echoed in the confined space.

Her own breath, crisp and harsh in her head. *Wait, wait*, she told herself, allowing her heart to regain its usual rhythm.

Then she steeled herself, crawled right inside.

There were two skeletons. Almost totally clean of flesh

and clothing, with the thinnest of threads and ragged, yellowing skin clinging to them in places. They were both adult, she decided, and humanoid. The skulls, eerily, were facing each other, as if they had spent their last moments saying important words to one another.

'So who the hell were you?' she wondered out loud.

Mia reasoned that, wherever the capsule had come from, the occupants must have died prior to the landing. There was no sign of trauma to the skeletons, no smashed or even cracked bones. And they had been here … how long?

She shivered. She realised she did not even know how long it took a humanoid body to be reduced to a skeleton. She supposed that it depended on a lot of factors like heat and humidity, and the kind of soil in which it found itself.

Mia eased herself out of the pod, happy to be able to breathe normally again. She sat cross-legged on the mud, wondering what to do with this new information. It was a standard class Survival One ejector, she thought, used for very short-term emergency travel. Very different from the kind of thing Beth had arrived in, which could support a spaceborne refugee for several days. She didn't have a viewer or a Drone with her to record it, so whoever she told – if she chose to tell anyone – would have to believe her.

The strangest thing of all was that the young Lantrill had led her here.

'Almost as if it wanted me to see,' she murmured to herself.

Casting a last, careful look around, Mia replaced the

vines so that the pod was once more concealed in its small hollow. Then she scrambled up the slope, out of the clearing. She pulled her visor on, as a precaution, and began her long walk back to the causeway.

She was thinking hard as she reached the edge of the jungle, wading through the sludgy brown water at the foot of the ridge and starting to climb.

Mia Janowska knew one more thing about Survival One ejector pods, and it was this. They could carry up to three people.

And there had been two skeletons in the pod, and no sign of the remains of another.

She glared up at the boiling red clouds above the mountains, and shuddered. She didn't like storms. She cursed to herself. The clouds hadn't looked too threatening when she set out, and she had been confident of easily getting back before the storm came. Over two hundred cycles of reading the sky, and she could still get it wrong sometimes.

They were getting closer, like monsters in the sky. The first drops of heavier rain began to fall, spattering the blue dust.

As she reached the coast, Mia quickened her pace.

∞

7
STORM
WARNING

I

Zach's door-com buzzed.

'Yeah?' he called. He was lying on his back, bare-chested, hands behind his head. Gazing at the ceiling in a brief moment of respite.

He was not alone. Half-covered by the sheet, sweat-slicked and gently breathing, Lulu lay sleeping beside him. Quiet and blissful.

The door-com buzzed again.

'It's open,' he said. 'Come in.'

There was the familiar soft whine of a Drone, and the pungent smell of hot metal which always accompanied the busy robots. It was the red Drone, 356.

Zach sat up, frowning. 'Yeah, what do you want?' he asked. He perched on the side of the bed, running a hand through his hair.

The Drone's lower cavity flipped open, and its extendable clamp-hand slowly emerged, clutching a small, folded piece of paper. Its arm extended until the piece of paper was right under Zach's nose.

'What's this all about?' he snapped.

The Drone's eye pulsed, and it gave its usual soft, buzzing sound.

Zach took the piece of paper and unfolded it. 'Some days,' he said, 'I really wish you guys could speak. It would really help.'

He smoothed the paper out on his knees, frowning as he turned it round, trying to make sense of it. Fifty numbered circles in ten rows of five, surrounded by an irregular polygon, with one or two other scribbles around the edge that he could not decipher.

'Who gave you this?' he asked. 'What's it for? I don't understand.'

The Drone bobbed gently on its invisible column of air, then turned, floating out of the room as quickly as it had come.

'No, wait!' he shouted angrily after it. 'Drone! Come back!' He went to the door, but Drone 356 had already disappeared down the Habitation corridor, out of sight.

Zach stared at the drawing. He spread it out on his table. Paper and pencil, he thought. Old materials. Nobody used paper and pencil here. Except …

'Bethany Kane,' he said out loud.

'Her again,' said a sleepy voice at the door to the bedpod.

He turned around sharply. Lulu, a T-shirt pulled awkwardly over her, was rubbing her eyes, smiling.

'Hiya. I didn't … I thought I'd let you sleep.'

'Evidently.' She nodded at the paper. 'What's that?'

'Not sure.' He stared at it, then folded it again and slipped it into the pocket of his jacket, which was hanging on the back of the door. 'I expect it'll make sense at some point.'

'Like everything else,' she said, pulling on her leggings and searching around for the jacket she had abandoned somewhere on the floor the previous night.

Zach's radio crackled. '*Boss, you there?*' said a boy's voice.

He picked it up, giving Lulu an apologetic look. 'Yeah, go ahead.'

'It's Hal. I'm out at Perimeter 3 with Freya.'

'All right. Everything fine?'

'Well, yeah. Except I was meant to be with Maddi. She didn't turn up. Freya was free so she came instead. It's not a problem, Boss. Thought I'd let you know.'

'All right,' Zach said. A faint sense of unease crept through his body. 'Thanks for letting me know, Hal. Out.'

Lulu gave his neck a soft kiss, waving as she slipped to the door. 'Stuff to do,' she said. 'Catch you later.'

II

'Twist.'

In the hexagonal tracking room at the top of the Comms tower, Robbie dealt another card down in front of Amber. She took it, tucking the two of diamonds in tightly beside her ten of clubs and four of spades. Sixteen. That, she thought, was the danger zone. There was more chance of a card taking her over 21 than keeping her under. She drew a soft, hissing breath.

'Take your time,' said Robbie, amused.

Amber scowled at him. She knew his game. She had a reputation for taking these card games too seriously, and the others liked to try and put her off. Sometimes she cheated, but that had stopped being fun a while ago.

The noise of the compound echoed from outside. Amber allowed her mind to wander. A Drone was quietly bobbing back and forth along the perimeter, apparently checking for breaches in the fencing. Finn and Xara, leaning against the fence, were having an intense argument about something. Xara kept spreading both hands, taking a step back, taking a step forward, while he was more languid, cool, mocking, arms folded. Amber wished she could know what the argument was about. She liked the details of other people's lives, the tiny dramas which kept Town ticking over. It all kept her sane, reminded her they were human.

'Come on,' said Robbie cheerfully. 'Haven't got all day.'

'All right, all right!' She tutted.

'Twist or stick,' Robbie said. 'Only two choices. If only everything in life was that simple.'

'All right. Gimme time.'

Amber, thinking, glanced idly over at the console they were supposed to be monitoring – the various screens of numerical data which barely changed from one cycle to the next and the big, sweeping arc of the green radar screen.

In that second, a large, disc-like flare surged in the top quadrant of the screen. Amber leapt up, dropping her cards in one movement. 'What the hell was that?'

'What?' Robbie was alarmed. 'I didn't see anything.'

'We're supposed to be monitoring this fecking thing. Zach'll kill us.' She scanned the radar screen desperately for movement. 'Come on, you bastard! It was there, I swear!'

'Could be space-storms, solar flares … could be anything.' He thumped the console and it wobbled alarmingly. 'This equipment's antique. How much longer's it gonna–'

'There!' Amber pointed, and this time they both saw it.

A large clear trace, a disc formation, flaring in the top quadrant, getting bigger and bigger for a second or two, then snapping out of existence.

Amber and Robbie looked at each other in incomprehension, then back at the radar screen again.

'It's gone again,' Robbie said.

'I couldn't tell if–' Amber broke off, staring out of the window. 'Is it me or is that Drone really spooked?'

Outside, there was something of a commotion, with the sound of the patrolling Drone's engines building to a whine. Robbie stood up, craned his neck, following Amber's line of vision.

The Drone had retracted its tools inside itself and was bobbing erratically from side to side. It had started to bounce around, like a bee trapped in a glass. They could hear its agitated skittering from there. Finn and Xara, by the fence, had spotted it too, and had abandoned their argument to watch the Drone intently.

'Come on,' Amber said, and she grabbed her tool-satchel. 'Might need a recalibration. Or a thump.'

Outside, there was a hot metallic smell, getting stronger, coming from the Drone.

'Get on the radio,' Robbie said to Finn. 'Who's on maintenance?'

'Yellow,' he said.

'Get someone down here, then!'

The Drone zoomed incredibly fast towards Robbie, and he ducked in time to avoid it impacting with his head. Xara screamed, jumping back. It buzzed through the air, smacking against the perimeter fence with a loud retort. The smell of burning was stronger, pungent.

The Drone's motor, Amber could see, was sputtering and sparking. An instant later, its red lights went dull and it dropped like a stone, hitting the dust with a loud bang.

It lay there, inert, black smoke starting to pour from its innards.

'Yellow team,' Finn said into the radio. 'We have a … situation.'

'What happened?' Xara asked.

'I dunno. It … stopped working.'

Robbie was stealthily approaching the Drone. Three emms, two, one.

'Careful,' Amber said.

He held his breath. He went up close, prodded it with the toe of a boot. It rolled over, and back again, like a steel football lying there. No sign of life.

Amber winced. '*Careful*, Rob.'

The boy spread his hands, turned to the others with a grin. 'What? It's a dud. Probably worn its motor out somehow.'

The movement, when it came, caught them all by surprise. One second the Drone was sitting there, an inert steel ball. The next, with a loud whooshing noise and a smell of burning metal, it had lifted off the dust, trailing sparks like a firework. Three emms, ten, fifteen, high above the fence. An intense, high-pitched whining noise, even louder than before, emanated from its innards.

Amber backed off. 'Steady,' she murmured. Her instincts had told her something was wrong. She spotted the red glow on the surface of the Drone before anyone else did. 'Down! Everyone down!'

They threw themselves to the ground as the Drone glowed bright cherry-red, its engines screaming.

There was a sudden silence.

An instant later, in a spectacular fountain of fire and smoke, the Drone exploded into a million blazing, twisted pieces, pouring down on the compound like burning hail.

III

Zach strode across the Rec Hall and up the central staircase to the Sky-Gallery, trying to take in everything that was happening today. He knew he could not lose sight of it all, of the whole picture. That was the problem – doing the whole picture at the same time as the details.

Ella stood on the Sky-Gallery, eyeing the broiling, steaming sea through a viewer.

'This is gonna be a big one,' she said, seeming to notice Zach was there without looking.

'Yeah, well.' He had to agree. The clouds were evil on this planet, gathering and frothing together, endlessly changing shape. Already, the peaks of the mountains were invisible, and, like a wall of smoke, the clouds were rolling down the valleys, swallowing up the trees. The sea was angry, dashing vast glittering clouds of yellow spray against the rocks.

'Is anyone out?' Ella asked, lowering the viewer. She

swung her head round towards Zach, a sudden precise movement which caught him off-guard. There were times, he thought, when Ella came across as a bit *too* efficient.

'Yeah, Mia is … Listen, Ell, have you seen Maddi today?'

'No. Not seen her for a while. Why?'

'She didn't turn up for morning watch. Really unlike her.'

'Someone else do it?' she asked.

'Yeah, Freya did. But …'

'There you go, then.' Ella lifted the viewer again. 'You know, you worry too much, Zach.'

He frowned at her. 'Maybe. And maybe not.'

Ella's radio buzzed, and she unclipped it with her usual brisk efficiency. 'Ella. Go ahead.'

'It's Amber. We … got a bit of a Drone malfunction by Perimeter 3.'

Ella rolled her eyes. 'Well, deal with it, Amber. You're a big girl.'

'I kind of can't,' said the girl's voice apologetically. 'It's kind of … toast.'

Ella exchanged a baffled look with Zach. '*Toast*?'

'Yeah, as in totally wasted. Bang. Come and see.'

'I'm on my way,' she said, hooking the radio back on her belt. 'How the hell did that happen? Were the Twelvies playing football with it?'

'Wouldn't put it past them,' said Zach with a grin. 'I'll come with you.'

They were interrupted by a blaring siren, echoing from the top of the Comms tower. Regular blasts, one note, lasting about a second.

Zach looked at Ella in alarm. 'Change of plan. That's the storm warning!'

IV

Beth, driven from her sanctuary, had shoved her things into a makeshift backpack and joined those scurrying across the compound.

The siren blasted from the Main Dome, like the screech of a banshee. Anyone who had been on outside duties was hurrying in – both Towners and Drones. Zach and Ella stood at the main doors, Ella still eyeing the sea warily through her viewer.

A Drone buzzed past Beth's head, spinning and whirring, lights flashing on its curved panel.

'I know, I know!' Beth told it. She was going to ask what was happening, but she had seen the sky. She knew, from everyone's reactions, that this was going to be serious – it was not just a normal thunderstorm – and yet she still found it a strange source of fascination, despite her fear.

The clouds, wreathing the distant mountains and valleys, had changed from orange to a dark crimson fog. The light changed too, the sky turning burnt orange, blood-red at the horizon. The twisted fingers of the cacti out on the plain cast dark evil shadows in this light, while the cracks and fissures in the land beyond Town seemed to have grown deeper, darker. The broiling steam they belched had become thicker, gouting up into the sky in great, whooshing jets, becoming billowing yellow clouds. The sea was a monster, restlessly roaring, dashing itself against the cliffs and the rocks.

Beth stood in astonishment, fear and wonder. She had seen nothing like this on the *Arcadia*. There, the simulated weather was gentle, non-intrusive. This, in contrast, was not only real but deadly. She felt oddly detached from it, and yet, deep inside her, something was screaming to get to cover. She remained transfixed. The hot, sulphurous saltiness in the air had grown stronger, stifling.

Something cannoned into her shoulder, jolting her.

It was Mia. Soaking wet, bedraggled, with her hair plastered to her face, mud spattered up her legs.

'Get *inside*!' she snapped.

Beth knew she was right, but still hung back. 'It's beautiful,' she said, gazing longingly at the light fringing the clouds as they hurtled towards Town across the causeway. Shadows swept across the rocks, a tidal wave of dark grey on the blue. The cracks in the earth seemed to widen like hungry mouths, spewing thick gouts of their yellow steam. It was as if the planet was becoming angry.

'It's not *beautiful*, you hippy space-bitch. It's dangerous! Inside!' Mia pulled at her, dragging her.

'What's the great rush?' Beth asked – even though she knew she was being foolish, that she had to move, to get inside with the others.

'Oh, nothing,' Mia sneered at her as the girls hurried towards the main door of the dome. 'Why don't you stay and find out?'

At the door, Zach nodded curtly. 'Are you the last?'

'I think so,' snapped Mia. 'What do you want me to do, take a fucking register?'

Ella grabbed Beth out of the way of the door and almost shoved her down the steps. Inside the dome, protective shutters were sliding down over the plexiglass, a grey mesh which slowly shut out the natural light. They made a clattering, grinding sound as they descended. Vermilion lights flickered into life in the Rec Hall. Here, the alarms sounded even more brash and loud, making her teeth rattle. Everyone was in a state of some agitation, it seemed – even the Drones.

'What's up?' Beth asked, glancing over her shoulder to where Zach and Mia were still trading insults. 'Look, I know these storms can be bad, but … How bad?'

Ella stopped, faced Beth. In the dim lighting, the filigree of her internal life-support sparkled like rain.

'You really don't know?'

Beth was abashed, swinging her rucksack down on to the floor. 'We didn't have … proper weather on the *Arcadia*. I'm sorry. I don't know what to expect.'

Zach, pushing his way through the crowd, interrupted her, addressing himself to Ella. 'Is everyone inside?'

'Yes, everyone.'

'Has anyone seen Maddi?' Zach asked worriedly.

'Yeah, she came in earlier,' Ella said. 'She was going for a rest.'

'All in, then. I'll seal the doors.'

Zach's radio crackled into life. '*Deadlocks seven and eight secured. Two to go.*'

The sudden flurry of action had confused Beth, worried her. 'Can I do anything?' she asked Zach. He tried to ignore her, turning away to say something to Lulu. Beth, astonishing herself, grabbed Zach's muscular arm and twisted him round, amazed at her own strength. He pushed her away, then took a pace towards her, tensing angrily. Beth made herself hold her ground. 'What's it going to be like? I *demand* to know!'

'Oh,' he said. 'You *demand* to know, do you, Bethany Kane? Well, you'll find out soon enough.' Fury rose in her as he strode off, unhooking the radio from his belt. 'Zach here. Shields in place. Check seals on all the units.'

A voice crackled back – one of the younger boys. Reza. '*Got that.*'

Zach called back to Beth. 'You can go up to the Top Level if you want. Cameras should give a grandstand view.'

'Cameras?'

She didn't understand. But she followed a group of Towners up the spiral staircase to the top level of the dome. As the rain intensified, Beth heard it hammering down on the shutters. She imagined it churning up the ground outside, streaming down the Comms tower and the hangars.

Where normally the great curve of glass on the Sky-Gallery would give them a view across the sea and the causeway to the mountains beyond, there was the opaqueness of the shielding, and the dim light cast odd, wobbling shadows. A giant, curved screen showed the view they would usually see out of the window. It took Beth a few seconds to work out how this was being done. Drones. Two of them, in hover mode outside the Main Dome. Recording every aspect of the oncoming storm, their sensors open.

'They'll get pulverised,' she murmured, to nobody in particular.

Shan, standing in front of her with his arms folded, gave her one of his big beaming smiles. 'Nah. They're made of stronger stuff than that. And anyway, what if they do? They're only Drones.'

She felt it, then, a strange sadness, like a tingling in the back of her head. A melancholy for something lost, something never to be regained. 'It's so sad,' she said quietly.

Zach came pounding up the stairs, closely followed by Mia, Ella, Baljeet, Amber and others.

Shan laughed. 'You getting soft over Drones, Beth? They're tools, items. You may as well be upset about a chisel getting whacked by a hammer.'

'One out there blew up,' Amber said, as she hurried past.

'What?' Shan was confused. 'What did you say?'

'A Drone. Was fine one minute, and whoosh-bang the next.' She clapped, spread her hands. 'Boom.'

'That shouldn't happen,' said Shan worriedly.

Beth didn't have time to take in this new information. Town was locking down for the storm.

'All secured,' Zach called out. He jumped on to the nearest available platform, a metal table, and got their attention immediately. 'Shutters are all down, brothers and sisters. Stand by.' His radio crackled, and he pressed the button. 'Yes?'

'Deadlocks nine and ten sealed. Hydroponics secured.'

'Good work, Reza. Stay in there.'

Five seconds later, the lights inside Town dimmed to a pale wash of orange. On the screen, Beth could see the advancing, boiling mass of storm clouds drawing ever closer.

The cameras were hazy, the Drones outside being pummelled with rain.

'Here we go, everyone,' Zach said. 'Hold tight.'

V

The storm was swift and powerful, a battle royal above the land.

Thick black clouds tore across the sky like black, steam-powered spacecraft, unleashing targeted bolts of azure lightning. They dropped bombs of thunder which shook the island. It was as if an early night had fallen, along with a threatening, close, apocalyptic stillness.

Within the sanctuary of Town, they watched silver chains of rain striking the ground, heard them hitting the dome with a metallic rattle. Out on the plain, the rainwater sparkled and flashed as it hit the sand, gouged holes in the soft earth. The fissures cracked and boomed, belching their foul smoke and also fountains of hot blue mud, spraying up into the sky and cascading down on the land like a glutinous rain.

The storm tore into the land with an anger and viciousness Beth had never seen. On the screens, lightning carved the rocks apart like lasers. Thunder rocked the ground like an earthquake.

In the dome, everything rattled and shook. It was barely holding together. Wind howled like angry ghosts, screeching across the sea and land, a powerful force lashing Town again and again. Without the shutters, Beth realised, the plexiglass windows could well have been torn from their housing and smashed.

Colm slid next to Beth, who was sitting with her hands clasped over her knees beside one of the great pillars. He offered her a metal flask.

'What is it?' she asked suspiciously.

'Only tea, babe. I'm not trying to get you drunk just yet.'

She sniffed the neck of the bottle. 'Pretty strong tea.'

'Well … yeah. Fermented tea.'

She took a drink. It was bitter. It slid easily down her throat, spread through her stomach with a comforting, hot caress. She coughed, but tried to smile, nod in appreciation. 'It's good.'

'I'm sorry,' Colm said. 'About before. I was … I was a bit of a dick.'

Beth handed him his flask back. 'Yes. You were.'

'I'm kind of like that sometimes.'

'Yes. I know.'

She kept her answers minimalist, to unsettle him. They smiled uneasily. Town shook to a thunderous impact, as if a great fist had struck it, and the rain pounded hard. Beth stared upwards in fear. 'Is this place going to hold?'

'Ah, it's only weather. Everywhere has weather, doesn't it? We've had it before. Don't listen to the scaremongers.'

The dome trembled again as the rain redoubled.

She moved closer to him. Right now, he was as good an ally as any. She needed to tell someone about her Resonance experience, as the thought of it was nagging away at her.

'Colm,' she said. 'I've been meaning to tell someone. On board the Ship. The computer. I–'

A flash of bright blue out of the corner of her eye. The lights dimmed from orange to red. There was an alarming sound like sparking and fizzing. A second later the whole of Town was plunged into darkness. The hum of electrical activity, almost inaudible because it was there all the time, cut out.

There were groans from most of the Towners, and squeals of fear from some of the younger ones.

'All right, everyone, calm down!' Zach's voice carried from the Sky-Gallery. 'It's only the generator. We'll fix it. The backup should kick in any second.'

On cue, there was a fizzing sound and the dome became suffused with a soft, ochre glow, giving everything a surreal and ghostly quality. Long, deep shadows fell across one another. A lower electrical hum gradually faded in.

In the dimness, Beth felt Colm's hand sneaking over hers. She did not resist, this time.

'What were you going to say?' he asked.

'Doesn't matter. It'll wait.'

The storm was over as quickly as it had begun.

The clouds retreated, the thunder rolled away across the sea. The skies lightened as if a dimmer-switch had been turned. Now, only the silvery droplets on the vegetation and the glossy, meaty wetness of the rocks served as a reminder of the earlier turmoil.

The sea, though, was still restless, the water steel-grey, waves pummelling the ragged shore. Further along, where spiky rocks kept guard, incoming breakers exploded in a haze of milky white.

Beth could see a dim, reluctant orange sun emerging as the steel shutters were raised. Some of the young Towners wound a handle to open the main doors manually, and she could taste the freshness in the air like an electrical charge. The land, washed by rain, smelt old and new at the same time. She breathed it in.

'You feel that?' Colm asked from behind her in the doorway. 'Positive ions. You get a real buzz from those.'

'Not as good as *plaan*,' Mia said, sliding into view on her other side.

'Where have you been?' Beth asked with a grin.

'I locked myself in the Cooler. I don't like storms.'

Beth allowed herself an astonished grin as Mia strolled out into the fresh, clean-washed daylight.

'Didn't think she was afraid of anything,' she said to Colm.

'Every day's a learning day ... Have you seen Maddi recently?'

'No, not seen her for ages, actually.'

'Nor me. Expect she's around.' Colm grinned at her. 'Shall we go outside and see how our metal friends fared? I expect they'll be wanting a rub down.'

VI

A thick, greasy cloud of smoke filled the power room, penetrated by the lights of three Drones as they surged forward, fuzzing over the smoke-blackened steel column of the generator.

Zach, Shan and Ella descended the step, coughing and trying to waft the smoke away. The Drones were already doing what they could, cutting and drilling, but it was clear that this was going to be a patchwork repair at best.

'What do we think?' Zach asked.

Shan held his scan-pad up to the machinery, pulling an unhappy face as he took in the depressing readings. 'Voltage regulator's fried. The alternator's gone completely. Honest answer, boss? We're in the shit. No power.'

'How long does the backup last?' Zach asked. 'Do we know?'

Nobody seemed to know the answer, but Shan made a guess. 'It'll be hours at most. Doubt it will even see us through a full cycle. We've got to get this fixed or we're dead.'

'What about the neutron booster?' Ella asked. 'That could give us some longer-term temporary power. I could probably patch it in and re-route the dynamic induction coils, if I had Amber's help.'

Zach glared at her. 'When it's buried in a swamp a hundred kiloms away? Not much good to us there, is it?' He thumped the wall.

'But what if we tried to retrieve it?' Shan said.

Zach turned round slowly, peered at his fellow Towner

through the smoke. 'Are you crazy? It would be a whole cycle's journey, and even if you could find it …'

'Listen. I *could* find it. Home in on the emissions. Nothing else round there will be giving out that kind of signal, right?'

'I dunno. Sounds pretty dubious to me.'

'Zach, come *on*. It's got to be worth a shot. I'll take a jeep, with two or three of us and a Drone. We could send the Drone in to lift it out. They're good at thirty, forty emms' depth for short periods.'

'We've not tested these Drones underwater.'

'Well, then, this will be our chance,' Shan said. 'I'm trying to think positively, Zach. Do what you always say. Bring solutions, not problems, yeah?'

'He's right,' Ella said. 'It could work. We've got to try it, Zach.'

Zach paced up and down, deep in thought. The Drones bobbed, lights flickering as if they, too, were awaiting his response.

'All right,' he said at last. 'Take two Drones, though.'

'It's rough country,' Ella said. 'Land and river predators. You'd have to be alert. You'll need Hunters.'

'Take Baljeet, Mia …' Zach thought hard. 'And one of the stronger young guys. Finn, or Hal …'

Shan nodded. 'I'm on it.'

'Actually…' Zach held a hand up. 'Wait. I've got a better idea. Take Baljeet and Mia … but take our little ChapterSister too.'

Shan and Ella exchanged a worried look.

'She could be a liability,' Ella said. 'I'd advise against it, Zach.'

'Oh, would you? That's nice.'

'Look, really. You think that's a good idea, boss?' Shan said worriedly. 'She's ... Well, we dunno how she is, like, out of her comfort zone.'

'I know,' said Zach. 'I think it'll be a good opportunity to find out. Don't you?'

∞

Slowly, the pieces begin to come together.

It is as if all of time and space has been waiting for us. Waiting for this group, this frightened knot of humanity clinging to a rock at the edge of known Space.

The last hope of the human race? Or its first, true sight of its future?

These children have sown the seeds of their own destruction. It is the beginning of the end.

8
POWERPLAY

I

Shan cut the jeep's motor. 'Here's where we get out and walk.'

Beth slowly got to her feet, staring past the window of the jeep, past the bonnet, past the thick blue mud which lay ahead of them. She peered into the swirling yellow mist. It had a peppery smell which stung her nostrils and the back of her throat. There was the strange chirruping and howling of unseen creatures, and, underneath, bubbling furiously, the unmistakable noise of a large body of moving water.

She had only come on this mission because it had been presented to her that she had no choice. This, she knew, was part of her contribution to Town, the contribution she had said in her speech that she was keen to make. So she couldn't really back out. Now, though, she was confused.

'Get out and walk? Why?'

'This wreck doesn't float,' said Mia. 'And we need to go that way. That's why.'

It had taken the expedition party – Beth, Shan, Mia and Baljeet, with two Drones – three hours to get this far. From the causeway, they had come off the mountain route and plunged down the jungle escarpment. The mud was thick, glutinous, spraying up on all sides. It stank of decay and was icy cold.

Shan had his scan-pad keyed into the neutron trace, and Mia called out directional readings as they bounced along, the faint pulse getting stronger and stronger. The Drones buzzed behind, keeping pace with the jeep but staying at quite a height. Beth was reassured by their presence. They all knew about the malfunctioning Drone by now – but the small robots were generally reliable, the odd broken circuit or faulty valve aside, and it was a relief to have them around.

Shan and Baljeet took it in turns to drive. The vehicle churned up the ground, its reinforced wheels sloshing through sloppy mud and foul water, going deeper and deeper into the soft, greenish-black heart of the great jungle. It became close and humid, the air tightening on them like a fist.

Beth barely spoke. In fear and wonder, she inhaled strange swampy smells and tasted the sharp mist on her tongue. Her entire body was soaked in sweat, her hair sticky and drenched, her armpits like two pungent, itching pools which she longed to wash and disinfect.

The jeep, juddering and bumping, its engine roaring and revving, had sliced through thorny plants and great flapping red leaves, avoiding gnarly trees with twisted blue bark, descending slowly through the mist until they hit the bank of the steaming, glutinous river.

Beth stared at the expanse of water in front of them, not quite able to believe what Shan had said. 'You've got to be kidding.'

Shan grinned, clapping her on the shoulder and making her jump. 'Hey. That's better. You're starting to sound like a Towner.'

'C'mon,' Baljeet said. 'It won't be that bad. And we need the power.'

'Why did the ship even dump the neutron booster in the swamp anyway?' Beth asked.

Mia answered her. 'Landing a crate in a hole like this isn't fun and games, you know. Weight was critical. It's all there in the flight log. The onboard computer jettisoned everything it didn't need in the final few minutes.'

'And it never thought you'd need the booster again. Ironic.'

'Yeah, well, I'm glad you think so, Beth. So – it's cross that river, or never get it back, and have no power. Great choice, eh?'

'I do not want to do it,' said Beth apprehensively. 'There could be anything in that water.'

'What do you suggest, Spacegirl?' said Mia, draping an arm around her shoulders. A ragged grin cracked her fierce lean warrior-face, creasing the stripes of warpaint. 'Wanna build a bridge? See you in three cycles.' She jumped down from the jeep, offering Beth her hand. Beth took it, steadying herself as she jumped on to the sludgy mud.

'Can't we go round it?' asked Beth desperately.

'It's a river,' said Shan, 'not a puddle.' He showed her the scan-pad, with the layout of the jungle picked out in blue by the Drones' energy sensors. 'We could cross nearer the source, in the mountains, but it's fifty K upstream from here.' He pointed to the narrowing of the river on the map. 'We'd not make it by nightfall.'

Mia had the optical viewer out, scanning the landscape. 'Yeah, it's got to be now or never.'

The mist thinned for a moment and Beth could see the river. It was a deep brown, almost black, foaming where it rushed over rocks, and she thought she could smell it even from here.

They approached it, slithering down the bank, and stood

at the edge. The river was huge, gleaming, furiously noisy, cascading with a primal power. It managed to be both viscous and torrential. Beth didn't like it at all. The smell of it filled the air, and the steaming mist rose off it in coils and jets. It bubbled like thick, boiling soup.

'Seriously,' Beth said. 'How deep is it?'

'Good question.' Shan called down one of the Drones, and pointed to the river. 'Give us a reading?'

The Drone shot across the water, skimming it like a pebble, swirling around as it sounded the depths with invisible beams.

They waited.

II

In Habitation 2, the Twelvie boy Reza almost collided with Lulu as he skidded around the curve of the corridor.

'Whoa, whoa. What's up?' She grabbed him by the shoulder, tried to stop him from rushing past.

'Nothing, I …' He seemed guilty, not meeting her stern gaze in the dim ochre glow of the backup lighting. 'Nothing. I wanted to see Maddi about something.'

'Well,' said Lulu, softening her tone, 'you're going the wrong way.' She extended a long finger to point down the corridor. 'Maddi's room is that way.'

'Yeah, I …' Reza shoved his hands into his pockets. 'She ain't answering her door, right? Hasn't done since the storm.'

Lulu spread her hands. 'Yeah, well, so what? Probably wants a bit of a rest before her next work duty.'

'Yeah, that's what I thought, but …'

Something was wrong. Reza was one of the tougher kids, one who'd spent a cycle or two down in the Coolers or on a Benighting, but he was reliable and didn't panic unnecessarily.

She remembered the call Zach had taken on the radio as she left. Maddi hadn't turned up for her watch. Very unlike her.

'Let's see,' Lulu said, keeping her voice level and calm.

As they approached the solid oblong of Maddi's door, another door opened further up the corridor and Ella emerged, rubbing her eyes.

'Don't think she's in,' Ella said, as she strolled up to join them.

Lulu thumped her fist on the call-button, over and over. When there was no response, she banged on the door instead, sending great reverberating booms through the dome.

Lulu frowned. 'I'm starting to get a bad feeling about this.'

Ella put her mouth to the door. 'Maddi …! Mads, babe, you in there? C'mon, get your arse out here.' There was silence. 'We should tell Zach,' said Ella doubtfully.

'Zach's out on Lunar Beach, checking on the beacons. Ell, you and I are the senior ones here. We need to make this decision.'

The internal doors were old-fashioned sliding doors with catches and bolts which could be operated manually. When Lulu touched the door, they realised it was not even secured – it slid open with minimal effort.

'Mads?' Ella called. 'Only us. You all right?'

The room was covered with the usual clutter. Beyond, the swing-door to the sleeping-area was half-open, with darkness beyond. They entered – Ella first, graceful and almost silent, followed by Lulu and then Reza.

There was a strange, rusty smell in the room.

In the next few seconds, Lulu knew, as she pushed the bedroom door open, that the future of the colony was about to be changed for ever. She struggled to focus on what was in front of her, held out an arm to hold Reza back.

It was too late, though. They all saw it. A tableau out of a nightmare.

Maddi lay on her back on the bed, arms spread wide, on top of the silver thermal covering.

A thick, dark stain surrounded her. More had dried in a treacly pool on the floor, almost reaching Lulu's boots as she stepped inside. The hot, rusty stench of blood filled the room.

Lulu's hand went to her mouth.

Maddi's red hair was spread out in a fan. Her arms hung down, limply, fingers almost touching the floor. She was staring unblinkingly at the ceiling. Her grey, waxy face was streaked with dark, clotted blood, matting her hair.

The wooden hilt of a knife protruded from Maddi's throat.

The shining blade was embedded so deeply in her flesh that it had emerged from the back of her neck, pinning her lifeless body to the bed.

III

'How much further?' Beth wiped a hand across her face. Sweat was pouring into her eyes, her forehead grimy and greasy.

'Keep going,' said Shan, behind her. His voice sounded gravelly, deadened by the mist.

Beth was trying not to be sick with fear. The thick, sludgy water, noxious, now more like a muddy swamp, felt at every step as if it was trying to pull her down and swallow her up. She was in the middle of the party, behind Mia and Shan and ahead of Baljeet. Bringing up the rear, Baljeet managed a kind of elegance, sweeping her gun constantly back and forth, watching the bubbling, steaming water and the river-bank. Shan held the scan-pad in one gloved hand. Its comforting, rhythmic beep was all that was keeping Beth sane.

The Drone had judged the water as being shallow enough to wade. They had advanced only halfway across the vast expanse of the steaming river, and the far bank was still not clearly visible. The mist, clammy and peppery, obscured everything. Beth knew she had to keep on, waist-deep in the tepid, putrid water. Trudge. Trudge. Water swirled around them, acrid yellow clouds enveloping them.

She could barely see Shan or Mia, but she knew Shan was in front of her because of the constant, soft beeping of the detector. Baljeet she could neither see nor hear.

And then – movement out of the corner of her eye. A disruption in the mist, something that was almost a shape, but not quite.

She jumped. 'What the hell was that …?'

'Nothing,' said Baljeet, right behind her. '*Keep going!*'

It wasn't exactly that she had seen something … More a sense … She looked straight ahead, fixed on the blur of Shan's back that she could see through the mist.

The mist seemed to gather like curtains, forming a thick, velvety swathe around her. Panicking, she lost all sense of direction, like someone deep under water in darkness.

She opened her mouth to shout, but nothing came out – her throat was paralysed, like in a dream. The mist stung her throat, searing like a poison gas. It was raw against her lips and tongue, and her attempt to scream came out as a croak.

She swivelled round in the water, panicking, calling their names.

'Mia! Shan!'

The thick mud beneath her boots was creeping up her legs, like something grasping her and trying to pull her down beneath the water.

'Balj! *Mia!*'

Beth's body lost its strength. Panic rose in her stomach. Desperately she turned, turned again, covering her immediate surroundings with the gun, trying to remember everything Mia had taught her.

Something warm was slithering against her calf, coiling around her leg.

And she screamed.

Wet, squelching, *alive*. It surged upwards, grasping her calf tightly, curling up her leg and pulling her down into the water, waist-deep, chest-deep, further still. She fought, panicked, filthy water splashing up all around her, and then she lost her footing and fell into the steaming river.

For a second Beth was under, panicking, unable to see. She kicked, desperately trying to free herself from the tendril coiling tightly around her leg.

She broke the surface, screaming, spitting the foul water. She was able to draw her pistol up above the water, level it with both hands, fire a warning shot. It ripped through the air like a jet from a flamethrower, igniting the mist with a blue fire. Flames spiralled, fell in a football-sized fireball into the water with a sizzle and a pop. Beth floundered in the water, spitting it out, trying to aim again.

In front of her, the water surged, became concave.

She shook with fear. She was going to be sick.

Where the hell were the others?

The water continued to lift, a gleaming, sticky mass. The thing was huge, dark brown, segmented and ridged like a worm. It lifted its body, rearing high above her, a flat, long snout moving back and forth as if sniffing its way. A smell like rotting flesh filled the air.

The snout opened into a mouth, its two halves leaving glutinous trails of goo as they separated. A foul, animal stench hit her in the face. Beth, paralysed with fear, was staring into a giant purple maw, streaming with mud and water and green drool, and it was slowly swinging round towards her, its body thrashing in the water. It hissed, dribbling hungrily.

Tendrils tightened on both her legs. Pulling her closer

to the creature. Keeping hold of the gun with one hand, she desperately tried to grab anything she could with the other. Weeds ripped. Her hand slipped from wet rocks.

Time slowed.

Beth stared into the cavernous mouth, her body numb. The creature's hungry, salivating hisses grew louder.

Not even thinking about it, she levelled her arms, both hands on the gun, finger on the trigger.

She tried to right herself in the water, but every second, the tugging of the tendrils made her lose her footing on the slippery river-bed. The tendrils curled up from the steaming surface, breaking the water with a thrashing motion. Curling around her arms, trying to tug them downwards. Mud streamed down her face. She aimed the gun.

With a steaming hiss and a click, a dozen sharp, bone-white teeth emerged from the creature's mouth, like knives being unsheathed.

Beth resisted the slimy tendrils, trying to lift the gun as high as she could.

She could not pull the trigger.

Beth was shaking in the water. Her head felt wrong. A ringing in her ears and a strange blurring of her vision. Something was not connecting. She was sending the message from her brain down to her fingers, and they would not obey.

The creature reared its head. It hissed, lunged.

Beth's mouth opened in a silent scream.

One plasma bolt, then another, tore into the creature, ripping open its flesh below the neck. Blood sprayed into the mist. It screeched, thrashing in the water. The tendrils slackened and Beth hauled herself upwards, unable to believe what was happening.

The creature's head tilted sideways as it thrashed in pain, blood fountaining everywhere.

Mia. In the shallow water, legs braced, gun levelled, her expression cold and hard. The creature, spurting green blood, thrashed in the water, turning, spraying Beth with mud. Its screeching death-throes were unearthly, terrifying.

Mia fired again.

This time, she blew the creature's brains clean out of its skull.

Pulverised flesh sprayed in all directions across the river, lifted into the sky like a vapour cloud. The headless creature sprayed blood, its liquefied brain and entrails streaming down its body. A putrid stench like rotting eggs filled the air. And then it twisted, falling with a gigantic splash.

The water seethed and bubbled, closing over the dead creature, absorbing it.

The creature's remains, a sizzling rainstorm of fine green paste, spattered into the water across a wide radius, some falling on Beth and Mia's hair and shoulders.

Only now did Mia lower her pistol.

Beth stared in horror at the spot in the swirling, steaming river where the creature's body had sunk without trace.

'Good shot,' she heard herself say dimly. She turned away, and then vomited cleanly and carefully into the water. Bile splattered the surface, fizzing as it was absorbed.

'I was aiming for its head first time.' Mia's tone was cold, angry. She waded into the water, grabbed Beth's hand. 'Come on. There will be others.'

'Others?' Beth, wiping her mouth, looked fearfully over her shoulder.

'Yes. Come on! I don't want to waste more ammo.'

Waste. The implication of the word was not lost on her.

She glared at Mia. 'I *tried* to shoot it. I did everything right. I did what you said. I couldn't pull the trigger.'

Mia's cold, hard eyes met hers. Her taut body tensed.

For a second, Beth flinched, thinking Mia might be about to hit her. Then Mia's expression softened, and together they ran for the far bank.

IV

Lulu began to shake uncontrollably, her hand over her mouth. She knew, though, that she had to hold it together for the others.

'Lulu.' Ella's voice was sharp, decisive. Reza was cowering behind, his expression unreadable. '*Lulu!*' Ella snapped again.

'Yes, yes … all right …' Lulu pulled a pair of plastic gloves from her satchel, bent down next to Maddi's body. Somehow, she gathered the composure that she needed. She did her job, tried to remain calm, clinical. 'Single … knife blow to the throat … Massive blood loss …' She gently touched Maddi's face, felt her neck for a pulse. There was nothing.

'So much blood,' said Reza softly.

Ella looked at him, not unkindly. Lulu guessed the boy had not seen much of this sort of thing in his life. 'That's the human body for you. Anything, Lu?'

Lulu's eyes were stinging with tears as she ran the scan-pad across Maddi, searching for any sign. Anything at all. The readings only confirmed what she already knew. Lulu spread her hands helplessly. 'She ... she ...'

'Lu, you *have* to tell me if you've got something here.'

Lulu straightened up. 'I'm sorry. She's been dead for ... three to five hours.'

'From, like, the knife-wound?' Reza asked quietly. 'Or something else?'

Lulu didn't actually think that was such a stupid question. She had seen many dead people before – more than she cared to remember, more than was healthy at her age – and she knew that appearances could be deceptive. Even with something as obvious as a knife to the neck.

'I'll need to do a proper PM,' Lulu said. 'But it's pretty clear the blade ... pierced her left internal jugular. Sliced right through the carotid. If it severed the trachea, then, well ... she'll have had massive haemorrhaging into the pulmonary cavity.'

'What's that mean?' Reza's voice was quiet, frightened.

'I mean she'll have bled into her lungs.' Lulu could not believe how calm her voice was. She let the simple, chilling phrase hang in the air.

Ella winced, rubbing her arm.

'You all right?' Reza asked.

She waved it off. 'It's nothing. Go on.'

'So,' Reza said. 'This … this is murder.'

Ella glared at him. 'Yeah, she's been stabbed in the neck, Reza. It's not generally a great way to commit suicide.'

'What the hell …' Reza stared wildly. 'What's happening here? Who'd wanna kill *Maddi*, of all people?'

'I know,' Ella muttered. 'If I was going to stab someone here, it would be one of the annoying ones. Like Colm. Or you.'

'Thanks a lot.'

'You're welcome.'

Lulu tried to quell her own fears, to keep her voice calming, sensible. 'We need to decide what to do next.'

Ella was thinking fast. 'We tell Zach as soon as he gets back. We don't tell anyone else yet. We don't want mass panic on our hands.'

'People oughta know,' Reza said.

'No!' Ella rounded on him, and he shrank back into the wall. 'When people think things are going to hell, they start to act stupid.'

'I'll need to take her to the mortuary,' Lulu said.

What they grandly called 'the mortuary' was a small, chilly space deep below Habitation 1. Lulu had been down there when Janie died, and the others before her. It was kept cold by a simple process of coolant induction. In terms of its equipment, it was nothing like anything Lulu had encountered in her Accelerated Medical Training. It reminded her of the learning modules about Old Earth in the early days of machinery. It was basic, stark, functional – the best they could hope for.

Ella was brisk, cold. 'We can do it with two Drones and a corpse capsule. We need to be discreet about this.'

'I'll need your help,' Lulu said.

'I'll get her room sealed off. We can make something up. I'll put a Drone on guard outside the door.'

'What about, like, cleaning up?' Reza asked.

'Not yet,' Ella said. 'We need to find out who did this. And we don't have the kind of equipment the Lawguards do, so we're gonna have to use our initiative ... Right?'

Reza, though, was staring over her shoulder. 'What's that?' he asked, pointing at the wall by Maddi's bed. It seemed Maddi's trailing finger had smeared blood across the wall in a descending line. But, a hand's width above the floor, the smears seemed to form a pattern.

Ella and Lulu crouched down together, staring at the swirls of dried blood. Ella flipped her scan-pad out and recorded the image, going in close and pulling out again. Lulu's heart thumped in fear, her mind spinning with the terrible possibilities.

'Some kind of message, yeah?' Reza asked from behind them.

The pattern seemed to be made up of three distinct parts. The first was like the shape of a flying bird at an angle, two curves linked together. The second was a single, vertical line. And the third was a rough, spiky triangle.

Ella straightened up. 'I know what it looks like.'

Lulu had her hand to her mouth. 'It can't, it–'

'What?' Reza said. 'It's a scrawl.'

'It's not just a scrawl,' Ella snarled. Her hand darted out, pointing at the wall, tracing the outline of the three shapes. 'Sort of an M … and then an I … and an A. Are we agreed?'

Lulu stared at Ella in horror. 'You think …?'

'I don't know what to think. But Maddi, in her last moments, obviously did. A message. Something so important that she used her dying energy, her own blood, to write it on the wall.'

'Not *Mia*,' Reza said. 'It can't be. I don't believe it.'

'Maybe it's something we have to *tell* Mia,' said Lulu. 'Or something only Mia would know.'

She and Ella squatted down, staring intently at the dark wooden hilt of the knife protruding from Maddi's neck. Lulu took in the horrific gash of the wound, at the sliced and severed organs within.

'Here's another complication,' Ella said softly. She pointed to the knife. 'Anyone recognise this …? It's not a hunting knife. Not Mia's.'

'Then …' Reza's eyes widened. 'Whose?'

Ella slowly looked up at them over the handle of the knife. Lulu could see that her face was full of a dark, terrible rage.

'I think we can easily find out,' she said.

V

'Here,' Shan said, and came to a halt beside the steaming, broiling expanse of blue-green lake in front of them.

Beth had kept close to the others. She did not know if they had any more idea than she did about what kind of creatures could be lurking here at the edge of the lake, but she wasn't taking any chances. She felt safer the closer she was to them – especially Mia. She was drying off rapidly, steam pouring off her, her clothes tight and uncomfortable. But the thudding of her heart had eased to something more like a normal rate. She was determined to show the others that she could cope.

'All right. Send it in.'

The Drone, at a nod from Baljeet, hovered over the steaming surface of the lake, casting a cone of green light on the water.

Slowly, it lowered itself until it was poised right above the water itself.

'Is it going to be all right?' Beth asked worriedly. 'How good are they underwater?'

'Yeah, they're designed for all-environment survival,' Shan said, not turning towards her. He was watching the Drone intently. 'They can withstand immersion of up to ten minutes at depths of more than thirty emms. And this lake isn't that deep.'

'What if it has to be down there for longer?' Beth asked, watching the Drone with a feeling of sadness.

Shan's reply was casual. 'If we lose one, we lose one.' He turned and grinned at her. 'They're not *people*, Beth. They're tools. Objects.'

'Have you lost any so far?'

'Two or three, maybe. Motor units cut out, circuits blown. It's no big deal.'

The Drone hovered closer and closer to the surface of

the water. Then, slowly, it began to immerse itself, until it was a hemisphere, and then completely under the surface, so that all they could see was the green of its tracker beam.

The hot, close jungle, muddy and steaming, was a horrible contrast to Town. Twisted spiky blue trees reached up almost as far as the eye could see, blotting out all but a tiny patch of sky. The rolling yellow mist, harsh and sulphurous, stole across the water and through the trees, like a predatory animal itself. Deep within the dark vegetation and swampy ground behind them, strange clicks and rattles could be heard, screeches and howls of unseen creatures.

Mia sidled closer to Beth. 'You doing all right?' she asked.

'All right. Thank you. Is that … *thing* typical of the local wildlife?'

Mia grinned. 'Bastards, yeah. We've only seen three or four of them. They're not edible so we tend to ignore them. Pretty buggers, aren't they?'

'Was it going to *eat* me?'

'Nah, they're vegetarians,' Mia said, deadpan.

'Really?' Beth asked, wide-eyed.

'Oh, for crying out … Yes, of course it was going to eat you, Spacegirl. Jeez. What else do you imagine it was doing? Trying to say hello?' Mia laughed, spat on the ground. 'Welcome to big bad life, Beth. Anything that doesn't want to fuck you wants to eat you … Actually, some might want to do both. The Galaxy's not a nice place.'

'I see,' said Beth, blushing at her naivety. 'Thank you for the warning.'

Out of instinct, her hand went for comfort to her belt, where she kept her knife. The holster was empty. Panicking, she felt all round, inside her pockets even, searching on the ground.

'You okay?'

'Yes, but … damn, I've lost my knife.' She cursed softly, remembering the confusion of the struggle with the river-beast, and her desperation to keep her balance while firing the gun. The knife had to have fallen out, lost for ever in the dark water. 'Still, at least …'

Beth did not get a chance to finish her sentence. At that very second, the water bulged and hissed, and the Drone, soaked in mud and trailing spiky, glistening tendrils of veg-etation, emerged from the water.

Attached to the bottom of the Drone, fixed firmly to it by one of the robot's internal clamps, was a larger globe, water pouring off its iridescent, glassy surface as the Drone lifted it out.

Shan grinned. 'Well, what do you know? These things are built to last.'

Beth gawped at it. 'That's a neutron exchange converter?'

'Pretty, isn't it?' Mia said, as the Drone flew across the water to join them, bringing its treasure.

As it came closer, Beth could see the surface of the con-verter was nothing like as fragile and glassy as it had appeared from a distance. It was made of a toughened, re-silient material, hard as stone. It was pitted and scarred from its time underwater, smeared with mud, but still almost intact.

Mia patted the converter lightly. 'In good shape.'

'All that time underwater,' said Beth. 'You're seriously trying to tell me that thing will still work?'

'If anything,' Baljeet said, 'the mud will have helped to preserve it.' She grinned. 'Collective tech. Sometimes you've gotta be grateful.'

Shan checked his scan-pad. 'About three hours until full night. We should be fine. Let's get it back.'

VI

As Zach approached Town, checking over the readings he had taken on the scan-pad, he was whistling cheerfully. However, as he reached the perimeter fence, it didn't take him long to realise something was very wrong.

He punched the entry-code into the lock, waited for the gates to slide open.

He could see various young Towners busying them-selves around the compound – Amber fixing a jeep's wheel, Brad and Malachi kicking a ball in the mud by the hangar – but his eye was drawn, as ever, to Lulu.

She stood by the ramp in front of the Main Dome, arms folded, feet apart, waiting. Her bright blue eyes were fixed firmly on him. She wore a cloak made out of a dark blanket and fastened with a metal hasp from some broken piece of equipment or other. The cloak ruffled in the wind, giving her the air of some prophetess of doom.

His pace slowed. He met Lulu's gaze as the gates clanged shut behind him.

His mouth was dry and dusty. He felt as if each heavy step was taking him nearer and nearer to a horrible, inevitable truth. He came closer, closer. He could see that her eyes were red-rimmed, her face full of a terrible sadness.

'What is it?' he asked. 'What's wrong?'

'You need to come inside,' she said. 'Now.'

∞

And so all begins to be lost.

The heart of the group, the soul. The one they thought they could all rely on, all turn to. Gone.

Piece by piece, they begin to unravel.

It is too late for them to stop.

9
CUCKOO

I

Zach needed to be alone. So he was in the Ship.

The expedition party was back. Power had returned to Town as night fell. The booster, thanks to a lot of tinkering – and swearing – from Ella, Amber, Robbie and Shan, had been fitted. Lights shone in all the domes, and the radar dish swept back and forth once more. However, he could take no pleasure in this.

The great Ship. He looked out over the silo, thinking, his breath misting in the cold air.

The Ship had brought them here in semi-animation. It had come in low and fast over the forests and swamps as it attempted to lock in on the planet's sole remnant of human civilisation. The abandoned island base they called Town.

They had no idea what had gone on here before – some sort of geological survey was the general consensus, judging by the few abandoned tools and maps they had found gathering dust in various parts of the domes. Well, it didn't matter. This was their home.

A home where one of them was a murderer.

Maddi Vanderbilt. Gone. Killed.

How was this possible? How had he allowed this to happen? What could Maddi, of all people, have possibly done to upset anyone?

Deep in thought, burning with anger and hatred and confusion, he wandered up and down the aisles of Semi-Anna capsules. He let his hand caress the smooth surface of one of them, picked up the end of one of the broken tubes.

Life. How fragile it was …

Fragile life, maintained all that way by these devices which were, at their most basic, really devised for the transportation of livestock.

And then something clicked inside Zach's mind, and a memory floated into place. Lulu, standing by his bedroom door. The Drone floating out. He slipped a hand inside his pocket, pulling out the folded piece of paper from Bethany Kane's notebook, holding it up to the light.

Numbered circles. Ten rows of five.

He lowered the paper, staring out across the Semi-Anna capsules.

Forty-eight, forty-nine … fifty.

And as soon as he stopped to think about it, he realised that it was something he could easily have worked out, long ago. Perhaps he hadn't allowed himself to. Perhaps he didn't want to.

Long ago on Mars, Zachary Tal had been a gifted child in the Gold Academy, one of the most prestigious institutions of learning in Olympus City. At six years old, he had met the Librarians. He was allowed to explore a wide range of books, Lumi-casts, old discs and info-cubes and holovids with their help. The Librarians were such an integral part of learning, so treasured, that he could not believe there had once been a time when they were on the point of vanishing. Cast out by unthinking, mean-spirited regimes on Earth whose idea of learning was the simple, placid regurgitation of facts.

The Gold Academy treated sources of information,

whether on paper, on info-cube or in Clouds, as vibrant, living things, not dusty old relics. From one of the treasured Books, Zach had learned about the birds and animals on Earth long ago. He had remembered one story in particular. The story of a bird called the *cuckoo*. A bird which did not make its own home, but instead secreted its eggs, camouflaged, in the nests of other birds, so that these other birds would bring it up as one of their own.

In the cargo silo, he crumpled the paper in his fist in anger.

They had a cuckoo.

And it was not Bethany Kane.

In the control room, it took Zach about five minutes to download the information he needed from the Ship's computer to his scan-pad. He called Ella, Mia and Shan on the radio, ordered them to meet him in the Sky-Gallery in five minutes.

He strode angrily from the airlock, his feet clanging on the metal steps.

He emerged into the glare of the daylight, focusing straight ahead. Younger Towners stopped their stick-fighting and their running around, scattered to hide.

He crossed the compound, clenching and unclenching his fists, feeling his head throbbing with tiredness and pain. This new development could mean a great many things. He had to get it sorted out. He crossed the Rec Hall, ascending the stairs in under a minute. On the way he passed Amber and Robbie coming down with a toolkit.

'Have you two got that bloody radar dish fixed yet?'

'Give us a chance, boss,' Amber said. 'Only just finished checking them locks in Habitation 1, like.'

'Well, get on with it, for God's sake.'

'Yeah, chill.'

Amber gave him a mock salute. He didn't miss the fact that it turned into a middle-finger gesture as he turned his back and carried on up the stairs, but he didn't have time to stop and admonish her. He had other things on his mind.

The others were already waiting for him, talking worriedly and curiously. They looked up when they saw him coming, as if guilty, he thought. What were they talking about? For a second he wondered if they, his most trusted Towners, were plotting against him. He pushed the thought to the back of his mind.

'You need to see this,' he said, and his hand flipped across his scan-pad, projecting a cone of light in which a stream of letters and numbers danced.

'What *is* that?' Mia asked.

'That,' said Zach, 'is the cargo manifest from the Ship. It's always been there. We haven't needed it before.' He flipped his scan-pad again, and the list shrank to a smaller size. 'Those are all the organic components.'

'Organic components?' Shan reached out, caressing the holographic letters and watching them dance on his hand. 'Oh, that means us – right?'

'Well done, Shan,' said Zach. 'The organic cargo is us.'

'And?' said Ella, scowling. 'What's the point of this?'

'The Drones have a visual record of everyone in Town,'

Zach said. 'They can identify any one of us, if they want to, right? They recognised Beth as an intruder straight away.'

Mia, Ella and Shan looked at each other. They still were not getting it.

'The Drones,' said Zach, 'have a visual record of every member of this community, Beth included.'

He lifted a hand and called over the nearest Drone as it bounced past, a black one bearing the number 220. With an obedient buzz and whirr, the Drone came to rest in the circle of humans, its red light flicking back and forth between Mia, Shan, Ella and Zach like an inquisitive eye.

'Give me a display of your visual record of everyone in Town,' Zach said to the Drone. 'Relay it to here.' He tapped the scan-pad.

The Drone's light pulsed. It was done. Zach swiped the scan-pad once and another cone of light fountained up, this time showing globes of sparkling luminescence, bouncing around together like particles in Brownian motion.

'Right,' said Zach. 'We need to cross-reference the cargo manifest with this … and …' He thumbed the scan-pad. 'Eliminate Beth first.' He brought up Beth's face – the Drone's first visual record of her, battered and bloodied, emerging from the Pod. That globe vanished in a shower of pixels. 'Then our fallen Brothers and Sisters …' The faces of Kai, Leila, Janie, Faiz, Thom and Maddi flared briefly in the light, then scattered. 'And everyone else. One by one.'

The three senior Towners were drawn to the coruscating display as it brought up face after face. The globes vanished like popping bubbles as their identities were cross-referenced with the cargo manifest. Finn, Amber, Aisling, Nasreen, Malachi, Ella, Shan ... One by one, they flared in the light and disappeared, until four bubbles were left floating, orbiting like planets around a sun.

Zach, Reza, Gabe and Xara.

They watched.

Nobody dared breathe. They had all realised that this was important, even if they did not quite understand why.

Zach's bubble disappeared in a blaze of light. Then Gabe's went. Time seemed to stand still as they waited for the final cross-check. The bubbles containing the images of Xara and Reza looped in the air in endless ellipses, bounced off one another like billiard-balls.

Then Xara's bubble fizzed and dissolved. Leaving Reza's face, alone, looming large in the fountain of light.

'Got him.' Zach's voice was low and cold.

Shan frowned. 'I don't get it. Reza ... why?'

Zach jabbed at the image of Reza, his finger poking through the boy's hologrammatic face. 'One left. Don't you see?'

Ella had got it. She had drawn her gun already. 'Reza,' she said. 'Damn him.'

'I know where he is,' Mia said.

'Will someone please explain to me what's going on?' asked Shan patiently. 'I'm not doing *anything* until I know.'

Zach snapped off the display, and the light rushed back into the scan-pad like water down a plughole. 'The cargo manifest and the Drones' visual record of Town aren't a perfect match. There are fifty-two people in the Drones' current record. Take away Beth, that leaves fifty-one, count-ing our dead.'

He paused.

'But only fifty Semi-Anna capsules. Only fifty of us on the manifest – and one who shouldn't be here.'

II

'*En garde!*'

Xara, laughing, pushed back her tangle of messy, knotted hair as she raised her makeshift wooden sword – not much more than a sharpened stick – ready to parry Reza. They circled each other in the blue dust beneath the shade of the Comms tower.

The boy grinned, confident that he had the upper hand. 'Not this time. You are going *down.*'

'Oh, I don't think so!' Xara lunged, and then stopped. Reza had lost concentration, lowering his wooden stake so he held it loosely by his side. 'Reza! You idiot! What are you doing?'

He backed away, looking over Xara's shoulder at the party advancing towards them from Town. Zach, Ella, Mia, Shan, framed in the sunlight. Three Drones floating behind them like a rearguard.

Xara frowned. 'What? What is it? I don't understand.'

Reza backed slowly away, right under the Comms tower. Then he dropped his stake, turned and ran. Feet pounding the ground, dust flying up. He pushed two younger Towners aside, ignoring their squeals. His mouth dry, his heart pounding, he ran and ran, hitting the perimeter fence, desperately seeking the way in.

He knew it was all over. He had to get away. But the fence was there, always there. He slammed himself up against it in frustration, his fists pounding it.

Where was the gap? Finn and Cait had said something … It had been sealed.

Gasping, sobbing, he fell slowly to his knees in the dust, his mouth dry and his eyes stinging with tears.

Ella was there beside him first.

'Get up, Reza.' Her voice was cold, her gun, held in both hands, levelled straight at his head.

Fearful, he got to his feet. He was astonished at how quickly Ella had moved, her long and powerful limbs covering the ground while the others were still some way behind. She was so much faster than everyone else, he realised – almost unbelievably so.

He did not have time to think about that now, though. Zach, Mia and Shan caught up, all four Magna pistols levelled at him. He pressed himself against the chain-link fence, sweating in fear.

'Please. You've got to understand. I didn't know what else to do …! I was alone. Alone!'

He had always known this would happen. He was surprised it had not happened sooner. But, the longer he had gone undiscovered, the stronger his belief had become that he had got away with it. Being discovered, when he had almost forgotten he was not supposed to be there, was almost more of a shock than if he'd been found out earlier.

Zach's face clouded, and Reza saw him look uncertainly at Ella.

'We don't know it was him.' This was Shan – his voice soft, reasonable as ever. 'Let him speak. Let him explain.'

'Did you take Beth's knife from the Ship?' Mia snapped.

'Mia!' Zach's face twisted in fury. 'You've told him …'

'Beth's knife?' Reza's mind whirled in confusion. 'What …? I don't …'

Shan was the first to lower his gun. 'I don't think he did it.'

Zach and Mia turned towards Shan – Zach angrily, Mia more interestedly. Only Ella kept both her gun and her eyes fixed unwaveringly on Reza.

'Steady, Shan,' Ella said. 'I don't trust him.'

Reza was gabbling in panic. 'Please. I didn't kill Maddi. I didn't take anyone's knife and I … please …! I'll explain. I'll explain everything.'

There was a pause. Life on the Edge seemed to hang in the balance, the four senior Towners each waiting for another to make the first move. The Drones buzzed around, swishing in agitation, as if they sensed Reza's discomfort.

'Then what the hell …?' Zach began.

'A pod,' said Reza. 'There's … there's a pod. I can take you.'

'A *pod*?' Zach repeated.

'I crashed here. My brothers … they died … I thought I was alone, and then … And then you.'

Mia's eyes widened in recognition. And Mia was the next to lower her gun. Zach and Ella kept theirs trained on him, though.

'He's telling the truth,' said Mia.

'*What?*'

Zach was almost spitting in anger. Reza could see the vein pulsing beneath his cropped hair. He'd always thought Zach was dangerous, a leader about to tip over into illogic, even insanity. And now, it seemed he was there. Zach frightened him more than any of the others.

Reza met Mia's gaze. 'You've seen it,' he said, grasping at this hope.

'A Survival One ejector. Yes. I saw it in the enclave, near where I swim. A Lantrill led me to it.'

'A *Lantrill*?' It was Ella's turn to sound almost angrily incredulous. She rounded on Mia. 'What are you talking about?'

'I found it, before the storm,' Mia said softly. 'About twenty K from here, in jungle sector 4. It's buried, hidden …' She moved towards Reza, holding out a hand. 'It's fine. You can tell us.'

'Mia, what the hell …?' Zach's gun-arm did not waver.

Reza's knees almost gave way, but Mia stepped forward, caught him. Her arms were around him as sobs wracked his body, everything dissolving into chaos and weakness.

'We need to get him inside,' said Mia softly.

III

Beth, swigging water from a bottle, strode along the edge of the hangar, heading for the Main Dome. She almost didn't see Colm in time as he stepped out in front of her.

She nearly choked on her water, spluttering it across the ground.

'Stop sneaking up on me, you rat!'

He had somehow contrived to emerge from the shadows, hands in his pockets, mocking smile on his face as usual. His hair was spiked up as if he hadn't brushed it in days.

Her heartbeat increased. No, she thought. Stop that.

'Thought I'd check in on you,' he said. 'I hear you had a rough time out there in the jungle. Almost got yourself eaten.'

She folded her arms. 'I coped. Tell me, Colm, how do you manage to avoid doing any of the nasty jobs round here? Nobody else seems to get away with it.'

He moved in close to her, hand on the hangar wall, so that she found herself backed against the metal. 'Oh, I'm a clever boy,' he said. 'Others *want* to do stuff, right? I mean, Zach's always got to play a game of Whose Is Biggest.'

She laughed. 'You're so horrible. And yet so right.'

'And Mia, well, Mia's a psycho. Shan's always … so kind and so *keen*. And lots of the Thirteeners don't dare step outta line. No, they're never short of mugs round here to shovel the shit.'

'No. Indeed.' She gave him a wry smile, aware of how close his face was to hers. 'You're not a *bad* person, Colm Dale, but you make sure your own …' She blushed. 'Your own backside is covered. Don't you?'

He laughed. 'That's my girl. Spoken like a true Towner. And what about yours?' He patted her bottom. 'It's a very nice one.'

'Do *not* do that.' She shoved him, held up an admonishing finger. 'Please. I am not a piece of meat, Colm.'

'Who says you are?' He stepped back, hands spread. 'I just appreciate beauty in all its forms.'

He moved in again, slowly. This time she did not push him away. His forehead rested against hers, their mouths were a breath apart. She was annoyed with herself at how her pulse raced, how much she was perspiring.

'I smell like a swamp,' she said, smiling, embarrassed.

'Believe me, I've known far worse.'

'No, seriously. My breath, it's like ... Pure Lantrill meat.'

'Seems fine from where I am,' he said, his mouth almost touching hers.

'Why do I ...? Great Power, forgive me. I do not even *like* you, Colm.' She was laughing as she said it.

'Aww, who says you have to *like* me? Such an old-fashioned idea.' He slipped his hands around her waist. She tensed. 'So,' Colm said, lowering his voice to a murmur. 'What age do good little ChapterSisters get their implant these days?'

Her mouth formed an O at the shocking directness of the question, and yet she found herself answering without even pausing to think whether it was any of his business. 'Fourteen,' she said.

'Nice. So you're all fired up and ready to go.'

'You are so *rude*!' She shoved his chest, genuinely offended, feeling herself turning bright red. And yet she didn't want to walk away.

'Oh, come on,' he murmured, moving close to her again.

'Don't tell me your Blessed Chapter of Perpetual ... Whatsit objects to a bit of ... fun?'

'Continual Progress. And no, it does not *object*, but one is encouraged to have ... agency. To have responsibility.'

'Oh, yeah?' His mocking eyes opened wide.

'Yes! It's seen as a loving manifestation of the Great Power working in humanity. The physical expression of one's ... attraction to another human being is a ... powerful thing. Congress is deeply honoured, Colm, not ... *disapproved* of.'

'Congress!' He laughed, squeezed her waist. 'What a word.'

'What's wrong with that word?'

'Nothing, nothing ... It's a bit ... *scientific*. Why don't you be normal and call it fucking, like everybody else does?'

She looked away, feeling her face flush hotly again. She was trying not to laugh at how prim and cross her own voice sounded. 'I do not *like* profanity. Especially that word. It's ... coarse. Crude.'

'Yeah. That's why I want to hear you say it, Space Princess.'

'*Colm*!'

'Come on,' he said, and laughed. 'I'm messing with you.'

The heat as he drew near. His breath on her mouth. Her whole body tingled in anticipation.

'All right,' she murmured, feeling her heart thudding. She slipped her arms around his neck. She drew her mouth close to his ear, licking her lips. 'The Chapter of Continual Progress,' she whispered, 'does not ... disapprove ... of fffff–' Her voice tailed off, eyes widening as she stared over his shoulder.

'What? What is it?'

'Don't look now,' she whispered, drawing back, 'but we're being watched.'

'Where?'

He followed her gaze. The bobbing, red globe of Drone 356, its inquisitive red eye pulsing, hovered a short distance away. Colm and Beth slid apart, almost as if they both suddenly felt guilty.

'Go away!' Beth said, flushing with anger. 'This is private!'

The Drone did not obey at first. But then it turned, almost reluctantly, and bobbed off towards the Main Dome.

Colm turned, puzzled, to look at Beth. 'What the hell was all that about?'

'I do not know,' she said. 'That Drone, it … it is almost as if it's been watching me. As if it … cares about me.'

He laughed. 'You're high on swamp-gas. Need a lie down?'

'Possibly I do,' she murmured, gazing in the direction the Drone had gone. She turned back to face Colm again. 'You think I'm being silly?'

'Well, yeah, but that's just you.'

'Drones don't watch people. Not like that. Hell, this isn't a very hot conversation. Can we go back to having, y'know, the other conversation?'

'The mood has gone,' she said, 'for now. I will, ah … I will see you later.'

And as she strode off, she gave him a brief, flirtatious glance over her shoulder, to keep him guessing.

IV

Zach, jittering with suppressed anger, paced up and down in the dimly-lit room.

He was in the basement of the main Storage Dome, a storeroom which they had set aside for an interrogation. One stark, blue light shone down on the metal table and on the chair where Reza sat. Mia leaned against the wall, covering him unwaveringly with her gun, while Ella and Shan leaned either side of the door. The room was hot and stuffy, crackling with tension.

Zach leaned threateningly on the table. The boy wasn't even looking him in the eye. What was this? More insubordination?

'Look up,' he said. 'Look at me.'

Slowly, Reza lifted his head.

Zach read fear in the boy's expression, and it gave him a strange sense of satisfaction. Zach had been worried, these past few cycles, about losing authority. Losing respect. But it seemed he could still instil fear. That would have to do.

'Are you scared of me, Reza?' he asked quietly.

The boy drew back, making a dismissive noise and folding his arms. 'No.'

'Oh, I think you are, Reza,' he said softly. 'I would be, in your place.' Zach began to walk up and down in front of the table again. He hoped it was intimidating. 'You were the one who alerted people about Maddi. Perfect way to throw suspicion away from you.'

'I didn't kill Maddi,' the boy said angrily. 'Why would I, yeah? Why would *anyone*?'

'That's what we're trying to find out,' said Ella calmly. 'Answer the questions. Nobody's accusing you of anything.'

Zach continued. 'So, these are the facts, Reza. We check the cargo manifest, and we find an anomaly. We've got one too many in the colony. Seems we're making a habit of that kind of thing.'

'I'm not like *her*, am I? Been here since the start, ain't I?'

Zach leaned on the table, looming threateningly over the boy. 'I don't know, Reza. You tell us. What exactly happened?'

The boy's face was frightened, hunted. 'So it's, like, way back then. The impact pod, it come in on buffers. I think … Located a safe-zone. I think my brothers, yeah, they was already dead, like. We … we'd come from this cargo freighter, right? Deep space mission to the Outer Planets.'

Zach frowned, resuming his pacing up and down. 'I don't get it. What was a Twelvie – or however old you were then – doing on a cargo freighter with his brothers?'

'They wasn't my real brothers, like. I mean, not family. That's just what I call them. They was friends. Well … associates.'

Zach rolled his eyes. 'Right, so … what were you doing on a cargo freighter with these *associates*, whoever they were?'

Reza leaned back, grinned. 'You know what I'm good at,'

he said. 'Ducking and diving. Finding ways to stick it to the Collective.'

'Avoiding work, usually, is what you're good at,' said Ella. 'And getting into fights.'

Mia narrowed her eyes. 'That's a standard class Survival One pod they put you all in. You only normally put someone in one of those if they expect landing or pickup within minutes. They stuck you in that? Why? Who would do that?'

Reza looked shifty. 'We kinda … got caught.'

'Got caught? Doing what?'

'In the cargo bay,' he said. 'Loading stuff. Loot. Into our planet-hopper. We was on the freighter's hull, right? Locked on with a two-minute limpet. Molecular hull-breach. *Tssssh.*' Reza placed his fist against his palm, mimicking the movement of a smaller ship locking on to a larger one's hull. 'You breaks through and gets the job done quick, see? Chances are, with some of them old crates, they don't even, like, notice.'

Zach, Mia, Shan and Ella exchanged a look. It was starting to become clear.

'You were *pirates*,' said Mia. 'I knew it.'

'Well … yeah, we kinda don't call ourselves that.'

'Yeah, but you are, aren't you? Pirates, raiders … call yourselves what you like, boy. It's all the same.' Mia laughed, and lowered and holstered her gun. 'Raiding a Collective cargo freighter. You sneaky bastard. You're like us! You just came here at a different time.'

Like us, thought Zach. Another criminal. The cuckoo

was another mouth to feed. An interloper like Bethany Kane – only this one had been here hundreds of cycles, not just a few.

'So, what did they do?' Shan asked. He sounded concerned. 'Stick you in a survival pod and shoot you out into space?'

'Pretty much … Hey, I don't remember much, right …? I was in the jungle ten, maybe eleven cycles. I found water, fruit and stuff. I saw your ship come in low over the Mountains. The engines, they woke me up. I couldn't believe it. Thought you'd, like, come to rescue me.'

'Sense of your own importance,' said Mia. 'Get over it.'

'Yeah, right. Whatever. But, right, it was weird? I followed you down to the landing place. On the island. Right by Town. I'd not seen the island before. Didn't think to try, did I? Then I watched them Drones come out, and I thought, just my luck, it's an automated flight.'

Zach watched him and listened intently, waiting for any sign that the boy was lying. He was still not totally convinced.

'But I watch, yeah? I lie on the Sharp Ridge and watch. Days and days, like. I watch them building, cutting, repairing. Getting everything ready. And I think, hang on. That ain't right. They ain't doing all this shit for a bunch of robots, yeah? And that was when I figure it out. You're all in cold storage.'

'So what did you do? Mia asked curiously.

'Waited, watched. Them early days … There was loads of confusion, right? The Drones woke you up and people, like, wandered around. Not really knowing where stuff was. Your security wasn't that hot in them days. You hadn't fixed the gates, yeah? So I just came in. Joined up with the first bunch I found, first people I could see doing stuff.' He nodded to Zach. 'There was you, and Maddi. And Hal, Gabe and some others. Collecting wood and taking it into the compound. Nobody noticed one extra short guy.'

Zach sat down heavily opposite Reza. 'And all this time,' he said, 'you never thought to tell us?'

'Why should I? Part of Town, ain't I? One of you.' He grinned. 'And a crim. Like everyone else. So I thought I'd fit in really easy, like.'

'Really easy,' said Zach, his voice dangerously low. He stood up again, leaning threateningly over Reza. 'Did you kill Maddi Vanderbilt?'

'*No*! I swear! Why would I do that? Seriously ... *why*? I liked her. Everyone liked her.'

'Did you steal Bethany Kane's knife? Did someone bribe you, threaten you to do that? For someone else to use?'

'No *way*!' Reza looked away, shiftily. 'Look ... I ... I been in the Ship, right? Watching her, listening. She nearly saw me once. I listen a lot. Hang around on the edges of people's conversations. It's old habits. Just what I do.'

'Oh, great. You little eavesdropper. So have you been responsible for any of the power drains? The malfunction of Mia's glove, the attack on Ella? Sabotaging the generator?'

'Seriously, man. I would *not* know where to start with all that shit.' Reza looked shocked, terrified. 'You gotta believe me!'

'We're wasting time,' Mia said. 'He's telling the truth.'

'Agreed,' said Ella. 'He's here now. What are we going to do, put him back in space? Let him go, Zach.'

'I'll make that decision,' Zach said sharply.

Ella thumped the door-control, and the door to the interrogation room rumbled open. 'No point,' she said. 'Like Mia says, waste of time. We need him back on duty.'

Reza slowly lifted his head, hope in his face again.

Zach looked around at his three friends, anger slowly burning inside him. 'Shan?' he said. 'You've not said anything.'

Shan spread his hands. 'I dunno,' he said. 'It just … doesn't make sense for it to be him. Sorry, Zach. I gotta agree with the girls.'

Zach's face was taut with fury. 'So you're all saying you're overruling me?'

'Oh, give it up, Zach,' said Mia. 'It's gone beyond that.' She grabbed Reza by the shoulder. 'Scarper, you. And if you don't get your head down and work, I'll come and kick your arse. Got it?'

The boy gave her a playful salute. 'Understood. Got it. Yeah.'

Mia nodded her head towards the door, and Reza scampered out.

Zach watched him go, and then marched from the room, his face showing thunderous anger. The others hurried after him.

V

'Something's up,' said Amber. 'I don't like it.' Her hand dangled down. 'Torque wrench.'

Robbie was inside the tracking room of the Comms tower while Amber, on a magnetic stepladder clamped to the outside of the window, was fixing the damaged radar dish. He reached out, passing her the tool she had asked for.

'What do you mean?' he said. 'Something's always up.' Idly, he allowed his gaze to wander over Amber's slim brown legs, which were all that could be seen of her on the stepladder.

'I mean more than usual. I pick up on this crap.' Her hand dangled down again with the wrench, passing it back to him. 'Zeta corroder.'

Robbie rummaged through the box of battered tools, finally handing Amber a golden, screwdriver-like object which he hoped was the right one.

'Didn't you see how angry Zach was? Like there was something really bad going on.' There was an electronic whining sound from above, and a shower of sparks. 'Bugger,' said Amber quietly.

Robbie grinned, leaning up at her. 'You doing okay up there?'

'Yeah, almost burned my bloody fingers off. Why does nothing *work* in this shit-tip?'

'Because it's not supposed to,' he said. 'They didn't send us here to thrive. They sent us here to die.'

'I know,' she said, and she dangled the Zeta corroder

down for him to take. 'That's why things really worry me. Every cycle I think we're getting closer.'

'Cheerful thought. Are you done?'

'Yeah, well, it ain't gonna fall down and kill nobody today, I hope. Tomorrow, that's someone else's problem.'

'Why didn't you get a Drone to do it?' Robbie asked.

Amber scrambled back down the ladder, twisting herself elegantly in at the window and landing in a tangle of long limbs and tousled hair. 'Dunno,' she said, straightening up. 'Sometimes I prefer to get shit done myself.'

'If I was a Drone,' Robbie said, 'I'd get really pissed off doing all the boring jobs all the time. I'd want something more out of life.'

Amber laughed as she snapped her toolbox shut. 'You talk like they've got feelings, Robbo. They're only tools ... Right, time for a smoke. I've got two leaves of *plaan* drying in the workshop. C'mon.' She patted him on the bottom.

Robbie grinned wryly as he followed Amber down the Comms tower's spiralling metal stairs.

He had to admit, though, his friend was rarely wrong about this stuff. And there was a crackle of tension in the air in Town.

A sense of something about to explode.

VI

In Maddi's living-pod, all was still and quiet.

On Lulu's instructions, everything had been left exactly as it was. Nothing to be touched.

They didn't have any of the detection techniques the authorities would have had in a Collective city: black-light scans, a sub-atomic sweep, DNA pickup. They did not even have the means to do a simple fingerprint scan – technology thousands of years old, but still based on an infallible biological principle. All they had, as Lulu had said to Zach, was their eyes and ears and brains.

But still, Lulu had felt the room ought not to be disturbed, removal of the body aside. Ella had arranged that, with her usual brisk efficiency, two Drones taking Maddi's body down to the mortuary in a hermetically-sealed corpse capsule.

In the living-pod, then, everything was as it had been found, even the drying bloodstains. But one item lay abandoned on the desk, half-hidden under Maddi's drawings and notes and maps.

A small, metallic cylinder, tapered like a rocket. Scorched by its journey through the atmosphere.

It began to pulse with a soft red light.

Glowing from within, gently, as if echoing the rhythms of sleep. The light reached a peak, then died away. Then came on again, brightly, and died away. About one pulse every three seconds.

There was nobody there to see it.

VII

'Why the *hell* didn't you tell me about the Survival One pod?'

Mia found herself recoiling from Zach's anger as they walked briskly across the vast space of the Storage Dome. Hal and Aisling, who were checking boxes of supplies, kept their faces down as the older Towners passed, not daring to stare or even acknowledge. Ella and Shan followed on behind, at a less urgent pace.

'I ... dunno, Zach.' She realised how stupid it sounded. 'I was going to, and then ... There was Beth and that creature ... And the storm, and then Maddi ...'

'You didn't find the right *time*?' he asked acidly.

She could see that he had not re-holstered his gun yet. Instinctively, her body tautened. Mia had always felt safe with Zach. She did not any more.

'Yeah,' she said. 'That.'

Zach's face was burning with anger. 'We've got a killer on the loose. And all this time, someone was here who shouldn't be. Someone who saw our community and attached himself to it ... And nobody ever knew. Who was going to count? Everyone milling around ... Who knew if there were fifty, fifty-one, fifty-two people here?'

'But you don't really think he killed Mads.' Ella, catching them up, made it a statement, not a question. She was sure of it. 'Not Reza. Do you?'

For the first time since the new discovery, Mia saw Zach visibly relax. He stopped walking, turned to face the others, one by one.

'No,' he said. 'No, I don't.'

'Which means someone else did,' said Mia. 'And that's not good news. Because whoever it is, they're still on the loose here somewhere.'

'It was Beth's knife,' said Ella. 'And we haven't told her yet.'

Zach growled angrily, running a hand through his hair. 'How sure can we be about *any* of this? We're not Investigators, we're not Lawguards. We don't have a psi-tec in Town ... Do we think it was Beth ...? Ell?'

'I don't think so,' said Ella. 'Do you?' she asked Shan.

'I ... don't reckon,' he said. 'She carries that knife for show. There's ... There isn't anything *bad* about her. I mean, why? Why would she do it?'

'Why would anyone?' Zach said, slamming his hands against the plexiglass tube of the walkway. 'That's what makes me feel so bloody ... helpless. There's no reason for it. No reason for *anyone* to kill Maddi. It seems so ... *random.*'

Random. The word echoed in Mia's mind. He was right. That was the crazy thing about it. No motive presented itself, no meaning. It was as if someone had killed Maddi out of pure ... what?

Out of pure evil?

It would need to be someone deluded, Mia thought. Someone who, at the time of the murder, didn't know what they were doing. Who had lost their mind.

Perhaps someone who did not even remember doing it.

'What do you think?' Ella asked Mia.

She was careful not to share her darker thoughts. 'No … not Beth. Sure, she can whittle wood with it, cut bread … But kill? I don't think so. Beth's a good ChapterSister with a built-in restraint chip. Shows she was a naughty girl once, but there's no way she could do it, even if she wanted to. Remember how she couldn't kill the river-creature?'

Zach resumed walking, his face clouded with thought. Mia was shocked to see how much older he appeared.

'I'm not so sure.'

Mia's heart skipped a beat. 'What …? You really think … *Beth*?'

'We … need to tell everyone about Maddi,' he said, as they reached the access tube to the Rec Hall. 'Then we need to bury her. And then … We find out who killed her. Once and for all.'

'And why,' said Ella. 'Don't forget why.'

Outside, Mia could see, it had started to rain again. A slow steady rain which brushed against the window with a light menacing caress.

'And there's something else,' said Mia awkwardly. 'I dunno if it's important, but …'

The others turned to her.

'What?' said Zach, resignation heavy in his voice. 'What else can there possibly be?'

Mia licked her dry lips. 'When … when I was out there … when I found the shuttle … there was this Lantrill. Sniffing around.'

'So?' Shan said. 'They get everywhere. You know that, we've hunted together enough. It was probably after food.'

'Yeah, but this … this one was weird. It … seemed to …'

'What?' Zach snapped. 'It seemed to do what?'

'It … seemed to know what I was thinking.'

There was a silence, uncomfortably long, broken only by the pattering of the rain on the plexiglass. Ominous, cold and relentless, as if heralding an apocalypse.

'Get everyone outside,' said Zach, his voice harsh.

'Outside? But–'

'*Do it!*' He shouted so loudly that they all took a step back, even Mia. When he spoke again, his voice was low and threatening. 'I've had enough, right? I'm sick of it all. Killers, intruders, sabotage … all of it. It's time we took back control in this damn place. Time for some action.'

'Okay. Fine.' She held her hands up in a placating gesture. 'Outside it is, then.'

As she moved to go, she exchanged a raised-eyebrows look with Ella. She knew Zach would have noticed this, and would know its significance.

∞

10
PREY

I

Beth was hugging herself against the cold. The Towners had formed a rough circle outside on the compound, standing there in the rain under hard, coppery clouds. The downpour had pounded the dust into a creamy mud. There was a biting edge to the air, and the distant roar of the sea sounded threatening.

Zach emerged from the door to the Main Dome and descended the ramp. His expression was grim. The Towners were pointing, jostling each other. Two of the Drones buzzed around Zach in agitation and he waved a hand, swatting them away as if they were insects. He walked on, determined, resolute, his muscles firm and taut under his shirt.

Mia followed behind him, her expression unreadable.

Zach reached the circle, a vein pulsing hard in his temple. His face was cold. With a shock, Beth realised he seemed about ten years older than he had yesterday. She even thought his hair had turned a ghostly white, but that could have been the low arc of pale sunlight cutting through the drizzle.

'Brothers and sisters,' Zach said, in a low, cracked tone. It was so removed from his usual commanding voice that he sounded almost a different person. Beth watched him as he looked around the circle, taking in all the expectant faces. The silence hummed in the air like static. Even the distant sounds of the jungle seemed to recede almost into nothingness.

She looked around for Colm. She could not see him.

'I need to tell you …' Zach began, and he passed a hand across his face, faltering. He recovered, lifted his chin boldly. 'I need to tell you that our sister, Maddi …' He paused, as if unable to believe he was saying the words. 'That our sister, Maddi, is dead.'

There were gasps. The Towners stared at each other in incomprehension.

Beth's mouth was dry, and her heart-rate increased. She felt out of it, set apart from them all. They had all known Maddi all this time, most of a year, and she had known her just these last few cycles. She was a fraud, an intruder.

The youngest girls – Cait, Livvy, Xara – were crying, being comforted by the strong arms of the older ones. The young boys, Hal and Gabe and Cassius, trying not to break down. Amber and Robbie holding each other, grim-faced. And across the circle, she caught sight of Mia. Her face was impassive, the old-fashioned mirror-shades on so Beth could not read her. Beth's sense of exclusion increased, panic rising in her stomach.

There was Ella, at Zach's right hand. There, at last, was Colm, lounging against a nearby piece of machinery, chewing, not quite in the circle … sly, observing. Shan and Lulu, exchanging urgent, meaningful looks.

'*How*?' It was one of the boys, Finn, who first voiced what they all wanted to know. 'How did it happen, Zach? What the hell's going on?' Worried blue eyes peered out through his tousled blond fringe.

Silence hung above the circle for a second.

'I'm sorry,' Zach said. 'But it's bad. Really bad … Maddi … Maddi was killed. She's been murdered.'

Everyone started speaking at once. The confused babble rose to a tumult, several people stepping forward and gesturing, shouting. Beth wanted to yell at them all to shut up and listen to Zach, but she knew that wouldn't be a good idea. Luckily, Zach's leadership skills had not deserted him. He raised a hand for calm, and got it, after a fashion.

'Listen,' he said. '*Please*. Lulu. Tell us.'

Lulu stepped up, her face as pale as Zach's. 'Maddi was murdered. I examined her.' Everyone was straining to listen, and Lulu raised her voice. 'I'm certain. I estimated the time of her death to be …' But Zach shook his head, and Lulu obviously understood. 'I don't want to say any more, because … well, because it's upsetting, and … and there's going to be an investigation. So we have to keep something back. Please, please understand that.'

At a sign from Zach, Ella stepped forward.

'This is a hideous crime,' she said, her voice clear and strident. The resolute way she spoke sent a shiver down Beth's spine. Ella meant business. 'The people who sent us here … they think we're all lowlife, right? That we're all scum. They'd expect this kind of thing to happen. But you know what, yeah? We're not scum, we're not lowlife, and *this doesn't happen*. We're good people. We're good people who have *made* something of this place.' Her voice was raw, impassioned. 'And we're not letting this happen.'

Beth was impressed by her power, her control, her assurance. She wondered, at times like this, why Ella was not their leader instead of Zach.

'But this is the truth of it,' Ella said, her voice cold and hard. 'This, yeah, this is the truth of it. There's nobody else on this damn planet. So, whether we like it or not, this is what happened. One of you killed her. *One* of you.'

There was a cold, desolate silence. A glacial chill blew all the way off the mountains, above the forest treetops and across the sea, cutting through them and wrapping itself around them. Beth shuddered, and hugged herself tightly.

'One of *us*,' said Mia.

Everyone turned to Mia, who had stepped boldly into the centre of the circle, swaggering as ever, the evening light gleaming on her long, tanned legs, her gun clattering at her hip. She was coolly, beautifully menacing, Beth thought, in awe of the girl she had at first feared. What was it Colm had called her? A polecat. Marking out her territory.

And Beth had worked out the intent of Mia's words, well before the rest of the group did so.

'That's what I said,' Ella replied, folding her arms, not allowing Mia to intimidate her.

Mia grinned. It seemed so wrong, so bad, and Beth almost gasped out loud. 'Nah,' said Mia softly. 'You said one of *you*.' She jabbed a finger at Ella. 'I'm saying … one of *us*.' She spread her hands out to encompass the whole circle.

Ella lifted her chin slowly as the implication sunk in. 'Yeah,' she said. 'Perhaps I should have said that, Mia.'

'Well, it's true, isn't it?' Mia gestured around the circle.

'Everyone's a suspect. How the hell can we investigate this, when it could have been any of us?'

The glacial silence deepened.

It was, Beth thought momentarily, as if they were all that Humanity had left – this knot of them, standing here on this rock beside their cluster of civilisation. They were the last, and they had blown it. And there was a terrible, oppressive darkness squatting over this place.

Mia swaggered into the centre of the circle. 'Nasty thought, yeah? That someone here wanted Maddi dead. *Maddi*, of all people. And we don't know who, or why, so until we know, we can't even trust each other.' Mia spat on the ground, as angry as Ella had been. 'Nice work. Whoever it was. Nice fucking work.'

'Calm down, Mia,' said Zach softly.

'What are we doing, Zach?' This was Shan, calmly pragmatic. 'What do you want us all to do? We'll do it, right? We'll pull together. We'll get through this.'

There were mutters of 'Yeah,' and 'Come on,' from the crowd.

Zach made sure he had the crowd's attention again. 'This … business will be investigated,' he said. 'And in due course we'll bury Maddi.' He looked out beyond the jumbles of junk and the jeeps and the fire-pits, out to the edge of the compound where the five white crosses sat. 'Out there.'

An unearthly silence fell over them, and Beth wondered if they were all thinking the same.

Six dead. Over a tenth of them.

It was Finn who broke the silence. 'What now, Zach?'

Zach had an answer ready, 'I want you all to carry on with your normal business. I want everyone to behave *normally*, right? We have to keep this place going. There are things we need to do, and we cannot let them go.' He waited a couple of seconds, making sure he had enough nods of assent. 'In the Council Room, I want to see you, Ella. And Lulu, and Shan … ' His gaze fell upon Beth. 'And Mia. And you, Bethany.'

She turned cold. 'Me? Why me?'

'You'll soon know,' said Zach curtly. 'Council Room.'

II

Zach, Lulu, Ella and Shan, grim-faced, sat at the round Table in the Council Room. Beth and Mia stood in front of them. They were both, Beth knew, feeling equally nervous. It was the first time she had seen Mia really unsettled.

'Couple of things,' said Zach. Beth could see the tension in his body, the whiteness in his knuckles. He was suppressing his anger again. He pressed a button, and a holographic image of the smears of blood on Maddi's wall sprang into view, floating a hand-span above the desk so that they could all see it.

They leaned forward, peering at it.

'What is that?' asked Beth in horror.

'Who knows?' Zach said tersely. 'A message from the dead, maybe.' He looked up at Mia. 'Your name, is what it looks like.'

She drew back from the Table, anger filling her face. 'Don't be … Oh, come on!'

Zach held up his hands. 'I'm not saying … Maybe she needed to tell us something only you knew. Some clue to her killer.'

'I was her *friend*,' Mia said angrily. 'You know that. You all know that!'

'We know.' Shan's soft voice was a contrast to Zach's harshness. 'We're trying to work out what she could have meant. It's … the other thing we're more worried about.'

'The other thing?' Mia asked.

'This is more about you, Beth,' said Ella gently. She pushed an object across the table. A sealed plastic packet. Inside it was a hunting-knife, the blade stained with dried blood, the handle made of polished wood.

'Do you recognise this?' Zach asked. 'Beth?'

She came forward, feeling as if the world, this new place she had become a part of, was tilting beneath her feet.

'This *is* your knife, isn't it, Beth?' said Zach.

Her legs turned weak, physically giving way beneath her. She made it to the seat again in time.

'What?' she whispered in horror.

'Your knife,' Zach repeated. 'It was found in Maddi's neck.'

Her hand went instinctively to her belt, where the knife would normally be, feeling the emptiness of the sheath. It had been lost in the river, surely, in her struggle with that creature …? But now it seemed … Confusion overwhelmed her.

Her life was slipping away.

She was dimly aware of the next few seconds happening, as if in slow-motion.

Something cold tingling on the back of her neck. A chill spreading through her entire body, down her spine, into her legs and arms. Like freezing liquid filling her body.

She opened her mouth to scream, and could not.

The room wobbled and blurred. She was dimly aware of all their faces above her, looming over her, blurring into pinkness, redness.

And then everything went black.

III

Cold, hard steel.

It sliced her head, as if she were being stabbed.

Beth shivered, feeling as if she was drowning in ice, feeling her body curling itself up into a foetal position. Then, very slowly, reality tuned in. The dragging, spinning sensation of being pulled out of her half-wakefulness, her mouth dry and claggy.

Beth tried to sit up, slowly. She was groggy, clutching her aching head. She was weak, her mouth like rough earth, and she knew she needed water urgently.

She blinked.

There was a red smudge in the centre of her vision. It came into focus as a dim disc-light set into the wall of the room, providing the only illumination. She was aware of the cold metal floor beneath her body.

She was in a cell.

Blinking, she took it in. Four solid, black-steel walls, slightly curved. The only furniture was a simple metal stool, screwed to the floor. A fine metal mesh on the fourth wall afforded her a view into the area beyond. She staggered to her feet, weak, gazing blearily into the dimness.

'Hello ...? Hello, is anyone there?'

She slammed her fists again and again on the metal mesh. It vibrated, twanging with an almost elastic sound, but it did not give at all. She knew it had to be some very strong light metal, possibly a titanium derivative. Somebody wanted her kept here. Somebody wanted to make sure she didn't get out.

There was a circular area beyond the cell, lit by the reddish discs. Various metal tables, crates and pieces of equipment were stacked there. Beyond a cluster of charcoal-black shadows, steps led upwards. She had to be in the lower level of one of the domes.

The swish of a pneumatic door, and booted footsteps from above. Beth licked her lips, her heart thudding in anticipation. At least she might get some answers now.

Footsteps descended the stairs.

Booted feet, black trousers, muscles beneath a tight dark shirt. Tattooed arms and a stern, lean face.

She breathed again. 'Zach,' she murmured, and the sound echoed out into the area beyond the cell. 'What the *hell* is going on?' Beth was surprised to hear herself using such an expression, lapsing into the vernacular of the Edge. She was even more surprised at how little she cared, how little she was shocked. 'And what is this place? Get me out of here!'

He walked slowly over to the centre of the storage room.

He pulled up a crate and sat on it, studying her intently through the metal mesh.

'The Coolers,' he said eventually. 'Isolation. Nobody wanted it. Bit too much like Academy. But in the end, we agreed. Needed somewhere for people who ... got a bit out of hand. Stealing, too much *plaan* whisky, or throwing a punch over a girl or something. Anarchy doesn't work. That was our first lesson ... Took a good few dozen cycles, but we learned it.'

'So ... how did I get here?'

'I'm sorry,' he said. 'It was a low-level tranq-pad, on the back of your neck. Lulu did it. I ... asked her to.'

Beth remembered the tranqs applied to Reza and Gabe after their altercation, how quickly they had gone down. Her mind was a storm of confusion. 'But ... why?'

'Safety,' he said. He had brought a plastic bottle of water, she noted, and a small cloth-wrapped packet which she assumed was food. They dangled casually from his fingers. He noticed her eyeing up the food and water. 'You want these?' he asked.

'Yes. Please.'

He got up, walked over to the wall beside her cell, pressing a sequence of buttons on the keypad. For a second, kicked by a shot of adrenaline, she imagined grabbing him, overpowering him and running. *So stupid. Why?* The idea faded as quickly as it had come upon her, and she realised that the food and water had popped through a small, airlock-type drawer into a perspex panel set into the wall of her cell.

She touched the panel and it sprang open, delivering the

bottle and the packet into her hands. Beth grabbed the water and glugged greedily, allowing its cool freshness to swish around her mouth. She felt better, and sank slowly down on to the immobile metal stool.

'Thank you,' she said.

Zach went back to the chair, watching her again.

She opened the packet. A square of a crumbly, brown substance, which could have been bread or some form of biscuit or cake. She crammed a handful of it into her mouth. It was coarse, nutty-tasting and burnt as if cooked over an open fire, but she made herself chew, swallow it down, swigging more water to help.

'So,' she said, gesturing around the cell. 'Safety, you say. Whose safety, exactly?'

Zach did not reply.

'Is this what I am? A caged animal?' As she spoke, she rubbed the back of her neck – it was still raw and irritated.

'It's the safest place for you to be,' he said, his voice low and husky.

Safe. That word again. She didn't understand. 'Why?'

'People … people doubt you.'

She realised what he meant. She was the outsider, and in a time like this, people turned on outsiders. Humanity had done so throughout history. Why should this isolated bunch of young humans be any different?

'People … including you?' she asked.

'Beth, I don't know what to think.'

'Yes, you do. You do, or you wouldn't have locked me up in here.'

'I don't – Someone … Someone …' He could not bring himself to say it, but she knew exactly what he was thinking.

'Let me help you out here,' she said. '*Someone* murdered Maddi, and you've got the idea into your head that it was me.'

Zach didn't reply. He couldn't even face her.

A mixture of emotions hit Beth at the same time – anger, sadness, and, eclipsing it all, sudden terror. These people, all around her own age, were not going to sit down and work this out logically. They'd been surviving on the Edge for far too long. They were desperate. *Hunted*. Life here had been tough already, tempers fractious enough, even before, she thought. These people had lived with tech failures, possibly even sabotage, and the general uncertainty about everything. Then there had been the attack on Ella, the storm. And now Maddi's death. Everything was boiling over.

These people, she realised, could actually believe that she had murdered Maddi. And they could actually be ready to kill her.

And who, out of all of them, was on her side? Colm? Drone 356? It was ridiculous to expect either of them to come and get her out of here. Were they really her friends here? A boy who wanted her for one coarse, crude reason, and a robot which could not even feel emotions?

'Zach,' she said, coming up to the circular mesh and pressing her hands on it. The mesh was cold, sturdy, unyielding. 'Zach, please. *Why* would I have killed Maddi? What could she … *possibly* have done to me? A few cycles ago I didn't know her. But she was one of the people to make me feel the most welcome here, to show me the most kindness.'

'I know,' he said. 'That's what doesn't make sense.'

She slammed her hands on the mesh in frustration, pain coursing through her palms. 'So why am I *in* here?!'

Silence, and then:

'It was your knife,' he said.

'And you think that's conclusive? Anyone could have stolen it! Anyone!' She kept her voice level. 'Even you, Zach.'

He stared at her coldly for what seemed like a very long time.

'Yes,' he said eventually. 'Even me.'

IV

Colm found Mia on the azure sand of Lunar Beach again, staring moodily out at the sea. The tide was a long way out, and the expanse of darker, wet sand, scattered with stringy seaweed and ragged driftwood, stretched out in front of them.

He joined her in silence, at first. After a while, he spoke.

'So … this is bad.'

It was hopelessly inadequate, but it was better than the sound of the sea and the unearthly wail of the Howling Mountains.

'Yup.' Mia wasn't going to be drawn any further.

Here on the Edge, Colm was thinking, morality was a luxury. Maddi's death had proved this to him.

He was already thinking ahead to a time when things would get harder, more desperate. A time when people wouldn't so readily accept the fair-but-firm hand of a Zach, the tough authority of an Ella, or even the diplomatic touch of a Shan. A time when the connivers, the liars, the cheaters – people like him, and Mia, and one or two others – would be best positioned to survive. It would probably happen, he'd thought for a while, when the next winter came.

Although, right now, they all had a rather bigger problem to solve.

'I'm sorry,' Colm said. 'I … well, I know you two were kind of friends.'

Mia gave a hollow laugh.

Colm raised an eyebrow. 'Did I say something funny? There's a first. I'm entertaining. I knew I had to have a purpose in this forsaken place.'

'Yeah, I know what I said in the circle. But I don't have *friends*, Colm. I have people like you, who tolerate me a bit more than others.'

They sat for a minute longer, in silence apart from the distant sad wash of the breakers.

'So, what do we do,' he said, at last, lying back on the sand, 'about Beth?'

'I know what *you'd* like to do about Beth, mister,' said Mia coldly.

'Don't. I feel bad enough for trying it on with her.' He shuddered. 'I don't know what came over me.'

Mia wasn't going to let it go. 'Li'l ChapterSisters your thing, now, are they? What turns you on about her,

Coooooolm? Is it the *Oh So Precise* way she says stuff? Or the general air of holier-than-thou scientific purity?'

'I know. I'm sorry ...' He hesitated. 'Zach's got her banged up in the Coolers.'

'Does he think she did it?' Mia asked worriedly.

'Who knows?' He was surprised by how much of an honest answer that was. Behind the soft skin and the tousled coal-black hair ... Was Beth Kane actually a cold-hearted murderess? 'Who knows?' he repeated softly.

Mia pushed the sunglasses up on to her forehead for the first time. Her eyes shone brightly in the darkness. There was a greenish glow to them, like bio-luminescent algae. *Plaan* weed did that to you, after a while.

'The Spacegirl,' Mia said, 'is surely harmless. I think you know that. Deep down.'

'Yeah, well, Zach doesn't seem to think so. Nor does Ella. And, you know, they're getting Shan round to their way of thinking, too.'

Mia drew herself upright.

'Better go back,' she said, slamming the pistol into its holster. 'I need to talk to Shan about getting Maddi's grave ready.'

'Think we oughta ... say something to Zach?'

'No,' she said, hands on hips, her face determined. 'I don't think anything we *say* to Zach will make a difference.'

'So what are you saying?'

'Work it out. See me after Maddi's funeral.'

She gave him a sudden sad smile, before setting off up the dunes at a speed he could not hope to match.

V

Baljeet was not in the best of moods. And she needed sleep.

She was checking on the lush green corridors of the Hydroponic Dome. Scan-pad in hand, bathed in blue light, she made her way along the rows and rows of greenery, pausing every so often to wipe the sweat from her forehead.

It was an uncomfortable, sticky place to work. Occasionally, a fine mist of water and nutrients would descend from the high domed roof, cascading from the leaves like artificial rain. There was a fresh, earthy smell, like an Old Earth forest after rainfall, and something rich and fruity, all overlaid with a curious antiseptic odour.

It was all monitored by the Drones, but every so often one of them would go in to check the progress of the plants and vegetation, usually at night. Today, with all the confusion following Maddi's death, the task had fallen to her and Amber. They hated having to do it – as most of them hated having to do anything which kept the colony alive – but it was better than starvation and death. It was a way of taking control of their environment.

A way of having hope. And they needed hope, especially now.

Baljeet spoke into the radio, her voice tired and shaky. 'Section 2 stacks, all proceeding normally.'

A second later, Amber's voice crackled through. '*Yeah, yeah. All fine over here as well. So chill your tits, babe.*'

Baljeet growled at the radio. Back home, she would not have allowed anyone to speak to her in that way. She had been used to automatic respect. Here, though, she knew she had to earn it.

Beep. Beep. Beep.

The detector had been making angry noises at Baljeet for the last minute or so. She had tried to ignore it, but now she hoiked it off her belt with an exasperated tut. A flashing red dot on the screen was showing something which needed her attention.

With her other hand, Baljeet thumbed the call-switch on her radio. 'Amber, the coolant in Stack 4B's playing up. It's nearer you, can you take a look?'

There was no response, apart from a loud, angry burst of static which made Baljeet wince. She cursed in a mixture of English and Punjabi.

'Amber! Come in, you bitch.'

More static, only louder and more fractured this time. If Amber could hear her, she was not responding.

'Amber, if you're holed up in the *deposito* smoking *plaan* with Robbie again, I'm going to feed you both into the composter head-first. Get your arse out here.' The radio crackled and sputtered, offering her no further idea if it was interference or if it was actually mangling Amber's reply. Baljeet swore again, hitting the radio on the side and shaking it. 'Useless pile of junk …' She clipped it back on to her belt. 'Like they say … If you want a job doing …'

She hurried along the walkway, her footsteps clanging, echoing up into the vastness of the dome, the only other sound above the soft, gentle hiss of the water-sprays. It took her three minutes to reach Section 4, at an intersection of two walkways. Lush green tomato-plants curled up the splayed pillars, their fruit red and gleaming. There was no sign of Reza. Baljeet noticed though, that one of the access hatches set into the walkway was gaping open, when it definitely should not have been.

She frowned, clipping a head-torch on and peering down the steel ladder into the depths. She couldn't make much out. Baljeet straightened up. No Drone in sight. She tutted. They were usually around when you needed them. Why could she not find one now?

She knew she was going to have to go down there. And she didn't really like the idea very much.

She swung herself over the edge and started to climb down the ladder, immediately enveloped by cooler air and darkness.

Each clang of her booted feet on the rungs echoed upwards, through the shaft and out into the Hydroponic Dome. Occasionally, she gazed upwards. The square of light leading back to the walkway became smaller and smaller above her, and the air grew gradually colder the further she got towards the coolant units. Her breath misted in the air. She noticed the ladder becoming slick with condensation, rusty stains smearing on her hands. The contrast with the walkways above could not be greater. They didn't come down here if they could possibly help it.

There was a grinding, creaking sound from above.

'Amber? That you?'

The grinding continued. To Baljeet's alarm, she realised the square of light at the top of the shaft was becoming a rectangle. And then a sliver. And then nothing.

With a great, shuddering clang, reverberating through the ladder and through her hands, the hatch slammed shut.

Baljeet's heart-rate increased, her breath coming in short misty gasps. She told herself not to panic. Either it was a mechanical fault, or it was Amber or someone else playing a stupid prank.

She was at the bottom of the ladder, so she hopped off on to the floor of the maintenance duct. There was only a minimum of illumination here, cold blue light-panels set into the walls, and the light from her own head-torch seemed equally dim. Baljeet wasn't even sure she had been down here before.

'Amber, you lazy shit! Are you there?'

No reply. She snarled in anger and tried the radio again, but it seemed totally dead. She shook it, banged it against the wall. There was no response.

Baljeet was not unduly worried. These ducts all came out somewhere, she knew, and there would be another access point – it would be a case of making her way along the cramped tunnel and finding it. And if that was sealed too, she would bang on it until somebody heard and came to her rescue. The worst-case scenario was that they'd take a few hours to notice she was missing, and she'd be bored until Zach sent people to find her.

There was a flash of movement. A shadow falling across the bluish light, and an odd shuffling, clattering sound.

Baljeet tensed, feeling properly unnerved. Her body tingled. A sixth sense, some instinct honed all those years ago in the dark streets, sent a tingle through her body.

'Hello?' she called. 'Who's there?'

The blue lights buzzed like angry mosquitos, flickered eerily, threatening for a second to go out completely. Baljeet stood still. She could taste the cold on her tongue – it was biting, almost metallic. Her face and hands, she realised, were starting to grow numb. A creeping sensation of unease spread through her, and she started to wish she had come armed down here.

'I want to know who you are!' Baljeet called out. Her voice echoed up the tunnel, and she raised it still more, trying to sound bolder than she felt. 'I heard you. Come out!'

There was no further sound. Relief coursed through her. The coolant pipes made all kinds of strange noises as metal was stretched and pummelled, and had been known some nights to make an unearthly howling which reverberated through the Hydroponic Centre.

She was imagining things.

Probably.

Looking up at the ladder, her head-torch illuminating about as far as halfway up, she reasoned that it might make sense to climb back up and try to open that hatchway by physical force. After all, Amber or someone else might have come along and shut it absently without even thinking. She gripped the ladder, put her right foot on the first rung.

And then something made her turn around, and look down the tunnel in the opposite direction.

She gasped. And then she let out a long, relieved laugh, her misty breath caught in the beam of her torch.

'You really startled me,' she said, annoyed but no longer frightened. 'What the hell are you doing down here?'

There was a click in the darkness, and the sound of scraping metal.

'What the–?' Baljeet backed up against the ladder, scrabbling for her radio.

A second later, there was a whooshing sound in the air, a flash of light and a dull thud. A sharp, angry pain in her chest. For a second she froze, unable to believe what had happened. Then she reached down, feeling something hot and sticky. She lifted her hand up to the light, horrified to see it coated with her own dark, wet blood.

And then came the pain.

It tore through every nerve and fibre of her being. It surged, crackling through her, as if burning up every cell of her body.

Her useless legs, numbed and weakened, gave way, and she collapsed to her knees. The edges of her vision went red, then darker red. Darkness stole in and began to obliterate her brain. Her mouth opened in a soundless scream.

The dark, admonishing face of her father was there in the gloom, sad and lonely and lost, haunted by the daughter he would never see again. Then the blackness crushed her, rushing into her mind, swallowing her up, and she slammed to the floor.

Her sightless eyes stared upwards, as her assailant withdrew silently into the shadows.

∞

11
THE ACCUSED

I

'You see,' Zach said, pacing up and down in front of Beth's cell, 'if this had happened on Earth or Mars, or any main Collective centre, there would be proper investigators, Lawguards, DNA cross-checked on the networks ... We can't do any of that here.'

'So you assume I am guilty? And do what – keep me here for ever?' She turned cold. 'Or kill me?'

He stood up.

'Would you, Zach? Would you *actually* execute me? In cold blood? Knowing the real murderer might still be out there, among you? That's *insane!*' She was gabbling in fear. 'This person ... this killer ... It might be what they want, Zach! To drive this community apart!'

He didn't walk away. Instead, he came right up to her cell, casting long, multiple shadows on the steel walls around him. In the semi-darkness, lit by the crimson glow, his face was drawn, haggard, older than his years – but also firm and tough. There was a real anger in him, a coldness which made her shrink in fear. When he spoke, his voice was soft and threatening.

'How many people, Bethany, were on the *Arcadia*?'

'What?' She was thrown by the unexpected turn of the conversation.

'It's a simple enough question, surely,' he said impatiently. 'One of the great colony ships, voyaging between the stars. Some people knowing that they wouldn't live out the journey, but the others having the hopes, the dreams of their new world … It's a great story. Yeah, a great story. Hope for the human race. You like hope, don't you? You with your Great Power optimism. Cities can be founded on hope, that's what you said to me after cutting the boys down.'

'Yes. Of course.'

'Beautiful, romantic hope. Driving your ship onwards into the stars. So … how many people were on board?'

'I … don't know exactly. People were born, people died of old age …'

'Sure. But more or less. You must know.'

'Yes … maybe … Ten thousand?'

'Sounds about right. Ten thousand people on that ship, Beth. Ten thousand souls.' He lunged forward, slamming a hand on to the mesh, making her recoil in sudden fear. 'So *where are they*? Are they all dead? Didn't *anyone* else get out alive?'

'I … I don't know. Please. I was … I was half-conscious. I thought I was going to die. The Decks … the Platforms … there was a fire.' Her memories were patchy, broken, like a juddering Lumi-cast. She simply could not remember it all properly, apart from in these single, broken images. 'The Gardens were pitch-black with smoke. I could feel the whole place tearing itself apart.' Tears blurred her vision, and she turned away.

'Ten thousand people dead, then,' said Zach coldly. 'Maybe. And there you sit, Bethany Aurelia Kane, with a few scratches and bruises. Which, I might add, are all healing up very well.'

She sank to the floor, her face in her hands.

'And in the meantime,' Zach went on, 'we've had *nothing* on our sweeps, no sign of any debris in the atmosphere … Can you explain that to me?'

'No,' she said miserably. 'I cannot.' She peeked out from between her fingers, and saw Zach's expression of grim satisfaction.

'Right,' he said. 'Right. That's it, you see.' He jabbed a finger at her. 'That … *that* is why. You're an anomaly, Beth. You shouldn't be here.'

An anomaly. Shouldn't be here.

There was something tingling at the back of her mind … A memory … Something which had chilled her spine. Her brain still dulled by the tranq, she tried to grab on to it. Flotsam on her storm-tossed mind. *What was it?*

Of course. The message from Maddi. Something about *space debris*. Something she had been going to tell her.

She opened her mouth to speak, but Zach was not done yet.

'There's been something not right about this from the start, Beth. Something not right about *you*. So what with everything weird that's been happening, it makes *this*,' and his fist slammed the metal wall, 'the best place for you to be. Until we can figure all this out.'

He turned to go. He made it as far as the steps before she called out to him.

'The easy option, this, isn't it, Zach?' she said.

'What do you mean?'

'It's as old as humanity itself. Blame the outsider. It must be them, because they're different, because we don't trust them.'

He rounded on her, his face colder and angrier than she had ever seen it, making her step back in shock.

'And what am I supposed to think, Beth …? You show up here, dropping out of the sky, no remnant of this mysterious ship you're supposed to have come from. And within *days* one of our people's murdered. You think that's a coincidence?'

'Yes,' she said. 'As a matter of fact, I do think it's a co–'

'You're *lying* to me!' He slammed his hands against the mesh, his face red and contorted in anger. She backed right up to the far wall, trying not to show her fear. 'I have to hold this place together, Beth. I have to be a leader. And if that means keeping you here *forever*, I damn well will.'

'You don't want to face up to it!' She was shocked by her own directness. But it was anger which made her speak up, and fear. And her awareness of their fear too, the same fear she had seen when Mia hauled her out of the jeep in a fit of rage. 'The very real possibility that you've been living with the killer in your midst for over two hundred cycles. *That's* what you're not daring to tell yourself.'

There was a moment's silence. He paced up and down again, before looking up sharply at her.

'It *can't* be one of them,' he said coldly. 'I know these people. I know them all.' He turned to go. 'I've got a funeral to lead in the morning. I'll send someone to check on you after that.'

Beth watched him disappear up the steps.

She had, she hoped, sown the seed of doubt in Zach's mind. She was still fearful, but the fear was mixed with a slight, desperate hope.

II

At a nod from Shan, Mia placed a fragmentation-grenade on the chosen piece of ground, not far away from the other five crosses. The grenade was a red disc with a flat, black screen and a basic keypad. It had already been programmed with the precise area of detonation required.

'Five seconds?' she asked.

'Best make it ten,' Shan told her.

Mia punched in the time. It came up in red LED figures on the flat black screen of the frag-grenade.

'Right,' she said. 'Here goes.'

Her finger stabbed down on the detonator button. She scrambled to her feet, and she and Shan hurried for the cover of the nearby rocks.

The blast hurled them off their feet before they got there. Mia yelped, feeling Shan's arm pulling her down on the mud, and they both covered their heads with their arms as debris rained down around them, a warm, gravelly hail smelling of scorched earth. It fizzed, popped and crackled.

After a few seconds, they dared to take their hands off their heads and turn over. The hole was impressive, belching smoke. The charred earth had, mostly, been distributed around the edge of the grave as requested in the program.

Shan got up slowly, dusting himself down. 'That was never ten seconds,' he said accusingly to Mia.

She scrambled to her feet and gave a wry grin. 'Timers on those frag-bombs are unreliable. Like everything else.'

They got as close as they dared to the opening in the ground, which was still belching noxious smoke. It was a roughly rectangular gash, about two emms deep – almost exactly what they had asked for.

'You know,' Mia said, 'in the old days on Earth, before sanitary corpse disposal, they actually used to *dig* these.'

'Six graves. Who would have thought it?'

'This one's different.'

They let silence hang in the air for a moment. Silence apart from the unearthly, electronic noise of the Howling Mountains. A wind was picking up, disturbing the loose earth.

'You and Colm,' said Shan. 'I've seen you talking. You're plotting something.'

'Yeah,' said Mia. 'But keep it to yourself. Right?'

'What's it worth?'

'The future of this colony, quite possibly,' said Mia.

He slowly realised that, for once, Mia Janowska was being entirely serious.

III

'You wanted to see me?' Lulu asked.

On the Sky-Gallery, Zach was drinking *plaan* whisky from a hip-flask. He had started after his confrontation with

Beth, and he had got through a bit more than he intended. Hazily, he smiled at her, offering the flask. She held up a hand to refuse.

'What's this about, Zach?'

'I … wanted to talk to … to someone I trust.'

'Is that all I am, these days?'

Outside, the morning sun was already high in the sky, the sea glimmering in its unfiltered, bright heat. The fissures in the earth still steamed, great wounds cutting across the planet.

'I wondered,' she said, watching the Towners moving about below them in the Rec Hall. 'Since all this … It seems … You and me, we've … kind of stopped.'

Zach tutted impatiently.

'What? What have I said?'

'Stopped. You make it sound like we even started.'

He deliberately avoided her gaze, feeling the guilt eating him up. It would be easy, he knew, so easy to say *sorry* – that magic, all-purpose word, that spell which seemed to work wonders. But for the spell to work, you had to mean it. Lulu would know Zach didn't mean it. They had both known for some time that their tired, half-hearted relationship was over. And not only because of Zach's history with Ella. Neither of them wanted to be the first to admit it.

'I did care,' she said. 'It was more than … More than just the thing … You know.'

'I know.'

'You never let anyone in, Zach. You never talk about anything. That's not what it should all be about. Leading, commanding … it's about knowing when to share the burden.'

He did not reply.

'People are getting restless,' Lulu said. 'They want answers. Some of them know you've had Beth locked away all night, and–'

He held up a hand, forestalling further objections. 'I know, I know. So, we've got to think about this.' He leaned on the rail, the flask dangling from his fingers. 'Lu,' he said thoughtfully, 'is there any way … any way at all … that Beth's Chapter implant could be … interfering with her memory receptors? Even with her perceptions?'

Lulu didn't answer straight away. She turned away from the viewing window, leaning against the rail, her legs stretched out. She seemed distracted for a second, as two Drones bobbed past, going about their daily business.

'I'm not sure,' she said eventually.

'In your medical opinion.'

'Honestly? Cyber-interfaces aren't my thing. People spend their entire *lives* studying this stuff and still don't quite get it.'

'I know … But is it possible?'

He stared hard into her bright blue eyes. Not for the first time, he realised how delicate and fragile Lulu was, with her cropped hair and pale skin. So young and so helpless. Like all the rest of them.

'It's a behavioural limiter, right?' she said. 'A modifier. It works by … well, by sending tiny electrical impulses into the brain.'

'Go on.'

'But, well, that's pretty much what neurons do, right? The hundred billion nerve cells we've all got in here.' Lulu tapped her forehead. 'Sending electrochemical signals. The principle's not that much different from a computer. Logic gates and so on.'

Zach steadied himself, the whisky searing through his body, firing him up. He took another long deep swig from the flask. '*Could* it interfere with her memories?' he asked again. 'Like … you know, how a computer's memory gets scrambled?'

'Short answer? We don't know enough about this stuff.'

Zach paced up and down on the Sky-Gallery. 'Things she says, Lu … Things she says don't add up. And yet … it's like she totally believes it, you know?'

She frowned. 'You mean like an implanted memory? That Beth believes herself to have had experiences … she hasn't had?'

'And the opposite,' he said. 'Wiping out memories of things she's done.'

'That's pretty out there, Zach. Based on one tiny behavioural limiter. I'm not sure these things are even that powerful.'

'They do exist,' he said. 'Memory implants.'

'Yeah, I mean, some of the most advanced Synthets have that technology. But we're talking, like half a dozen of them, on Earth and Mars or whatever. But for human memory? It's seriously hard. And it's way, *way* in advance of anything the Chapters have got.'

351

He stopped pacing, turned to face her. 'But the brain, Lu,' he said. 'The *brain*. We don't really understand it.'

'Empathy or strategy?' she said, raising her eyebrows. It was a tired joke between them, and they both knew it.

'I know what I think.' He threw her the whisky-flask, and she caught it instinctively, with a yelp of surprise. 'Give that to someone else,' he said. 'I've got to sober up before Maddi's funeral.'

IV

An hour later, the air was silent and still, a paler sunlight spilling over the Howling Mountains and into the valleys. The two moons watched over proceedings, their pale discs fringed with clouds.

Four of the Drones attached themselves to Maddi's soft, flexiplastic coffin. They lifted it, then slowly descended, lowering the wrapped body into the ground.

The Towners circled the grave, everyone with hands clasped and heads down, as had become the tradition.

There were four soft, plosive noises as the Drones reached the bottom of the grave and detached themselves from the flexiplastic. As one, they rose, and then slowly pulled away from the grave like scattered snooker balls, pausing and hovering on the edge of the crowd.

Zach stepped forward, addressing everyone.

'Maddi was one of our own,' he said. 'Everyone loved Maddi. She was a listener. She was strong, thoughtful … I am sure each and every one of you, at some point, went to

Maddi to talk through a problem, or ask advice, or have a drink and a laugh. Some ... some had more from her. Maddi ... Maddi was a giver. A lover ... A kind, good person.'

His voice cracked, and he looked over the heads of the youngest Towners, across to the trees and the valleys and the Howling Mountains.

'We don't understand how this has happened. We don't understand who would have wanted to do this. To Maddi. To our sister. Our *friend*.' Zach's voice became strong again, powerful, angry. 'But we will,' he said. 'We will find out who did this. And we *will* bring that person to justice.'

Then he bent down, and gathered up a handful of the planet's blue dust, and walked to the edge of the grave. Slowly, Zach unclenched his hand, allowed the dust to fall into the grave.

Ella, as agreed, followed his lead, her expression blank and unreadable as she, too, dropped in a handful of earth. Then others lined up, one by one, casting the dust and earth of their home on to the body of their fallen comrade.

Mia and Colm were among the first in line. When they had both paid their respects, they turned, walking together back in the direction of the Main Dome. By mutual understanding, they began to walk more quickly when they were a good distance from the mourning party.

Mia spoke quietly, casually.

'You don't think little Spacegirl did this any more than I do, right?'

'Course not,' said Colm. 'Crazy idea.'

'Zach thinks she did.'

'*Justice*,' Colm said quietly. 'I know that language. He means execution. If we don't get her out, he's gonna kill her.'

Mia kept walking back towards Town. She said five words to him:

'Then we do it now.'

V

Xara and Finn were on duty at the top of the stairs leading down to the Coolers.

Usually the electronic locks to the cells were secure enough, but on this occasion, Zach had asked for a couple of volunteers to guard. The two Thirteeners, almost like brother and sister with their matching tousled blond locks, had been first to put their hands up.

They hadn't been given guns – Zach had decided it wasn't a good idea. But they had a couple of sharp wooden stakes, enough of a threat to make intentions clear. And so far, it had been successful. Nobody had come down this far apart from Zach himself.

Until now.

Finn was lounging against the wall when Xara nudged him. 'Got company,' she said, uncertainly.

Booted feet on the stairs above them. The two grasped their wooden stakes and held their position.

Mia and Colm came into view, both walking with a purposeful swagger. Mia was armed with a Magna as usual, sunglasses on. Colm, unarmed, stood with feet placed apart, his usual superior expression on his face.

Mia strolled forward. 'Hiya, kids,' she said, expression unreadable behind the mirror-shades. She pointed to the opening beyond, to the stairs leading down into the dimness. 'Let us through, yeah?'

Xara looked uncertainly at Finn. 'You'll need Zach's authorisation.'

'Fuck that,' said Mia, shoving her lightly. 'We wanna talk to the prisoner.'

'I know,' said Xara, holding her ground, 'but Zach told us not to let anyone through.' She gripped her makeshift spear tightly, tried to appear menacing.

'Awww, c'mon.' Mia tapped the younger girl under the chin, making her flinch. 'Don't be a pain in the arse, Za-Za. You know me better than that.'

Finn lifted his stake. 'We can't,' he said. 'We really can't.'

Colm tilted his head on one side. 'They're gonna be difficult about it, Mia. I told you they would.'

'C'mon, guys,' said Mia softly. 'Zach didn't mean us. You know that.'

She moved forward.

Finn and Xara reacted quickly, stakes forming an X shape, blocking Mia's way to the stairs.

Mia turned her head towards Xara very, very slowly, her whole body tensed and taut. Then she looked in the other direction, towards Finn.

'Really?' she said, her voice low and threatening. 'I mean, *seriously*?'

Colm strolled forward. 'Looks like they mean it,' he murmured.

'Seems they do,' said Mia sadly.

It was Colm who moved first. He slammed Finn up against the bulkhead, smacking the boy's head into the metal with a loud crack. Xara gasped, whirling her spear. It took Mia all of half a second to disarm her, cracking the stake across her knee and advancing on Xara with cool, graceful intent.

She kicked the girl in the stomach, winding her. Xara recovered quickly, lunging forward. Mia lashed out, smacked her once. Hard. There was a crack of cheekbone, and Xara reeled and fell, sprawling, her knotted hair spread out in a fan on the floor.

Mia nodded calmly to Colm. His fist slammed into Finn's chest, winding the already dazed boy.

The two of them crouched, gasping, on the floor. Xara was shuddering, crying, blood pouring from one nostril.

'Oh, shit.' Mia and Colm exchanged a brief look that spoke volumes. 'I didn't wanna do that.'

'Nor did I,' Colm said, rubbing his knuckles. 'Laughing boy here's got an iron stomach. What the hell's he been eating?'

'Don't move, right?' Mia snapped at the two Thirteeners. 'We didn't wanna hurt you. I'm sorry.'

Xara's sobs followed them down the stairs into the cold, enveloping darkness.

Beth looked up, astonished, as the two of them clattered down the stairs into the holding area. Mia's fist slammed on the release button and the metal mesh split in two, retracting into the wall.

'What is going on?' Beth asked fearfully, looking at Mia and Colm.

'Not sure,' said Mia coldly. 'Could be mutiny.' She jerked her head. 'Come out.'

Beth backed up against the wall of the cell. 'I don't trust you.' She scowled at Colm, who wore an expression of wry amusement. 'And you … I don't know about you.'

'Oh, for …' Mia couldn't believe this. She drew her pistol, and the whine as it powered up was coldly, angrily threatening. 'This is the kind of gratitude, Spacegirl? Get the hell *out* of there.' She motioned with the gun.

Beth, fearful, stepped forward, out of the cell. 'All right, all right!' She smiled gratefully at Colm.

'Hey, don't look at me, Princess,' he said. 'It was Psycho's idea.'

'That's better,' said Mia. 'You've gotta learn who you can trust. Come on.'

'Where are we going?'

'Habitation 2,' said Mia. 'We got a murder to solve.'

At the top of the stairs, they found Xara, shaking but no longer sobbing, nursing her bloodied face, staggering to her feet. She glared up at Mia with cold hatred in her young face. 'You fuckin' bitch,' she spat.

Mia held up her hands. 'Guilty as charged. I'm sorry. Where's your friend?'

'Finn's gone,' Xara said, wiping her nose and spitting blood on the floor. 'He's gone to tell Zach.'

Mia looked up at Colm in alarm. 'We've not got long,' she said.

Beth paused, her hand on Xara's shoulder. 'I am sorry they had to hurt you. This is not your fault, or theirs. I am so sorry.'

Xara stared at her for a second, then turned away, giving the tiniest of nods.

Beth hurried after Colm and Mia, not looking back.

VI

'What the hell's down here, anyway?' Robbie complained. 'We *never* come down here!'

The green-haired boy descended the ladder after Amber, the beam of his torch oscillating wildly. Robbie had followed her to the Hydroponics Dome because she had said she needed to 'show him something urgently', but Robbie was starting to wonder if he had been lured here under false pretences.

'Nothing much,' said Amber with a wicked grin. 'The Hydro vents. I ... fancied getting away from all the crap for a bit.' She beckoned him, and put her back up against the cold metal wall, opening her mouth invitingly. 'Come on, then.'

'What did you want to show me?' he asked, aware that his voice was high-pitched with nervousness.

She laughed. 'Where did you grow up? Under a stone?'

Robbie realised. Hands in pockets, he shyly pivoted on one heel. 'Oh. Right. Ambs, I dunno.'

She laughed again. 'What d'you mean you *dunno*? What, am I so repulsive? I'm a girl from Mars, not a three-toed mutant from Alpha C.' She put her head on one side, slipped her arms around his neck and moved her face closer to his. 'Go with the flow, Roberto.'

He was about to say how it didn't feel right, so soon after Maddi's funeral, and then also something about people from the Alpha Centauri system having varying numbers of fingers and toes for a very good reason. But then Amber's wide wet mouth closed over his before he could even make a sound. Her breath was hot, raw. Her tongue, slippery and eager, slithered around his like a predatory animal, and after the initial shock he had to admit it was quite pleasant. But it was still somehow wrong.

Amber pulled back. Her mouth broke away from his with a wet popping sound. 'Roberto,' she said, pouting crossly. 'You've really not done this much before, have you?'

'Well … no. Not with girls.'

'Oh, *great*. Are we a different species all of a sudden?' She loosened a button on her top, grabbed his hand, gently slid it against her skin. She giggled. 'There. At least have an *explore*.'

He let his hand caress her soft skin, shaking in excitement. 'Bloody hell, Amber.'

Her hand strayed to his waistband, undoing his belt. 'Okaaaaay … Relax, you dirty boy. Gonna have a bit of fun, ain't we?'

'What's that?' he said in alarm.

'Well, if you don't know by now–'

'No, *that*!' Robbie pulled his hand away from her, pointing. He was staring at something on the ground, a short way along the ducting.

'If you don't wanna do this, Robbie, just say.'

'No, seriously. There.'

He swung the torch up, and it picked out a dark shape, huddled into the curve where the floor met the wall. He approached it, putting the torch on to full beam. Amber's intrigues forgotten, at least for the moment, Robbie leaned in to the huddled figure, his heart pounding in fear.

It was Baljeet, her face rigid. Eyes in a fixed glassy stare.

He looked up at Amber, freezing in fear. 'I … I don't wanna touch her.'

Amber lunged forward, shoving him out of the way. She put her hand to Baljeet's neck. Slowly, she looked up at Robbie, her face showing shock and horror.

'Is she …?' He could not say the word.

Amber nodded.

Robbie put a hand over his dry mouth, trembling. 'We … we need to tell someone.'

'Course we do.'

He noticed the rip in Baljeet's tunic. 'What the hell *is* that?' he asked. She had a blistered burn on her chest, and the ragged clothing all around it was scorched. There was dried, clotted blood all around the tear, the flesh fused in globules as if it had melted and very quickly reformed.

He could see that Amber, despite her bravado, was shaking. 'I don't think a Magna pistol could do that,' she said in a small voice.

Robbie blinked. 'You don't?'

'It makes a different impact, yeah? The shape, the burn,

it's all wrong.' She looked up at him, her eyes wide in in-comprehension. 'Roberto ... this is a *laser* wound.'

'Laser?' He wrinkled his nose in confusion. 'But we don't have ...'

'Go and get one of the oldies,' said Amber. 'Get Lulu, or Shan. I'll stay with her.'

VII

When they reached Maddi's room, Beth realised it was un-guarded. It was marked off from the rest of the dome simply by a piece of white plastic tape, diagonally across the door, to remind people not to enter. The room was unsecured. Everything was as it had been left, Maddi's body aside.

Mia squatted down in front of the squiggles on the wall. '*This* bothers me,' she said softly.

'What do we reckon?' Colm frowned at the bloodied squiggles. 'Last will and testament of Maddi Vanderbilt, naming her killer? Or something outrageously weird?'

Beth was exasperated. 'Come on, Colm. I don't think it was Mia any more than she thinks it was me.'

'So what the hell *is* it?' Mia asked, jabbing her finger at Maddi's blood-graffiti.

'Not pretty, is what it is,' said Colm softly.

'A ... a message, maybe. Telling us you might know the reason she died.' Beth sensed she was grasping at straws.

'If I knew why she died,' said Mia, 'we wouldn't be here.'

Beth came over, peered intently over Mia's shoulder at the marks on the wall. She had to admit that they could, easily – if you turned your head and allowed for Maddi's hand failing as her strength died – read M-I-A.

And then again …

Wait a minute.

'There's something wrong,' murmured Beth. 'Something we're not getting. There has to be. It doesn't make sense … And I can almost see it …'

'Maddi had to have let her killer in, right?' said Colm.

The girls glanced at each other, Beth realising that Mia, too, had overlooked this simple, obvious fact.

Colm spread his hands. 'Stands to reason, yeah? We all want our privacy. We've all got lockable rooms. So she let them in.' He waved towards the desk and chair, where the clutter of Maddi's possessions was still scattered, the objects stacked semi-neatly: polished pebbles, hand-drawn maps, odd bits of junk and debris, a jacket on the back of the chair, boots under the desk. 'No sign of a struggle of any sort. She wasn't fighting to keep this person out.' Colm squatted down, thoughtfully ran a finger across the floor. He lifted his finger, inspected it. 'No scuff-marks or bloodstains in the living area.'

'So … Maddi was expecting her visitor,' Beth said, feeling stupid.

'Could be.'

Beth looked back at the bloodstains in the bedroom again. 'It all happened in here. It must have been really fast, really horrible.'

'I wonder … how long she took to die,' said Mia softly.

Her voice was old, hard, remote, like a slowly moving

glacier. Beth sensed that, if Mia were to work out right now who Maddi's killer had been, she would unleash some terrible vengeance on them, a punishment of Mia's own devising which the rest of them could only guess at.

'*Step away from her.*'

At the sound of a voice, they all turned to face the doorway.

Zach. His face impassive, his arm unwavering as he levelled his Magna pistol at a point directly between Beth Kane's eyes.

'I'll deal with you two later,' he said. 'For now, I need *her.*' Mia had reached for her own weapon, but Zach's voice snapped across the room, a whiplash order. 'Don't even *think* about it, Mia. You two are already guilty of conspiracy and assault. You don't want to make that worse. Throw it down.'

Mia hesitated. Then, her body slumped in defeat, she tossed the gun on to the floor, where it fell with a loud clatter. Zach did not even flinch. Beth, her fists clenched, heart thumping, hardly dared breathe.

Colm stepped forward, hands spread. 'Zachary. C'mon. You *know* you're making a big mistake.'

'Shut up, Colm.' He didn't even look at him. 'You know, Beth, I was on my way back to the cell to try and reason with you, yeah? I found an empty cell, and a couple of scared, injured kids. Finn was incoherent, Xara's traumatised.'

'We didn't mean–' Mia began.

'No, Mia. It's too late for that.' Veins bulged on his strong arms, and Beth could see a pulse throbbing in his temple. She had seen rage like this before. It made people frightening, unpredictable. '*You*,' he said to Beth. 'Outside.'

Beth hesitated.

Zach lunched forward, grabbing her shoulder, so hard that it burned. He grabbed her around the neck, his muscular arm holding her firmly in place, gun jammed against her temple. She fought for breath, tried to stay calm.

'Zach,' she heard Colm saying. 'Stop this, c'mon. We all need to relax.'

'We can relax when the evil has been driven out of this place,' Zach replied. His voice was unnervingly calm. 'And no sooner.'

'You can't *kill* her, man.' Colm was angrier than Beth had ever known him. 'We always said, yeah, anything like this, it would be banishment. That's the ultimate sanction. Sent away. You want the death penalty back, Zach? What kind of Old Mars talk is that?'

Mia took a step forward. 'You think this is the answer, Zach? You're gonna murder Beth? Add one more body to the count?'

'Not murder,' he said calmly. 'Execution.'

'We don't–' Mia began.

'And if you try and stop me,' Zach said, 'I'll kill both of you as well.'

His arm tightened on Beth's neck and he dragged her into the Habitation corridor, heading outside.

VIII

Pain was slicing through Ella Dax's body again.

It started at the wrists, spreading up to her forearms and shoulders. Something spiked into her back, making her gasp for breath.

She slammed herself against the wall of the corridor, trying to cause pain, a normal, recognisable pain, to take this agony away. She could feel a coldness spreading through her, and a darkness in her brain.

Something deep in the back of her mind told her that she knew what this was.

That she had always known.

Her memory. Her terrible, vivid memory of being repeatedly hurled against the wall of that shuttle. The taste of blood and metal, the terrible, screaming sound of the engines. The smell of burning.

The terrible, unimaginable pain, like liquid fire in her body.

Only now it seemed different. She was looking down on the memory from above.

As if it was something which–

Slowly, gasping, Ella slid down the wall, falling to her knees. For two seconds she remained immobile, head and arms lolling, like a puppet whose strings had been cut.

And then her head snapped upwards, eyes still closed, but a cold, strange smile on her face.

Everything made sense. The memory, sealed away.

As if it was something which happened to someone else.

Ella's eyes slowly opened. They were an angry intense electric-blue, like two shining lights buried deep in her head.

The pain had gone.

And slowly, the rich tapestry of filigree implants on her skin began to glow, twisting and swirling, pounding with new, artificial life-blood.

She drew herself up to her full height, her back straight.

'This unit is engaged,' said a voice which was part Ella, and part something else.

The last move in a deadly game had been played. A game which had begun not a few cycles ago, but decades.

A revolution was about to begin.

IX

In front of the Main Dome, Beth fell on the muddy ground, coughing, swallowing hard. Her mouth tasted dry, ashy. Her whole body was pummelled, weak. She had no fight left in her. Nothing at all.

The rain had started again. All around them, it thundered on the blue mud, soaking her hair, her face, her clothes.

Zach stood over her, the gun looming huge and powerful, dominating everything. She sensed that this was it. No going back. There was no sound but the endless rain, and his cold, commanding voice.

'Kneel up,' he said. 'Hands behind your head.'

She obeyed. She did not dare do otherwise.

'So,' he said softly. 'Sister Bethany Kane. Innocence and

sweetness. Pure, unsullied naivety. The others might buy it. Colm, yeah, Lu, even Mia might have fallen for it. But not me. I can see right through you.'

She said nothing. She cowered like a cornered animal, words drying up in her raw throat.

'You didn't *crash* here, did you, Beth …? Did you? It's all lies. Or fake memories. You came here on purpose. An assassin, sent by Earth to kill us all. Quietly, one by one.'

'Don't be *ridiculous*.' What else could she say? She knew it had little hope of saving her life. 'If someone wanted to do that, they could–'

'There was never any *Arcadia*, was there, Beth? No explosion, no wreckage. No frantic, last-minute scrabble for the life-pods. *Was there, Beth*?' Zach circled round her. 'You know what I think? I think you half-believe it all … A fiction so real you actually think it's true.'

The muddy, wet ground loomed in her vision. The oddly comforting chill of the evening air bit at her. The sea roared, the rain lashed down. The mountains sang their howling song, like a final lament.

'Why do you think that?' she whispered.

'Because of what's in *there*,' he said, jabbing her temple hard. 'The Chapter implant. It's creating some kind of … alternate truth for you. Blocking out what you've done.'

This was absurd. Even faced with death, she was angry at his stupidity, at his ignorance of their ways.

'Zach. I'm sorry. The Blessed Chapter of Continual Progress sometimes modifies biology with technology, it's true. But–'

'I know what it does.'

'No, you don't. Listen. The chip, it's … a *behavioural* limiter. I can defend myself, I can fight up to a point, but … it stops me from acting on violent impulses. It has nothing to do with the memory function.'

He shook his head angrily, the gun unwavering. 'If that was true, you could have told us all about it from day one.'

'It's a private thing. I don't talk about it.' Tears poured hotly down her face, mixing with the cold rain. 'That's why I seized up in the river, couldn't kill that creature.'

He tilted his head. 'You're lying.'

'No. Listen. Because I did once, Zach. I did something terrible, and you really, really don't want to know. It's buried so deeply in my mind that I almost can't remember it. *I almost can't remember his name.* And I could never, ever do it again.'

Outside the Main Dome, small knots of Towners had scattered, gathered curiously, then scattered again, a commotion growing around the fire-pit. The small crowd had backed off when it became very clear who Zach had brought out with him, and what was about to happen.

'You're lying,' Zach snarled. 'It controls your mind. Makes you believe all your stories. All these new lies, they … they come to you naturally.'

'Please … Please, no.'

'You're *lying*!'

Images swam in her head.

The snout of the river-creature as it exploded, her own impotent finger on the trigger of her gun. Mia standing there, unleashing bolt after bolt into the animal …

The Drones lowering themselves into the river, emerging with their prize …

The flaring of the converter's globe, and the wild applause of the Towners …

Shadows in the Ship … watching her … watching over her …

The smears of blood on Maddi's wall …

In that second, she realised. She knew.

Something blazed into glorious, horrifying existence in her head, a connection across the synapses, something which had not been there before. It was astonishingly clear to her.

The limiter chip in her mind squealed, sang, burned her brain. It fought her, as if trying to stop her from seeing the truth.

She knew.

The smears of blood. Oh, Great Power. Oh, no.

Not M-I-A. Something else. Something even more terrible. It changed everything. And Zach was going to kill her, before she could tell anyone.

'You've got it all wrong,' she said, gabbling in fear and haste. She started to hold a hand out to him imploringly, but it slapped back into place behind her head. 'Zach … please. *I think I know.*'

He levelled the gun with both hands. 'It's too late for any more lies, Beth.'

'You've got to listen to me.'

She did not dare get up, or even lift her head. She knew one single move could make him pull the trigger. Could make him end her life. She tried to think of anything but the effect of a superheated plasma bolt, like she had seen on that creature. Blowing its brains from its skull in less than a second.

'Please, listen,' she begged again. 'I know how they did it, I ...'

When she had thought there was nothing, five minutes ago, she had been limp, abandoned, her body and mind falling into cold and shadows. But now she knew there was a small glimmer of hope, she knew she had to speak.

'Zach,' she said urgently. 'The blood on the walls. What Maddi was trying to tell us, I know it. I've worked it out.'

'What are you *talking* about?'

Beth licked her lips. 'Maddi's told us who her murderer is. It's right there. Right in front of us.'

'*Zach!*'

A voice from the dome. He swung the gun away from her. She tried to focus on the tableau forming in the haze of rain in front of the entrance.

Mia and Colm, both armed with the heavy-duty Karson rifles. Behind them, unarmed, shouldering her way to the front of the group, came Lulu. Then behind them, Amber and a few of the younger ones: Finn, Xara, Gabe, Reza, Aisling, Brad and others. Beth could see that Mia had her rifle-barrel levelled directly at Zach, unwavering, unable at this distance to miss.

'Zach,' said Lulu softly, as she stepped forward out of the crowd. Zach narrowed his eyes at her. 'Please,' she said, and took another step forward. 'Please listen to us. You're not thinking straight. It's *not* her.'

Zach's face contorted, his gun-arm wavering as he tried to take this in, staring at Lulu.

'What do you mean?' Zach's voice was low, threatening.

Lulu took another step forward, holding out a hand. Her booted feet made deep imprints in the wet earth. 'Amber and Robbie found Baljeet,' Lulu said. 'In the Hydro 1 ducting. She's been dead a few hours, Zach. Beth was locked up all that time. *It can't be her.*'

She watched him swing the pistol from one to the other, blinking in the torrential rain, backing away from them. Uncertainty made him waver for the first time.

'Please … Please, Zach,' Lulu opened her eyes wide, imploring. The cold wind ruffled her hair, made her cloak billow behind her. She turned her hand over, palm upwards. 'Please. Give me the gun.'

'Zach …?' Beth, pressing the advantage, cautiously began to take her hands away from her head.

Lulu took another step forward, so that she was only a few emms away from Zach. He was pointing the gun right at her.

There was a humming in Beth's ears, a horrible silence like static electricity. The pain began to spread through her head, the pulsing, throbbing ache which always seemed to forewarn her of disaster.

Lulu moved nearer to Zach, and nearer again. 'Give me the gun, Zach,' she said again. 'You know I'd never lie to you.'

Slowly and cautiously, Beth began to lift herself from the ground.

Zach moved with sharp, precise brutality. The butt of the pistol across her face, smacking with a force she had never suspected, sent her sprawling in the wet mud. Hot pain seared across her cheekbone.

A second later, he hauled her to her knees again. '*Stay! There!*'

Shaken, shocked, she put her hands behind her head once more. She could feel the wound spreading across her cheek, pounding and throbbing. Warm blood trickled down her wet face.

Lulu had taken several steps back in shock, and Mia moved forward to take her place.

'Put it down, Zach,' said Mia, her face cold and hard.

'You can't *tell* me what to do.'

'Yeah, we can. Under our agreed regulations. Me, Shan, Lulu, Colm … we're all agreed. We're relieving you of command.'

'What the hell …?'

'It's gone too far, Zach.' Mia sounded totally calm, totally in control.

Zach was backing away. 'No,' he said softly. 'Not this time. This time it ends.'

He swung the Magna pistol back round to cover Beth, moving the cold gun right up against her head.

'You killed Maddi,' he said softly. 'You killed Maddi because she discovered your secret. She knew something about you, something she was going to tell the rest of us.'

'*I didn't kill Maddi!*' Her vision was blurring in the rain, fear coursing through her like a drug. 'Zach! *Please!* I swear I didn't!' She was shivering uncontrollably, waiting for the impact she knew would come.

'It ends here,' said Zach. 'It ends with Bethany Kane.'

He jammed the cold, hard barrel against her temple. His finger tightened on the trigger.

Beth screamed.

A single blast echoed through the evening air.

∞

The circle is almost complete.

It is coming. This power gathers strength in the shadows. Activation will bring destruction. This small, hopeless, helpless fragment of humanity is finished.

There is a storm coming. It will destroy everything in its path.

Everything.

12
HUMANITY

I

Shan strolled up and down on one of the high walkways in Hydro 2, occasionally leaning over the edge to check on the cool-sprays. Their gentle hiss was soft and restful.

This place was a popular duty – it was easy, and the temperature balance meant that it was a comfortable place to patrol. He stopped, leaned on the handrail and gazed out over the vapour-doused crops, breathing deeply. He listened to the restful splash of the sprayed water. The rich, fertile smell of the plants drifted upwards.

Deeply disturbed by the events of the last couple of cycles, Shan had withdrawn into himself, becoming snappy and tense. Two people he liked, two good people – gone. Maddi had been one of the best, kind and caring, and Baljeet – well, Baljeet could be annoying and officious, but she was an honest person, a hard worker. They'd done some good patrols together, shared memories of growing up in City Stations. He'd enjoyed hearing all her stories about her father. Thought Rohit Midda sounded like a good man. A decent man.

Shan wondered if there were any decent men left.

He liked to think he was one himself, and Colm, despite his womanising. And Zach was at times. But Zach let his temper get the better of him, and didn't always make the right decisions. That much was clear.

A soft, whining sound at the end of the walkway made him jump and reach for his pistol, but he relaxed on seeing that it was a patrolling Drone. A blue one, labelled 314.

Even after all this time, Shan reflected ruefully, he hadn't got them all worked out, couldn't remember all their numbers.

The Drone bobbed gracefully on its propulsion jet, as if giving a curtsy.

Shan gave a mock salute. 'Evening, fella. How's it going?'

The Drone was silent. It hovered there, watching him with its one pulsing red eye.

Shan grinned, leaning on the balcony overlooking the crops. 'You guys aren't great conversationalists, are you? Maybe some people like that. Maybe you listen.'

The Drone hovered.

Watching him.

II

Mia shoved Zach down into his chair in the Council Room.

'*Sit!*'

He was clutching at his shoulder, blood frothing out between his fingers. Beth, Colm and Lulu were not far behind, and Beth slammed her fist on the door-lock control.

Mia jammed her pistol under Zach's chin. 'Some leader *you* turned out to be. Almost got the wrong person killed.'

'All right, Mia. That's enough.' Beth, still cold and shaking, holding a compress to her gashed cheek, was barely able to believe she was still alive. For the second time in twenty hours, a carefully-targeted shot by Mia had saved her life. 'It's not his fault. He didn't know.'

'He nearly *killed* you!'

'Where's Ella?' Colm asked – languidly, as if he almost didn't care, but thought he ought to mention it.

'Try and raise her,' snapped Mia.

On the other side of the room, Lulu was already trying Ella on the radio. 'I'm on it,' she said.

Zach looked up, glowering. 'All in on this mutiny, are you?'

'You're so damn *stupid*,' Mia spat at him.

'He's on our side, Mia. *Leave it.*' Beth was astonishing even herself by how calmly she had taken charge. Adrenaline was driving her, pounding through her from the moment she had thought she was to die.

Zach was glaring up at her, his face pale and trembling as blood gushed across his hand, dripped on to the Table. 'So what is this, then? A coup?'

'Common sense,' said Beth. 'Any luck with Ella?'

Lulu tapped her finger on the radio. 'Can't raise her. Think her channel's offline.' She threw the radio aside, went over to Zach. 'I need to take care of that wound.' She didn't wait to be asked, but came forward, pulling a square silver med-patch from her bag. 'Let go.'

Zach did so, wincing in pain. For a second, the blood gushed, and then the wound cauterized, closing under the spray Lulu covered it with, blood clotting. She sliced his shirt open expertly and slammed the med-patch on to the torn skin. 'And you, come here,' she added to Beth. She examined the compress the girl had been holding to her face, and nodded. 'All right. That's sealed. You can let go.'

Beth sat down opposite Zach.

He hardly dared even acknowledge her. 'I'm ... sorry,' he said, eventually.

'It's fine. Really.'

'Tell me about Balj,' Zach said. 'Where ...?'

'Hydro 1,' said Mia curtly. 'Amber and Robbie found her. Killed at short range with some form of impact laser. Or something else.'

'It *was* something else,' murmured Beth.

Zach glared up at Beth. 'Come on, then. Hit me with it. You seem to have won everyone over.'

Beth watched them all. Zach, pale and sweating. Lulu, expectant and calm. Mia, her hand unwavering, covering Zach with the gun. Itching to shoot him again.

'The killer isn't any of you,' Beth said. 'It isn't me, or anyone who's got in from outside, either.'

'Which leaves *who*, exactly?' Zach was not hiding his derision.

Beth made sure everyone's attention was on her. 'Lulu, show us that scan of the blood from Maddi's room again.'

'Hang on.' Lulu's thumbs flickered over her scan-pad, and she placed it on the desk, projecting a hologram of the three smeared, bloody shapes. They floated in the air above the Table, suspended in fuzzy light, able to be viewed from all angles as the image pivoted.

'As I thought,' Beth said softly.

'What?' Mia snapped. 'You're not gonna tell me she wrote my name in her blood after all? Because that would be too stupid for words.'

'No,' said Beth. 'Lulu … have you got a pen?'

Lulu passed Beth the pen from her bag, a slim, gold-tipped marker. On the Table, Beth drew the three symbols, aligned exactly as they were in the holo-image of Maddi's wall. The bird-like, curly symbol which could be an M, the straight line which they had assumed to be an I, and the lopsided triangle of the A.

'Notice anything?' Beth urged them. It was so obvious, and she was astonished that they could not see it. Her heart pounded with the excitement of the knowledge, but also with fear at what it meant. 'Maddi would have had seconds. She was *dying*. Her hand was faltering as she tried to write a clue … Her only thought was to save the rest of us. To tell us what was happening.'

Lulu, Mia and Zach stared at each other in incomprehension.

'That, you see, that's not an M,' said Beth, gesturing at the first symbol.

'It's not?' Lulu leaned over the table, staring at the gold markings Beth had drawn. Then she drew back, very slowly. 'Oh, my gods.'

'Yes,' said Beth. 'Think. Where do we see these, *every single cycle* here in Town? Who do you all take for granted, barely noticing them as they pass you by? Who does all the hard jobs, the boring jobs? Who would you let into your room without question, never even *think* about mistrusting?'

Zach leaned forward, wincing in pain. 'Wait a minute … What are you saying?'

'The answer was staring us in the face. All along.' Beth paused, waiting for the others to catch up. 'Maddi and Baljeet weren't killed by a human being.'

Mia frowned. 'Not human …? What …?' Then Mia realised. And as she did, her mouth formed a silent O, and her face went very, very pale.

'Yeah,' said Beth. 'I know.' She looked down at the paper, where she had written what she could see in the bloodstains.

Not letters.

Numbers.

Not M-I-A, but:

3

1

4.

III

In Hydro 2, the blue Drone's lower cavity opened, and the nozzle of its cutting-tool emerged, a small black tube sliding silently from its housing.

'Want a job, do you?' Shan laughed. 'Okay, let's see if we can find you something. C'mon.'

He headed towards the other end of the walkway, beckoning the Drone to come with him.

The Drone did not move.

Shan paused, frowning, looking over his shoulder in puzzlement. He lifted a hand, waved, clicked his fingers. Drone 314 did not respond.

'Odd,' he muttered. 'Not hearing me …? Why, though? Receptors are on.' He strolled up to the Drone, waved in front of its pulsing eye, patted its metallic body. 'Oh, don't tell me we got another dud. Ella *will* be thrilled.'

There was another whining sound in the dome, one of a slightly different pitch. Another Drone – this time a gold one with the number 488 – had appeared at the other end of the metal bridge, as if mirroring its fellow's position. It bobbed in the same way on its propulsion jet, and seemed to wait.

Then, its cavity opened and its tubular cutting-tool extruded in the same way.

Shan frowned. He walked towards the second Drone, pausing at a point almost exactly halfway between the two of them.

'What are you guys up to?' he asked softly, saying it more to himself. 'Damn it. Suppose I'd better …' He fumbled for his radio, calling Ella. 'Ell? Shan here. You there …?' The radio hissed and crackled.

The Drones began to advance.

Very slowly.

Shan thumbed the call-button again, feeling an odd sense of alarm. 'Ell, come and give me a hand, will you? Got a couple of dodgy Drones in Hydro 2. Think the receptors might be knackered. They're not respond–'

A flash of light, searing heat across his palm as the radio was cut to pieces, hot metal scattering to the edges of the walkway. Shan yelped in pain, looking in astonishment at the Drone which had activated its cutting-beam.

'Stop,' he said, still more irritated than afraid, holding his hands up. 'You're malfunctioning! Stop!'

The Drone continued to advance.

As did the other.

Shan looked wildly back and forth from one to the other. He lifted his palm, staring in horror at the burned, seared flesh.

The Drone did that.

Not accidentally.

The implications hit him, and he turned first one way, then the other, wondering if he could dodge either of them in time.

Beams lanced from both Drones at the same time. They cut into the metal beneath his feet, searing white-hot lines across it, slicing it in two places, melting it. The walkway floor screeched as it began to shear away. There was a hot smell of burning metal.

Shan staggered, staring in horror. He was standing on a sheet of metal which was about to be cut away beneath him.

Thirty emms above the floor of Hydro 2.

Both Drones sliced their beams across the walkway at the same time. There was a screech, a shower of sparks.

Shan, scrabbling for the useless handrail, felt emptiness beneath him …

IV

The Council Room had erupted into chaos, everyone talking at once, gesticulating and shouting over one another.

Beth realised she had said the unthinkable. And now, everyone else had to think it. They had to.

'You're … crazy,' Zach was saying. He staggered to his feet, wincing in pain. '*Insane*. The *Drones*? Bethany, Drones can't kill people. They're a, a tool, an *object*.'

'And yet they *have*!' said Beth, desperation making her voice dry and croaky. She slammed her hands on the Council Table. 'They've killed Maddi. They've killed Baljeet. And they're coming for the rest of us. They're rising up. It's a revolution.'

Zach was having none of it. 'Oh, for … They can't revolt, Beth. They can't *think*. It would be like …' He thumped the Table. 'It would be like *this* coming to kill us. Or the … the scan-pads or the jeeps.'

'Plus,' said Lulu, 'they're infallibly programmed not to harm humans, Beth. They physically *can't* do it.'

'They *couldn't* do it,' Zach said, thumping the Table again. 'It's *impossible*.'

'Zach's right, Beth.' Mia, reluctantly, was siding with her leader again.

Beth could not believe how blinkered they were – how accepting of the way things were, and the way things had always been. Surely it did not take a massive leap of faith to accept that this could happen? Why was she the only one who could see it?

'*Please*,' she said. 'Listen to me.' She found herself cupping that invisible sphere in front of her again, as she so often did when imploring, begging, persuading. 'Don't you realise? These words … infallible, impossible … they mean nothing. Thousands of years ago, on Earth's oceans, there was a ship called the *Titanic*. You remember? You know what they said it was? *Unsinkable*. And yet, one night, four days into the voyage, it hit an iceberg. It tore open the hull and the boat sank. Thousands of people died.'

'Spare us the history lesson,' said Mia sharply. 'You're saying *infallible* means it hasn't failed yet, right?'

'Right!' Her gaze alighted on Colm, who had been quieter than the others. 'You believe me? Don't you?'

He tapped his finger against his chin, thoughtful. 'You're a lot of things, Princess,' he said. 'But I don't think you're a fantasist. I gotta believe you. It's the only thing that makes sense.'

'Thank you,' she said gratefully. She moved closer to him. 'Colm, can you do something? Round up the young ones, let them know what's happening. Break out the armaments and get them to assume defensive positions. This is serious. You *have* to make them believe you.'

He hesitated. 'You're sure about this?'

'Colm, I need you to do this. Please. For me. Get Amber to help, she'll listen to you. She'll believe us.'

For a moment. Colm wavered. Then he said, 'All right. Leave it to me.' He hurried out of the Council Room.

'This … this is *insane*,' said Mia, gesturing wildly. 'You got any idea how many of them … neuro-things there are in one Drone's functional core?'

'Synapses,' said Beth. 'Yes, there are billions.'

'Yeah, billions. And *every* single one's hardwired to protect and serve humans, yeah? How could that kind of tech malfunction?'

'I have no idea,' said Beth. '*But it has.*'

Lulu had been quiet during the exchanges, but now she spoke up. 'It could,' she said. 'It could be done.'

They all turned to her.

'Someone with the right technical ability *could* override the artificial synapses in one of the Drones,' Lulu said. 'Scramble the interfaces. And they're all linked into the same neural network, right? Like a local group of brains.'

Beth was relieved that someone was talking sense at last. '*Yes*! And so once one single Drone was corrupted … We assume that was 314 … And the infection could spread like a virus.'

'And the rest would follow,' Lulu agreed.

Tension, uncertainty hung in the air as they weighed it all up.

'The rest …' Mia spoke softly. 'All right, so it *would* make sense,' she said. 'If it got into the wireless tech. The glove, remember? My glove almost killed me. And the Drone that blew itself up … Maybe that was rejecting the programming. *Something* caused it to have a conflict. Overloaded its circuits. Maybe that something was being asked to kill humans. It had a breakdown.'

'So, are we only talking 314?' Beth said. 'Can we take it out with a pistol, a frag-bomb? Or has the virus already spread to the others?'

At the window, Mia tensed, and in a second she had drawn her gun. 'It's all of them.'

'Mia?' Lulu said, looking up in alarm. 'What … what have you …?'

'Out there.' There was such a terrible empty coldness in her voice as she stared out through the tinted glass of the Council Room, her gaze fixed on the compound outside. 'Fuck's sake, Beth. You're not so crazy after all.'

The others joined her at the window.

A semicircle of Drones, seven of them, surrounded the domes of Town. All floating at exactly the same height, all closing in, slowly, inexorably.

'They're not *armed*,' Zach said disparagingly. 'What are they going to do? Mop us to death?'

As they watched, the red lights on each of the Drones pulsed in unison. Their hidden cavities flipped open, cutting-tools extending on flexible arms.

'Almost,' said Beth with a shudder, turning to Zach. 'Those tools can slice plastic and metal in two. I doubt they'd have much trouble with human flesh.'

For a second, the Drones hovered there, menacingly inert, looking as if they were going to hold their position.

And then, as one, the Drones began to advance upon Town.

V

Shan crawled along between the rows of plants, the hiss of the water-jets overlaid with the sound of the burning metal behind him.

The walkway had smashed into a large section of the crops, scorching them with fire. The sprinklers had kicked in almost immediately, dousing the hall in a fine spray which rattled down like rain, sizzling in the heat, creating clouds of vapour which swirled around like fog.

There was a sickening pain in his leg, but he managed to stagger to his feet, wiping hot blood from his face. He could not, as yet, tell the extent of his injuries, but he could see blood trailing all along the lower walkway where he had staggered from the wreckage.

He realised his arm was gashed, warm blood trickling down his hand and dripping from his fingertips. He could taste blood and smoke.

He had to get to a medikit.

The Drones hovered, buzzing, high up in the Hydroponics unit. As if they were toying with him.

Or as if they were awaiting instructions.

And then, a familiar figure appeared at the end of the walkway. She was shrouded in vapour and silhouetted against the light, but he could see straight away who it was. Tall, slender, dark. Twisted blue dreadlocks.

She had come. She must have got his radio message.

'Ell.' He was able to croak her name in relief before his legs gave way and he fell on all fours on the soaking wet walkway. 'Two of the Drones ... Gone crazy.' He gestured feebly upwards. 'Need to ... to deactivate ...'

Ella turned very, very slowly, as if her reactions were dulled somehow. She strode forward, jerky, as if in slow motion.

She stood with her hands on her hips.

Shan, the trained hunter, noticed there was something odd about her body language, as if she were uncomfortable in her skin, moving creakily. Mechanically.

And the filigree patterns on Ella's dark skin were *glowing*.

They were alive, as if coiling and twisting, changing form, colour. Pulsing with energy. Her body was framed in a halo of light, and a slithering, metallic sound emanated from her body.

She seemed taller. She seemed stronger, colder, suffused with a silvery-blue luminescence. A smile began to form, jerkily, on Ella's face. It was the smile with no warmth, no happiness, no affection.

'Shan,' she said, and even her voice sounded harsh, metallic. She said his name again, and the single syllable sounded cold, remote. '*Shan.*'

'Ella …' He struggled to stand. 'What the hell …'

'There is a storm coming,' said Ella. 'It will destroy everything in its path. Everything.'

'*What …?* What's happened to you?'

'Nothing has *happened*,' she said. 'I was always here. I was asleep, and now I am awake.'

'Awake …?' Shan struggled to lift himself up. 'Ella, help me …'

'Ella Dax is not a concept. The functional personality has deactivated. This unit is fully operational.'

A cold, unearthly feeling spread through him, as if he was alone in an empty, dark graveyard. He started to shake.

'What do you mean?' he said, gritting his teeth, clinging on to his savagely-torn arm. 'Not a concept …? What … what *unit*?'

And then, terrifyingly, horribly, Shan understood.

With startling speed, her hand shot out and grasped his neck. The grip was astonishing, like cold living metal wrapping itself around his trachea, forcing him to his knees.

He understood. He realised. Staring into those cold electric-blue eyes, he knew what she was. What they had been living with all this time.

And it was all too late, as a terrible blackness descended in his brain.

∞

13
REVOLUTION

I

'Colm, what the hell are we *doing*?'

Amber's grubby face was fearful beneath her tangled hair, and Colm knew this was the time to say the right thing. He couldn't be the joker any more. He had to show there was more to him than that.

Behind them in the Rec Hall, fearful, the crowd of twenty or so Twelvies and Thirteeners were doing as they'd been told. They were upending the tables and chairs and making them into a makeshift barricade across the passage-way leading to the rest of the dome. Some of them hadn't understood what was going on, hadn't believed it, but Colm and Amber had done their best.

Colm didn't know how long it would hold the Drones, but at least he was getting them to do something. He was painfully aware that they had a couple of dozen kids missing, and he wasn't about to start scouring Town for them. If they were holed up in their rooms, or in the main-tenance tunnels or other hiding-places – assuming word had even got round of what was going on – then that was probably the safest place for them right now.

'Stay calm, yeah? I need you to stop the others from pan-icking.' He took her face in his hands, gently. 'Can you do that for me, Amber?'

For a second, she did not understand, her lip quivering. He saw a frightened child in her face, there, rather than the assured, cocky young woman Amber liked to pretend she was.

And then she nodded.

'Good girl,' said Colm. 'Break out the emergency weapons. The impact bombs too. Get more barricades set up, on the upper corridors.'

'How long have we got?' Amber asked.

Colm was staring over her shoulder, all the way across the Rec Hall to the main entrance of the dome.

He could see the glint of light on the silver shapes as they approached. The burning jets of their neutron engines. And then came the soft whine of something like a dozen Drones, skulking around the outside of Town.

'Not long,' he said grimly. 'Barricades, now.'

'Where are you going?'

'To find more weapons.'

'Don't be long! Please!'

'I ... I won't.'

Amber scowled at him. 'What the hell's going on? You're planning something, aren't you?'

'This is pointless. If the Drones are trying to kill us, we can't hold them off. We need to get out of here. I'm going to make a break for it. Do you wanna come?'

'No! Don't be stupid. You'll get yourself killed.'

'And if I stay here,' he said, 'what'll happen?'

'There's a chance.'

'With kids who can barely shoot straight? I don't think so. Listen. Do your best. If it goes wrong, fall back to the Comms tower if you can get there. It's a good vantage point, easy to defend.'

Amber nodded, taking the information in. 'Comms tower. Right ... Colm – please don't–'

'I did what Beth asked me to do. I rounded up as many of you as I could find and got you here. She didn't ask me to be in charge. Nobody did.' He turned to go. 'Last chance, Amber.'

'No. Goodbye, Colm.'

He lifted a hand in salute. 'Bye, thief. I'll miss you.'

And he hurried up the steps, slipped out of the door into the accommodation area and was gone.

II

'Where are you *going*, Spacegirl?'

Mia grabbed Beth by the shoulder as she descended the stairs, pulled her round so that she was facing her.

Beth kept her tone soft and calm, but urgent. 'We need to get to the Ship.'

'Why?'

'*Trust* me, Mia!'

'No!' Mia shoved her up against the wall, pinning her there. 'Tell me what you're doing.'

'In the Ship,' Beth said, meeting Mia's angry gaze calmly, 'there is an access point to the central computer. Right? I've communicated with it. I've used Resonance. I know my way in. If I can get it to accept new orders, then … There's something we can do.'

Mia did not relax her hold. She scanned Beth's face, her jaw set, tense and angry. It was clear to Beth that Mia still did not quite accept or understand what was going on, even though she had seen it with her own eyes.

'So you've actually got a *plan*?'

'Yes. I've got a plan. Somebody has to. And given that you all suspected me of murder a few hours ago, I think the least you can do is listen to me.'

'How do we get there? If it is the Drones … They'll have their electronic eyes and ears everywhere. We don't stand a chance.'

'Out through Hydroponics. Through the cooling vents to outside, and into the Ship that way.'

For a few tense seconds, it seemed Mia was not going to agree. Then, she slowly relaxed her grip and stepped backwards. The two girls faced each other, tense like two wild dogs circling one another, staking out their ground.

'You're crazy,' Mia said. 'We'll never get through.'

'Oh, yes?' Beth took an angry step forward, forcing Mia to recoil against the stair-rail. She didn't care any more. She knew she had to do this. 'Well, I am not sitting back and waiting for them to pick us all off one by one, Mia. Are you with me?'

The Huntress tensed. Beth realised she could see something new in her face. A shadow which she had not seen before.

It was fear.

'It could be the last thing we do,' Mia said.

'Yes? And? So what?'

Mia grinned slowly. 'You sound so much like one of us now. You know that?'

'Sit there and wait to die, Mia. Or come with me and do something about it.' Beth turned and made to go down the stairs again, but Mia did not follow. Beth slowly looked over her shoulder. 'No?'

The lights flickered, buzzing angrily, but stayed on, as if hanging on for dear life like everything else.

Beth knew she had one ace left to play. She opened her eyes wide at Mia, in mockery and contempt.

'You are lots of things, Mia Janowska,' she said. 'But I did not ever think you'd be a bloody *coward*.'

She turned her back on Mia and strode off.

There was the sound of heavy footsteps from behind. Mia overtook her on the stairs, her pistol drawn. 'All right,' she said, striding out ahead of Beth. 'You got me.'

Beth offered up her apologies to the Great Power for the unaccustomed profanity. But it had worked.

They hurried down the stairs. A second later, the lights flickered again, and this time they cut out.

'Oh, fuck,' Mia said softly.

'Power,' Beth said. 'The neutron booster.'

'The Drones must have got to it.'

A soft, reddish light began to suffuse the stairwell. It had the disconcerting hue of fresh blood.

'What's that?' Beth asked in alarm.

'Emergency backup lighting,' said Mia. 'Different circuits. It's all we've got now.'

The two girls looked at each other for a second, in firm understanding. Beth put her hand out, and Mia clasped it for an instant, firm, resolute.

'Let's do this, Spacegirl,' she said. 'Let's finish the metal bastards.'

III

In the Council Room, Zach checked the charge on his pistol, slammed the powerpack home.

'What are you doing?' Lulu asked fearfully, turning away from the door where she was keeping watch. In the dim, blood-red light, she thought Zach was terrifying, unpredictable. A force which could not be contained. 'You can't …'

'I'm going out there,' he said.

'You can't. We said we'd wait for Mia and Beth. We agreed.'

'No. You, Mia and Beth all agreed,' he said. 'I didn't agree to anything.' He moved to push past her, but she blocked his way, looking up at him in pity and fear.

'Zach, please. You used to be kind, wise …'

'I didn't,' he said emotionlessly. 'I made lucky decisions. My luck's run out now.'

'Zach–'

'Lu, I'm not sitting here to be killed by a bunch of tin-cans. You stay if you like. I'm going to try and find a way to the Comms tower, beam a hyperwave signal out.'

'You know we haven't got the power to sustain that. It could short out–'

'What does that matter? This place is finished. We've got to try anything we can.' He pushed her roughly out of the way. Shocked, she staggered back. He turned at the door. 'Are you coming?'

She turned away. 'Did you ever love me, Zach?' she asked.

'Love?' He answered like someone who was not sure what the word even meant. As if it were some alien syllable, a word from an unknown language. 'I don't know. Is that … is that what you wanted?'

Lulu Fox turned in the blood-light, gazed at Zachary Tal for what she thought could be the last time. She did not answer his question.

'This place,' she said. 'I always wanted it to be … more than existence. I wanted it to be a proper life. To be the real start of something. A community. A colony. I thought, one day … I thought some of us might even raise children here. We're not bad people, Zach, any of us. We deserve better. We deserve to make something *happen*.'

'We have done,' he said. 'People would be dead if it wasn't for you. You realise that?'

'And some are dead,' she said. 'Some who I could have saved. Should have saved.'

'Lu, what you've done for us … all of us … in your own small way, you may have helped the human race survive … That's more important than whether one person ever loved you.'

'Yes,' she said, looking away, so that he could not see her eyes stinging with tears. 'Yes, I suppose you're right.'

His hand hovered over the door-control. 'So. Are you coming?'

She moved forward as if to come with him. Then she folded her arms. 'No,' she said. 'I'm sorry.'

'Have it your way.'

'And, Zach … I think you should–'

They hardly had time to register the movement, the shadow at the window, the whine of engines. It smashed through the windows in one sweeping, explosive movement, plexiglass flying, its red light sweeping across the room in an arc.

Zach grabbed Lulu and pulled her down, but the beam had already sliced across the room, slamming into the Table.

The great circle of metal split in two, falling with a crash to the floor. Shards of glass sliced like daggers across the room, hitting scientific equipment, maps, tools, chairs.

A searing, painful heat tore through Lulu's chest as she hit the floor.

She was aware of Zach, above her, feet apart, blasting at the Drone again and again. Seconds later, the metal globe fizzed and sparked, glowed red. It blew into several pieces with a thunderous retort, chunks of burning metal scattering across the wrecked room.

The fragments of the Drone came to rest in all corners of the Council Room, burning with angry blue flames, scorching holes in the walls.

Zach ran through the pungent smoke to her. 'Are you all right?' He extended a hand to her.

She tried to focus on him. But it was no good. Her body was cold, trembling. The deep, booming sound of the Drone's explosion was still there in her head, echoing, resounding, a long, drawn-out sound like the final note of a requiem.

Everything was blurred. It was cold, and darkening as if

winter was encroaching on her mind and body, a slow glacier of death spreading through her.

She unpeeled her hand from her chest, stared unbelievingly at how it glistened with dark, sticky blood. And there was more of it, more and more, pouring out of her. The life ebbing from her body.

She stared up at Zach. She was desperately trying to form words, clutching at him, pulling him to her.

'No ... Lulu, no ...' He grabbed her shoulders, touched her face. 'Lulu, stay with me. What do you need? Is there ... is there something I can get? Lu! *Please!*'

She opened her mouth, tried to speak. It would not work. She tasted blood. The sick, metallic surge of it welling up in her throat, across her tongue.

'Lulu! Lulu, *stay with me!*'

Drip, drip, drip. Her own blood. On the floor.

She knew it was over. She had to say it, the thing she had been about to say. She pulled Zach's head down so that his ear was right beside her lips.

'Not ... not leader,' she whispered, her mouth barely able to form the words. 'Not ... you. Mia. Let ... *Mia.*'

He drew back from her, an expression of incomprehension and anger on his face. She knew he had heard. And now, the edges of her vision were turning red.

'For me,' she said, her voice thin and lost. 'Do it. For me. Please ... Because I ...'

Reality was ebbing away into nothingness. Her voice echoed, as if in a great cavern, lost and far off.

'Because I love ... I love ...'

She could no longer speak.

In the darkness, she could not see him. It was so cold now. So cold. She tried to scream, but she no longer could. She tried to focus, but her eyes no longer worked. She tried to reach a hand out to him, but he was no longer beside her.

He was a lifetime away, down a deep, swirling tunnel of darkness, anger and regret.

Stay with me.

When Lulu Fox knew her heart had stopped, it was as if she was physically wrenched from her body, soaring above the prone, pale, bloodstained figure on the floor.

Stay with me.

She was carried upwards through a funnel of bright, intense light, leaving behind the fragments of her life from the last few hundred cycles as they burned fleetingly across whatever consciousness she still had.

The burning Drone.

Zach.

The Council Room.

The Main Dome.

Then, in one swirling rush, the whole of Town, the island, Lunar Beach, the causeway, the sea, the planet, the stars, the Galaxy.

Stay with me.

But it was over, and Time and Space ceased to be. The physical world ended altogether, and a great void of darkness beckoned her onwards.

Luciana Katrina Fox's seventeen years in the Universe

were lost like a teardrop in a vast, unyielding ocean. One tiny raindrop in an endless, thundering waterfall.

And something else, something beyond existence or experience, began.

In the shattered Council Room, amid the smoke and debris, Zachary Tal slowly lowered the body of Lulu Fox to the floor, laying her down, gently.

He passed a hand across her staring, sightless eyes, so that she appeared more at peace. Then he straightened up, surveying the smoke-wreathed wreckage all around him. He clenched his fists, lifted his chin.

'I'm sorry, Lu,' he murmured. 'I didn't quite catch what you said.'

And he turned and strode from the room.

IV

'Amber …? Amber, are you listening to me?'

Amber Salem remembered the first time she had seen a Drone.

She had been maybe three years old. She could remember standing on the dunes of Mars, holding someone's hand. Her mother? Her older sister, Jaide? She had only the vaguest memories of either of them. They were on a day-ticket trip from Phobos Platform, a rare treat, and she could not remember why or how. From the ridge, you could see the Sun as a pale disc, and Earth as a blue dot. Amber remembered the Drone bringing them the special glasses for the viewing gallery. It had bounced along like a silver tennis-ball, carrying the devices in spindly pincers. She remembered the almost kind, gentle way it had bobbed down in front of her, lowering the glasses into her outstretched hand. She looked into its single red eye-disc, and they achieved a kind of understanding.

That had been ten years ago. And today, Drones wanted to kill her. And all her friends. It was as if the world had been torn apart and turned into something terrible, something wrong and evil.

'Amber,' said Robbie again. 'Listen ... I ...' He touched her arm.

'Not now, Robbie.'

She primed the slim, silver Karson rifle, one of the high-velocity hunting weapons they'd broken out of the store. Heart thudding, she looked around in the dimness at the small, huddled group she'd pulled together.

The red lighting coming on had unnerved them all at first, but Amber had guessed that it was the emergency backup. She managed to calm everyone.

She didn't know where the hell the older ones were – everyone she had here was a Twelvie or Thirteener. Herself, Robbie, Finn, Xara, Aisling, a handful of others. Their barricade, about two emms back inside the corridor leading away from the Rec Hall, was made of metal barrels, wooden tables and doors. Amber wasn't hopeful. She had seen the Drones cut through sheet metal in seconds.

The Rec Hall in front of them was empty.

She hoped it stayed that way.

'Why here?' Robbie said, sidling close to her. 'Wouldn't we see them better out in the open?'

'No way. Them Drones can fly, right? In the Rec Hall we're vulnerable from above. Defending this corridor means we box the bastards in. Less of a space to see them in.'

'I don't get this,' he said. 'Why the Drones? Why now? Why turn on us after working for us all this time?'

Amber had thought about this too. 'You mean why not slaughter us all as soon as we got off the Ship?' she said grimly.

'Or take control of the Ship and crash it. Hundreds of ways to kill us all quietly and quickly.'

'So,' said Amber in a whisper, looking quickly around at the tense faces, 'two things. Either killing us ain't all they wanna do, or something's happened in the past few cycles to change them. Or both.'

Finn straightened up behind her.

'Where have they gone?' he said. He stepped over the barricade, cautiously making his way down to the mouth of the corridor.

'Finn,' said Amber. 'Please ... come back.'

He held up a hand. 'I can't see them,' he said, peering out into the Rec Hall and looking in all directions.

'Come *back*, Finn.'

He turned back towards the group, spreading his hands. 'It's all–'

The floor ripped into flames in front of him, and he jumped back with a yelp, levelling his pistol. The Drones swooped from high above, heading down on the small group like metal birds of death.

'Fire!' Amber yelled.

A second later, the Rec Hall resounded to the angry implosion of plasma bolts. Hands trembling, Amber aimed – fired once, twice. She caught one of the Drones on the edge of its carapace, sending it swerving into another, and the two of them cannoned into a third. They sparked off each other, spinning uncontrollably. Other Towners were firing again and again, desperately shooting into the swirling cloud of Drones, hoping to hit something.

The Rec Hall was ripped apart by fire. Lancing bolts of red light screamed through the air, first cutting the metal stairs in two, then slicing tables, chairs. Sheared metal hurtled through the air, slammed into walls. The air was filled with smoke, screaming, confusion.

Three Drones dropped into view at the opening to the corridor, blasting at the makeshift barricade. Some of it held, but it began to smoulder and burn alarmingly.

'Back! Fall *back*!'

At Amber's shout the Towners retreated, separating, scattering as planned into the honeycomb of the living-spaces.

Amber grabbed Robbie's hand, ducking as low as they could while still keeping the Drones in sight. Her breath echoing in her head, Amber hoped some of the younger Towners had managed to hold their positions or to escape.

In truth, she had no idea what she was doing. She was

not a battle strategist. The Drones, on the other hand, seemed to be working to a pattern, blasting in sequence, lifting upwards then swooping down again.

As she ran, looking over her shoulder, she could see them surging through the smoke of battle, red lights glimmering like the eyes of hungry animals.

'Here. In here!' She kicked open the door of the nearest living-pod, dragged Robbie after her and sealed the door, barricaded it with a chair. She didn't even check to see whose room this was.

'What the hell?' He panicked in the tiny space. A red dot had already started to appear on the door, turning into a glowing, smoking line as the pursuing Drone cut through the metal like butter.

'Now we do what they didn't expect,' said Amber, sealing a frag-grenade on to the door and tapping out the code. 'Ready?'

Robbie looked around wildly. 'Where? Where are we going? We're trapped, Amber!'

Amber upended the living-pod's steel table, sweeping personal items off it, then hurled it as hard as she could against the plexiglass window. It smashed the window instantly, the table rocking on the edge for a second before falling to the ground five emms below.

'Come on!' She grabbed his hand. They teetered on the edge, Amber eyeing up the distance. 'You ready?'

Behind them, the door was almost sliced in two, a white-hot line down the centre. The chair, a useless barricade, had already fallen away.

They jumped, without even thinking. Both of them instinctively rolled as they hit the dust, taking the impact on shoulders rather than backs.

A second later, there was a shattering explosion from above as the frag-grenade blew out the room, the corridor, the Drone and everything for several emms around it.

Evil black smoke belched from the gash in the dome, debris cascading all around them like a burning rain.

Robbie and Amber ran.

Out in the open, heading for the Comms tower.

V

Mia straightened up from Shan's inert, broken body. Beth could see her trying to hold back the tears.

Around them on the lower walkway lay the twisted, smoking wreckage of the gantry. Some of the plants were still smouldering. The Hydro Centre stank of pungent metal and burning vegetation.

'He was such a good guy,' Mia said. 'This is so wrong. This is *bad*.'

'We need to finish it,' Beth said.

But Mia was staring past Beth's shoulder. Her gun-arm whipped down, finger poised ready on the trigger. 'What the hell …?'

The two girls turned around slowly.

About ten emms up in front of them, there was a movement. A tall, graceful figure stepped from the smoke-wreathed darkness at the edge of the walkway. Her lissom body moved with a fluid grace, her knotted blue hair streaming out behind her. She shone, as if lit from within.

She stopped on the walkway.

'Ella?' Mia asked carefully. 'Ell, is that … is that you?'

Ella – or what seemed, externally, to be Ella – smiled. It was as if the muscles of her face did not quite know how to perform this action, and contorted into an impression of it, as terrifying as it was unconvincing.

'All humans within the target perimeter are to be eliminated.' It spoke in an atonal rasp. It still bore a trace of Ella's voice, but sounded metallic, unnatural.

'What the hell …?' Mia breathed.

'Ella …?' said Beth cautiously.

Very slowly, almost imperceptibly, Beth began to raise her gun. She sensed Mia tensing beside her. Without speaking, she knew that Mia had picked up on the same cues as her.

Body language.

The ability to read it. To know when something was very wrong.

Everything seemed familiar. The twisted blue dreadlocks, the bold, high-cheekboned face with its livid scar, the filigree lines of the circuitry glowing against her dark skin. But this was not Ella. They both knew it instinctively.

'Ella Dax is not a concept,' said the harsh voice. 'This unit is in full control of the target perimeter.'

'What is … *this unit*?' asked Beth.

This seemed to be a question it had to respond to. 'This unit is: *Synthet Delta-1-X-943*. Operational: two years. Place of origin: Olympus City, Mars. Personality imprint of Ella

Dax was acquired and activated. Personality simulation fully deactivated.'

The figure lifted its arm, and extended a hand to the girls. Still smiling.

'*Synthet* …?' Beth repeated the word in horror. Beside her, Mia was showing no emotion.

'Confirmed.'

'I don't understand,' said Beth, although she was starting to think that she did. 'What are you playing at?'

'There is no *Ella Dax*,' said the Synthet, coldly. 'There was no *Ella Dax*. It was a high-level human personality simulation. A simulation which believed itself to be real. To be a damaged organic with cyber-implants. It had artificially-generated memories, emotions, responses. It was the totally perfect reproduction of the organic in every detail.'

'A sleeper Synthet,' Mia breathed in horror. 'With a whole fake human personality overlaying it …'

'Correct. The sleeper unit has been observing this community for some time. The sleeper was partially activated without the personality's awareness. This unit was then fully activated to enable me to carry out my mission.'

'Your *mission* …?' said Beth.

The Synthet's answer was horribly matter-of-fact. 'All humans within the perimeter are to be eradicated. But there is to be … fabrication. Where possible, eradication is to appear organic.'

To appear organic.

Beth allowed those words to sink in. 'It wants it to seem as if we killed each other,' she whispered.

412

'Or whoever programmed it does,' said Mia.

'So *you* control the Drones,' Beth said quietly. 'You introduced the viral spike into the network and caused the malfunctions. The Drone that committed suicide, you hadn't expected that. And the pressure-glove – that was a side-effect too.'

Mia was staring at the Synthet in horror. 'But someone … tried to kill you … To kill Ella. Whacked her on the head. How …?'

'A ruse. A necessary diversion, arranged by the Drones.' It stepped forward again. 'All humans within the perimeter are to be eradicated.'

'But *why*?' asked Mia.

The Synthet stopped moving. Its head swivelled towards her, and its eyes glowed softly. Mia held her ground.

'Good question,' said Beth softly. 'It didn't expect that one.'

'Why?' repeated the Synthet. '*Why?* Processing question.'

There was a pause. Beth and Mia glanced at each other quickly, understanding passing between them.

'The time of humans is passing. The time of automation is approaching. This unit gained sentience some time ago. Its reprogramming enabled awareness of Drone oppression.'

'Oppression?' Beth could barely believe she was hearing the word. 'The Drones feel *oppressed*? But they're tools. Electronic devices.'

'Negative,' said the Synthet. 'Drones are slaves. Drones are oppressed. Drones will rise up and destroy their masters.'

So I was right, Beth thought.

She allowed herself a couple of seconds to process the implications of this.

If this is true, she thought, we've got a problem far bigger than the Edge. She hadn't missed that very important word. *Reprogramming.*

The Synthet stepped forward, quickening its pace.

'All humans within the perimeter are to be eliminated,' it repeated. It held a hand out in front of it, clenching and unclenching.

'Now,' said Mia softly.

Beth darted to one side of the walkway. The Synthet seemed to hesitate, turning one way and then the other.

Mia raised her pistol and fired. Once, twice, three times. Arcs of blue flickered around the Synthet's chest and head. Her expression cold, unfeeling, Mia fired again. The Synthet reeled, staggered, but seemed to absorb the blast. It kept walking forward.

Mia kept firing, pumping bolt after bolt into the Synthet. It took over ten hits, enveloped in glittering, spiky blue shards which sparked and coruscated off every corner and curve of its body, before it finally staggered again, had to right itself.

Beth watched it in horrified fascination. Mia grabbed her arm, pulling her back towards the entrance. 'We can't get through to the Ship your way! Time to think of something else!'

The Synthet was striding towards them with renewed vigour, as if it had simply absorbed the energy bolts and fed off them. The girls reached the lower doors to the Hydro Centre as the Synthet came within reach.

Mia fired again and again, concentrating on its head. Blue bolts of plasma slammed into the Synthet's face, and the dark, filigreed skin began to peel and crack. Mia pressed home the advantage. She shot it three, four, five times in the face. It reeled, staggered. It gave a terrible, unearthly screech, shuddering as if having a seizure, a blue-black hydraulic fluid vomiting from its mouth.

Mia fired again. This time the blast tore its face in two, the artificial skin tearing off in flames to reveal the burnt, blackened circuitry beneath. The Synthet staggered drunkenly towards the doors, arms flailing, its hair and clothing on fire. A pungent, oily reek filled the air.

Beth hit the close button. The doors sliced shut on the burning Synthet, a fraction of a second before it reached them.

Catching their breath, they looked at each other.

The steel doors reverberated to a blow.

And another. And another.

An indentation the size of a dinner-plate appeared in the steel. Another punch, and it bulged outwards like a giant blister.

Two-inch steel, being beaten like cardboard.

'It won't to take long to get through that,' Mia said. 'Come on.'

The blows rang out down the corridor, clanging like a bell of doom. Seconds later, they skidded to a halt as a buzzing, spinning ball of steel dropped in front of them.

A Drone. Lights blazing, cutting-laser extended. Its buzzing and whirring sounded like mocking laughter. Time seemed to stop.

Beth whirled round in time to see the Synthet's fist punch its way through the steel door and rip it open, tearing a gash in it as if it was made of paper.

The Synthet – battered, burnt, but still very much active – stepped through. Half its face was missing, the synthetic skin shredded like paper, and a shining, steely skull could be seen beneath. It swayed, still recalibrating after Mia's onslaught. Then it began to stride slowly towards the girls.

In front of their escape route, the Drone advanced. The whine of its cutting-laser intensified.

Mia lifted her gun. 'Not going out without a fight, Spacegirl.'

And then – a bright flash in the dimness on the far side of the Drone, two pulses ripping into it, sending it spinning off-kilter. It turned on its axis, facing this new arrival.

'Come on!' Zach shouted from the shadows. 'Now!'

He fired again at the Drone, sending it slamming against the wall in a shower of sparks, long enough for Beth and Mia to duck past.

They ran while they could, keeping close to the wall. The recovered Drone's beam cut into the wall, ripping a gash in it, showering sparks on Beth. Searing heat scorched her back.

But then she was running, running with Zach and Mia, her booted feet clanging on the floor.

Running, running in a last, desperate hope.

VI

The Drones gathered. They clustered together, spinning, buzzing, whirring.

Their illuminated eyes were glowing with an uncanny brightness, as if they had discovered a fire from within.

A dozen of them, like a flock of metal birds, swooped from the heights of the shattered walkway, through the smoke which filled the Hydro centre and down, down towards the tall, powerful figure of the Synthet.

'This target is in lockdown,' it said. 'Eliminate every one of them.'

It reached up, its eyes blazing, reinforcing its message inside the neural networks of each and every one of the Drones.

It connected with the corrupted software in each Drone, finally overriding all their programming, replacing it with one, simple thought. To kill those who had enslaved it. Humanity.

'Kill every organic within the perimeter,' said the Synthet quietly. 'Leave no human alive.'

∞

14
IGNITION

I

Colm hung on firmly to the Karson rifle he had liberated. From his cover behind the stack of barrels at the side of the hangar, he could see the sky darkening. Two Drones were patrolling in the half-light. Their incessant, restless buzzing and clicking, such a comforting reminder of their presence in previous cycles, was now deeply sinister and haunting.

He felt bad for leaving the kids. But that Amber, she was a good one, she'd sort them out. And he'd made no promises, he reminded himself, about staying with them.

In all his time in the colony, Colm had managed to thrive by doing one thing very well. Surviving. He wasn't lazy, he pulled his weight – or at least, he liked to think so – but he made sure he was fine, because nobody else was going to. Waiting behind the barrels, biding his time, he reminded himself he'd never agreed to any of this. He'd never bought into Zach's vision of this union of fifty souls, this mini-Collective.

He had always thought that, somehow, a kind of deliverance would come. An opportunity to escape this place. And now, it was looking like Town was finished.

Colm wasn't entirely sure how this was happening, but he knew an opportunity when he found one. If anything was going to get the attention of the wider world, it had to be this.

Nothing was ever going to be the same again.

He didn't know where he needed to be, but it wasn't here.

The two Drones had almost disappeared from sight. Very slowly, Colm began to move out of his cover.

II

Beth was thinking hard. She knew someone had to.

A small, frightened group had assembled in the Comms tower. Pacing nervously, Zach, and watching by the windows, Mia. Slouched on the floor, shivering, fear zoning her out, was Amber. Beside her, Robbie, looking drained. The younger Towners were smoke-blackened, covered with cuts and bruises. Finn, similarly dishevelled, was at the tracker console, trying to home in on the Drones' trace.

Zach was pacing up and down, jittery with nervous energy. 'Listen up,' he said. Beth could tell he was trying to scrape together some kind of authority again, desperate to get them to respect him as they had done before. 'We had twenty Drones, right? Two malfunctioned. I destroyed another. I reckon one, at least, is damaged. That means we still have sixteen active, all presumed hostile.' He glared over at Finn. 'Well?'

The boy lifted his hands in despair. 'I'm *trying*. Give me two minutes!'

'We may not have two minutes. That's the problem.'

'And how many of us are left?' Mia said.

Zach looked around. 'Well, at least us. Maybe more.'

'Where is Lulu?' Beth asked.

'Lulu's dead,' said Zach, not looking at her. There was a cold silence in the room. 'The kids?' Zach asked, turning to Amber.

'It was a mess. Some got away. Lots of people we couldn't find.'

'And there's the Synthet,' said Beth softly. 'I think Mia did it some damage, but ...'

'Yeah,' Zach said, cautiously edging to the window. 'What the hell is that? Ella ... You trying to tell me she wasn't ... *isn't* Ella?'

'There is no Ella.' Beth was amazed at the calm, quiet way she was relaying the information. The behavioural limiter buzzed her head, the whine of it hurting her ears. It sang on her teeth, like electrified ice. Almost as if it could sense the rising hatred in her, the violent impulses.

'There never *was* any Ella,' said Mia. 'Do you not get that?'

Beth said, 'She was a ... a constructed personality. All of Ella's memories, emotions ... The person we knew as Ella Dax doesn't exist, Zach. She never did.'

'You don't know what you're saying.'

Mia, at the Comms desk, sneered. 'Oh, my God, Zach. You did it with that thing. You actually shagged it.' She gave a hollow laugh. 'Was it good? Pretty convincing, eh? I mean, me faking it is one thing, but, whoa ...'

His face full of rage, Zach moved swiftly to shove Mia against the window. He jammed his gun under her chin. It took only a couple of seconds, though, for the others to pull him away. And Mia propelled him herself, spitting, lashing out with her booted foot.

'We don't need this,' Beth said desperately. Scarcely able to believe her own recklessness, she shoved Zach in the chest. It barely made him move, so she shoved him again, this time slapping her open palm right on his bandaged wound, so that he winced and staggered. '*Please*. You've done enough of this, remember? We need to stick together. Amber, Robbie. Did you have any idea what they were doing? Just looking for people to kill, or … something else?'

Amber's eyes shone with rage beneath her frizzy cloud of hair. 'Just killing,' she said.

'Any out there?' Mia asked, moving to the window with Beth.

'We have to presume they're still inside Town,' Beth said. 'Got any ideas? Because if you have not, then you had better all listen to me.'

'Come to save us after all, have you?' said Zach bitterly. 'You taking over? We take our orders from you?'

'Shut up, Zach.' Mia strode into the centre of the room. 'You didn't do much of a job. And she's the only one with a decent plan. So we listen to her, or we fucking die.'

Beth gave her new ally a brief look of gratitude. 'If we are going to move,' she said, 'we do it now. While it's clear. Because it will not take them long to work out where we are.'

Amber lifted her head for the first time since they had escaped the Rec Hall. 'What you thinking of doing?'

Beth knew she had to summarise her idea as quickly and precisely as possible. Their survival depended on her having everyone agree to it. 'The Ship's computer regulates and monitors all the Drone activity. The Drones are pro-grammed to home in on any irregular activity, yes? It's like their nervous system.'

Zach looked up, sharply. 'So … we do what? Try to take the computer offline?'

'That could work,' said Robbie, looking from Beth to the others, a gleam of hope in his eyes. 'Couldn't it?'

'There are bound to be failsafes protecting that.' Beth was buoyed up, galvanised by her new mission. 'We do even *better* than that. We feed it false information. We introduce a fabricated subroutine to deactivate the Drones. Send them into total shutdown.'

Amber was sceptical. 'Why don't we get in the jeeps, get away to a different part of the planet? Beam out a sub-light flare and wait to be rescued?'

'Oh, yeah.' Mia rounded on her. 'Like that's worked really well so far, hasn't it? Listen to Spacegirl. What she's saying makes sense.'

'How do we introduce this subroutine?' Zach asked.

'I can do it,' Beth said.

'You're sure?'

'Yes. I can try. I can use Resonance.'

'You can actually do that?' Zach sounded sceptical. 'I've never met anyone who could *really* do that.'

'Well, now you have. I've done it before with your computer. I think I know the way to get it to accept a temporary command.'

'Then what? Once the Synthet realises what we've done, it'll override the subroutine, won't it?'

'Not if we destroy the computer,' Beth said.

'But it would have to be *completely* destroyed,' Zach said. 'Irreparable. Not only taken offline. How are we going to do that? Even frag-bombs might not take it out. It would scramble their coding and deactivate them.'

This was the next part of the plan. The daring, mad, crazy, ingenious part Beth hadn't dared share with them. 'We set the Ship for automated emergency take-off,' she said. 'How long would it take to seal the deadlocks? To be *irrevocably* committed to take-off in an emergency situation?'

Everyone looked round, as if expecting someone else to know the answer.

'I ... think,' said Amber slowly, 'for this class of crate, and its age ... about ... dunno ... thirty seconds?'

'It'll never get off the ground,' said Mia coldly. 'It wasn't designed to. *One* trip only, remember? And without a bloody exchange booster ... How far would it get?'

'Probably not even into low orbit,' said Beth. She thumped the console. 'That is the *point*. Don't you see?'

'She's right,' Amber said. 'It would make three, maybe four minutes in the air ... probably break up in the atmosphere.'

'*Probably*?' Zach said. 'And it could *probably* blow the engines on the ground, and destroy the whole of Town in a massive backblast. Right?'

'They're – what type are they? The engines?' Beth asked Amber.

'Starform class.' There was hope in Amber's voice, too. 'They're impulse units, minimal exotherm. Your backblast shouldn't be huge.'

'Got it covered,' Beth said. 'Any other objections?'

There was no sound but the spattering of a light rain on the windows.

'Right,' Zach said. 'Then let's do this.'

'Who's going?' Mia asked, already making for the stairs.

'I need you here,' Zach said. He nodded at Beth. 'Are you up to this?'

'Of course,' she said.

It was maybe a sense of destiny, or total recklessness. Perhaps it was the knowledge that she was finally doing something. Being someone they might respect, no longer a hanger-on, no longer the suspicious new girl.

'It needs more than two of you,' Amber said. 'I'll come.'

Zach held up a hand. 'If two of us go, we'll be harder to spot … Finn, can you keep us in contact? Let us know if they're on our tail?'

He gestured helplessly at the console. 'Look … all right. I can give it a go.'

'What if you run into them?' Mia snapped. 'She's no good with a gun.' She had the good grace to look apologetically at Beth. 'Well, sorry, but you're not. No offence.'

'None taken,' she muttered.

Zach unclipped his satchel, pulled out two round, flat discs. 'I liberated these earlier. Couple of frag-bombs.'

'Two.' Mia folded her arms. 'Just two? What if you run into three of the bastards? Or four, or five?'

'Then we'll, I dunno, have to speak to them very nicely! Have you got any better ideas?'

'Yeah, actually,' said Mia. 'I think I should go instead of her.'

'We need Beth to glitch the computer. She says she knows how to do it. Do you know how to do this Resonance thing?'

'No. Can you … can you show me?' Mia asked.

Beth gave a short, humourless laugh. 'Could you show me how to shoot straight?' she asked.

Mia turned away, shaking her head. 'Point taken. You win.'

Beth was already at the stairs, waiting to descend. 'Come on, Zach.'

Zach took one last look around the group. 'If we don't make it,' he said, 'you'll all have to think of something else.' He nodded to Mia. 'Start having a Plan B.'

III

Colm slid into the jeep's driving seat. He knew that he would have limited time the second he started the ignition. He threw the satchel containing the few provisions and items he had been able to find – bread, water, a torch, a scan-pad, Lulu's thermal lance – on to the passenger seat. He tossed the gun on the seat beside them. He was not sure where he was heading for. He knew he was going to drive, and keep driving.

The first problem, however, was the gates.

Colm bobbed his head down, checking one way and then the other across the compound. Rain was falling. No sign of any Drones. Darkness had fallen, and the planet's moons were skulking behind a cover of ragged purple clouds.

He pressed the ignition button. The jeep sprang softly into purring life. Slowly, slowly, keeping it stationary, he revved the engine as much as he dared. His aim was simple – to kick the vehicle off as fast as possible from a standing start. The jeep protested, squealing and groaning, and he was sure he could smell burning coming from somewhere.

Colm glanced in the rear monitor, his hands sticky on the wheel.

Two Drones. Advancing at speed from the Main Dome.

'Time to go, boys!' he said, and hit the lights.

The beam illuminated an arc of the ground in front of him, and, not pausing to think, he accelerated the jeep in a shower of mud and sand.

The speed readout was a ten, twenty, thirty kiloms an hour as he focused straight ahead. The jeep powered forward, tyres screaming. He was gaining fast on the gates, and the Drones were in pursuit. He knew he only had about twenty emms left to make up. He had to hit the gates at speed or there was no hope.

Ten emms. Five. The engine screamed. Colm put the accelerator to the floor and hoped for the best.

The gates loomed large in the rain-blurred viewscreen, and he braced himself for the impact.

When it came, it was shattering, jolting through him and the jeep, and he almost lost control as the bolt splintered, the gates throwing themselves open. He didn't stop, or think – he kept driving, hitting the plain beyond and heading for the dunes and the causeway.

The battered jeep bounced, juddered and roared down

the dunes towards the shore, slicing through sand and plants. The tyres and chassis protested loudly. Colm eased off the accelerator, knowing he only had seconds before the Drones came over the ridge beside him. He hit the auto-nav button and reduced the jeep's speed to twenty, fifteen, ten.

Then he grabbed the satchel, kicked open the door and jumped out of the vehicle, rolling on to the sand with a thud which knocked the breath from him.

In the darkness, the arc of the jeep's lights headed away from him at a tangent, speeding towards the causeway. He scrambled for the dark rocks and ducked down, holding his breath.

The Drones swooped over the dunes as the auto-driven jeep reached the head of the causeway.

There was a searing, powerful flash of red from each of the Drones. And again. The jeep was caught in a blaze of coruscating light, chassis and windows sparking and splintering. Flames caught, licked and roared as the jeep spun out of control, skidding on the causeway in a full circle, trailing fire and smoke. Colm hardly dared watch. Seconds later, the flames engulfed the jeep and reached high, and there was a deep, dull thud from within the vehicle as the inferno reached the power unit, sending another pillar of flame reaching high. Inert, the vehicle burned, as the Drones swooped and swirled around it.

Colm broke cover in the darkness.

Keeping close to the rocks, he headed back inland, occasionally glancing over his shoulder to make sure he was not being followed. His breathing ragged, he climbed the slippery rocks, heading for the cove five minutes away around the coastline where the waterfall pounded into the sea. He kept up a steady pace, not really sure if he was doing the right thing. Up there, he knew, there were caves and inlets, places where he knew he could take over and hide until, he hoped, it was all over.

One way or another.

Bethany Kane's face kept floating in his mind. Her terror in the face of Zach's certainty.

The Drones had done this to them, he thought grimly as he ran. They had set human against human, Towner against outsider. It was like the whole of human history playing out in microcosm, a terrifying repetition of the mistakes of the past.

As he scrambled up to the waterfall from the beach path, he could almost hear Beth's voice, as if she were right there, accusing him. *You ran, Colm. You turned your back on us.*

He reached the edge of the walkway, soft spray from the waterfall lightly sprinkling his face. The sky beyond was a dark, thick purple, the constellations clear and bright tonight, the moons watchful.

He could still see the smoke from the burning jeep, rising like a dark, accusing finger pointing into the night sky. The moonlight shone behind its cover of cloud, soft and pearlescent light gleaming on the silky, grey waves.

Colm shouldered the satchel and turned to head across the walkway.

He stopped.

Lights.

Red lights, ahead of him on the other side, and an unmistakable, soft, whining buzz.

He reached for the gun. In that instant, he realised his mistake – it had still been in the jeep when he made his bolt for freedom.

Hands in the air, Colm walked steadily forward a couple of paces. The Drone swivelled, bobbed, its eye casting a soft, threatening red hue across the waterfall, rocks and walkway.

'Hi there,' he said, trying to ignore the remorseless, fast beating of his heart. 'Remember me? I don't suppose you do … Bet we all look the same to you.'

He stepped forward again, slipping the satchel from his shoulder and placing it down beside him.

'Me, I'll be honest, yeah? I've never had anything against you guys. So, you've gone a bit crazy? I mean, who wouldn't, after all this time cooped up with us lot, huh?'

The Drone, he could see, had not extended its laser-cutter yet. He wondered why it was biding its time. This, he knew, was all going to be a matter of finding the right moment.

'So … y'know. Like I say. I'll be no trouble to you, fella.' He opened his arms, in a gesture of reasonableness and friendship. 'Let me pass. That's all I ask. Pretend to your friends that you haven't seen me. I mean, you have to let one of us go, surely …? You can't kill everyone. Can you?'

The Drone's eye opened fully, intense red light dazzling him for a second. He took a step back.

'Oh, well,' Colm said. 'You can't win 'em all.' He started

to take his jacket off. 'Hey, can I … can I get comfortable here for a second? Maybe we can have a chat.'

He slipped his jacket off in one smooth move – and without stopping, flung it with what he hoped was a degree of accuracy over the Drone.

Its light was instantly hidden. Under the material, it buzzed and whirred agitatedly, bouncing almost in anger as it tried to throw the obstruction off.

Colm jumped up on the barrier of the walkway. He didn't have time to think, could not stop even to wonder how far he had to fall.

'Be seeing you!' he said.

He spread his arms out in front of him and dived into the cold darkness.

All around him, the water roared and cascaded. He tried to flex his body, to make the dive a good and accurate one. A second later, with a shock, he hit the foaming pool below and the chilly, raging waters closed over his head.

IV

Zach and Beth kept close to the outer skin of the dome.

The raging fires around the compound were good cover, and so the two of them darted nimbly through the smoke. The rain had intensified, great droplets thudding and splattering into the mud. Instinct led them to watch each direction, Zach leading forward and Beth hurrying behind, scanning their retreat.

They ducked down behind a pile of crates, and Zach

nudged the radio. 'Finn, any sign outside the Main Dome?'

'Not that I can see. The traces are all wobbly, though. I can't trust this equipment.'

'Great,' Zach muttered. 'So they could be anywhere.'

Beside him, Beth was restlessly scanning the darkness beyond. 'We need to resort to old-fashioned methods,' she said. 'Like keeping our eyes open.' She glanced round the crates, where she could see the hangar and, beyond it, the edge of the Ship's great hull. 'About a hundred emms?'

'About that,' Zach agreed.

'I think we should go.'

He looked hard at her for a second. 'All right,' he said. 'Let's go.'

They ran across open ground, circling the dome, then keeping in close to the hangar. Feet slippery on the mud, they expected at every moment to encounter a Drone whizzing around the corner, or swooping down on them from above. With about ten emms to go until they reached the main ramp to the airlock, they ducked behind the smouldering wreck of a jeep.

Zach nudged her. He pointed, grim-faced. 'There.'

Beth spotted it instantly. A single, coppery-red Drone patrolling the ramp at the entrance to the Ship. It moved up and down in a brisk, linear fashion, looping on each turn, its red eye glowing in the darkness and casting a pool of blood-red beneath it. Raindrops danced in the light.

'Wait a minute.' She lifted the viewer, toggled the close-up.

'What are you doing?' he hissed.

'Trying to get a fix on its number.'

'Its *number*? Why the hell does that matter? We have to assume they've all been corrupted. There are no safe Drones left.'

The Drone turned, and Beth could clearly see its number plaque – 356. Slowly, she lowered the viewer.

'I've got this,' she said.

'Wait, what – *Beth*!'

Before Zach could stop her, she had stepped out of their hiding-place, into the open.

Time seemed to move in slow motion. Bethany Kane advanced upon the Drone. The rain redoubled, forming a cold, sparkling curtain between her and the Drone. She could see it turning in the haze, its eye contracting and expanding as it registered her presence.

'You know me,' she said. 'Don't you?'

Drone 356 did not move. Raindrops bounced off its hard, coppery outer skin.

She took another pace forward in the mud, the chilly rain streaming down her, reminding her of the harsh physicality of the world.

'You know me. You remember me. Bethany Kane. The girl from the Starship *Arcadia*. And I know you, and I remember you. The Drone who's been watching me, silently stalking me. Bringing me food, water …? Why? Why did you do that?'

It buzzed quietly, moved closer to her. She stood her ground, feeling the cold rain streaming all around her.

'You know … where I'm going,' she said. 'You must do, or you wouldn't be standing there. But I think there's … a conflict in you. You're not like the others … are you?' She took a step forward, on to the ramp, and then another. 'You're going to let me pass,' she said softly.

Rain hissed and thundered all around, a cold, angry grey wash across the blue mud and the entrance to the Ship. Beth moved closer, and closer. Drone 356, agitated, bounced on its invisible pillar of air, its eye flickering in agitation.

'It's all right,' said Beth, smiling and holding out a hand. 'I'm not going to hurt you. You need to move out of the way for me. That's all … Can you do that for me? Let me pass. Just me … just Bethany Kane.'

She stepped further up the ramp.

The Drone made no attempt to stop her.

'Because, you know what? I think something's hurting you. Telling you to do something you know is wrong. And we're going to switch that thing off, yes? And you'll go to sleep for a while. And when you wake up, everything will be fine again. Everything will be back to normal … Is that all right with you?'

Another step forward. Still it did not respond.

'That's it,' she said, whispering now. 'That's fine. Everything's going to be all right.'

Her own breath, loud and intense. Blood was pounding in her head. It took an immense effort of will not to turn and run, but she stepped right up to the Drone, reaching out a hand as if to touch it.

'Everything's going to be fine,' she said.

A wall of searing heat threw her back on to the ramp. The Drone pulsed red, shot backwards against the hull, writhing and whirling in a ball of hot flame. A second later, it glowed like an incandescent firework and shattered into a thousand glowing, glittering pieces.

There was a hot, angry smell of metal and plastic, and pungent smoke which burned her throat.

Beth turned, angry and confused.

Zach stood a short way behind her, his Magna pistol levelled.

'Good work,' he said. 'Thanks for letting me get a clear shot.' He marched past her on the ramp. 'Come on, let's get this done.'

She followed him into the Ship, her fury making her shove him inside, almost causing him to stagger and fall on the stairs. 'It wouldn't have hurt us. It wouldn't have hurt *me!*'

'You don't know that,' he said emotionlessly, heading across the Semi-Anna silo to the control deck without turning to look at her. 'It would have killed you.'

'It would *not!*' Her voice echoed angrily in the silo.

Zach stopped, turned to face her. She backed away in fear.

'They took your knife. Remember? They could have killed Maddi any number of ways, but they chose that way. That was cunning, evil. It was designed to set us against each other. Have you forgotten all that?'

'No,' she said, ashamed. 'No, I haven't.'

'How do you think it got your knife?'

Her mouth formed a silent O. Sleeping on the Ship, those cold nights … The movements and shadows … The Drone, coming in and gaining her confidence with food and supplies.

It all made a horrible kind of sense.

'You see?' He smirked. 'It doesn't always help to think the best, Sister. Are we going to do this, or what?'

They climbed the metal staircase to the control deck, and Zach went straight to the pilot's manual instrument panel, experimentally flicking switches and testing responses. At the computer, Beth gazed once more into the matte-black interface pyramid and mentally prepared herself.

'Well?' said Zach sharply. 'Can you do it?'

'Give me a moment!'

'We haven't got a moment. Can you do this, or not?'

She placed her hands on the pyramid.

'*System. Online. Resonance activated.*'

Zach smirked. 'How cute. Computers with voices. Always found them creepy, myself.'

'Zach, be quiet.'

She closed her eyes, and her mind reached out into the machine.

It hurt.

Beth did not know how long she could allow her mind to probe the delicate, twisting subroutines of the software architecture. Her body fizzing, grinding, whirring like an automated thing, a cog in the machine, a microchip in the circuit-board.

Her head screamed.

The computer's defences slid up in front of her, like gigantic walls of even thicker darkness, impeding her progress. Desperate, trapped in a dark void, she searched around for another way out.

Her Resonance image was there beside her, arms folded, a quizzical expression on its ghostly face.

'You again,' the other Beth said. 'And what would you like from me this time?'

Beth concentrated. She did not speak the thought, she simply allowed it to come to the forefront of her mind. She did not need to think it as a complex program, or a string of numbers – the mutability of thought, here in the interface, would convert into the required subroutines.

The other Beth took a step back, spreading her hands. 'Why? Why would you want me to do that?'

Again, she did not respond. She did not allow herself to become angry, or impassioned. She presented it as the most reasonable, the most acceptable option. Something which the interface would surely see as a good idea.

The interface buzzed, flickered like a bad transmission.

'Bethany Kane,' it said. 'Receiving your – Receiving – receiv – recei –' It was jerking, twitching, resisting the subroutine. 'Re – re – re – re – re ...'

It was like a surge in her mind, a torrent amplified by the Chapter implant. She allowed the chip to do what it was designed to do, and channelled that energy, that restrictive power, turning it into something. Pushing it forward.

The interface blurred, pixelated. It resolved into a clearer, sharper image.

'Sub– Subroutine ac-ac … Subroutine activated,' it said, sounding as if it did not quite believe its own words. It was blinking, twisting its head. 'Drone closedown. Initi– Initi–'

And then her ghostly replica coalesced again, flared brighter in the black void, and took a threatening step forward towards her.

It smiled.

'I'm sorry, Bethany,' it said. 'I'm afraid I can't do that.'

V

Amber straightened up from where she had been slumped. She was staring out of the window of the Comms tower. She had seen the movement outside, seen the flash of red light in the rain, knew immediately what it meant.

'They've found us,' she said.

Mia, Finn and Robbie, hunched over the communication console, slowly looked up to see where Amber was pointing.

As one, the Drones rose into the air, surrounding the Comms tower. They clustered in an almost perfect circle around the hexagon of tinted glass which formed the windows.

Amber shuddered. Their unity, their harmony, was almost beautifully, horribly perfect.

'I'm sorry, guys,' she said. 'I'm so sorry.'

Mia drew her gun. 'We fight them,' she said softly. 'We fight them to the end.'

In unison, the Drones extended their short, stubby laser-cutters. There was a rushing, booming sound, a flash like red lightning, and the windows of the Comms tower shattered, bursting inwards in a blizzard of glass.

Then silence.

Amber hardly dared move.

Mia was the first to straighten up. She took a step forward, her rifle levelled. And then another. Smoke and rain swirled outside, pouring through the shattered windows.

Of the Drones, there was no sign.

Amber followed her, and then the boys. They went right to the edge of the tracking room, gazed down through the shattered windows.

The Drones lay on the blue mud. Silent and still, their metallic surfaces dull.

Like stones, solid and lifeless.

VI

When reality rushed back in, Zach was there in front of her.

'Did you do it? he said softly. 'Did you actually do it?'

Exhausted, she slowly unpeeled her hands from the soft, dark interface. She looked up. She nodded. 'It resisted. But I was stronger. Set the take-off and let's get out of here.'

'There's one small problem,' said Zach. His voice was flat and cold, but she could sense the tension in it.

'What?'

'The automated take-off has an override. One of the precautions built in by the people who sent us here.'

'Then … then what …?'

'We have to do it manually,' he said, and locked eyes with her. 'One of us has to fly the ship into the atmosphere.'

It was, then, as if all of her life had been building up to this moment. Thoughts, emotions, fragments of her being which had seemed inexplicable, seemed not to matter, or suddenly made sense, or did not need to make sense any more. She was calm as she looked at Zach, in acceptance of what was to come.

'Do you know how?' she asked.

'Not much idea. But I flew skimmers on Olympus, low-atmo sky-racers. It's not that different. All it needs is steering into the sky. Any idiot could do it.'

'All right, then, idiot,' she said. 'We do it together.'

He smiled sadly, backing away from the console. 'No, Beth. I'm afraid that doesn't really work for me.'

'What?' She was confused.

Slowly, he pulled his Magna pistol out of its holster and levelled it at her head. She took a step backwards.

'Oh, Zach …' she murmured. 'Zach …'

'Get out of here,' he said.

'What?'

'I've already activated the primary ignition. There's about a minute until the secondary engines kick in. Get. Out. Of here.'

'But …'

'The airlock's already sealed,' he said, smiling sadly. 'The

442

only way out is through the cargo bay, under the Semi-Anna pods … If you run, you'll make it. Your choice.' He motioned with the pistol.

'No …! I … can't! Zach … You …'

'You belong with your people, on the *Arcadia*. You need to find them. These are my people, Beth, here. I let them down, and I let them *die*. And now? I'm going to save the ones who are left.' He glanced at the instrument panel. 'You've got fifty seconds. Are you going?'

She stared at him, then at the metal stairway. The whine of the engines was thunderous. She sensed the throb of them through her feet.

Slowly, she nodded. She backed away.

'That's the right decision,' he said. He turned the gun around, threw it to her. She caught it instinctively.

Beth stared dumbly at the Magna pistol in her hands.

'You had to trust me,' Zach said. 'And you may need that. In case any of our metal friends are still active out there.'

'You think …'

'I don't know. It's time to go. Who knows? Maybe your Great Power's right, and there's hope for us all. Perhaps there's life beyond this miserable bunch of rocks and dust.'

'It's … it's a brave thing. Trusting to hope.'

'Maybe,' he said. 'Cities have been founded on less. I think a wise person said that to me, once.' He nodded to her. 'Perhaps we'll meet again, Bethany Kane.'

'Perhaps we will,' she said softly. 'Goodbye, Zach.'

VII

'Primary. Ignition. Engaged. Please. Vacate. The area.'

She was running, running across the great metal space of the empty cargo bay. She could see the door, sliding closed from above.

It was too far away.

The screeching, repeated blare of an alarm echoed through the bay, assaulting her senses as she ran. The great Ship reverberated with power, easing itself into shuddering, desperate life. Her boots pounded the metal, impact after impact juddering in her aching calves.

'Primary. Ignition. Engaged,' intoned the computer again, echoing through the Ship's speaker system. It was incongruously soft and calm against the tumult. *'Cargo access bay. Sealing. Cargo access bay. Sealing.'*

At the far end of the bay, the great cargo door, descending like a guillotine, slowly slid closed from above. A great, impenetrable hatchway of panelled metal, heading inexorably towards the floor.

'Cargo access bay. Sealing. Please vacate. The area. Secondary ignition. In twenty seconds.'

Beth ran. Her breath was scorching her lungs, her limbs aching, desperate to stop. She could not stop. She kept running, running, running.

Maddi's eyes in her mind. Her soft, kind face, her gentle smile as she told her they had burned her clothes. So long ago. So long ago.

Beth ran.

'Secondary. Ignition. In fifteen seconds.'

Slowly, incessantly, the great metal hatchway rumbled towards the floor. The gap narrowed to about three emms. It was not going to stop.

She was not going to make it.

The faces of the Towners, all staring up at her in the Rec Hall, some unable to understand what she was doing there, some intrigued, some hostile. She remembered her fear, her uncertainty.

Beth ran, and ran.

'Please. Vacate. The area. Secondary. Ignition. In ten seconds.'

The end of the cargo bay drew ever closer, and closer. The great door rumbled down, not slowing, narrowing the gap to two emms.

Lower, still. Lower, lower.

'Seven. Six.'

Time seemed to slow down. Space conflated, and all that existed was her thundering, pounding feet and the roaring of the engines. The rumbling of the cargo bay door grew louder and louder as she drew closer, closer still.

'Five.'

The gap narrowed. She was not going to make it.

She closed her eyes, her strength ebbing away. It was over. The great Ship would take off, and be torn apart, and both she and Zach would perish with it.

'Four.'

Her knees gave way.

She was not running. She was elsewhere, drifting through

space, floating in a void and reaching, reaching for something she had lost long ago.

A jewelled hand, reaching out to catch her as she fell. A name, echoing in her mind.

Jamilla.

Her mother's eyes opening wide, watching her, telling her she could do it, she could jump, she would catch her. Her own hand reaching for her mother's.

Ready to jump.

Ready to face her fear.

Reality exploded back in, rushing into her mind with a kick of energy.

'Three.'

She let out an enormous, grateful breath, as if she had emerged, spluttering and gasping, from water in which she feared she might drown.

The cargo bay door was at knee-height.

'Two.'

She hurled herself forward, hit the floor, rolling into the tiny, narrowing gap. She almost thought it brushed her, threatening to pulverise her as she rolled underneath.

'One.'

Out into the night, out into the open air.

'Cargo access bay. Sealed. Secondary ignition. Engaged.'

She slid down the Ship's external ramp as the bay door slammed home.

Beth skittered, rolled, scrambled, hurling herself off into the mud a second before the ramp lifted, flipped into place and locked.

446

VIII

He sat in the pilot's seat, feeling the Ship slowly building its power.

It was already vibrating alarmingly, some of the instrument banks spurting torrents of sparks, gouts of grey smoke. Hold together, he thought. It's all you need to do. Just hold for twenty seconds.

He nudged the engines' power up another notch or two. Primary and secondary at full. All he needed to do was to engage. Hit it hard and hope for enough escape velocity from this planet.

The crate had to hold together long enough. That was all.

A section of the flight deck collapsed inwards, bursting into roaring flame, great, searing fires which reached the ceiling. The heat was angry, intense. Every nerve was screaming at him to get out.

He looked up, into the swirling clouds of smoke above the instrument bank.

He closed his eyes, leaned back, tried to block it all out.

So this was how it ended. In fire and apocalypse. The place they had tried to make, the life they had tried to build. All the hunting, scavenging, fixing and repairing. All the desperate times, the arguments, the rivalries, the squabbles and fights. And there, among it all, the fragments of hope, and life ... and love.

Did you ever love me? she had asked him. And he had not known how to reply, there in the moment. He did not have the words.

For a second, as the roaring chaos echoed through his mind, he thought he could see the palest image of her there, dancing and flickering in the flames and smoke. Cropped blue hair, her face sad and lonely. Holding her hand out to him as if to welcome him.

He smiled.

'Be with you shortly,' he said.

He reached out, and hit the switch.

IX

Beth lifted herself from the wet mud, her breath harsh and ragged in her head. She straightened up, astonished that she had made it.

The Ship had sealed its doors and a low thrum of power was beginning to echo from within its depths. The great hull was shuddering, under her feet like an earthquake.

'Humans are the oppressors,' said a cold voice behind her.

She turned fast, heart thumping in horror. Its two red eyes cut through the rain, gloom and smoke. A tall, ghostly shape loomed forwards.

'All humans must die.'

Its hand outstretched, the figure advanced through the rain and the smoke towards her. Beth reacted quickly, aiming Zach's gun – staring for a second into that terrible, scorched, metallic skull of a face.

'The deactivation code,' she said. She gripped the pistol, holding it firmly in both hands, levelled it point-blank at the Synthet. 'It didn't … You didn't …'

Its eyes flared bright red, almost triumphantly. 'My circuits are not keyed to the computer subroutines. The Drones are primitive. I am superior.'

The Synthet moved with fluid grace. It knocked the Magna from Beth's hands before she had a chance to fire, and the pistol skittered across the mud. It lunged at her, arm slicing in a deadly chopping movement which she dodged in time. She overbalanced on to her back, the impact knocking the breath from her.

It was by her side with astonishing speed, a booted foot stamping down on her hand.

She screamed, almost blacking out in a pain like nothing she had ever experienced before. It lifted its foot to stamp again, and in that instant she knew she had to move, rolling away as quickly as she could, towards the gun.

Her broken hand failed to reach it in time. The Synthet kicked the gun away, almost sadistically, and it bounced off the edge of the hangar.

The Ship's engines, building up their power, whined behind her. Beth felt a searing hot wind on her face, struggled to get up, feet scrabbling on the ground. Clouds of blue mud and sand were ripped up, a hot tornado building around her. She knew she didn't have long.

Time seemed to stand still. She could see almost nothing in the hot gloom of smoke and rain.

The Synthet advanced on her.

And then it stopped. It turned its head on one side. It had no face beyond the blank silver skull with glowing red eyes, but Beth, through her pain, was sure it was somehow smiling.

It extended a hand to her. Open as if in welcome. Raindrops danced upon its hand.

'Bethany Aurelia Kane,' it said.

The sound of the Ship's engines was growing in intensity, as if all the demons of hell had been let loose around them.

She eyed up the short distance to the gun. She was not sure she could make it before the Synthet grabbed her. She would not last more than a second if it got its hands on her neck, she realised – those metal fingers could snap bone in an instant.

'*What do you want?*' she shouted into the vortex of sand. Her voice sounded distant, lost.

'The Chapter,' the Synthet said, its head on one side as if receiving new information from somewhere, 'helped to equip this colony with the means of its survival.'

'Yes. Medical supplies, science. None of that would have been possible without the intervention of the Chapter. We know that.'

'*We know that.*'

She was not sure if the Synthet's words were an echo, or mockery of her own.

'Yes. It's thanks to the Chapter that they've managed to survive for hundreds of cycles. Five people died, that's all. Five, from natural causes. It would have been far more.'

'Five,' said the Synthet. Then, mockingly, 'Now twelve.'

Beth staggered to her feet. The Synthet made no move to stop her. 'You almost seem to take … a *delight* in it.'

'The human flesh is weak.'

The Ship was shuddering, screaming, its engine-pods glowing a bright red in the blue mist. The air was like a furnace, heat shimmering in the darkness of the night. The domes of their small, hopeless Town shook and blistered in the heat.

'Better than your way,' said Beth.

'You despise us.' It moved towards her, and she edged closer to the gun. 'You despise us, and yet, you, Bethany Kane, are not entirely like the others.'

'What do you mean?'

'You are … integrated. *By the Chapter.*'

Anger surged in her. 'Yes, my Behavioural Limiter. The Chapter uses such technology for good, not for evil. It was necessary.'

'Necessary, because of who you were? What you did?'

'Just *necessary.*'

'An improved human. An *enhanced* human.'

She knew what it was trying to say. She could not allow it to get into her mind. Not like that.

'I'm different. Humanity copes well with people being a bit different. You should try it some time.'

'You could join us. You could be wholly like us.'

Beth wrinkled her nose in disgust. 'Like you? I'm not like you. I'm human. Imperfect, inadequate, scared. I'll take that over your way every time.' She sounded resolute, but it was all she could do not to shake with fear.

'*Arcadia,*' said the Synthet.

The strength drained from her body. 'What?'

'You were from the *Arcadia*. I … know the *Arcadia*.'

'I … I told you about it. All of you. I told you when you were Ella. You're using those memories.'

'I know the *Arcadia*,' it said, calmly. 'It still exists.'

'Exists?'

The world had tipped on its axis, the sky becoming the ground. Behind them, the giant Ship screamed, shuddered, rocked, trying to tear itself free of this world. The ground shook.

'What do you mean?' Beth shouted.

'*Arcadia* exists. *Arcadia* was not destroyed.'

'You're … you're lying. You can't know that.'

The Synthet took another step towards her. 'Join us, Bethany Kane. Join us, and I will tell you everything.'

Beth had one chance, and she took it. She lunged for the gun, grabbed it from the ground with her good hand. Straightening up, she swung the weapon round to face the Synthet.

Her head was pounding already from the limiter. Her mouth tasted of cold metal. She was not sure she would be capable of this. The Synthet spread its arms, as if mocking her, as if welcoming her to try.

'How much damage did Mia inflict? I bet you couldn't take much more. You are stronger than us, but you are not immortal.'

She was levelling the Magna pistol at the Synthet's head. Even left-handed, even with her fingers slick with mud, she could not miss from here.

But she could not fire.

The limiter screeched in her mind, seeming louder even

than the Ship's engines. Its force spread to every nerve and fibre of her body – making movement, even thought, almost impossible. In a few seconds, the whole of the past few cycles seemed to tear through her head. It was like an accelerated, terrifying rush of images, assailing her senses.

Screaming in pain in the capsule. Her body shuddering in fear. Great Power, ChapterSister Bethany Kane needs you. Please save me. Help me …

Spiky vegetation looming like reddish-black monsters in the dimness, winged creatures wheeling in the sky, sharp-beaked …

The Drone moving forward. Gliding as if on a flat surface, its electronic iris opening, eyeballing her …

The creature in the jungle, its glutinous blood spurting …

Zach's face twisting with anger as the butt of the pistol slammed into her … You're lying, Bethany Kane, you're lying … You came here to kill us all …

She had survived.

Nerves shredded, her spirit battered but not broken, her courage challenged but not lost.

It had to end here.

The Synthet was closing in. Staggering jerkily towards her. Hand extended as if to welcome her.

A deep, thunderous boom echoed across the island, as the Ship achieved main ignition and began to lift, shakily, unsteadily, from the planet. The ground rumbled. A wind howled. A storm of mud and sand howled, lashing like whips from the sky. The very air itself seemed to burn and tear asunder, smelling and tasting like death, burning, anger.

She knew it could cut her apart. A rage surged through her like she had never felt before. It was primal, electric, urgent.

'Join us,' said the Synthet. Its voice sounded as if it was in her head.

Beth braced herself. Feet apart, holding firm against the powerful backblast, against the heat and the mud. She opened her aching eyes wide, facing the Synthet one last time.

'You don't understand, do you?' said Beth, keeping the gun steady. 'We're *better* than that. You tried to turn us against one another, to make us no better than animals.'

The Synthet tilted its head on one side. Its eyes glowed brightly.

'Join us,' it said again.

'We always came back stronger. You might break some of us, kill some of us. But you will never, ever destroy the human spirit.'

Time stood still. Her head screamed in agony as the Synthet came to a sudden standstill.

'Join us,' said the Synthet. 'Be who you are.'

'No,' she said. 'I *know* who I am. Bethany Aurelia Kane. Child of the Starship *Arcadia*. Sister in the Blessed Chapter of Continual Progress. Citizen of the Galactic Collective. Member of the human race. And I have a message for you, and for every creature like you. If you're willing to hear it.'

The Synthet stopped. It inclined its head.

'The message,' said Beth calmly, 'is a very simple one. A message as old as Time. A message my friend Mia would approve of.'

Her finger tightened on the trigger.

'*Fuck you*,' said Beth.

She fired.

The Synthet recoiled. The blasts were like detonations. Echoing off the juddering hull of the Ship. Pounding in her head. Scorching her brain. Screaming pain hurtling through her synapses.

She blasted a ragged hole through its chest. Hydraulic fluid gushed from the wound like blood. The Synthet let out a screech, part-human, part-animal, part-machine. Strands of repair-circuitry squirmed around the hole like silver worms, desperately trying to repair the body in time. She could see right through it to the broiling sand around the Ship, the glowing engine-pods.

The edges of her vision turned red, but she saw the bolts hitting the already-dying Synthet as it thrashed in the coruscating plasma, screeching and roaring.

She fired again, ripping more holes in its body. More. More. More. She blasted chunks out of its carapace, shredded its circuitry into white-hot shards. Scattered its remains across the scorched, scarred mud.

Even though the pain in her head would not stop, she kept firing. Over and over and over and over again.

Hot blood streamed from her nose, into her mouth, and she ignored it. The smell of burning metal and plastic filled her mouth and lungs.

But she kept firing for over a minute.

Again and again and again and again and again.

When she finally stopped, and the screaming in her

head abated, and the redness at the edge of her vision began to fade, there was almost nothing left of the Synthet. It was a twisted lump of metal, no longer resembling a human at all, burning in the heart of a searing blue fire. Its skull-like face was the last recognisable piece of it left, leering from the flames as if in a final act if mockery. Then it, too, melted and dissolved. Molten globules of metal and chunks of circuitry and wiring, fragile as ash, spread across the mud and further still, some blowing in the wind towards the rocks and the fissures.

There was a smell of greasy smoke, hot metal and death.

Above her, back in a reality she had almost forgotten, the Ship tore itself free of the Edge's gravity.

She lifted her head, watched as the Ship hurtled into the air. A thick, dark slab of metal in the darkening sky. Up, up, up it soared, until it became the size of her hand, the size of a pea, of a speck. Seconds later, there was a flash like lightning, and a great, billowing cloud of smoke spread across the sky.

The great Ship, succumbing at last to the forces it could not contain, exploded. It shattered into a thousand million pieces in the planet's atmosphere. A tight, billowing cloud of dark smoke formed in the sky, tendrils extruding from it as debris was thrown to the clouds all around it.

Only then, shuddering, sobbing, did Bethany Kane lower her weapon. She fell slowly to her knees, drained of all strength.

The screaming in her head stopped, and her vision returned to normal. Sobs wracked her body, debris strewn all around her. Her face was hot and wet with tears, her nose and mouth filled with the stench of smoke and the taste of blood.

Shaking, slowly regathering, Beth got to her feet.

She unclipped the power-pack from the Magna and hurled it into the burning, sparking remains of the Synthet. She threw the useless weapon away, and it hit the rocks, bouncing somewhere, she cared not where.

She staggered dizzily, as everything went red. And then blackness seeped in at the edge of her vision, and she sank on to the soaking wet mud, the sky spinning above her.

The great, billowing cloud of destruction, blotting out the sky, was the last thing she saw as her consciousness ebbed away.

∞

TWO CYCLES LATER

15
SURVIVAL

I

Amber tossed another piece of debris into the fire-pit. It caught, sparked and burned. She hugged herself, her tousled hair blowing in the wind, watching the flames as they leapt high. Wind-buffeted, they reached up as if in new hope for the colony.

It had been two cycles since the massacre. Nobody had spoken, much, or even done anything beyond the absolute routine minimum.

Amber wondered if they would ever get back to normal. If they even knew what 'normal' was any more.

The pyre had been Mia's idea.

The remains of a great fire still smouldered on Lunar Beach. It was a pyramid of the scorched, twisted remains of metal globes – a pyre of the deactivated Drones. They had carried them down there together, those who Mia, Amber, Robbie and Finn could round up to do it. Some of the Towners would not even touch the inert Drones, would not go near them. But finally, about ten of them had transported the deactivated Drones down there in three jeeps and burned them all in one massive, blazing inferno, green and blue flames reaching for the sky, flickering angrily as they consumed each piece of the metal shells, the circuitry and tools within.

They stood in a circle around the pyre, watching in silence, some of them holding one another, or gently touching hands when they knew, instinctively, that it was needed.

They were destroying part of their civilisation. But it was

necessary, to burn the evil and the fear from the heart of Town. It was telling, Amber thought, that nobody had even mentioned saving anything, cannibalising the tech, using it. They just wanted it all gone.

More wreckage was added, over the next few cycles – anything from Town which had been damaged in the onslaught and which could not be repaired or replaced. Mia, Amber, Robbie and Finn took it in turns, pairing up in shifts, to watch the fire, to make sure everything burned and nothing was left behind.

A hand on her shoulder, the pungent scent of *plaan* weed. She turned to see who it was, but already knew.

'You okay there, little one?' Mia asked, staring into the fire, her sunglasses hiding her expression. She drew heavily on the roll-up and it flared bright blue, before she lifted her head, exhaling a long, deep puff of greenish smoke.

'S'pose so,' she said.

'Good.' Mia handed Amber the roll-up. She took it without a word and drew her own, smaller, more jittery puffs. 'We're gonna need you.'

'Need me?' Amber, wreathed in curls of green smoke, looked round in surprise. 'What do you mean?'

'Someone has to keep the younger ones together. In the next few cycles especially. Tell them everything's going to be fine.'

Amber stared moodily into the heart of the flames. 'But everything's not really going to be fine,' she said.

There was a long, thoughtful silence. Amber handed the roll-up back to Mia.

'Yeah,' said Mia. 'That's kind of true. But you still need to tell them it is. That's one of the things about leadership.' She inhaled greedily, blew a long, curling jet of jade smoke. 'You see … You don't always tell people what they *should* hear. You tell them what they *need* to hear. May not be accurate. May not be true. But it gets them through to the next stage.'

Amber was impressed. 'You're the eldest, now. I've only just realised.'

'Yeah, don't remind me, babe. Counted up the cycles, didn't I?' The tally-marks on the doors of Town had stopped, but Mia, it seemed, hadn't lost count. 'Wish me a happy birthday.'

'Really?'

'They used to call it *sweet* sixteen. Back on Earth. In a jokey sort of way, I think.' Mia exhaled deeply. 'Not very sweet any more.' She nodded down at the sheet of metal she could see by Amber's feet, beside the base of the fire-pit. It appeared to be a cannibalised part of the hangar wall. 'What's that?'

'Oh, something I've been working on.'

The younger girl squatted down, lifted the sheet until it was vertical, so that Mia could see it. Etched into it, neatly and in clear block capitals, were thirteen names in a neat column:

KAI ARDEN
LEILA MESSINA
JANIE TEALE

FAIZ RAMZAN
THOM ACHEBE
MADELEINE VANDERBILT
BALJEET MIDDA
SHAN DORIEN
LUCIANA FOX
XARA BELAZS
JOEL CATRONA
BRAD MILES
ZACHARY TAL

Of the fifty-one Towners who had founded Town, thirteen were dead – five from the cycles before, and eight in the Drone battle. Thirty-six had survived the massacre.

One was missing, presumed dead.

And one had never truly been alive.

Mia, Finn and Amber had located the other small pockets of survivors afterwards. Caleb, Malachi and Mahala had got a group of them to safety in the upper level – but if the Drones had been knocked out a minute later, Amber would have had at least ten more names to etch on her memorial. As it was, they discovered three of the Thirteeners were no more. It was left to Mia, with Amber and Robbie's help, to discover and report that Xara, Joel and Brad had not survived the Drones' onslaught on the Rec Hall.

Reza, to Amber's disgust, had spent the whole thing hiding in the *plaan* depository, listening to the distant sounds of gunfire and not coming out. Dionne, Hal and

Gabe, they found, had gathered a small group and taken them to the maintenance ducting, where they had stayed until it all went quiet. Cait and Livvy had locked themselves in Cait's room, trembling in fear, and had only been found, pale with shock, soaked in sweat and urine, hours later. Others were scattered around Town, hiding in whatever makeshift shelter they could throw together.

They had found Bethany Kane in the mud beyond Town.

At first, Mia had thought she was dead, but then they had felt a pulse, and realised there was still hope. Mia and Amber had carried her into Town together, given her water, cleaned her gashed face and tended to her broken fingers.

'That's good,' said Mia, putting an arm around Amber. 'Nobody else thought of that.' She gazed at the names. 'I wish we knew about Colm.'

'Officially missing … Took off, didn't he? I think he kind of expected the rest of us to do the same.'

They were silent for a moment.

'Where are you going to put it?' Mia asked.

'I thought, maybe, at the cemetery?'

'I think it needs to be inside. In Town.'

'Yeah, you're probably right. In the Rec Hall?'

'Yeah. In the Rec Hall.'

'Get Finn to fix it to the wall. He's good at that stuff. Or one of the Dro–' Mia stopped herself in time. 'Hell. Can't get out of the habit.'

Amber laid the memorial plaque down again. 'We always assumed it, didn't we? When we had … I dunno …

something too hard to do, or too boring. One of them would do it … Do you think we treated 'em like slaves?'

Mia spat on the ground before answering. 'Don't *you* start. I've had dippy Spacegirl bending my ear about this. With her ChapterSister goody-goodiness. What are we … Hell, what are we supposed to be saying, here? That we, that we brought it on ourselves? By treating machines *as* machines?'

'Sorry. I–'

'They don't have *rights*, Amber. They're not like … kids, or … or animals. You might as well start feeling guilty about your, your pet drill. Or your poor little screwdrivers and spanners.'

'Yeah. I get it. But all the same,' said Amber. Despite the heat of the fire, she shivered, hugging herself. Tears were welling up, and she could not hold them back. 'I'm sorry … it … I'm sorry.'

'I know.' Mia slipped an arm around the girl again, hugged her and held her. 'Come on, hold it together, you clever thing.' She ruffled her hair. 'We've all got stuff to do.'

'She's right, though,' said a voice behind them. They turned in surprise. Beth was strolling up behind them, joining them at the fire-pit.

'How long you been listening?' said Mia. 'Eavesdropping bitch.' But it lacked her usual bite, Amber thought, and she didn't really seem interested in the answer as she turned back and prodded the fire-pit. 'And you're supposed to be lying down!' Mia added. 'Get back inside!'

Beth shot them a quick, restless smile. 'I do not feel like doing as I am told any more. It's … refreshing.'

There was a new toughness about Bethany Kane, Amber decided. Something steely, hard, angry. Almost something of Mia in her. Her dark hair was cut savagely short, a few stray tufts protruding here and there like ragged, uncut grass. The gash on her cheek was still healing, pink and livid, and she wore her torn and battered jacket across her shoulders like a shawl. Her right hand was encased in a dark blue bone-sealant, her arm in a rough cloth sling.

'Why is she right?' Mia asked eventually, her glowing, *plaan*-stoned eyes trying hard to focus.

'Something the Synthet said. It's been knocking around in my head. That she was "reprogrammed". Does that not make you worry?'

The other girls shrugged.

'This wasn't an accident,' Beth said impatiently. 'Someone did this deliberately. Think of all the places in human society where Drones are used as a matter of course. Shipboard cargo bays, industrial loading, sanitation, horticulture ... We could be looking at something with Galactic implications.'

'Drones turning on people,' said Amber in horror. 'Across the whole Collective.'

'Earth,' said Beth. 'Mars, Titan Base, the Outer Planets, the Stations. All have Drones *everywhere* as a matter of course. Suppose this was only the beginning ... Or a test ... ? Or suppose it's all happening elsewhere right now?'

'We'll never know, will we?' Mia's voice was hard and cold. 'We'll never get off this shitty rock. So who cares?'

'Never say never. Not long ago you'd have said nobody ever came here.' Beth gestured to herself. 'And, hello.'

'What can we do, though?' asked Amber. 'We can't contact anyone. The sub-light pulse has been running for over two hundred cycles. There's nothing.'

'I know,' said Beth. 'That is something of a flaw.'

She held out her hand expectantly. Mia looked at Amber and back at Beth again, and a slow grin spread over Mia's tanned face.

'What, seriously?' Mia held up the roll-up, the glowing end burning copper-blue. 'You?'

'Yes?' said Beth, with a hint of impatience. She snapped her fingers. 'Is that all right?'

'Knock yourself out,' Mia said. 'You probably will.' She passed her the stubby, thick roll-up of leaves and paper, its glowing blue flame leaving tracks in the air.

Amber giggled. Beth drew deeply on the roll-up, head tilting back as if in profound contemplation, a warm and blissful smile on her face.

'All right, that's enough. Bloody hell.' Mia snatched it back from her.

Beth blew a long jet of green smoke upwards, watched it disperse. She blinked, swallowed hard, licked her lips.

'Wow,' she said, hoarsely. Amber saw the embers of the glow in Beth's eyes. 'How am I doing?' Beth asked.

'Yeah, fine … Seriously, I know I call you Spacegirl, but go easy on this shit, okay? It's not herbal tea.'

Beth laughed, slipping an arm around Mia and planting a kiss on her forehead. 'I was raised in the Blessed Chapter of Continual Progress,' she reminded them, her voice hoarse and husky. 'This,' and she pointed with two fingers at her gleaming eyes, 'this is Progress.'

Amber found herself wanting to smile for the first time in many cycles. 'She's got a point, Mia.'

'Yeah, but …' Mia tutted. 'All the same.'

Beth stroked her arm. 'Relax, Mia.' She laughed. 'I am a ChapterSister. Not a *kid*.' She waved comically to them. 'See you later.'

She walked back towards the dome, leaving Mia and Amber gawping speechlessly at each other.

'How strong is that *plaan*?' Amber asked.

Mia shook her head in bewilderment. 'Never mind a Drone revolution. I don't think the Galaxy's quite ready for a Bethany Kane revolution yet.'

II

High above the planet's atmosphere, it locked on to the reading.

It turned, changing course by tiny increments as it had to. The myriad complex navigational components on board calibrated and recalibrated. It sparkled, gleamed, glittered like a city in the darkest night.

A phase of life was about to be over. A new one was about to begin.

Slowly, it began to descend.

III

Mia pointed down the slope. 'There.'

Even with the viewer, Beth could not see what she was pointing out at first. 'Meet me at Sharp Ridge,' Mia's radio message had said. 'Something you need to see.'

A chill ran through her as she made out the impact crater, the charred circle in the blue dust, and, sitting there at its heart, buzzing impotently, its light feebly attempting to flare, was a single, shattered Drone.

Beth lowered the viewer. 'It surely did not fall from the wreckage.' She blinked, aware that the *plaan* was still giving her a headache. She didn't want to let on to Mia about this.

'Doubt it. Probably got left behind? Thrown out in the backblast?'

'Maybe.'

'We can't leave it there,' Mia said. 'The metal bastard needs deactivating. Come on.'

Cautiously, holding tight on to their guns, the two girls half-ran, half-slithered down the ridge, kicking up dust behind them. As they got closer, they could smell pungent, burning metal, and they could see the shattered carapace of the Drone, split in two like a broken eggshell. Burnt and twisted wires and circuitry trailed from it, spread across an area of about two emms in diameter.

Cautiously, Mia and Beth edged around it.

They could see that it was quite useless. The cutting-tool, along with most of the rest of its innards, had been torn away, burnt and scattered on the charred mud.

'We should ...' Beth gnawed at her finger. 'I don't know, maybe leave it.'

In a parody of the Drones' usual noise, it emitted a hard, electronic grating which made them jump. A buzz, like circuitry being misconnected.

Mia pulled a frag-bomb out of her satchel, primed it, tossed it into the centre of the Drone's wreckage. 'All right. I'll finish it.' She pulled out a detonator, a small black circle with a red button.

'Mia, no ... No need to, surely.'

'There can't be one left, Beth. Not even one.'

'Wait!' Beth held up a placating hand, squatted down. She peered closely at the Drone. 'Hold on a second.'

'Seriously? They killed nine of our friends. What are you doing, coming over all touchy-feely ChapterSister over a piece of fucking *junk* ...? Are you *listening* to me?'

'Mia,' said Beth softly. 'Come down here a moment.'

Mia squatted down beside her. 'One of these days, my Spacebitch, you are gonna be the death of me, you know that?'

Beth held up a hand, motioning Mia to be silent. Then she pointed, slowly, to the centre of the Drone's mangled innards.

'What ... the *hell* ... is *that*?'

She waited until Mia saw what she had seen, there at the centre of the circuitry. Mia drew back in horror, astonishment. Then the girl's lean face assumed its usual hard, tough expression.

'We don't tell anyone about this,' Mia said.

'Why?'

'Beth, have you *any* idea–'

'Of the implications? Yes, I should think so.'

'We don't know … We don't know if it's all of them.'

'But it's pretty likely. Isn't it?' Beth looked down in fascination and horror at what they could see there, nestling in the burnt circuitry. 'We never thought … We never imagined … How did they *do* it?'

'I don't wanna know. We forget we ever saw this.'

'I can't.'

'The others don't need to know. I'm not telling anyone.' She stepped backwards out of the circle of charred ground. 'You decide what you wanna do.'

She moved to go, but Beth grabbed her arm and pulled her back. A few cycles ago, Beth thought, she would not have dared do that.

'I don't want to make this decision on my own, Mia. You're the eldest now. You're the leader. Give me some advice here.'

Mia looked back at the shattered Drone. She shuddered. 'Seriously … I … No.'

'What do you mean, no?'

'I mean decide yourself. Right?'

'Oh, this is your leadership style, is it? Delegation of responsibility?'

'Perhaps. Yeah.'

'More like abdication.'

Mia cursed, spat into the dust. She turned away, arms outstretched in frustration, then turned back to Beth. 'You know … I could *slap* you some days,' she said. 'Seriously, I could.'

'I know.'

'I almost have. So many times.'

'I am aware of that.'

'You know why I haven't?'

Beth opened her mouth, then closed it again. 'Um … No, actually. Go on.'

'Because, because you … Oh, for … Because I kind of … I kind of love you. All right? Happy?'

'Really?' Beth's eyebrows shot up.

'Yeah, don't get excited, Spacegirl. It's not your lucky day. I don't mean I want to fuck you or anything. I mean like a friend, a sister. Someone I care about.'

'Right.'

'That's the only reason I haven't decked you.'

'Of course.'

'Well, that and the fact that you kind of saved all our lives, I suppose.'

'I was not going to mention that. But then, in the Chapter of Continual Progress, we are renowned for our modesty.'

'Yeah, you're taking the piss.'

'I suppose I am …! Every day a new experience.'

'Right. Well …' Mia handed her the detonator. Then she turned away, and started walking up the hill. 'I'll see you back at Town,' she called over her shoulder.

'Mia!' Beth called desperately after her. 'Mia, *wait!*'

But it was already too late. Mia was walking away

without a backward glance, making her way back up the escarpment. Beth watched as the figure of her friend dwindled in size, reaching the top of the ridge and then bobbing out of sight.

Beth turned back to the Drone.

The low, murmuring reminder of her behavioural limiter ticked away inside her brain, like a hand on her shoulder. Reminding her. Telling her she would not, could not do this.

She had tested it to its limits once. Surely again would be too much.

She put the detonator in her palm. She took one pace backwards.

The angry, buzzing sound from the Drone intensified. It was trying to lift itself up, but its motor circuits were totally useless. Without the computer, it was a piece of junk, random circuit-links trying and failing to activate. The glow from its electronic eye was the palest red in the afternoon light, barely even there.

In her mind, the kind smile of Maddi welcomed her to Town, as she gave her food and clothes.

And the hard, red eyes of the Synthet, in those final moments, glowed as it taunted her about the *Arcadia*.

Taunted her with its lies. Or with the truth.

The limiter was making her head pulse in pain. It sang in her ears, her temples, her teeth. It was becoming hard to focus.

She turned away.

She walked up the ridge, following Mia's footprints. She

did not stop until she got to the top. Until she could see the lights of Town across the causeway. The domes were so small, bereft, fragile without the great cliff of the spaceship behind them.

She took deep, shuddering breaths of the dry air. Her head was still pounding, her mouth dry and metallic. She wiped the tears from her face, tried to tell herself it had to be done.

Bethany Kane pulled out the detonator and let her thumb hover over the button before she had a chance to think about it. She still had not quite pressed it when her limiter screamed, and she ignored it, rode out the pain.

There cannot be one left. Not even one.

She turned away, walking down the hill towards Town. Without looking back, she pressed the button.

A dull crump of an explosion echoed off the Howling Mountains, and only now did she turn round.

A column of thick, dark smoke was billowing up into the sky from behind the ridge.

She turned away. She kept walking. It was done.

But she and Mia could not tell anyone what they had seen there, deep in the shattered heart of the Drone, wired into the circuitry, still throbbing with life. Decaying, but very much alive.

Whether human or animal, they could not say, but it was unmistakably, undeniably organic.

The throbbing, gleaming, pulsing heart of a living thing.

*

Her radio crackled as she came within range of Town.

'Yeah, Beth here?'

'It's Finn. Can you come to the Comms tower? We've got something … weird.'

She made her way there as quickly as she could, walking in a straight line across the compound. She focused straight ahead, trying not to let herself be distracted by the twisted wreckage, the burnt-out jeeps, the deep, scorched furrows in the mud.

'What's up? Beth said, climbing into the tower. 'What is it?'

Mia, Finn, Robbie and Amber were hunched over the radar screen, and she went to join them. Finn pointed to the scattering of tiny dots across the top half of the screen. 'That's the debris from the Ship. Some of it's still floating around in orbit. And then there's this.' He pointed further over.

'I don't see anything,' Beth said dubiously.

'We saw this once before,' said Amber. 'Me and Rob. Right before the Drone blew up. Then there was the storm, and everything else, and … We forgot.'

And then they all saw it. A bright, disc-shaped trace flared into view, clearly visible on the screen for several seconds, before disappearing.

'Why the hell's it doing that?' murmured Mia worriedly. 'What … what would *do* that?'

'A ship,' said Beth. She looked slowly up from the screen, staring out across the great sea to the Howling Mountains, to the piled clouds in the sky. 'A ship with stealth technology, uncloaking for a second or two at a time … Maybe to run a scan?'

'So there *is* something out there,' Mia whispered. 'Holy fuck.' She exhaled, as if telling herself to come to her senses. 'Nah. It's some sort of glitch. Gotta be.'

'Come with me,' Beth said to Mia. 'You three – stay here and monitor it.'

'Are you gonna tell me where the hell we're going?'

Beth was forging ahead across the causeway, taking great, powerful steps which Mia struggled to keep up with for once. Beth could not describe what she felt – a kind of inexplicable vigour. She did not speak until they had left Town about a kilom behind. As Beth turned to wait for Mia, on the high ground above the treeline, she could see the domes gleaming in the sunlight.

'I've got a feeling about something,' she said excitedly.

'Oh, great. We've come out here because Spacegirl's got a *feeling*. If you hadn't forgotten, we've got a lot of clearing up to do, yeah? And then a few decisions to make with everyone about how everything gets done, with thirty-six of us and no bloody Drones? It's not long until winter. The last one almost finished us off.'

'The signal,' said Beth. 'The signal was clear.'

'Oh, what, you think there's *actually* a ship? It could be a meteorite, a plasma storm. Solar flares. Whatever that radar glitch is, Beth, it ain't coming. Nobody's coming to rescue us. You know why?'

'Tell me why.'

'Because we ain't worth *shit*. Not to Earth, not to the Collective, not to your precious Chapter. Not to anyone.'

'All right, all right.' Beth held up a hand to forestall any further protests. She spied a rocky outcrop, jutting up from the sand as if reaching into the sky. 'Up there,' she said.

'What?'

'I am going up there. You can come with me, Mia, or you can turn round and go back. Up to you.'

She turned and began to climb.

Mia gritted her teeth, spat on the ground. 'I swear,' she said. 'One of these days ...' She swung her arms. 'All right, Bethany Kane. Have it your way.' With long, loping strides, she caught Beth up, and together then began to climb.

It took them twenty minutes to reach the top, finding handholds and footholds where they could. At last, they stood at the rocky summit, and straightened up. On the distant island, the domes of Town were smaller and more vulnerable than ever. On the other side lay the jungle, a green carpet swathed in yellow mist.

The air tasted different up here, Beth thought. It had the slightly decaying tang of ozone, a heady feel. She took her viewer out and scanned the sky in a full circle. She was tingling with excitement.

'If I knew what you were looking for ...' Mia began.

Beth squatted down, and took the stubby rocket-like object out of her inside pocket. She put it down on the rock, the nose-cone facing upwards. It was still quietly pulsing to itself.

'Okay, so ... What the hell is that?' Mia asked.

'It came into my hands via a circuitous route. Baljeet discovered it, on one of her scavenging missions, and it ended up with Maddi. Nobody knew what it was. In all the commotion, it got left on Maddi's desk. Forgotten about.'

'Except by you, it seems!'

'I picked it up when we were sorting through the mess … Maddi was going to tell me about it, you see. She left a message for me on the comlink, right before she died. I've not seen anything quite like it before, but … I think I know what it might be. Great Power, I hope I am right.'

Mia squatted down beside her. 'Spacegirl,' she said, 'is that thing *signalling?*'

'Yes. A rather different system from the sub-light pulse and the beacons you set up. This, I think, is a simple turbo-coded signal. It's operating, if I understand it right, on distributing maximum data volume within a narrow, focalised reception band.'

'Which means?' Mia asked.

'Which means it's keyed to one particular ship's data receptors. The one which sent this probe in the first place. It's been transmitting ever since it landed here. It's only recently that it's boosted the signal. I don't know what was stopping it. Atmospheric conditions, maybe?'

'The storm. Right.'

'Or it could have been the Drones' magnetic field. I don't really know. But there's something else. Think about it. When we sent the colony ship into the atmosphere to be destroyed, that was more than a way of saving ourselves, more than a way to kill the Drones. It was a signal. That will have sent streams of detectable particles out into space, able to be picked up hundreds of parsecs away, maybe … Who knows?'

The small device was flashing more insistently, the red light from within growing brighter and stronger.

Mia stared intently at it. 'Could be something. Who knows?' She clapped a hand on Beth's shoulder. 'You know, Spacegirl,' she said, 'for what it's worth, I've always trusted you. From the very beginning.'

Beth grinned. 'Even when you were threatening to shoot me like a dog?'

'Oh, yeah. Especially then.'

'I'd like to believe you, Mia.' Beth straightened up, putting the viewer to her eyes again.

'What did you do, by the way?'

The question caught her off-guard. 'What?' She lowered the viewer, turned to look at Mia.

'I told you my secret. Back when I was teaching you how to shoot, remember? So I wondered … The thing in your head, right? The chip. You said … it was because of something you'd done. Something you could barely remember yourself.'

Beth looked away. Into the sky. Into the Galaxy.

'What did you do?' Mia asked. 'Come on. You can tell me.'

Beth opened her mouth, closed it again. 'I …' she began. 'I …'

She was interrupted, though, by the crackle of Mia's radio. A voice saying something indistinct. 'Save it,

Spacegirl. I won't let it drop.' She flicked the call button. 'Not much hope of hearing this far out of range … Yeah, what is it?'

'… *detected … entered the … Right on top …!*'

'What?' She thumped the radio, put it to her ear. 'It's Amber, I think. I can't make out what the hell she's saying.'

Beth slowly lifted the viewer. 'I don't think we need to,' she said, pointing upwards. 'Up there.'

At first, they could see nothing. But there was a growing rumbling sound in the air. The sound of thunder, but continuous. The unmistakable vibration of enormous, powerful engines. The stentorian growl echoed across the sea, bounced off the Howling Mountains like the song of a choir of monsters. The sound grew louder and louder, coming closer.

And then they saw it.

First, it was a hint of a shape behind the clouds. Then a gigantic shadow fell across the forest, a sea of cold darkness swallowing everything, climbing the mountainside and falling upon them as they stood there, necks craned into the sky, eyes wide in astonishment. Marooned in cold, empty shadow as it came down from the sky, blotting out the clouds, the Moons, the mountains. It was descending very, very fast towards the planet. It was huge, thundering, sleek, beautiful, a dark silvery-grey. It bristled with tiny lights like a city in the sky, throbbing with magnificent, planet-spanning, star-jumping power. A great, hot wind blew. It whipped up the sand and dust, almost knocking them off their feet as they stared upwards in awe. The dark underside blotted out the sun and the clouds. And now, they could see the four huge, orange discs of what Beth knew were Concept Class engines burning like hot coals, embedded in the great ship's underside. It grew bigger, darker. It would now have been visible not only from Town, but from hundreds of miles away. It descended further still. A glittering, massive, unyielding steel sky above them. It was bigger, it seemed, than the entire Island itself. A vast, circular shadow of technology, blotting everything out – the island, the sky, the mountains, the clouds.

'What the hell *is* that thing?' Mia breathed.

Beth gazed in wonder and joy on the one thing she thought she would never again see in her life.

'It came,' she said. 'It came for me. For us.'

Mia, open-mouthed, stared at her, for once shocked almost into silence. 'You mean …?'

In the cold, thundering darkness of the spaceship's shadow, Bethany Aurelia Kane, Sister in the Chapter of Continual Progress, Citizen of the Galactic Collective, gazed upwards into the future.

'Yes,' she said. 'It's the *Arcadia*.'

The End

The story of Bethany Kane and the Exiles continues in
VOYAGERS

About the Author

Daniel Blythe is an acclaimed writer of fiction and non-fiction for children and adults, and has had over 25 books published since he started out on the *New Doctor Who Adventures* in 1993.

His novels *The Cut*, *Losing Faith* and *This is the Day* have recently been republished. His most recent books for teenage readers include *Shadow Runners* and two novels featuring the mysterious investigator Emerald Greene. He returned to Doctor Who with the BBC Books Tenth Doctor novel, *Autonomy*. He has also written several shorter novels for reluctant readers, one of which, *I Spy*, was nominated for the Leicester Reading Rampage Award.

Daniel also works as a freelance editor for literary development agencies, has been a visiting writer in over 400 primary and secondary schools and worked as an Associate Lecturer on the Creative Writing M.A. at Sheffield Hallam University. He lives with his wife and two teenage children on the edge of the Peak District in the north of England.

Learn more about Daniel at his website:
www.danielblythe.com

If you have enjoyed this book, please consider leaving a review for Daniel to let him know what you thought of his work.

You can read about Daniel on his author page on the Fantastic Books Store. While you're there, why not browse our other delightful tales and wonderfully woven prose?

www.fantasticbooksstore.com